SLOW STEPS TO LOVE

T0158261

SLOW STEPS to LOVE

A Novel by

Tew Bunnag

RIVER

BOOKS

First published and distributed in 2023 by
River Books Press Co., Ltd
396/1 Maharaj Road,
Phraborommaharajawang, Bangkok 10200
Tel. 66 2 225-9574, 225-0139
E-mail: order@riverbooksbk.com
www.riverbooksbk.com

Editor: Narisa Chakrabongse
Design: Suparat Sudcharoen and Ruetairat Nanta

ISBN 978 616 451 075 3

Printed and bound in Thailand
by Parbpim Co., Ltd

I would like to thank Narisa Chakrabongse
for her tireless work editing the text,
and, of course, for publishing this book.
I am also grateful to my son, Shane,
for providing the beautiful photographs
for the cover.

Part 1

Chapter 1

He yelled out in pain as he turned his head round to face her. The expression in his eyes was one of anger as he said, in a gruff voice: 'Are you trying to kill me?'

The old woman returned his gaze without showing any reaction to his words. If I wanted to, you'd be dead already, she thought.

Slowly and carefully, the man, who was known in that household simply as Khun Chai, propped himself up on his right elbow and began to move his neck carefully, up and down and then in a semi-circular motion. It reminded her of a tortoise. Still lying on his belly, he then began to rotate his left shoulder this way and that. After a while, he raised his body into a full sitting position with his knees tucked under him.

'I don't believe it,' he said, addressing the wall he was facing, which was covered with paintings and framed photographs.

Yai Li, with her hands folded in her lap, looked at the back of his head and the thin white hair that covered it. He's probably a bit older than me, she concluded.

Now she cast her eyes over the black spots that were dotted all over the pale, flabby skin of his back. They were not good signs. Then, briefly, she looked out of the window at the row of tall tamarinds and the swimming pool beyond them, all bathed in the gentle yellow glow of the garden lights. It was a place fit for a king – a real palace, she thought. How had she landed up there?

Khun Chai turned towards her as he adjusted the waistline of his faded, threadbare fisherman's trousers. Then he stretched his right hand over to his left shoulder and rubbed it energetically, lifting his elbow constantly as he did so. Now he reminded her of a bird opening its wing.

'What did you do?' he asked. The frown had left his face. 'I haven't been able to move like this for months.'

She shrugged. She had never been able to talk about what she did, nor ever wanted to. It was a gift that her father had, and before that his father. If pressed, she would describe it as *Jup Sen* (touching the nerve). It explained nothing, but it was enough for most people. But he did not seem to need her answer. He continued:

'I can't tell you the pain I've been through. Couldn't move this side at all. It was all locked up. I could hardly walk. I've seen everyone they wanted me to see. Paid loads of money to that fancy physio in the hospital over in Sukhumvit – can't remember the name . . .'

She kept nodding gently but was responding not to his words but to the sound of his voice. He was relieved, she could tell. He repeated the same actions with his neck and shoulder, with more confidence each time, and then began stretching his body as if to lie down again. But she put a hand up, and waved it from side to side.

'That's enough for now. Any more won't help you today,' she told him in a voice of quiet authority.

For a moment he looked at her, disappointed, before saying:

'Yes. I guess you've done a lot for me already this evening. Are you tired?'

She shook her head, and in reply she pointed her forefinger at him and waved it in the air to indicate that it was he who had had enough. He chuckled.

'Okay, Okay.' He said as he pulled himself awkwardly onto his feet and walked slowly over to the other side of the room. She was glad to see him move with less difficulty. When she arrived at the house earlier that evening he had been sitting in a wheelchair in the hallway and was helped off it by a strong looking young man who supported his left arm as they went into the room ahead of her.

She saw him now putting on the checked cotton shirt that the helper had taken off him and hung on the back of a chair by the huge teak desk, piled with books on one end, and with a huge computer on the other. When he finished buttoning up his shirt Khun Chai reached over and pressed a bell on the wall, then pulled open the draw on the right side of the table. When he walked back towards her, he was holding a white envelope that she took from him and put immediately into her shoulder bag. She drew her hands together and slightly bowed her head in a gesture of thanks, to which he replied in kind.

'Can you come again?' he asked. She nodded.

'When? Tomorrow?'

'No. I'll come back at the weekend.'

'Good,' he said smiling. 'I'll send the driver for you.'

'Not necessary,' she said quickly. 'Joy, my granddaughter, can bring me, like she did tonight. Or I can take a taxi.'

'All right. As you like. But this evening Sai will take you home. Joy has some work to do with my son. It's all arranged.'

Yai Li sat stiffly on the back seat. The car smelt of polished leather and jasmine, from the garland that hung off the rear mirror. There was room enough for a whole family, she thought as she climbed in. It was not the first time she had been driven anywhere by a chauffeur. But on previous occasions, on the way to the market or a shop when she had worked as a servant, she had always sat next to the driver. It was Khun Chai, leading her out to the huge blue vintage Mercedes whose engine was purring as it waited in the covered carpark outside the front steps, who opened the back door for her. She could have told him that she preferred to sit in the front, but his forceful politeness did not leave her room to contradict his wishes. Now she felt embarrassed at the thought of arriving in Klongtoey, where she lived, in the back of this grand limousine, like an ageing princess or the grandmother of a gangland boss, not the slum-dweller that she was.

Before leaving her house, she had been persuaded by her granddaughter to dress up to go to the mansion and she had put on a white blouse on top of her black slacks and worn the new, shiny patent leather slip-ons that had been bought for her. But nothing Joy said could persuade Yai Li to leave her shoulder bag behind and, instead, carry the leather handbag that had also been given her by Joy for her last birthday. It was shiny red leather with a silver clasp and looked expensive. But Yai Li insisted that she was going to take her shoulder bag. She had never been anywhere without it.

'Does that mean that you'll never use the one I got for you?' Joy had asked, unable to disguise her impatience. 'Maybe I should go back to the shop in Siam Paragon and change it for something else, something cheap and plastic. You never like the things I buy for you. And you won't ever go shopping with me, so I don't know what to choose. I don't see why you are so attached to that dirty old shoulder bag? It looks so scruffy.'

Yai Li smiled.

'No. Don't change anything for my sake. You should take the bag and use it yourself,' said Yai Li. 'It suits your style, not mine.'

She did not want to argue with her granddaughter, and understood why she was frustrated with her, as she often was. But the shoulder bag, which was faded red with a piece of embroidery sewn round the top edge was the most precious object she owned, along with the photo of her father. It belonged to her mother, and she had always kept it with her, all these years.

She fingered it now as she tried to make herself comfortable in the back seat. She sensed that Sai, the driver could pick up her unease. He seemed to be a sensitive man despite having the strong, muscular body of a boxer. As soon as they were through the tall metal gates that opened and closed by remote control, he caught her eyes in the mirror and said, reassuringly:

'It won't take long, Yai. There's less traffic these days at this time of night. Not like before. Sometimes it used to take me ten minutes or more just to turn out from the lane into the main road.'

He was right. She remembered this part of the city as being constantly clogged up with traffic jams when she came off her shift at the factory where she worked. It would sometimes take her hours on the bus to get home from there.

'Khun Joy, your granddaughter, brought you this evening, didn't she?' he asked.

It was an unnecessary question. He's trying to make me feel at home, she thought. Better let him know I am all right.

'Yes. She did,' she said flatly.

'She's a very nice person. I've driven her many times.'

This interested Yai Li. When? Where to? Why? she wondered. But she said nothing.

'Yes. She's a very polite and kind person.' Sai continued and glanced in the mirror once more for her reaction. She nodded at his eyes.

'In fact, the last time I drove her she told me: "If anyone can help Khun Chai, it's my granny." I must admit that I was surprised when she said that. I asked her if you were a doctor and she said no, but that you could heal people. She'd seen it with her own eyes.'

He left a moment for her to respond but she said nothing.

'Well, it looks like she was telling the truth.' He went on. 'You certainly helped Khun Chai. So you must be a kind of doctor. I've been wheeling him around for months, taking him to one hospital after another and to clinics all over the city. That's the only time he's left the house these days. Not like before . . .'

She let him drone on, but she was hardly paying any attention to what he was saying. She was feeling drowsy. She often did after giving someone a session. It drained her energy. But it was also the comfort of the leather seat and the coolness of the air-con that were making her want to close her eyes and sleep.

She must have dozed off. For when she opened them again, the car had stopped at the traffic lights in Phya Thai. She noticed that Sai had his head turned and was staring at something on the other side of the street, and her eyes followed his. On the pavement opposite a small crowd had gathered round a street food stall. The corner was well lit and Yai Li saw two young men gesticulating to each other and obviously shouting but she could hear nothing through the thick windows of the car. She could only catch the intensity of their interchange. Suddenly the fists and kicks were flying. One of them fell to the ground and the other looked like he was trying to stamp on him as members of the crowd started to get involved. At that point, with the traffic light going green, the loud, and aggressive hooting of a car horn behind them made Sai move quickly to put the car in gear and speed off.

Neither of them said anything for a while. The short, abrupt scene of violence had shocked Yai Li, and she wondered how Sai had taken it.

'Probably drunk or stoned out of their heads,' he said after a while. 'Everyone's on edge these days. Especially the young. All those demonstrations.' He shook his head as if in disapproval.

Yai Li did not want to be drawn into a political discussion. But she was curious about Sai's views.

'And what does Khun Chai think of it all?' She chose an oblique way to approach the subject.

'You mean the demonstrations? Oh, he's behind them all the way.' Yai Li did not show her surprise.

'And yourself?' she asked.

'I'm with him. But it's just that he tends to get carried away. Only the other day in that big one near the Victory Monument he wanted me to drive him there and push him out in the wheelchair. Imagine! He wanted to go and shout and protest like the people who were there.'

Sai was giggling at this.

'And did you?'

'No. I told him I didn't want either of us to get caught up with the police coming down on us and not be able to run away. But it wasn't easy to dissuade him, I can tell you. And now that he can move a bit more I'm afraid he's going to try and join the next demo.'

They were both laughing now.

'How long have you been with him?' she asked.

'A long time. Since forever. My family has been with his for generations. My grandmother was in his grandfather's household. I was with him even before he came back to live in Baan Suan.'

'Why? Hasn't he always lived there?'

'It's a complicated story,' said Sai cagily, giving the impression that he did not wish to elaborate on it.

Yai Li let it go.

'How old is he?'

'Well, they celebrated his sixth round four years ago. So, I guess he must be coming up to 76.'

By now they had turned off the main road and were crossing the railway track and about to go through the arched entrance into the district in Klongtoey where Yai Li lived, known to the locals as Jetsip Rai. But their way forward was momentarily blocked. Motorbikes were cutting across their path and two taxis were coming out of the narrow street that led in through the archway. There was no room for Sai to manoeuvre and she could sense him tensing with impatience.

'I can get out and walk. It's not far to my place from here.'

'No. It's all right, Yai,' he said. 'We'll get you there eventually,' he said confidently. 'Khun Chai told me to take you to your door.'

'But there's no way you'll be able to drop me at my house, because it's in a lane so narrow that you can hardly go through it on a motorbike.'

'Don't worry, Yai. Nobody can see you. In this car you can only see out. You can't see in.'

Even though he had misunderstood her, Yai Li was impressed by his remark because it showed that he was intuitive. For it was true that as they neared the district, she had again felt a pang of embarrassment to be arriving in this huge limousine.

'You're right,' she told him. 'I don't want to step out looking like some Khunying. All the same, I am going to get off here if you don't mind. It'll be easier for you. This car is so wide and there's a lot of traffic in the streets here at this time of night, not to mention the people. You've never been here before, have you?' she added as an afterthought.

'No,' said Sai. 'It's my first time.'

'Well, some taxi drivers won't even come into this area at night,' she said as she leaned over to pat his shoulder. 'Thanks for the ride. I'm sure we'll see each other again soon.'

With that, Yai Li opened the door and climbed out. As she stood and watched Sai reverse and turn the car before joining the main road, she half raised her hand to wave at him but remembered that she would see nothing beyond the window. She waved anyway.

From the archway it took her a good twenty minutes to walk to her little wooden shack. When she first moved there in the 1960s it would have taken ten at the most, even walking slowly. Nowadays she took her time and walked at a snail's pace so as not to put too much of a burden on her knees and ankles, which had begun to feel increasingly painful, particularly during the rainy season.

It was a Friday and the last week of July. People had received their pay packet that afternoon. The streets and alleyways were crowded. On any other evening at the same time, 9.30, it would have been much quieter but that night there was a festive atmosphere. Children were playing, the adolescents were strolling in groups, the boys and girls eyeing each other with sideways glances. All the small shops were open, including the hairdressers. There were queues by the food stalls and the air smelled of frying chicken and fish. Country music blared out from the bars where the taxi drivers, the dealers, the pimps and the local hookers gathered. The game halls were crowded and in the smoky back rooms the sessions of pool and billiards were in full swing.

Yai Li took all this in as she made her way patiently through the crowd. She liked the warm feeling of the community where she lived. It was getting rarer in other parts of the city. The further she got from the arched entrance the quieter it became. There were still as many people, but fewer shops and less business going on. She remembered that she had told Sai how some taxi drivers did not dare to come into the district at night. It was true, but now she regretted having told him so. The district had such a terrible reputation among the people of Bangkok who thought it was a den of vice, which it was, but no more so than any other poor district in the city. She should have told him that there was really nothing to be afraid of, because it was her home, at least for the moment.

She heard a voice calling out her name from an open window.

'Yai Li. Where have you been, all dressed up like that?'

It was a woman whom she had known when they sewed clothes together in the garments factory where she had worked until she retired.

'Out on the town, of course. Looking for a husband.' The other woman laughed.

'Why? Can't you find one around here?'

'Never in a month of Sundays,' said Yai Li. 'They're all junkies and layabouts.'

She continued down past the buildings that housed the NGOs, noticing that the lights were still on in the Mercy Centre, run by the Christians, and that a few of the older children were still sitting around chatting on the terrace. When she was nearer to the small alleyway that led to her shack there was only the pale light from an old streetlamp, flickering as it always did. She looked over to the dustbins just to check. Frequently, she had seen someone lying there comatose and she would call the police station. She had once come across a young woman who had died from an overdose. But tonight there was no one, only a mangy dog licking himself. She took her mobile phone out of her shoulder bag and turned on the torch. A large rat scuttled out of sight.

She could already see the distinct orange glow of a cigarette as she walked deeper into the lane, and heard the familiar hacking cough of her neighbour, Mae Da, ancient and toothless, who always sat on a low chair outside her front door at this time of night having her last puff before going to bed. As Yai Li approached Mae Da shouted out:

'So how was your prince? Was he charming and handsome?' She cackled.

Yai Li walked past her without replying and began to undo the lock of her own front door.

'I'll tell you about it tomorrow,' she said. 'Too tired tonight. I have to sleep now.'

'Are you going back there? Did you fix him up good and proper? Did he like you?' Mae Da threw out these questions in rapid succession. It was clear that she was hungry for gossip.

'Does he pay you well?'

Yai Li paid no attention to these last words. She knew they were meant to provoke her. But she did not want to enter into a conversation that she knew would drag on into the night. She was already through the door and turning the light on in her narrow room. She had no energy left to talk. She needed to lie down.

But she could not sleep that night even though she was tired. Her restless mind kept jumping to one thing and to another, none of any importance while she turned continually from side to side in her wooden bed. She tried to calm herself by listening to the rain that was drumming on her tin roof. It had begun to come down soon after she got in, heavily at first but it was now just a steady drizzle. At two in the morning, she heard Nai Lek, her neighbour on the other side, arrive at the entrance to the alleyway, turn off the engine of his motorbike and wheel it into his house, locking the door behind him. He usually arrived at the same time after his shift as a hotel porter. It was just after that when she suddenly realized what had been niggling her.

A memory shot up like the pain of an old wound never properly healed.

London. 1963. She is nineteen years old. The dinner party. There are half a dozen guests, including the ambassador, whose cook has come to 'help out'. This meant that she took over the kitchen because Yai Li did not know how to make the foreign dishes very well. She was assigned to the role of server that evening. No problem. In fact, she is relieved. The dishes were complicated. Serving was easy. Eyes down and don't spill anything. Be invisible. She remembered her aunt's advice.

The ambassador drinks whisky and soda, and is doing most of the talking. At one point, as she is about to enter the dining room with another large plate to serve, she hears his voice.

'She's good looking isn't she, Khun Chai?'

She pauses before going through the door in order not to let them know that she has heard this. When she puts the dish down, she raises her eyes momentarily and the ambassador is smiling over to the man called Khun Chai on the other side of the table. She had opened the door to him when he arrived that evening and noted that he was the only young person invited. He was neat looking and well dressed, and he had greeted the other guests respectfully; but she also noticed that they treated him with a certain subtle deference, normally shown to someone important, or to the son of someone who had more wealth, power or status than they did. The look that she sees pass between the ambassador and this young man is one of amusement, like a private joke they are sharing.

After the guests had left and she was clearing up the coffee cups from the living room, she heard Khun Benjawan, her boss's wife remark to her husband, as she was putting on her raincoat before leaving for the airport to fetch her mother, arriving that night from Bangkok:

'I hope Khun Chai enjoyed himself, sitting with all us grownups.'
'Oh, I'm sure he did,' said her husband.

'A little young to be drinking so much, isn't he? And he seems fond of it.' 'Yes. You noticed that too. Runs in the blood, I guess.'

The young man had exchanged glances with her as she handed him his coat in the lobby when he was leaving the apartment. It was a fleeting moment when their eyes connected, but she noted that his expression was intense and the look on his face was that of a much older person. There was something melancholic about him. All this in a second. Long ago.

Now as she lay awake, she knew what was bothering her. When she climbed the steps to the mansion and saw the old man in the wheelchair waiting for her and their eyes met as Joy, her granddaughter, introduced them, she thought for a moment that she recognised that same look she had come across in London that autumn evening all those decades ago. And then there was his name. Could this be the same Khun Chai? Perhaps. It was impossible to tell. It wasn'at even a name, but a title given to someone with royal blood. There must have been countless other Khun Chais all over the country. Why should this one be the same person? There was nothing about him that reminded her of the young man she had met in London. None of his features jogged any memories in her. The gentleman she treated that evening was an old man; white hair, sagging belly, wrinkled skin. She could not even remember what the young man had looked like, apart from his smart appearance. That one brief glance exchanged more than fifty years earlier proved nothing. Besides, she knew that it was not about whether she had met this Khun Chai before or not. This was not the issue. The possibility that their paths had crossed a long time ago was not what was troubling her and keeping her awake. It was the memory of London in 1963 and what happened to her there after that fateful dinner party.

Chapter 2

It was three in the morning. Khun Chai put down *The Complete Chekhov – Volume 1* on the glass table and stroked the cover. It was a beautifully bound, thick, blue hardback copy given to him by his son for his birthday two years earlier. He had been reading it constantly since then, taking time to enjoy each story in a way that he never did as a young man when he read everything hurriedly and almost casually, in order to get to the end. Even though he acknowledged both privately and publicly that of all the writers it was probably this Russian author who had influenced him most of all, he now realised that this was only true in a superficial sense. As a writer he had admired Chekhov's craft, the way that he wrote about people's relationships with such insight into all the possibilities and nuances. He had tried to do that himself. But recently he was discovering that there was much more to Chekhov that he had missed when he was young. What was filtering into his consciousness was different than before, and now he would sometimes dwell on a single page, rereading it several times to savour the master's skill. The stories he was familiar with had changed into a different narrative, and reading them brought home to him the fact that he was not the same person.

He walked over to the wooden railing of the balcony outside his bedroom, and stood watching the rain as he finished his cheroot. The sound of the water coming down on the trees and running through the gutters and cascading from the eaves mingled with the music that drifts out from the room – Ella Fitzgerald singing Cole Porter. It was a record he first heard when he was a student in England. The housemaster at his boarding school, who liked jazz played it to them. He remembered that he, an Asian, was the only boy who enjoyed the music. Her unique voice and the familiar, eloquent lyrics still delighted him, though he never managed to match them to her motherly figure and the serious schoolteacher's face that appeared on the record cover. He flicked his cheroot onto the lawn and inhaled the heady scent of the frangipani that grow abundantly in the garden. It is his favourite scent – the perfume of his childhood.

'It's so stupid to smoke,' he said to himself in a semi whisper and then remembered that he had had the same thought almost every day since he began to feel the pains in his chest, and still had not stopped smoking.

'You're an idiot,' he adds.

The rain was falling more gently by the minute. The leaves of the tamarind trees were sparkling as the light caught the drops of water. The bullfrogs that had provided their concerted call and answer earlier were now quietening down. Ung, Aang, Ung, Aang, Ung, Aang, they still echoed every so often, and it made him smile. He enjoyed the rainy season – all the more at that very moment because he had been able to walk out onto the balcony by himself instead of being wheeled there by his servant.

Khun Chai never slept before four in the morning. Sometimes he even stayed awake to catch the dawn light. It was a habit he established when he started writing his novels and short stories. He felt that he could only think creatively when the frantic energy of the city had calmed down. It was not a hard rhythm to maintain. He had always been a late sleeper, and in the days that he was going out to parties and driving round the city he was rarely in bed before the early hours of the morning. When he began writing fiction the routine served him well. Four novels, three collections of short stories and two screenplays were the fruit of these hours, and with them he had enjoyed moderate success at home and a clasp of appreciative reviews from abroad. But he had not written anything since he turned seventy, just notes and ideas scribbled down casually and often left dangling in mid-sentence. He had, in his own words, dried up. This was what he said when justifying his lack of output to anyone who cared to ask, and he would go on to explain that this drought had not happened overnight because of any writer's block, or emotional crisis, or from his being discouraged by falling book sales; although, of course if he had continued to have more success with his novels, or landed a serious contract with his screenplays, circumstances might have kept him wanting to keep working. It was more like water that had trickled away from a leaking well. That was how he described the process of gradually losing the energy to put down his thoughts with any coherence, and the perseverance needed to pursue any idea to the finish line; in other words, the motivation to go on telling stories. Fundamentally, it was about his age and nothing more complicated.

Those who were close to him were not convinced by this explanation, however many times he repeated it. On his previous birthday, Mitr, his son, had given him the latest desktop computer to replace his antiquated laptop and even paid for a technician to come over to teach him how to use it. Editing his text would now be even quicker on this new machine than ever before; cutting, pasting, copying in the blink of an eye, grammar and spelling corrected without even having to think about it. He could even speak into the computer if he did not feel like using his fingers to type and the text would appear instantaneously on the screen, complete with punctuation. This latest technology was incredible, he thought, and he was suitably impressed and grateful to be the owner of such a fine instrument. Another piece of modern magic, he jokingly told his son. But although he was touched by Mitr's effort to resuscitate his all but dead interest in writing he did not feel like returning to the task. The enormous, shiny new computer was left virtually untouched on his work desk for weeks, and when he eventually began to use it, he limited himself to writing emails, although this, too was a burden. The thought of writing to anyone was not one that enthused him. Those he would have liked to communicate with were either dead or totally resistant to the technology or, like himself, too lazy to keep up a regular correspondence. Instead, he often found himself answering messages from total strangers who questioned him about things he had written in the past, which meant that he would have to try to remember the characters born out of his imagination, as well as their names, and what they did or did not manage to do. This exercise in returning to his own inventions was not only increasingly tedious as time went by, but nearly impossible. It was difficult enough trying to recall correctly the names of his surviving family members let alone those of characters who had never existed in real life.

Given his insistence that he was through with writing it was, therefore, with a certain surprise that night – the sensation was one of being ambushed in a game of hide and seek – that Khun Chai, as he stood there enjoying the rain, looking out onto the garden that he had known and played in since he was born, found himself thinking of returning to it once again; not just doodling in the notebooks but producing something that had a beginning, middle and end. That night the ideas that had been dormant in his mind during the past five years began to stir once more. Stories and plots that had been lying around in the backwaters of his mind were floating up like the detritus from the bottom of a stagnant canal. Characters he had been thinking about over the years and parked in a temporary morgue were waking from their sleep like ghosts creaking back to life from their in-between realm.

It must have been something that the old woman, Yai Li did to him, he decided. Certainly, the fact that he was on his feet again and able to lift his left arm and walk with relative ease brought with it an empowering sense of relief, one that only those who have recovered from a serious physical handicap can fully appreciate, and with it a resurgence of hope and positivity. There had been moments during that year, when the pains seemed to be a permanent feature of his existence, that he felt so desperate that he even considered taking an overdose and ending it all. He was glad now that he didn't. It was not that he felt miraculously cured by what the old lady did, or that his limbs were fully functional. There was still the sense that if he moved without care all the symptoms that had been tormenting him could return in a flash. But right now, standing there where he was, he felt fine, even robust, once more free to move, and this freedom brought with it a sense of liberation on other levels of his being. It was as though a huge boulder blocking the entrance of a cave had been rolled to one side.

But what had she done, exactly? Once more he went over the session with her, trying to recall it in detail so that he could figure out the strange thing that had happened to him.

It lasted for not much more than forty minutes. She had been late because Joy could not get off work before eight o'clock that evening. He had been sitting in the wheelchair with Sai by his side, impatiently wondering when she would be arriving.

'It's the traffic,' Sai kept saying to placate him. 'Do you want me to call Khun Joy?'

'No,' he kept grunting back, unable to disguise his annoyance. It was not the fact that they were late. He knew how bad the traffic was at that hour. But the truth was that he was cross with himself at having agreed to the session in the first place. He knew it was because he did not want to contradict Mitr, who had intervened on Joy's behalf by saying:

'Come on, Pa. Give her a chance. It can't do you any harm. At least you'll get a good massage, I'm sure. You haven't had one of those for a long time.'

But Khun Chai was unconvinced that Joy's granny was going to make the slightest difference to his condition, since he had been seen by the best specialists that his son's money could buy. Nevertheless, as an erstwhile writer, he was curious to meet her as he'd never met a healer in the flesh before. He had often heard stories since his childhood of people with the gift to do extraordinary things, of monks with mystical powers and so on. He had even elaborated on these tales in one of his novels. But he had never come across any of these special people in the flesh, let alone received a treatment from them.

His first impression, when they finally arrived, was not a favourable one. As he watched Yai Li walk slowly and haltingly up the steps slightly behind her granddaughter, he noticed that she had a cloth shoulder bag slung across her chest that jarred with the modern clothes that she was wearing, especially the black patent leather slip-ons. He had been expecting someone in a sarong to turn up, looking the part of a traditional healer, not this old lady who was dressed like she was going to a temple fair. Her hair was grey and tied in a bun in the back, but not in a neat way. There were strands sticking out on both sides. She climbed the last few steps with difficulty, and this added to the general feeling of disappointment that Khun Chai felt on her arrival. How was this dishevelled woman, who was clearly not in good shape, possibly going to help me? he asked himself. When she was finally standing in front of him, she put her hands together in greeting and looked at him for an instant, very directly. He could not help but notice her fine features; the high, clean forehead, large eyes set wide apart, prominent cheekbones, an open relaxed expression, no wrinkles around her full lipped mouth. He thought for a moment that he was facing not someone who was probably about the same age as himself but a young and beautiful woman with the dark brown skin of someone from the South, perhaps. For a few seconds her gaze seemed to bore right into him. Then, just as quickly, she looked down towards the floor.

Their session took place in the large room downstairs overlooking the garden that Mitr had turned into a bedroom and study for him, so that he did not need to go upstairs to his own quarters. With Sai's help Khun Chai had obediently removed his shirt and was lying face down on his bed while Yai Li sat on a low chair beside him. He was hardly aware that she was touching him for a long time. It was only very gradually that he sensed a kind of warm tingling on his skin as her hands glided over his back, although he could not be sure this was what she was doing because he had his head turned away from her. The silence in the room was palpable, creating an atmosphere he found uncomfortable and oppressive. There were just the two of them. It was the first time in years that he had been alone with a woman in a bedroom, he realised. He felt the urge to break the spell by saying something. But he found himself uncharacteristically speechless. Then at some point he began to feel that her finger was on the side of his neck. It felt like the cold tip of a knife or an arrow. All of a sudden, images appeared in his mind; vivid scenes of a battlefield, of himself dressed as an ancient warrior, with a short sword in each hand. Then something pierced his neck from the right side. It felt like a sharp weapon and with it came the shock of stabbing pain. This was when he had shouted out. Then, to his amazement, he could move his neck freely again. She had done something no specialist with their training, technology and their medicines, had managed to do. It was truly unbelievable. Mobility had returned and now with it his creativity was revived. Even if this new spark of inspiration came to nothing, at least he was feeling something other than the depression that he had been suffering since his physical problems began to cripple him.

The rain finally stopped. The air was fresh and cool and scented. As Khun Chai wrapped the faded silk dressing gown that he had inherited from his father and tied it round his waist, he was thinking of how the old man would be complaining of the waste of money. In his mind he could hear him shouting:

'Why, for heaven's sake do they leave the lights on in the garden all night long? Do they know how much it costs?'

His father, who managed to lose one fortune through gambling and signed away a second through drunkenness, ended his life as a stingy man who counted his pennies and scrimped on everything, even, it was rumoured, to the point of rationing matches to the cook.

He himself had once brought up the question of the extravagance of having all night lighting in the garden with his son Mitr, who had answered, with his winsome smile:

'Don't worry, Pa. I can afford it. And isn't it beautiful?'

He had to admit that it was. Besides, he knew it was churlish of him to criticize anything Mitr had done. Without the huge amount that his son had spent on repurchasing the place and the necessary repairs and restoration work that ensued, Baan Suan, as the mansion was called, would not have been the jewel that it now was. The building would have been desperately run down and the gardens would have reverted to being a thick jungle. In fact, the whole place would have already been sold, or torn down like most of the old buildings in Bangkok to make way for a modern compound or another hideous giant condo. Khun Chai was grateful to his son for saving the property from this fate and for having converted it into the fine dwelling that it was now. He had no cause to complain. He was living in a house that was a distant dream for most of the inhabitants of the city.

Chapter 3

PART I

Baan Suan was built by Khun Chai's grandfather, Khun Luang Paiboon Thammawong (1880- 1931). There is no mention of him in any history book or journal of social history. There are a few copies remaining in private libraries of the text written for his funeral ceremony, but these would be hard to find. He is not even remembered by his grandson who never met him. But for his generation he was a well-known figure in Siamese society who, by the time he was forty, had acquired the dubious reputation of being both an eccentric and a degenerate.

The first description was the result of his decision to purchase a large piece of land to the north of the city. This involved sending his agents out to negotiate with the owners of all the small holdings in that area, which was in itself a laborious task that took patience, dedication and a considerable amount of ready cash. Once this was done, the construction of Baan Suan was begun. Family members and friends, who were on the whole conservative in their outlook, saw it as a decision not motivated by rationality but by an unnecessary wish to indulge a fancy that left them all bewildered. Paiboon was thirty-two years old, former heir to one of the largest teak companies in Siam, married to a high-born lady who had borne him a son, and already living in a fine house by the river in Thonburi. He had everything that any wealthy gentleman could want. He was a part of the social scene, a regular guest at all the grandest parties. He did not need another dwelling, particularly in Pakret, an area that was then considered to be the dark countryside with no streetlights or any civilized activity, difficult to access and, potentially dangerous. Why did he want to remove himself from society? But Khun Paiboon, as he was known then – the title came afterwards – was not one to be dissuaded.

The construction of the house began in the first months of 1912 and was finished in late 1915. An Italian architect, the esteemed Paolo Giacone, who had already been employed by several of the richest families to build their mansions, was contracted to design and oversee the project; to create a sumptuous Italian style villa suited to the tropics. There were numerous grand mansions already dotted over the city, but Paiboon wanted his to be the most impressive. Money was no obstacle. The result was a two-story building in pale pink marble imported from Carrara with a tower and a domed observatory that topped the whole structure. It could have stood on any one of Rome's most splendid avenues but had the airiness that suited the heat of the local climate. The garden, also designed in the European style, its formality blending with the tropical extravagance, included a croquet lawn that was later turned into the swimming pool. The interior of Baan Suan, which was the name Paiboon chose for his new dwelling, was lavishly elegant. Persian carpets covered the floor of the dining room. Vast chandeliers, brought over from Paris, hung from the ceiling in between the large circular fans. The West wing held a full-size snooker room with a long bar stretching the whole of one side. There were outbuildings for the servants and stables for the horses and the carriages that transported Paiboon and his guests to and from the city. Behind the house ran a wide canal that eventually joined the main river at Pakret. Beside it, a wooden building was constructed to house the boats that were used to ferry the servants to market and the guests from the pier on the Chao Phraya River. There was also a garage where the car that his father had imported just before he died was kept; a forest green Napier 40/50 HP. There was only one other model in the country and that was to be found in the royal palace. Paiboon used the car to drive round the estate and occasionally on the main road that led to Ayutthaya. But he did not enjoy driving it into the city. It attracted too much attention, and besides, he always preferred the rhythm and the sounds of the horse and carriage.

The property, which was about 500 acres of cultivated land, orchards and extensive kitchen gardens, was tended by the families who had been persuaded to sell their own allotments to him and who now carried on living on the estate, dependent on his patronage for their livelihood. All around there were paddy fields where water buffaloes wallowed in the irrigation canals. It was rich farming country. This was just before Don Muang, Bangkok's first airport was about to be constructed just a few miles to the east of the property. By the time it was completed many of those who had previously criticized Paiboon's decision to move there agreed that it was a shrewd investment after all, as they watched him add to his fortune by selling off chunks of his large estate to developers who were keen to see Bangkok expanding in that northerly direction.

As for Paiboon's reputation of being a degenerate, those who knew him blamed it on the education he received while in England, at Oxford University. As a young student there, the young Paiboon had been taken up by a group of the so-called aesthetes of his generation keen to have a handsome oriental among them. He was an exotic addition to their ranks and under their guidance he discovered the joys of theatre, of music, of poetry, of beauty, and of opium. Before his death he would admit to his son that such was his enjoyment of his time in Oxford that he had entertained the idea of remaining in England forever after obtaining his degree in Natural Science. But his overriding sense of duty to his father was what convinced him to return to Siam in 1903 at the age of 23. Only those Siamese students who had known him in England could have been aware of the radical change that he assumed by the time that he stepped off the boat after the tedious journey and onto the shore of his native land. Gone were the flamboyant clothes and the long curly hair. He was now soberly dressed and groomed, looking like the English gentleman that he was meant to be, returning to his native land to fulfil his filial duties.

On his return to Siam, he duly joined the business that had been set up by his father in Sam Ngao on the Mae Ping River in the 1870s, and eventually took it over when his father died in 1908. During those initial five years back in his homeland he worked diligently to turn the company into the one that the British traders preferred to deal with. It helped that he spoke the language perfectly whereas other Thai teak merchants at that time had to make do with interpreters who did not always act in their interest. Another advantage was that having been educated abroad, he was acquainted with the way the foreigners approached a deal and the subtle tricks they used to gain the most out of it. Within a few short years of returning to Siam, Paiboon had expanded the business and increased the family's wealth beyond anyone's imagination. In the meantime, he had married a minor royal from the line of Rama III, called Ying Mai; an elegant, shy lady who bore him a son named Wigrom.

With the death of his father things began to change. It was as if Paiboon now felt free of his filial responsibilities and the parts of himself that he had pushed aside in order to show that he was a grateful and loyal heir, began to emerge from the shadows. At first, he still took an active interest in the business but gradually he became happy to let his assistants do the work of negotiating all the deals in the north of the country while he stayed in Bangkok. Then, three years after his father's death, he made the decision to sell the company to a British firm based in Burma, called 'Johnson and Hargreaves', for a sum that made him one of the richest men in the country. His two younger sisters who were both married, one to a high ranking soldier and the other to a diplomat, received a generous chunk from the proceeds of the sale. It was with a small part of the rest that he built Baan Suan. Once it was finished, he moved his wife and young son, along with his large household of servants, out to the countryside. To his delight, his wife, Ying Mai, took to her new life with ease and grace and within a year had set up a small clinic in the village nearby, where she employed a doctor and his team to attend to the needs of the poor in the local community. Wigrom was already going to the Royal Pages School set up by Rama VI as a boarder, in preparation for being sent over to England to carry on the tradition of being educated in the same establishments that Paiboon had been.

The first years in Baan Suan were filled with endless social events. Guests that included businessmen, high ranking military, politicians and members of the royalty, rubbed shoulders with the foreign dignitaries at the lavish parties held on the lawn. The notables of Thai society spent long evenings in the snooker room discussing the state of the country and sharing the latest court gossip. This was a period of change and the opinions regarding its direction was divided. The 1912 palace rebellion highlighted the grievances among the ruling class as to what was best for their interests and for the country's. Although he himself had no ambitions to play a role in Siam's political life, Paiboon enjoyed being included in these private unofficial discussions in the company of those who had the power in their hands to influence the course of the country's history. But the years away from Siam had left him with a sense of being an outsider. He vaguely supported the king's policies and yet he felt no particular allegiance to the aristocracy. The liberal ideas that he had encountered and absorbed during his time in Oxford still influenced him. But he did not think that he had any part to play in reshaping his own country into a modern Western-style system. Siam was a world apart from the England he had known.

This initial golden period of Baan Suan lasted no more than five years. It was not that Paiboon became bored with the house he had built, or with his role as a country squire, or of being host to so many influential people. But the old habits that he had learned during his time as an Oxford student re-emerged, and now, with his immense wealth, there was no obstacle to indulging them. Gradually the gatherings at Baan Suan were held less frequently and he began to go back to Bangkok more often, to stay in the old family home on the river in Thonburi that had been kept as a pied-a-terre for whenever he had business to do in the city. This involved the projects to build schools for the children of the poorer classes that he had initiated a year after returning from England, and for which he was given the honorific title of Khun Luang, bestowed by the king himself.

The other business that now brought him back to the city was less motivated by social conscience. Soon after Baan Suan was finished Paiboon discovered a passion for the traditional performing arts. This happened one evening in the dry season when his estate manager, who was responsible for the entertainment of the guests, had arranged for a dance troupe, complete with musicians to come and perform on the stage set up on the lawn. Until then, Paiboon had thought of culture in terms of what he had seen, heard and admired in the theatres and other venues in London and Oxford. He had a slightly disdainful attitude to the music and dance in his native country which seemed to him, as a young boy, repetitive and obscure. But on that hot, cloudless evening he found himself enchanted by the spectacle. The costumes and the masks and even the music that had once bored him now took on a different meaning. He discovered an underlying mystery to them that intrigued him and introduced a dimension of myth and allegory that were new to him. There and then, on a whim, he decided to convert the part of the Thonburi house on the river that had served as the former headquarters of the teak company into a school of music and dance. Inevitably, once established, it attracted the most talented in the land and within a short time the dance troupe became the best and most sought after. Paiboon was thereafter known as a patron of the arts.

At first, he would be driven down to the city to visit from time to time and to check on the progress of his school. But gradually he would spend the weekdays in the Thonburi house, and the weekends with his family in Baan Suan. The reason for this change of routine was twofold and obvious to everyone. Firstly, his famous troupe consisted of extremely beautiful young men and women. Paiboon, who had always enjoyed his sensual pleasures and appreciated the charms of both sexes, in effect now had his own harem. The male and female dancers and performers returned his generous support by yielding to his sexual desires. The other reason why he now preferred to stay in the city rather than in his luxurious country mansion was that he rediscovered the drug that gave him even more satisfaction than sexual pleasure. Opium. It was something that he had tried with friends once or twice in Oxford, but which had not impressed him in any notable way. But when he began smoking it again in the opium houses that were still legal at that time in Bangkok, he knew that he had found the medicine that he was looking for. He enjoyed the drug that gave him access to the ethereal world to such an extent that he kept a special room in the house where only he and the manservant who provided the opium and prepared his pipes was allowed to enter.

Eventually, it was as though he had forgotten that he owned a house in the countryside. Baan Suan became a distant dream, from another lifetime. He left his wife and son living in style and well looked after by the army of servants at their disposal while he remained in the house on the river. By the time he reached the age of forty he never returned to Baan Suan. News of his life in the Thonburi house spread through Siamese high society and he was the object of constant dinner table gossip. His behaviour was considered scandalous by his relatives, and he was shunned by them. But he was oblivious to their criticisms. He was wealthy enough not to need their approval. It was harder when old friends and colleagues started to abandon him. But the opium smoothed over any sadness that he might have felt. In any case, he was now left with the company of his beautiful dancers who administered to his needs. Unfortunately, as his addiction grew, they took advantage of his dislocated mental state to do practically what they pleased. The discipline that had once been a crucial part of the running of the school turned into anarchy. Without leadership there were constant power plays, and internal rivalries often turned into violent conflict, so that gradually the house was filled with those who hung around like leeches while the serious performers found work with other dance troupes in the city. It was fortunate that Khun Luang could still count on the loyalty of one or two of his servants, who had known him since he was a child and who protected him as best they could from the vultures who were waiting to pick at the corpse. One of these retainers was Sai's grandfather. When Paiboon died in 1931 aged 51, an emaciated, hollow-eyed, prematurely aged man, there were rumours that his death was due to poisoning by one of his jealous lovers but no proof of this emerged. In fact, it was a lung disease that killed him.

PART II

Khun Chai's father, Wigrom, officially inherited the property in 1932, the year of the revolution that eventually turned Siam into Thailand. With his domineering, pious mother he had been running the estate from the time Khun Luang Paiboon abandoned them to their own fate in Baan Suan. As an only child he had known and enjoyed the deep affection of his father in his early years. But by the time he was at boarding school in the city, that paternal presence had all but been withdrawn. Whenever he did see his father as he was growing up, it was on trips to the Thonburi house, driven there in the Napier by the chauffeur. He would always find Khun Luang surrounded by the dancers and performers who, in his eyes, were wicked people who had only their own interests at heart, and he blamed them for encouraging his father, their benefactor, to sink deeper into the smoke-filled realm of his opium-fuelled mind. Often, he would find Khun Luang in a semi-articulate state, and their meetings were stiff and awkward, punctuated by long silences in which his father stared off into his private space. During these encounters, Wigrom would sometimes receive bits of vague manly advice handed out in a slurry voice to which he paid little or no attention. But he kept his patience and listened dutifully because the purpose of these visits was to remind his father to fill the old Gladstone bag that he took with him full of the cash that was kept in a safe in a back room. This bundle, never counted, was the material compensation that he and his long-suffering mother received for having been left behind in the mansion in Pakret, and he felt no guilt or hesitation in carrying it back there. Sometimes he would find Khun Luang in what he came to recognize as a limbo state when his father mumbled at him making no sense at all, either having just emerged from his smoking room, or so eager to be back there that he hardly acknowledged the presence of his son. On these occasions, sloppily dressed and unshaven, Khun Luang would slump into his wicker chair and recount to his son things that flowed spontaneously from his imagination mixed with the experiences he retained from when he was a student in England, and when he first worked for the teak company. In these ramblings the river Mae Ping merged with the Thames and the elephants pushed teak logs all the way through dead autumn leaves into the Surrey hills. Thankfully for the young Wigrom, these meetings in the Thonburi house were infrequent. There was enough cash stuffed into the bag from each visit to last for many months. What Wigrom really wanted from his father was for him to honour the promise made when he began going to the Royal Pages School; namely, that he would be sent one day to England. He had been fed stories about the place since he was a little boy. It was his dream to see London and ride on an omnibus, to visit the British Museum, and sit under the huge trees in Hyde Park. He even asked his father several times to make the necessary arrangements for his journey and to provide him with the letters that would get him registered at the English school where he was meant to be going. But none of it ever happened, not because of his father, who was ready to put his signature to anything, but because his mother would not let him go. She told him that she needed him by her side to help run the estate while she carried on with her charity work, looking after the poor and supporting the various monasteries that she visited regularly.

All these circumstances turned Wigrom into a bitter young man to whom financial wealth was synonymous with pain and disappointment. Because of this, by the time he was in his early twenties, without a formal completed education either abroad or in his own country, he turned his attention to the art of losing money as best he could. His trips to the city now included going to the card games taking place in one of the mansions or in the private back room of an exclusive restaurant in Chinatown. It was in these venues that he discovered his love for gambling. By the time that his father died, followed by his mother two years later from what was then known as consumption, he was already a familiar face on the circuit of habitual card players, whose lives revolved around the next encounter with chance. He had replaced his father's vice with his own addiction.

1932 is a date that marks a turning point that has set the tone for the political journey of the nation since then. Some would say it is the most important year in Thailand's modern history, one full of hope and confidence that the old ways were going to be replaced by a more just and equitable system. Democracy was going to take over from autocracy. For Wigrom it was also the most significant year of his life – one that was also filled with hope and confidence, although in his case this had nothing to do with social and political transformation. The way he explained it much later, when he had long ceased to have enough money to play with and to lose what he called 'a decent game', never ceased to amaze Khun Chai.

Khun Luang Paiboon's death the previous year had left Wigrom with a huge fortune. The first thing that he did when he received his inheritance was to sell the Thonburi house, which he had always hated for all that it stood for and the bad memories it held. He kept the servants he felt had been faithful to his father and disposed of the rest along with the dancers and the hangers on. When his mother died, he made sure that all her charitable projects would continue being supported although he would no longer take any active role in them. In Baan Suan he had the snooker room converted into two adjoining areas; one was furnished with card tables and the other became a dining space that also served as an extension to the card room. By the beginning of 1932 the work was finished. Now, every evening, there would be a group of visitors arriving either in their own chauffeur driven vehicles, ferried by boat from the main river landing in Pakret, or fetched in the Napier to enjoy a light supper before beginning the evening's activities. The wives would take a stroll out onto the balcony or into the garden before returning to the dining area after the tables were cleared. There they would play mahjong or sit around sipping tea and catching up on gossip. The men were shown into the large room to take their places round the card tables. On some of these the traditional game of Pai Tong was played. But poker was the game that Wigrom preferred. He had learned to play it at boarding school with his friends for mere ticals. Now the stakes were for real money.

The first year that these games were introduced to Baan Suan was the only year that Wigrom won on a regular basis, to the extent that some of his guests, especially the ones who lost consistently, suspected that there was some cheating going on. But this was never proven, nor was it the case. If anything, the inexplicable phenomenon of Wigrom's unbroken run of success was because he found himself in that rare state that sometimes comes to a gambler, or for that matter to anyone else; call it Grace or mere Luck, a rare moment when the gods favour you. Perhaps, like his father before him, he now felt released from a shadow that had been oppressing him, and this was the reason he kept winning. Whatever it was, for the first time in his life, he had the confidence to follow his intuition in every game he played and to trust in a force outside his control. It was thrilling for him to pick the right cards almost every time and to know when to hold back and when to push, when to call others' bluff and when to use the tactic himself. Whatever he did at the table that year, he could not fail to win.

In the meantime, events were evolving steadily towards the climax that would take place on 24th June 1932. Up till then in Baan Suan there were rumours and whispers and discreet conversations held at the dining table, or over drinks when the games were over, about what was coming. These took place on the long balcony that stretched the whole side of the house, and they were conducted along the same lines as a poker game. Nobody gave away the hand they were holding. Each intuited which side someone was on in the build-up to the actual events that were about to take place. Wigrom's position was as incoherent and contradictory as that of most of the people who frequented Baan Suan and who, like him, were members of the wealthy elite of Siamese society. Put simply, he was for the status quo even if he knew that some sort of radical change was inevitable. He did not trust the students who had studied abroad with their lofty *farang* ideas of democracy. Partly this was to do with his disappointment at not having been educated in England, as his father had promised. Having once dreamed of going abroad and, deprived from doing so, he now considered that the *farangs* had no superiority over the Asians, and that their political systems were as flawed as anyone else's. In any case, he was not convinced that a Western-style democracy was possible, or even desirable for Siam. In his opinion, there was no basis for it in a country where the majority of the population were still uneducated. But despite this patriarchal, reactionary view, he also wanted to see a shakeup in the infrastructure, a wider distribution of power so that those at the top would not continue to make such a mess of running the country.

During the months leading up to the revolution, the games at Baan Suan went on as normal and Wigrom continued to win. There is an anecdote related to this period that Khun Chai later learned of from one of the old servants. It goes like this:

One evening, a cousin of Wigrom's called Khun Tak came to Baan Suan to speak to him. But Wigrom was playing and was on a roll. Nothing was going to get him to leave the table. He was not particularly fond of this cousin and kept him sitting on the balcony waiting for more than an hour while he played game after game, winning each one. During a short break Wigrom, already informed of Tak's presence, and annoyed, goes out to meet his cousin and asks him what he wants. Khun Tak tells him:

'We need money urgently.'

Wigrom has been told that his cousin is a friend of the revolutionaries, and he knows that this money will be used to finance their adventure. He marches into the card room, sweeps all his winnings from the evening, which is a considerable sum, into a wastepaper basket, returns to the balcony and hands it to Khun Tak.

'Here. Take it. And don't show your face here ever again.'

The revolution itself was a successful gamble and set in motion a transformation of the country that might have benefited the population if the fine intentions of the revolutionaries had been properly carried out. The first constitution, written with the sincerity of ardent idealists stated: 'The highest power in the land belongs to all people.' In hindsight, this sounds more like a wish to be fulfilled rather than a description of any political reality. Unfortunately, the central notion of universal franchise put forward by the revolutionaries found little response in the people they meant to stir.

For Wigrom, it confirmed what he had been saying to anyone interested in his opinion: wait for the mess that's coming. But he took no satisfaction in being right. He wanted, more than anything, for the situation to be normalized so that the old routine of Baan Suan could be continued. But this was not to happen for several years. After the 24th June came and went, the initial euphoria of those who had managed to carry out their plan with minimum bloodshed, gave way to the reality of the situation, which was one of uncertain loyalties and private ambitions. With the confusion and the instability following the revolution, nobody was able to return to the lives they had known until the dust settled. Those who had been frequent visitors to Baan Suan were now caught up in the division created by the events that were spiralling out of control. The supporters of the monarchy held out for a compromise. Those who felt that it was time for radical change struggled to find a way that the fine ideas could be implemented, but without much success.

The country was never going to be the same, and Baan Suan never returned to the way it was before 1932. In 1935, after King Rama VII left Thailand for exile in London, Wigrom attempted to revive the card games. Compulsive gamblers like himself had made do with impromptu meetings in the intervening years but there had been no regularity, and the atmosphere was always coloured by the undermining tension produced by the conflicts of loyalty. By the time that the games were renewed in Baan Suan there were now fewer people who came to the house and among these an unspoken agreement was established – to avoid all political issues. If they were mentioned at all it was couched in language that was designed to avoid bringing up any political discourse. At first this created a tension at the meetings, but soon everyone who came seemed relieved to have an evening when they could forget about politics for a while, and they were grateful to Wigrom for providing this break from the confusion the country was going through. But for Wigrom these were not good years. From the time that he started inviting people back to Baan Suan, he began losing consistently and heavily. Week by week, month by month, he waited for his star – as gamblers call it – to change, and to feel that exhilarating flow that he had known in 1932 to return. But it never did. Eventually, in July 1941 Wigrom was informed by his foreman, Nai Samraan, that there was no money left to lose at the card table, nor to cover the expenses of running the house nor to support all the good works his mother had initiated. Fortunately, she had died and so did not live to see the collapse of all her projects due to the reckless addiction of her son.

Wigrom's unlikely saviour was an old gentleman called Khun Sombat, who as a young man had worked for his father in the teak company. Later he had branched out into the hotel business and made himself a fortune. He too liked to play poker and other card games, but, unlike Wigrom, he played for enjoyment and with great caution. When Khun Sombat learned of Wigrom's situation, which was by then common knowledge, he offered to help him financially to keep Baan Suan and the estate going; but on two conditions. One was that he would no longer gamble. This was a tall order for an addict. But Wigrom had no choice. The people he owed money to were serious about having their debts repaid and had already made thinly veiled threats about what would happen both to the house as well as to his person if these were not honoured. As for the second condition, Khun Sombat added it as a bonus to his generous offer – the hand of his youngest unmarried daughter, Taew, who was pretty and intelligent, but of a delicate disposition. This was the polite way used to describe her unstable mental condition, which would be called in modern terms a bipolar disorder. Khun Sombat was keen for her to be married to someone respectable who would look after her and provide her with a sense of stability. Although Wigrom was by now impecunious and unable to provide any security to anybody, let alone himself, he was respectable enough, being the owner of Baan Suan and the son of Khun Luang Thammawong, still remembered as a patron of the arts as well as a social benefactor, whose other less noble contributions to society had been conveniently forgotten. So it was that the marriage was arranged for that very month and Baan Suan was saved.

In December 1941, the Japanese invaded Thailand and by the following year, as a result of the treaty with the Phibun government, they were occupying Bangkok as Thailand's ally. One of their garrisons was near to Baan Suan and it was natural that they would requisition their food supplies from the estate. Wigrom willingly complied because he was an open supporter of the Japanese cause. They were Asians, like him, who would give back territory that the French and British had robbed from Siam and eventually ensure that the *farang* colonials would be kicked out of India and Southeast Asia altogether. He even set about constructing new granaries with the funds received from his father-in-law. These were to prove vital during the terrible floods in late 1942, when all of Bangkok was underwater.

Nobody thought that Wigrom was capable of it, but he kept his vow to Khun Sombat. He never played another game of cards again in his life. It is not hard to imagine how difficult this must have been for a seasoned, addicted gambler. In part, as compensation for his abstinence from the card table he began drinking regularly. At first this helped to lift his mood and to stave off depression. When he drank, he would feel relaxed enough to be kind and considerate to his wife, Khun Taew. The fact that their marriage was one of convenience meant that neither of them was together by choice nor by attraction. Nevertheless, Wigrom tried to honour his pledge to his father-in-law to look after Khun Taew as best he could, even though she remained a mystery to him until the day she died.

When she first moved into Baan Suan, she threw herself into the projects that Wigrom's mother had been involved with. But her enthusiasm was excessive, and she wanted everyone in the household, including her husband to become involved to such an extent that it had the effect of discouraging people from helping her. Fortunately, within three years of their marriage, by which time she had become totally exasperated by the lack of cooperation she encountered and deeply disappointed in Wigrom and those around him. But, then, in 1944 she learned that she was pregnant.

During the bombing raids by the Allies in June, a son was born prematurely to Khun Taew after a very strenuous and problematic pregnancy. It was only through Wigrom's contact with the military commander of the garrison that Khun Taew received treatment from a Japanese doctor who gave her a Caesarian section. Even as she held her baby in her arms the symptoms produced by her preeclampsia were worsening. The swellings in her legs and hands were painful and she was suffering from agonizing headaches, but she was determined to have her new-born by her side. His life was precarious. She had already given him a name.

'Khun Chai. We will call him Khun Chai', she told her husband emphatically.

'But he's only got a tiny drop of royal blood in him, from my mother, hardly enough to warrant him being given any title. He's not a Momrachawong, nor even a Momluang,' Wigrom said sarcastically.

'I don't care!' She shouted angrily. 'This is going to be his name. He is my little prince. He's my Khun Chai.'

There was no way to argue with her and Wigrom accepted her decision.

A few days after this exchange, Khun Taew suffered a high fever and died from heart failure. The baby was given over to the arms of Na Cheua, the wife of the gardener, who looked after him like her own child. After the death of his wife, Wigrom seemed to become uninterested in the world outside of Baan Suan. All that he cared about, apart from the alcohol, was his son, who became the source of his joy and delight. He would sit on the balcony in the steamy afternoons, sipping from his glass of whisky, watching Na Cheua feeding the baby with the milk bottle as they sat on the reed mat on the lawn under one of the shady tamarinds. Afterwards, she would bring Khun Chai up to be held in his father's arms and rocked to sleep. Wigrom had never thought that he could know such tenderness towards another human being until then. But none of this prevented him from continuing his alcoholic road towards oblivion.

The end of the war did not make much difference to life in Baan Suan or the estate. Those who had always planted the rice, and tended the orchards and kitchen garden carried on with their day-to-day work unaffected by what was going on beyond its confines. Wigrom had no income but Khun Sombat, in his capacity as father-in-law, and proud grandfather to Khun Chai, his only grandson, provided him with enough money to maintain the estate and his household of servants.

If during those post war years Wigrom was at all aware of the events taking place in the country, it was mainly through his foreman, Nai Samraan. Wigrom himself hardly read the newspapers that were delivered to Baan Suan, and preferred listening to music on the radio as he sat with his drink in his hand, rather than learn about the news. When Nai Samraan told him that the king, Rama VIII, had returned from exile in Switzerland, Wigrom raised his glass and gave thanks. On hearing of his death, the following year, he wore a black armband and lit a candle in the Buddha room as a sign of mourning before pouring himself another tall drink. When Rama IX ascended the throne, he toasted the occasion with another glass of whisky. He was a constant, loyal monarchist. But he was uninterested in the political turmoil, the successive coups and counter coups and constant changes in the government, recounted in detail and explained by Nai Samraan. These events were noted by him with a nod at the most and sometimes with a wry comment.

'I suppose we'll muddle through. We have no choice, do we, Samraan?' These words were the only show of optimism that he ever expressed.

PART III

Khun Chai grew into a lively child who had the run of the house and treated the estate as his playground. His father, once so attentive and loving when he was a baby, now paid little attention to what his son was up to. He turned increasingly inward and felt no inclination to introduce his son to other members of his family and their children. As a result, Khun Chai never felt that he had any family other than the one in Baan Suan. As the years went by, Wigrom also became more and more unpredictable, distant and irascible. It was obvious to everyone that this was because of the drink, but there was no one who could give him any advice. Nai Samraan, his foreman, would often be the person who helped him up to the bedroom and the one to rouse him in the late morning. Due to his father's increasing remoteness and ill temper, Khun Chai spent his days by himself reading and drawing, wandering through the wide empty rooms, getting to know the furniture and collection of paintings and sculptures, going up to the observatory, which was his favourite place in the house, to look at the stars, or spending hours with the servants in the kitchen and in the fields learning about their work through the seasons. He played with their children and shared his toys with them. In later life he would attribute his identification with the less privileged to this phase of his upbringing. His pleasure was sitting on the kitchen floor with Na Cheua and the cook and the serving girls, watching the ironing being done, eating curry and rice with his fingers, hearing about the latest exploits of the drunken gardener, Nai Noon. This was Na Cheua's husband and Khun Chai always felt sad for her when he heard these stories. On the days when his grandfather, Khun Sombat visited Baan Suan, Na Cheua would quickly make sure that he looked clean and presentable and then take him up to the dining room where he would sit stiffly by his grandfather's side while the old man interviewed him. These occasions were usually formal and boring for him, and he was always aware that he preferred to be in the kitchen.

Khun Sombat was a kind man, and blamed Wigrom's drinking on the grief at Khun Taew's death. It was partly true that Wigrom had developed a certain fondness for his strange wife during the short time they were together. But perhaps nearer to the truth was his longing to gamble again and the inability to do so that had turned him into an alcoholic. In any case, Khun Sombat chose the more charitable explanation that was closer to how he himself felt, and as a result was forgiving of all that Wigrom did or did not do for his son. He assumed charge of his beloved grandson's well-being, and paid for a tutor to teach Khun Chai at home, because ferrying him to school in the city every day and bringing him back would have taken too much time and effort. When Khun Chai was nine, Khun Sombat decided to send his grandson to be a boarder at Vajiravudh School, which was originally the Royal Pages School where Wigrom himself had been educated. Khun Sombat felt that it was time for the boy to learn how to mix with peers of his own class, acquire discipline and good manners, and be trained to be one of the eventual rulers of the country. For Khun Chai, the next years were far from happy ones. Away from the comforting attention of Na Cheua and the familiar surroundings of Baan Suan, he found himself, as a boarder for the first time, in an environment for which he had not been prepared in the least. He had never played with any children other than the sons and daughters of the servants and the people who lived on the estate, yet now he found himself among the sons of the elite of Thai society, many of who were scornful of his rustic ways and his ignorance of city life. He was teased constantly about his name.

'You're a fake Khun Chai,' he was told more than once. 'Your parents are both commoners.'

Fortunately for him, he was a strong boy and good at sports, and at Vajiravudh he learned to box, thereby discouraging any would be bullies of his own age from attacking him. Nevertheless, he was constantly the object of malicious pranks, all of which gave him a sense of being different from his peers, of not sharing their values, their manners or sense of humour. The only area where he won any respect from them was on the rugby pitch and in the boxing ring.

At the age of fifteen, on a visit back to Baan Suan, Khun Chai was told by his father that he and his grandfather had decided that he was to be sent to school in England, to the same school that his other grandfather Khun Luang Paiboon had been to, and from there to Oxford. His father, less drunk than usual that day, explained to him how he had always wanted to go to England himself but that it had not been possible, and how Khun Chai was lucky to be able to do so. Khun Sombat, who was present at the meeting in the study downstairs, also expressed his great satisfaction that Khun Chai was going to receive such a good education abroad. This would prepare him for work either in one of the ministries when he came back with his degree, preferably the Foreign Ministry, or in a foreign company if that was what he preferred. He, of course, would be paying the fees and giving Khun Chai his allowance. Khun Chai's own views were not even asked for. He sat silently while the two men mapped out his future and he realised, as he listened to them talking enthusiastically, that he was to be the one carrying out their dreams and compensating for the regret both held that they had missed out on an education in the civilised West.

In 1959, Khun Chai, dressed in an uncomfortable grey suit and tie, turned around to look at the house as the car wound down the drive on the way to Don Muang airport, where he would board the BOAC flight to London. When he said goodbye to Na Cheua, he hardly dared to look her in the eye in case the emotions he felt in his chest would spill out. He did not know that he would never see her again. But he sensed it, as it dawned on him that it would be many years before he returned to Baan Suan, with its pale pink marble glowing in the sunshine, its lush gardens crawling with life, its quaint tower and domed observatory where he had spent pleasurable hours watching the night sky. The sadness he felt at leaving the place that is so dear to him, and the people he had grown up with, cut through his heart like a cold blade. But he showed nothing on the outside as he sat stiffly in the large Mercedes next to his grandfather, smelling of German cologne, who would also have died before the year was out from cancer. His last backward gaze caught his father standing on the balcony in a white short-sleeved shirt and khaki shorts, one hand holding his glass of whisky and the other waving goodbye. The next time they were to meet would be in the heavy silence of a hospital room.

Chapter 4

It is almost dawn, four days after Yai Li's first visit to Baan Suan. A slither of light is appearing in the eastern sky. The air is cool. There is not a sound in the garden. Khun Chai sits perfectly still, as if in a meditative trance. Since their meeting he had spent the long nights in much the same way, in silence, absorbed in his own history and that of the house. Contemplating the past was nothing new. Revisiting the people and events he had known had been part of his work as a writer. He had constructed many fictional biographies that were born out of his own experiences. But it was a long time since he had returned to his past in order to construct a narrative. Personal reminiscing, analysis and interpretation of the past, were not things he found necessary. Over the years, he had heard people say that when you reached old age, and were edging step by step towards the horizon, it was natural to look back on the trodden path in order to try to make some sense of what had happened, and perhaps to discern some underlying theme. 'Life Review' was the grand phrase he had come across in an English language article on Death and Dying. But he could not help feeling that this was an indulgence, at best a waste of time. He trusted more in fiction, and reinvention. To him, there was nothing to hold on to from the past. Memory, in his opinion, was a neurological phenomenon that remained a mystery. A drift of overheard conversation, a scent lingering in the air, certain colours, and other sensorial moments had the power to provoke spontaneous recollections of events that he could not be absolutely convinced had actually taken place, and there seemed to be so many of these that he had made it a point not to give them any importance. In this respect he followed the advice that his old nanny Na Cheua, a devout Buddhist, had always given him when he was a boy. '*Aniccam, Aniccam*', Impermanence, Impermanence, she was forever telling him when he was growing up. Let it all go. It doesn't matter now.

Whenever she said this, she was usually referring to her husband's exploits. Even as a child he understood that what she meant was that she did not want to hold onto the pain that Nai Noon caused her with his drunkenness and his womanising. Repeating *Aniccam, Aniccam* was her way of coping. Those Pali words, rooted in the Buddhism that she practiced, were imprinted in his heart. He could hear her voice intoning them. And he recalled how he had never fully accepted what they implied. Of course, they were true in the absolute sense. We cannot go back to what has gone. But surely, we carry within us all that has happened, all that we have seen and experienced, as part of ourselves. This had been his argument as soon as he began to question the things that Na Cheua taught him. Later, as a writer his creative process involved an exploration of the past and of people's recollection of it; what might have been, what could have been. Out of this came the plots and scenarios that he spent so many hours inventing and elaborating; the fictional histories of his characters that were intertwined with his own memories. Yet, for all his scepticism about Na Cheua's way of dealing with the things that had been unpleasant for her, he never entirely rejected what she had transmitted to him. He could not deny that there was something skilful, even wise, about her strategy, because it had helped him many times to push the dark, painful events that he had known into a far corner of his mind. '*Aniccam*', for him, as it had been for his Na Cheua, was a kind of self-protective shrug that said: 'It happened. Now let's move on.'

But ever since he had felt Yai Li's touch on his skin, he found himself traveling back in time with astonishing vividness; to his childhood, to his father and grandfather, to the mother he never knew, to his youth. It was like a river flowing against the tide, returning to its source, retracing its course over the stones and the fallen bits of tree trunk, weeds and wild plants. Sometimes, as he sat looking across the garden, he could feel an emotion that he had as a boy when the gardener walked up and held a snake for him to stroke, or catch the smell of the flowers in the hospital room where his father lay dying, or hear an argument that he had with a colleague at the newspaper where he worked in his twenties as if it were being played out that very moment. None of these or all the other memories that welled up seemed to be triggered by anything obvious. Nor did they, for the moment, make any sense to him. There was no pattern that he could discern. They just surfaced willy-nilly from the depths of his consciousness, like bits of discarded waste bobbing up from the muddy bottom.

He tried to understand why it should be happening to him at all. There was something disturbing about being reconnected to the past in this chaotic, intense way. What's more, he seemed to have no choice in the matter, and he asked himself if it had anything to do with his mortality. Was there something that he had to confront, while he had the mental and emotional energy to do so? At first, the answer was a resounding no. There were no skeletons in the cupboard that he could think of. He had committed no crime nor anything that he had to be guilty or ashamed of, apart from having married his wife without loving her. Yet here too he could find nothing to feel guilty about. He had done her no harm, verbally or physically that he remembered. In fact, he had tried his best to be kind to her. It was she who had treated him badly.

As the scenes continued to appear in his mind, he realised that there was a feeling that came with them, of something unresolved that was demanding to be acknowledged. It was subtle at first, and he had no way of telling when it would steal up on him, like a fleeting shadow that he caught out of the corner of his eye when he was least expecting it. But as the days went by this shadow began to stay close by his side until slowly it appeared to him clearly like an energy made flesh, and he began to see that along with these memories there was the lurking sense of *Dukkha*. That Buddhist term covered all shades of suffering, but for him it took on a precise shape and meaning. It pinpointed the emotion that he had managed, up till now, to push deep into the recesses of his heart – grief. It was this grief that was now making itself felt with a poignancy that surprised him, and he realised that his avoidance of it had infiltrated every aspect of his life; his failed relationships, his inability to love, his constant lack of peace. Perhaps it was time to bring this unresolved part of himself that was so crucial into the light and the air. But how?

The whole of that week, Khun Chai found himself impatient to see Yai Li again and to question her about her powers as he was now totally convinced that she was responsible for the strange process that was reconnecting him to this grief. While he waited for her next visit, he spent the afternoons sitting in the wicker chair on the balcony, in silence, almost oblivious to his surroundings, absorbed in the flow of consciousness that was a replay of his life.

⁕⁕⁕

On the Sunday morning, the day that Yai Li was meant to come to give him his second treatment, at seven o'clock, when he should still have been asleep, Khun Chai was awakened by the sound of raised voices in the hallway outside his room. They were those of his son and Arunee, his wife. He heard Mitr saying:

'I told you, darling. I'll meet you there. I just have to pick up some papers from the office and warn the team that the visit to Cha-am is off.'

'But you can just call them, can't you?'

Khun Chai heard the annoyance in his daughter-in-law's voice.

'We were all going to go from there in the van. Anyway…'

She did not let him finish.

'Oh, never mind!' she said impatiently. Then Khun Chai heard footsteps and the front door opening and closing several times.

He lay in bed, now fully awake, wondering what had happened to make them talk to each other in that manner. He had not seen them the previous evening because they were attending a charity dinner in a hotel in the city. He had heard them entering at around eleven, and Mitr had poked his head in briefly to say goodnight without stopping for a chat, which he usually did. Their voices that morning had an aggressive ring that he recognised from his own episodes of conflict with Mitr's mother before they separated. Ever since they had been living together in the house, Khun Chai had never seen them having an argument or heard either of them sound less than polite and loving to one another. He had not noticed anything different about them in the recent months except for their growing concern about his health. Arunee had accompanied him to the hospitals and clinics like the caring, dutiful person she was known to be and dealt with all the logistics with calm and patience. He had never noticed any tension between her and Mitr and nothing in their behaviour towards each other up till that morning that might have suggested that there was any marital problem. In fact, they seemed perfectly suited to each other in every respect.

In his mind, the only possible cause of their misunderstanding could be Joy, his son's secretary. Naturally, he presumed that Joy was Mitr's mistress, although it was difficult for him to imagine his straight-laced, intellectual, socially awkward son going down that well-trodden road. But in Thai culture this kind of entitlement came with his status in society. It would have been more surprising if, as the CEO of one the biggest companies in the land, he had not taken a mistress or a male lover. And there was no doubt that Joy was attractive and intelligent. Did she, Khun Chai wondered, have any ambitions to consolidate her position? Was this the reason for Arunee's sharp tone that morning? Was she angry about their affair? But just as quickly as these thoughts arose in his mind Khun Chai immediately dismissed them because he was certain that Mitr and his wife had already come to an understanding about this issue, as they had done about not having children. He noticed the looks they exchanged when Joy first visited the house one Sunday a couple of years earlier, to do some overtime work in Mitr's study. She stayed over for lunch that day. He could not remember the conversation, only that it was light-hearted and entertaining. During the meal, Khun Chai got the impression that this was all for the sake of Arunee. Joy was being formally presented to her, for her appraisal as well as approval, and he could sense in Arunee's manner that day, that she not only complied with Mitr's wishes but almost congratulated him on making such a good choice.

Khun Chai, of course could not be certain that any of his perceptions was correct. In his time, he had seen so many different combinations and arrangements in his own family and those around him that Mitr and Arunee's mutual understanding was just one more possibility to be played out in the human comedy that he had been studying for the greater part of his life. He allowed himself to wonder too if the fact that Arunee's acceptance of Mitr's need to have a mistress came perhaps from her dislike of sex. It was difficult to be sure and Khun Chai did not dwell on these conjectures although he had noted that, for all her good looks and admirable qualities, sensuality was not one of them. There was a certain trait in her that he could not put a finger on until, one day, by chance he read an article in an English language magazine that contained popular psychology. In it he came across the term 'Obsessive Compulsive'. This described the quirks in her behaviour that he had constantly noticed. He would observe how the arrangement of objects and cutlery had to be precise and how she would push a chair an inch or so over to one side before she was satisfied with its placement, or how recently, whenever she had to enter his downstairs room with its mess of papers on the desk and his clothes casually draped over the chairs, he would see her wince and retreat as fast as she could. He had spent days trying to translate 'OCD syndrome' into Thai and in the end gave up. It was enough that he had at last found a term to describe what he recognised in his daughter-in-law.

That morning, when Mitr and Arunee had left, he continued to lie awake wondering about all of these issues and regretting that his sleep had been interrupted. His thoughts were interrupted by footsteps entering the lobby from the dining room, and he heard Sai's voice, although he could not hear what was said. He sat up in bed and shouted out:

'Hey, Sai. Ai Sai. Is that you? What the hell is going on?'

The door to his room promptly opened and Sai stood there dressed in shorts and a tee shirt, looking as though he had been pulled out of his bed in a hurry.

'Khun Chai,' he said excitedly. 'Khun Arunee's father has been taken to the Bangkok Nursing Home this morning. Khun Arunee has just left to go there.'

'Didn't you have to drive them? 'asked Khun Chai.

'No. Ai Fad took Khun Arunee, and Khun Mitr drove himself.'

'They didn't go together then?' Khun Chai asked, although he already knew the answer.

'No. Apparently Khun Mitr had to rush over to the office to pick up some papers or something.'

'Do you know what happened to Pansak?'

'No. Not exactly. A heart attack, I think, or maybe the other thing.' He frowned as he searched for the right term.

'A stroke,' said Khun Chai as he hauled himself off his bed. 'It's not the first time.' 'Do you want your breakfast now?' Sai asked him from the doorway.

'No. I'll have a shower first. It's going to be a long day.'

Later, while he sat on the balcony and slowly ate his usual rice gruel, pickles and salted fish, and sipped his black coffee, Khun Chai concluded that it was because Arunee was upset about her father that she had spoken that way to Mitr. He knew that she was very close to Pansak who, in turn, thought the world of her, his only child. Nevertheless, it did not explain her sarcastic tone. There was something going on that he had not caught, and he sensed that it was a serious issue.

Before his thoughts flowed into these pools of possible scenarios, the phone on the chair beside him buzzed with life. It was Mitr.

'Pa. It looks bad. Pansak might not last the day.' Khun Chai said nothing.

'Pa? Are you still there?' 'Yes. I'm listening.'

'Well, just in case we all have to rush to the temple this evening you'd better cancel that appointment with Joy's grandmother.'

Khun Chai agreed. But when he put the phone down, he wondered why his son felt that it was so urgent to do so when there was the whole day ahead. He walked into his room and pressed the bell on the wall and in a few minutes, Sai appeared, now showered and dressed in clean shirt and trousers.

'Do we have the old woman's number?' Khun Chai asked his helper. 'I have to cancel the meeting with her this evening.'

'There it is on the table. She wrote it down before leaving. Don't you remember? You asked for it.'

Khun Chai went over to the table and saw the scrap of paper on which Yai Li had left her number. He noticed that it was written in the hand of a child. Then he handed it over to Sai who tapped them into the mobile phone.

'She's not picking up,' he said after a long while.

Khun Chai sighed. 'What's the point in having a mobile if you don't answer it?' he said. 'Better call Joy then.'

'But what do I tell her, Nai?'

'Oh, for goodness sake! Tell her not to bring her granny over this evening because Arunee's father is sick and might die today and I might have to drag myself to the temple for the last rites ceremony,' said Khun Chai, unable to hide his general annoyance at the whole situation and the fact that he was going to miss the treatment he had been looking forward to that evening. He added, for good measure: 'The old woman probably knows all this anyway.'

Chapter 5

Joy stepped into the shower, squeezed the shampoo bottle as though she was strangling a small animal, then scrubbed her hair with both hands furiously while her face, covered in thick white lather, grimaced into a silent scream.

How many more times was she going to accept being humiliated? she asked herself.

It was a Sunday. No work at the office. Mitr had already told his wife that he was visiting a site they were developing in Cha-am. Everything was planned. She and Mitr were going to have a day alone with each other at last. Joy had been looking forward to this outing for days. It had been three weeks since they had spent any decent time together. She was tired of the lightning visits in the early morning to her place or an hour after work in a motel. She just wanted a little more with him. Was it too much to ask?

That morning, he had turned up at 7.30 and only after making love to her in his usual rushed manner, did he tell her that plans had changed. His wife's father had been taken in an ambulance to the emergency unit of the Bangkok Nursing Home just after dawn and he had to be there with her and the others in her family. There was no way he could get out of it. Joy knew that it was true. Mitr never lied to her. After the first time that they slept together he had told her:

'I am never going to leave my wife. You should know that. And if you are ever indiscreet, I will drop you. Don't ever forget it.'

With the same brutal honesty, he had gone on to tell her in what manner they would conduct their affair, exactly what he wanted from her, and that if ever she decided to finish it because she found someone else that she preferred to be with, then she was always free to go; they would remain friends and she could keep her job in the organisation, though not as his secretary. He made it all sound so simple and fair. She could take it or leave it. His terms were always spelt out clearly. It was how he did business. He was a man in total control of his life, ruthlessly unwavering about what he needed and what to discard.

She was not angry with him, but with her own stupidity. She, who prided herself on being an intelligent, independent modern woman was now in the banal situation of sleeping with her boss. She would laugh if it happened to any of her friends, and probably try her best to drum some sense into them before they became too heavily involved. She would switch to another series if she came across this scenario in a television soap opera. How had she let it happen to her?

She knew the answer perfectly well. In a word: Desire. Not for sex. Or money. It was the desire to be connected to someone special, someone who commanded respect, someone who was both rich and influential and who had a great future. Mitr was all those things; already a director of the most successful real estate development company in the country, the person that everybody said was going to go even further in the business world because he was so brilliant and had all the right connections; a man with political ambitions who could even one day run for the highest office. Everything about him was blessed with power and this was what had drawn her to him from the start. The desire be close enough to drink from that source, to absorb its heady scent, to be nourished by its unique energy. That was how she became addicted.

The fact that he was nearly thirty years older than she was, a married man, balding and bespectacled and a clumsy, ungenerous lover made no difference. From the first board meeting that she attended as his new secretary, she was impressed by his total confidence in what he was doing, and his command over others. It was charisma in action. She realised during those intensely busy weeks, during which a major deal was being finalized with a company from Shanghai, that this was the world she wanted to be a part of, and the man she wanted to be close to. When she found out that she had beaten others to the job of being his private secretary it felt like hitting the jackpot. This was the first step to the life she had dreamed for herself. By becoming indispensable to him she would one day begin to taste the sacred essence that he, and people from the same privileged background, held in their hands. She was fuelled by this ambition, but her plans did not include seducing him. Before she landed the job, she had just finished a stormy three-year relationship with a *farang* who could not decide which gender he preferred, or whether sex was more attractive to him than drugs. In the end, he had turned violent and she had finished their relationship decisively, with a threat to get him deported if he ever came near her again. Now she needed a rest from being involved with anybody.

It was during the celebration of the success of the project in the Peninsula Hotel on the river that Mitr had suddenly leaned forward and told her, as they danced to the rhythms of a Mexican band, that he had a room upstairs if she cared to join him. She was both surprised and delighted. It was totally unexpected. Till then he had shown no hint that he felt any attraction towards her. In fact, he had given her the impression that he was a cold fish who was only interested in the work that he was doing, and in his family. She did not hesitate in accepting his invitation. The party was in full swing. The champagne was flowing, and people were going off to snort cocaine on the terrace and in the rest rooms. They had slipped away from the rest of the crowd without anyone turning to see. In fact, that night she did not care if anyone even noticed their leaving. She was high from the success of the project, and from his words of praise, and this was a chance to be even closer to her goal.

That was two years earlier. She was now 32 and feeling an unpleasant mixture of weariness and doubt. On the surface everything was picture perfect. They adhered to the rules of the game agreed on at the start of their affair. At the office she played the role of efficient secretary with effortless precision, never putting a foot wrong as far as the work was concerned. In public they always behaved with restraint and propriety, knowing how easy it was for others to project their fantasies. Joy was aware that in a large organisation such as Siam Estate, the tongues would be wagging even when there was nothing concrete to wag about. It was a favourite pastime. But they made sure that their behaviour did not provide even the keenest gossipmonger with any tangible material to share. Their exchanges were strictly businesslike, no flirtatious jokes or remarks on his part, and absolutely no sign that she knew more about his preferences and habits than any well-trained secretary should. It was often intense at the beginning for Joy, who sometimes wanted to reach out and touch him gently or transmit her feelings for him through a look in her eyes or a smile. But gradually, over the months she learned to play her part with the skill of a trained actress.

They were never seen to leave together after work unless it was to go to a reception or a conference, and even then, their guards were kept up. She would never sit in the back of the car with him, but in the front with the driver, and she always walked slightly behind him, never by his side. When there was no official engagement, she would leave the office exactly on time, and then drive her blue Toyota to the motel near Don Muang, and wait there for him in the pre-booked room. In her bag she always had a bottle of wine and some cheese or olives.

Sometimes, after taking a shower she would open the bottle, watch the television or listen to music on her phone or read a magazine. Then he would arrive and strip off and make love to her with a sense of urgency, as though he needed to offload his tension rather than from any feelings of pleasure from holding her in his arms. After that he would take a shower and it was only then that would he begin to relax. He would lie down on his front, and she would massage his shoulders and his neck while he talked about things that had happened that day. It was always about work, and as she stroked his pale skin, she would listen to the projects he was drumming up in his mind, all of which were to do with converting Bangkok into the city he dreamed of – a truly modern metropolis along the lines of Singapore but more laid back, less puritanical. He would get rid of all the slums and clean up the canals and overhaul the infrastructure and the transport system so that there would be no more traffic jams that were a waste of time, money and energy. It would be the hub of Asia that had been talked about for decades.

With Harry, the Greek American boyfriend that she ditched, it had been a daily drama. Everything was unpredictable, intense and passionate, and should have been exhausting. But she had felt alive with him and constantly invigorated by their crazy relationship, drug fuelled on his part. There was no restraint on their emotions. They argued and shouted and fought, and then enjoyed their sex. It was only when the cocaine had become such a problem that he could not contain his erratic moods and his aggression, that she knew it was time to leave him. With Mitr there were never any arguments. Emotions were a no-go area. Neither of them created any waves. It was like an extension of the office. Everything was conducted with discretion and careful planning. Any hint of conflict or tension was immediately dealt with and dismissed, so that in the end there was no drama to play out.

Even when she was invited to his house for lunch one Sunday, when she first met Khun Arunee, his wife, her responses had been so well rehearsed – which meant he had told her exactly how to behave and what to say – that she did not feel any nervousness, particularly when it was obvious, from the first time that she caught Khun Arunee look at her appraisingly, that his wife was already in the know. There was nothing to hide because everything was being conducted according to unspoken rules, under a transparent blanket of politeness that came naturally to those who had nothing to lose. After that first meeting, which was followed by more lunches, and sometimes dinners, because there was work be done out of office hours, Joy even began to feel herself as part of the family. Mitr's father, Khun Chai courteously accepted her presence, and the servants treated her with the respect given to a guest of the family, although she suspected that they knew that her background was not much different from their own.

She had once or twice been on the point of asking Mitr if his wife knew about their affair, but each time she chose not to. Firstly, because she already knew the answer, and because the situation was so perfectly well balanced that any questioning on her part would only bring about a change to the equation and a necessary readjustment. So she resigned herself to the situation and stuck with the status quo that brought with it a serenity that she thought she needed after the tempestuous bout with Harry. Yet it was this very lack of any conflict or anything other than the anodyne interchange with Mitr that was draining her energy. Before she met him, she had not realised how much effort was needed to maintain the appearance of propriety that the elite of Thai society cared so much about. There were times over the two years that she got to know the family, and became familiar with their habits and their idiosyncrasies, that she thought at first that she detected, beneath the calm surface, the rumblings of a tsunami. But no evidence of it emerged, and she came to realise that it was her own projection. It was something she wished would be happening – a seismic movement to stir up the waters. But they remained calm. No waves. She alone was drowning.

The doubts that were creeping in on her were probably also her own construction. But she could not be sure. Mitr used her as his concubine. That much was plain to her. But was he beginning to tire of her? Was he on the lookout for younger flesh? She had, once or twice, caught his gaze stray towards a pretty girl walking through the lobby or coming out of an office building. Would he turn around and simply tell her one day that her services were no longer required? Those were, after all, the terms that he had set out for her at the beginning, and she had to presume that it included his own wishes.

Yet, outwardly, his behaviour towards her had not changed. He still seemed to need her receptive body and was with her as often as time permitted. Apart from their motel rendezvous, he had taken to visiting her at her apartment on his way to work whenever he could and would sometimes in the evening drop in on his way home. He had taken her abroad with him three times over the two years; to Shanghai, to Delhi, and Singapore. These were business trips and there was little time for pleasure. Their meals were taken with the clients and associates Mitr had to meet, and long hours were spent in the meetings that had been arranged. They would have separate rooms and he would visit her after the day's work was done. But he would never sleep the whole night with her, so in no way could she even remotely think of these trips as an excuse for them to spend time together. During the same two years, he took his wife to Paris twice for a holiday. It was her favourite city, Joy learned.

She had confronted her jealousy of Khun Arunee from the first time that they set eyes on each other. It was a curious emotion – one that she had not known before. It was she who had always been the object of other people's jealousy since she was a child, a pretty child, a *'loog kreung'* with pale skin, large green eyes, a straight nose, and auburn hair. At school there were those who treated her like some kind of star and others who went out of their way to be mean to her, and tease her about not being a pure Thai – as though anyone in Bangkok was. In any case, she felt special simply by being the offspring of a Thai mother and an English father. As she grew up, this seemed to give her a special status, a sense of entitlement that was, of course, enhanced by the fact that she spoke English better than most of the people she knew. In any case, jealousy pursued her through school and then in the first jobs that she held; so much so that she could see it coming and prepare herself adequately by learning how to win over the ones who directed their bile towards her.

With Mitr's wife she found herself in new territory. She was discovering what it felt like to covet what she would never have. It was not the looks, although she had to admit that Arunee had a fine, delicate, old-fashioned beauty and a certain innate poise while her own, often admired, looks were more like the flashy prettiness of an actress. But it was more than the appearance, or the fact that this was a woman married to one of the richest people in the land, who happened to be her lover. It was that Arunee seemed totally at ease with Joy's presence in their lives, and gave the impression that Joy was not worth the effort of worrying about, that whatever Joy did or did not do with her husband had no importance for her. This felt demeaning, and having many times tried to imagine herself in Arunee's position and having to admit that she would find it distressful if not impossible to handle, she was jealous of Arunee's power to rise above her husband's infidelity and treat it with disdain. It was as though she did not have to try to keep him to herself. He was already hers until she chose to let him go. This, to Joy was the power that she would never know, and it made her feel insignificant.

But, of course, with Mitr she played the role expected of her. To him she was all smiles and appreciation.

'You have a wonderful wife,' she tried to sound as sincere as possible. 'She is so beautiful and so calm.'

'Yes. I know.' was all he said in reply.

With her jealousy came the sense of humiliation every time Mitr made his wife's wishes and desires a priority over her own. And beneath it all was that emotion she knew all too well because it had been part of her makeup since she was a little girl. Anger. Always controlled but always there beneath her smile and the impeccable manners that she had learned to adopt.

Chapter 6

Yai Li heard the phone ringing and watched it rattling on the glass tabletop like an angry insect. She leaned over to see the number but did not recognise it. She had recently decided not to answer any number that she did not know, as it would probably be another telephone sale, and just saying no thank you to their clever, seductive pitch tired her every time. But as soon as it rang off, she thought that perhaps she should have answered it as her intuition told her that it was a call from Khun Chai. She had been thinking of him when she was in the market that morning and wondering how it must be living in that large house having people to look after you, and having, in turn, to pay their wages and take care of them. She was also wondering if she should see him again and thinking that perhaps it was better not to do so. After meeting him she found that she felt disturbed, and during the whole week she could not help returning to the memory that had come up the night when she had been unable to sleep. She did not want to be dragged back to an event that had wounded and marked her. What was the point of recalling the unpleasant things that she had known? She preferred to forget them, and had managed to do so for many years.

That week, like Khun Chai, she kept going back into her past, into the moments that she thought she had left behind for good. They now kept coming back to her from nowhere – things that had no relevance to her present life. For example, she found herself recalling how her aunt, who had worked in one of those wealthy households, had explained to her, when she got her into the service, all the different rules that had to be followed; how to talk, when to talk, how to appear and disappear, how to recognise the guests who had to be given extra respect, what never to do, and so on. It was all so complicated for a simple country girl that she found herself too nervous to be any good as one of the servants who were allowed to engage with the guests. She was relieved when she was kept in the kitchen as a helper, and later allowed to look after the young baby who was the grandson of the owner of the house. These were simple tasks. What she was not prepared for was still to come.

When the phone stopped its insistent noise, she began to put her shopping away in the cupboard and as she did so she could hear her neighbour, Mae Da, coughing her lungs out, through the thin wall that separated their dwellings. They had never been close friends. Yai Li partly blamed Mae Da for encouraging her husband, Maitri, to drink and take pills. She even suspected that they might have had an affair. But that was all in the distant past. After his death Mae Da, sensing her responsibility, had tried to make up to her with small acts of kindness and by showing interest in Yai Li's welfare. But Yai Li could not cope with Mae Da's drinking and the gush of pointless conversation that came with it, often ending in tears of self-pity. Recently she had premonitions that Mae Da was very sick and that soon she would be the one to help her to the hospital.

She was so lost in these thoughts that she hardly caught the faint knock on the door.

'You can come in,' she shouted out. 'It's not locked.'

The door swung open to reveal her granddaughter standing half in shadow and half in the blazing morning sunlight. Neither of them spoke at first. The remark that Joy had made the previous evening about her appearance still grated on Yai Li even though she had responded politely at the time. It was trivial enough and should have not upset her at all. But it hinted at something that had been simmering between them for the past two years, ever since Joy landed the job in the big company.

'What are you doing here?' Yai Li asked, finally breaking the silence.

'I just dropped in to tell you that Khun Chai has cancelled the meeting this evening.' 'Thank you. But you could have just told me that over the phone.'

'But I'm here, Yai,' said Joy frostily. 'Don't you want me to come and see you?'

'It's a Sunday. You're usually busy. I wasn't expecting you, that's all,' said Yai Li, defensively, immediately sorry for her coldness towards her granddaughter, the only living relative left in the world. She could tell that Joy was not in a good way. She guessed the reason.

'Come on. Sit down. Let's have a chat,' she said and reached out her hand and touched Joy's shoulder. The young woman took a step forward and buried her face in her grandmother's breast and started to sob. Yai Li led Joy to the sofa in the corner, then sat her down next to her and cradled her gently in her arms.

They had never been close. In fact, she had never expected to meet or know Joy in this lifetime. Maitri, her husband had died when Nuan, Joy's mother, was barely three. The years that followed were hard for Yai Li. She knew that it would have helped to find another man to be with who, apart from providing her with his company, could contribute to the day-to-day expenses. But none had turned up who did not make her nervous. One drunk was enough for her. She preferred to stay alone, and she took care of Nuan by herself, which was not difficult when Nuan was a young girl who was loving and obedient. But by the time she was in her early teens she had discovered boys and become familiar with the street ways of Klongtoey, and there was no controlling her daughter anymore. When she was sixteen, Nuan was already under the watchful care of a local pimp who was also a drug dealer. He was grooming her to be a major source of income. Yai Li was working in a clothing factory, leaving home early and coming back in the evening. She did not have the will or the strength to try to stop Nuan from doing whatever she wanted. The girl came and went as she pleased and seemed to have money to spend. One day she announced to Yai Li that she had found a good job on the other side of the city, without explaining what exactly it was, packed up her possessions and moved out after declaring that she was going to get rich and never come back to the slums again. It was seven years before she returned, and when she did, she came with a rucksack on her back and a pretty, seven-year-old, light-skinned girl, with enormous eyes and thick, curly eyelashes, trailing behind her. Yai Li was shocked to see that her daughter had lost so much weight that her ribs stuck out under her thin cotton blouse. It was obvious that she was sick.

Yai Li could not take care of either of them. It would have meant giving up her job and looking for work in Klongtoey, which was easy enough, but it would not bring in sufficient money to pay for them all. It was Mae Da who suggested that Yai Li take Nuan to the Mercy Centre where she worked part time as a cleaner. This was where people with Aids from all over the city, and even from towns outside of Bangkok, had been taken when they had nowhere else to go. Yai Li walked past it every day on her way out to the bus stop, and, sometimes, over the years she would see a family arriving by taxi or in a pickup truck and climb out with an emaciated man or woman or a young child who could hardly walk. At such times she would feel a sadness well up in her. It was such a terrible disease, and everyone was afraid of getting it from someone who was sick, by sharing the same cutlery or drinking cup, or just by being near them. In the factory where she worked near Don Muang, there were women who had been infected and who were shunned by the others and eventually sacked from their jobs. In the lane next to hers there was a young man who had come out of prison and died from the disease.

She never asked Nuan how she caught the disease, but she guessed that it was from her work – that was going to bring her the wealth she craved. But she was relieved to know that her granddaughter, Joy, had been born before she was infected, so she was free from the disease. Yai Li wanted to do all she could to look after this beautiful child in her house but there was no way this was possible. The day after their arrival, she went with Mae Da to the office of the centre with her daughter and granddaughter and met with the kind, bright woman in charge of the hospice who took the details and then led Nuan into the women's ward. Then another woman, older and radiating warmth, talked to Yai Li and Joy and showed them a large bedroom on the first floor and the bed that was covered with a colourful patchwork blanket and two rag dolls lying on the pillow.

'Would you like to stay here?' the woman asked her. But Joy merely looked away.

'You'll make lots of friends. There are eight girls in this room. They are all the same age as you. You can go to school with them and play together. Would you like that, Joy?' But still Joy did not respond. Instead, she walked over and hugged her grandmother's thigh and began to sob quietly, the same way that she was doing now, and Yai Li felt the tears welling up in her own chest, as they had done when Joy was a little girl about to start her first day at the Mercy Centre.

She visited them every day at the Mercy Centre for the next three months. In the early morning she would stop to buy a packet of sweets or cookies to give to Joy and watch her climb into the school bus, and then she would visit Nuan in her ward and see what she needed. At the beginning, she saw that Nuan seemed to be benefiting from the proper care that she was receiving as well as the medicine she was taking. There was scant communication between them. Nuan was so weak that sometimes she hardly acknowledged her mother's presence, and whenever Yai Li did try to talk to her she made it obvious she did not want to talk about her past, and Yai Li did not insist. The only thing that she was curious about was who Joy's father was. This did not come up until one Sunday, when Yai Li, on her day off, was sitting with Nuan on the terrace outside her ward when a *farang*, a volunteer at the centre walked by. She noticed Nuan's gaze follow him as he walked away from them after saying a few words of greeting.

'Do you know him?' asked Yai Li.

'No. Somebody who looked a bit like him. But not really,' Nuan answered.

'The father of your child? Joy's father?' Yai Li slipped in her question spontaneously.

Nuan nodded and then told her mother how she met this *farang* from England in the bar where she worked and how he fell in love with her, how they got married and lived together in a nice apartment in the Laadprao area, and how she thought they were going to be together forever because when Joy was born he seemed so committed to them both. He even registered Joy at the British embassy. But then, one day when Joy was still about four years old, he disappeared without leaving a word, just an envelope full of money. And afterwards, when the money was nearly all gone, she went back to work and paid someone to be with Joy.

Before Yai Li could ask her any more questions, Nuan had put her hand up and said abruptly:

'But I don't want to talk about any of this anymore. OK?'

A month later, Nuan had a bout of pneumonia. Mae Da knocked on Yai Li's door one evening when she had just got home from the factory and said:

'They don't think your daughter's got long.'

She remembers rushing through the street and running up the steps of the centre. Nuan had been taken to a side room and there she found the male nurse and two assistants sitting by the bedside. One of them got up as she arrived and whispered to her.

'We didn't know whether you wanted Joy to be here, to say goodbye to her mother. We would have asked Nuan but …'

Yai Li stared at her, then at her daughter, whose breathing sounded like a bubbling well.

'Yes, please get her,' she said quietly, and in a few minutes Joy was by her side. The assistant gently tried to steer her nearer the bed, but Joy stood frozen like a statue for a long while staring at her mother, then turned to go. Yai Li went out with her into the garden, and they sat down on the bench. Joy said nothing but kept looking ahead into space. When Yai Li reached over to put her arm around her Joy, she jumped up and said:

'I've got to finish my homework.' With that she disappeared into the building and up the stairs.

They never mentioned that evening again. Nuan died and was cremated in Wat Saphaan temple on the river. During the months that followed, Yai Li continued to visit her granddaughter every day, until one morning Joy told her bluntly:

'Yai, you don't have to come so often. I'm all right here with my friends.'

From then on, Yai Li went to the centre only on weekends, taking clothes that she bought from the market and, always, a bag of sweets. She could see that Joy was being well cared for. There was little that she needed to do for her granddaughter, and the warmth of kinship that she could offer did not seem to be needed by the little girl. The centre had become her family. She was just the relative who had no special place in her life.

Joy's father had spoken to her and sung to her in English since she was born, and she had retained the language. Because of this she was chosen, at the age of ten, to be one of the girls who received a scholarship from an international school off Sukhumvit road, that supported the centre financially and sent some of their students there to volunteer. Yai Li saw even less of her now because on weekends Joy would be on a school trip or doing extra classes. It was during these years leading up to her teens when Joy began to display the traits which Yai Li disliked. Whenever she visited her granddaughter Joy now spoke to her in a sultry offhand fashion, often with a certain haughtiness at her grandmother's ignorance, and impatience with her appearance and her mannerisms in general. This in itself did not upset Yai Li. She understood that Joy was now a girl receiving a good education whereas she was only just literate, and had never shaken off her rural accent or her simple, unsophisticated way of looking at the world. Joy had a possible future in the big city if she carried on doing well at the school, while she would never be more than a factory worker at best. It was natural for Joy to want something better than what she could offer. These things she accepted. But what did upset her was the way that she saw Joy now behaving to her friends at the centre; the ones who had been kind and generous and supportive to her since she arrived, and whom she now treated with condescension and mockery. There was no way Yai Li could stop her from doing this, so she watched in silence and felt a deep disappointment in her granddaughter for her behaviour and in herself for not having given her proper guidance.

When she finished at the international school, Joy went on to do a degree in Business Studies at the Asian Institute of Technology and, on completing that, joined an investment company where she was assistant to one of the senior brokers. Her language skills were better than most of her age, even those who had gone abroad for their education. But it was her *loog kreung* looks that made her stand out from the crowd and she was aware of this. People noticed her wherever she went, including people in power who wanted to have her beauty as part of their personal and corporate image. By the time she was in her early twenties, Joy knew that doors would be open to her and that all she had to do was to stay on top of her game and not slip up.

Yai Li hardly saw her granddaughter during these first years of her career. Joy had moved out of Klongtoey into a little apartment in the Hwai Kwang area. She would visit Yai Li once every couple of months, bringing gifts – stuff for the house, clothes, a television, a new mobile phone. Sometimes, if it was a weekend, she would take Yai Li out to eat in a restaurant nearby. But the distance that had been there from the beginning could not be bridged by these deliberate acts of generosity. Yai Li did not feel comfortable with Joy's displays of kindness because she never felt that there was any genuine warmth behind them. They struck her as coming from a sense of duty rather than love. She would have preferred to have a decent conversation with Joy. But that never happened. The restaurant meals they shared were marked by awkward silences. Sometimes, Joy would talk about her work at the office and how much she was making for her company. Yai Li did not really understand what it was that Joy did, only that it involved dealing in money. It sounded like such a different planet from the factory, where she worked sewing shirts and trousers, that she did not share her own stories. In any case, it was obvious that Joy was not interested in hearing about her grandmother's time in the factory or in her life in the slums.

In time, as if by mutual consent, the visits grew less and less frequent. News of Joy now came to Yai li through Nong Maew, a girl Joy had grown up with in the centre and who now worked there as a secretary. She was the only person who remained in contact with Joy, and she lived not far from Yai Li. They bumped into each other from time to time in the street and Maew would give her an update on Joy's progress.

'She's aiming high, your granddaughter,' Maew once told her. 'But she hasn't forgotten us, Yai. She told me that what we're doing here at the centre is the most important work, in her eyes. She says that one day when she's rich she is going to give us a huge donation. That's her ambition.' Yai Li was both glad and surprised to hear this.

Then, two years earlier, just when Yai Li was becoming used to the fact that her granddaughter had vanished from her life, just as Nuan had done, Joy's visits resumed. She arrived in a small blue car that she parked nearby and again came to the door with her arms piled with gifts; only now they were expensive ones, fancy silk blouses, shoes, even perfume.

'I've got a new job,' she announced on her first visit, without explaining why she had been absent for so long. 'It's exactly what I was looking for. And I have got myself a new apartment.'

Yai Li noticed that a lot had changed in her granddaughter in such a short time. Apart from the trendy haircut and the expensive clothes and shoes she was now wearing, there was an unmistakeable confidence in her and the way she behaved towards her was less tense and forced. On one of these visits Joy drove Yai Li from Jetsip Rai to Bang Na to a condominium and showed her the new apartment that she was renting. It was light and roomy with indoor plants and a huge television hanging on one of the walls in the living room.

'Do you like it, Yai?' she asked.

'Oh yes. It's very nice. Do you have someone to help clean the place?'

'Yes, of course I do. I don't have time to do any of that stuff. I have a maid from Myanmar who cooks for me too when I need her to.'

Yai Li knew she was meant to be impressed, and she nodded appropriately. Her granddaughter had indeed risen in the world. She could now afford to employ a maid!

'You know. You could come and live here with me if you like, Yai.' she said with a sincere smile on her face. Yai Li saw that she was not saying it to be polite. It was a genuine offer. She paused before replying:

'Thank you for thinking of me. But I think I'll stay where I am. I've lived there for so long. I have friends there. I am used to the life there. I know no one around here. It would be lonely for me.'

She had expected Joy to be disappointed. But she saw that Joy was frowning now. It was a look she had learned to recognise as her granddaughter's mix of impatience and annoyance.

'But you can't stay there.'

'Why not? I've been there most of my adult life.'

'You know why not. You must do. Everyone in Klongtoey knows. And it's been all over the newspapers.'

What Joy was referring to was the news that Klongtoey was up for development once more. This had been on the cards since the Taksin government. At that time someone – probably from the port authority – had leaked the plans to the community leaders. As the rumours spread, it was believed that with investment from other Asian countries as well as the Middle East, luxury hotels, a floating casino, a heliport to transport the visitors were all part of the plan. There was anger among the Klongtoey inhabitants. Mae Da, who was involved with one of the community leaders at that time, and vocal about her opinions, persuaded Yai Li to join the movement to stop this wholesale takeover of the district that had been home to hundreds of thousands of people, and the effort to turn it into a hedonist wonderland. As luck would have it, or thanks to the prayers uttered at the sacred tree – whichever narrative you chose – the demise of Taksin meant that the plans, whatever they really were, had to be put on hold. But now it seemed that they had been resuscitated and there was already heady talk of converting the district into a mini 'city within a city' that would confirm Bangkok's status as the hub of Southeast Asia once and for all.

Yai Li had read the papers and was aware, like everyone else, that the huge tractors were already in place ready to encroach on the area at the far borders and that, if the developers wanted to, these monstrous machines could flatten the whole area in a couple of days. It was conjectured that the fact that they had not done so was due to the lack of agreement among the interested parties as to their share of the cake. Some of the locals were convinced that the prayers at the tree were making a difference, as they had done before, and that the development would again be stopped in its tracks. Yai Li, who had retained her rural beliefs, had been to the tree along with her neighbours and made offerings.

'Do you think they will succeed?' she asked her granddaughter.

Again, the withering look.

'What do you mean, Yai?' she snapped back. 'Do you know how many billions are involved in this project? Our firm is right in there. Khun Mitr has already cut a deal with the Chinese investors to turn the whole space behind here into the largest shopping complex in the country. No prayers are going to stop it from happening. Yai, you've got to face reality. Otherwise, you'll find yourself homeless one day and they will just move you to one of those ugly housing estates out in Rangsit. You'll be given a small room in one of those blocks they have been building. I've seen the plans. Do you want to end up there?'

Yai Li shook her head. Jetsip Rai had been her home for nearly half a century. She could not imagine being anywhere else. She liked the lively, dusty streets, the narrow lanes, the sounds and the music, the mix of people, the life of the markets. She was happy to end her days there. The thought of being cooped up in one of those flats far above the streets filled her with horror. But she was not convinced that the spirit of the tree would let this happen.

'Give me time to decide,' she said to Joy in an attempt to placate her.

'But there is no time left, Yai.' Joy was shouting with frustration now. But then she softened.

'Well, the offer is open if and when you are ready to take it up.'

'But won't I be in the way? I mean…' The words were out of her mouth before she had time to check herself. The two women looked at each other in silence. In a way that she could not explain, Yai Li had intuited that her granddaughter's relationship to her boss went beyond the work she did for him. It was something about the look that came over her every time that she mentioned his name. She sensed that Joy wanted to share this secret with her but was shy of doing so.

In reply to her question Joy now giggled.

'Not really Yai… I mean…'

It was the first time that Yai Li had seen Joy blush and be lost for words.

'I won't be in your way, 'said Yai Li and smiled as Joy reached over to touch her. 'But I haven't decided to live with you yet.'

They had both laughed.

Now as they sat side by side on the sofa, Yai Li held Joy in her arms and felt her granddaughter's pain. She said gently:

'What has he done to hurt you?'

Joy pulled away and quickly dried her tears.

'Nothing, Yai.' She said, sighing. 'He's done nothing.'

Chapter 7

It was late afternoon. Dark storm clouds hung over the city that evening, and the wind was getting stronger. The lay helpers at the temple were already preparing for the rain and putting up the awning outside the *sala*. The monks had not yet filed in to do their chanting. Inside, there was a constant, bird-like chattering of half-whispered conversations. Guests were still entering through the wide sliding doors that led out into the courtyard. Khun Chai sat in the wheelchair in the front row, trying to look calm, as he politely returned the greetings of those who passed him on their way to the coffin to pay their last respects and then on to the altar to bow to the Buddharupa before returning to their seats. But beneath his blank expression, which broke into a forced smile every time he had to respond, he was anything but tranquil. He hardly recognised any of the people, but they all seemed to be aware that he was Arunee's father-in-law. Occasionally, someone he had known from the past would kneel by him and ask him how he was, which he found annoying since it was obvious, being in a wheelchair, that he was not in good shape. They were unaware that he was trying to cope with the constant pain that felt like intermittent stabs on the left side of his neck and shoulder, and down his leg. The pills he had taken earlier did little to lessen his discomfort. But duty could not be denied, especially because of his special connection to the deceased.

Pansak had not survived the weekend. By Monday his white, embossed coffin stood on a raised platform in one of the newer, air conditioned *salas* in Wat Thattong where shoes did not have to be taken off and there was ample seating inside for all the guests. It was bedecked with flowers and surrounded by elaborate wreaths that were being brought in daily from every corner of the city. Such was Pansak's standing in Thai society that a television crew was there at the entrance to the temple to film those arriving in the early evening to attend the ceremony. Even by the standards of what was expected of such occasions this was a lavish event. Uniformed attendants were on hand to show the important guests to their seats and to serve out the drinks and prepare snacks for the post-chanting gathering that would take place before everyone dispersed.

Khun Chai had been coming to the temple since the first evening's ceremony, walking in from the carpark with only the aid of a stick. But that Friday the old symptoms were back, and Sai had wheeled him through the temple grounds and into the *sala* to take his position. As he sat there waiting for the ceremony to begin, between the brief social exchanges, he kept regretting that he had cancelled the meeting with Yai Li on the previous Sunday. He longed for her to do her magic on him so that he could walk out onto the balcony again as he'd done after her first visit. Being in a wheelchair, dependent on others to help him, made him feel, yet again, an outsider to the whole proceedings as well as a captive participant in a ceremony he wished he did not have to attend. He could not just walk out politely like some of the other guests, with an unspoken excuse of having another ceremony on the other side of the city to go to. He would have to wait till the very end for Sai to wheel him away. The only advantage that being immobile gave him was that he did not to have to go up and bow to the coffin or at the altar, or crawl on his knees to put the offerings on the monks' trays, or participate in the ritual that was all too familiar to him.

He had already been to several other less elaborate funeral ceremonies that year, of friends and distant family members, and others he only vaguely knew but to whom he was indirectly acquainted. Such was the custom of the land, and he had no objections to it. In fact, he enjoyed going to the temples he'd known as a boy and seeing how they had changed, how much richer some of them had become, or how run down. Even though he never learned the meaning of the chants, only that they were to do with Impermanence and the other tenets of the Buddhist teachings, he always enjoyed the trance-like state that they produced. But there was a point at which the repetition of the rituals, the walk up to the funeral pyre and the rest of it produced a sense of deja-vu, and along with that a feeling of over familiarity. Besides, each repeated ritual underlined the realisation that one day in the not-too-distant future it would be him lying in the coffin that was to be slid into the burning furnace.

By the time he had to attend Pansak's funeral, Khun Chai wished he could have sent someone to impersonate him. This was not only because he would rather have been in Baan Suan sorting through papers or reading his Chekhov stories, but because he had never got on with his in-law, and his presence there in the temple was dictated merely by social propriety. Even though he knew that part of the purpose of the funeral ceremony was to recall the impermanence of our earthly existence, and to forgive the person who had died and so finish with our karma with them, he felt less than generous in spirit towards the man who he had detested intensely. And now here he was having to stare at his coffin, pretending that his feelings had changed. The sense of hypocrisy and insincerity weighed heavily on him every evening that he had to attend the ceremony, but especially that Friday evening.

Over the years, he had often wondered why Pansak evoked such antipathy in him and why he bothered to feel so annoyed and upset by him, even long before knowing him personally. He would refer to him in conversation many times, before they became official in-laws, as 'that slimy toad', or 'that ridiculous buffoon'. On the surface it was obvious. Everything that Pansak stood for – his politics, his values, his lifestyle – was diametrically opposed to Khun Chai's own. Furthermore, he saw in Pansak's career the essence of all that was wrong with Thai political life; the cynical conniving, the corruption, the amorality, the barefaced lust for power. He knew others who had similar views to Pansak's and whose actions were just as venal and self-serving, but who did not manage to provoke such a negative reaction in him. At one point, during the years when he was writing fiction, Khun Chai was so intrigued by his feelings of distaste towards Pansak that he decided to turn him into a character in one of his novels. For months he did his research because he wanted his character to be authentic, and to reflect someone his readers would easily recognise. But in the end, after he had finished his investigation, he decided to omit the character altogether. After all his efforts at unearthing the scandals directly or indirectly associated with Pansak, he could find no satisfactory way of describing the fictional character he was inventing without it sounding like a far-fetched caricature of evil.

Now as he sat staring at the coffin surrounded by flowers, he took time thinking of the dead person lying inside it, and he tried his best to follow the popular guideline, and to be as charitable as he could.

The man's past was well known. He had been involved in the student movement in the nineteen seventies, and been one of those who had sought refuge in the mountains after the bloody suppression of the students in 1976. He returned after the amnesty in 1978 but had given up all trace of radicalism by the beginning of the eighties. This abandoning of the ideology of his youth was worn like a badge of honour rather than anything he had to apologise for. After his radical years he gradually reinvented himself as a political fixer, although many saw him more as an enforcer who would do the dirty work of politicians who did not want their own hands soiled. In the process he had also become a television celebrity who would tell his eager listeners how he had learned first hand of the danger of extremism. He would constantly stress that the middle ground was what underpinned the values of our Thai society, and he was the one who stood in the middle. This prompted a joke in one of the newspapers of the day whose caption read; '... And the one in the middle creams off from everybody'. The quip was made in reference to the reputation he had as not only an unscrupulous politician, but someone who used his connections to establish himself as one of the key figures in the euphemistically named entertainment industry, which to Khun Chai and many others was understood to mean that he trafficked in young men and women.

The Asian economic meltdown in 1997 ruined many businesses, including Pansak's, who had spread his entrepreneurial grasp far and wide. The tourists stayed away. Debts could not be paid. Money was not being lent. Investors pulled out overnight. The flesh industry that catered to both Thais and foreigners suffered a serious setback. In November of that year, a reporter who had been following Pansak's career in politics had gone to his house in Bang Na to try to interview him and found it empty. No servants in sight, not even a caretaker. It seemed that the man had disappeared into thin air. Cynics said that he had run away from his debtors with a stash of cash in his suitcase. But subsequent investigations revealed that his businesses had been terminated according to the proper legal procedures. All was in order. Some said that his bankruptcy had led him to commit suicide. But there was no evidence of this. The more compassionate commentators spread the word that Pansak had retired to a monastery in the north-east. This last version was the one that came to be accepted since there was no other explanation, and it was presumed that, if it was indeed the case, then he would have gone to a small temple somewhere in the mountains where he could not be traced and where he could depend on people to respect his wish to have time to pursue the Dhamma.

But the truth was that he had left Thailand in a private plane for Singapore to be with his daughter who was studying there, and whose guardian, a Singaporean entrepreneur, had been a major investor in his transport company. Long months were spent planning for a profitable way out of the financial crisis. By the end of 2000, at the age of 52, Pansak was back in Bangkok giving his first press conference in the large reception area of a newly opened commercial centre in Sukhumvit; not to talk about his absence but to launch his new business venture. Those in the press corps who were curious about the missing two years of his life were reluctant to let the matter drop without some sort of explanation, but Pansak dodged the questions with his usual aplomb.

'Let's say I needed time to myself,' he answered, with unctuous sincerity.

'You are looking so fresh and renewed,' tried another with a different tack. Could it be from his time in the monastery, from eating one meal a day and doing hours of meditation?

'Yes. I have been on a kind of retreat,' Pansak replied vaguely.

Khun Chai had caught this press conference on the television, and it made him nervous because it was common knowledge that Pansak had returned from his so-called retreat with his political ambition revitalised. There were already rumours that he was planning to set up a new political party with the collaboration, not so much of military heavyweights, but of like-minded businessmen and women. His politics did not belong to the left or to the right. He unashamedly described himself as a populist. He was the voice of the common folk. Khun Chai remembered thinking that only in Thailand could an untrustworthy rogue reinvent himself as a spokesman for the people and get away with it.

He never dreamed that ten years later this same person would be the man with whom he was clinking a glass of champagne by the river on the terrace of The Oriental Hotel to celebrate the wedding of his only son to Pansak's only daughter, Arunee. Pansak had insisted on this grand venue, and on paying for the whole event, which was attended by the rich and famous, the beautiful and the mighty of the land. In the intervening years he, with hefty investment from other Asian partners, had set up a company that supplied the best quality food and beverage to the hotels, spas, and entertainment centres that had resprouted all over Asia in the post-crisis years. The name of his company was 'Fine Catering', or FC to those in the industry, with a turnover of over forty billion baht a year.

It was a month after the wedding that Pansak had his first stroke, which ended his political career. But with his immense wealth, he still retained a significant influence that he continued to use in order to pressure the leaders into accepting his vision of where Thai society should be headed. Khun Chai could not understand why anyone felt this need to be in control of others and to think that he should persuade them into going along with his opinions. This obsession with power and influence, personified by Pansak, struck him as the key feature of Thai political life, and the main obstacle to anything approaching democracy.

As he continued to stare at the coffin, Khun Chai could not help thinking that, in the end, he had no right to judge Pansak, or anyone else, for what they had or had not done. He was at an age when he no longer felt superior to anybody else. Pansak was a different creature from him. That was all. He had been a player in the country's events, while he, Khun Chai, had always remained an outsider who observed and chronicled them. Pansak had taken risks on his unsavoury road to wealth and power, while he had only known the safety of a bystander. Even during the students' movement in the 1973/74 period that briefly filled people with hope and enthusiasm, he could not throw himself into what was happening without retaining a distance, not so much from suspicion of the leaders' motives – which he definitely felt – but from his fear of the violent backlash that was to come, and that eventually did.

These thoughts were playing in his mind just as the monks were taking their seats on the wooden dais and the hall went quiet. Then, after the preliminaries were completed, the ceremony began. The head monk, old and wizened, sitting behind his ceremonial fan began to intone the wise words of the Buddha's teachings about the impermanence of life and his fellow monks followed suit. Then just as they were getting into their stride a shaft of lightening flashed into the sala, immediately followed by a loud clap of thunder. Khun Chai looked out and saw the rain begin to pelt down onto the awning, and the tiled courtyard. It made him smile to think that some of those present would take this to be an auspicious sign. For him it was as though the heavens were saying 'good riddance' to Pansak. Now the fat drops were pelting the roof all but drowning the monks' voices. Khun Chai stopped thinking about the dead man and his feelings towards him. He put his hands together and let his mind be taken over by the rhythms of the prayers and those provided by the heavens.

Chapter 8

Joy threaded her way carefully through the heavy evening traffic. The trucks that passed her sprayed the windscreen making her lose her vision momentarily. Even though the rain had stopped, the streets were covered by a black watery layer that reflected the bright lights from the billboards. The motorbikes were weaving in and out of the vehicles through the puddles at breakneck speed, unconcerned, it seemed, by any thought of danger. In her concentration she almost forgot that her grandmother was sitting next to her. They had not spoken since she drove out of Klongtoey just as the storm was ending. She glanced over at her now and saw that Yai Li had her hands folded together and her eyes closed, as if she was meditating. She was relieved that they did not have to make any chit chat.

It had been a tiring stretch, from the time of Khun Pansak's death to the final day of the funeral ceremony. As Mitr's secretary she had to make sure that all the arrangements were perfect. Every aspect of the ceremony – the coffin, the wreaths, the hiring of the *sala,* the catering company's job, the invitations and guest list, the attendants, liaising with the temple to ensure a special chanting – all of it was in her hands. Khun Pansak's own team could have taken care of these logistics, but Mitr insisted that he would be responsible for all of it, out of courtesy to his father-in-law. This meant that Joy had to deal with an area that was totally new to her and for which she had not been trained. It was, she felt, as if Mitr wanted to challenge her with this task, and she wanted to show him not only that she was up to it, but that she could carry out her job better than anyone else. But it had been stressful, with so many details to get right. In the end, she was satisfied that she had done an excellent job, for which the least she could expect was his thanks. But he had said nothing. In fact, they had not seen each other outside of the office and the temple that whole week, except for a few occasions when she felt it safe enough to make some contact beyond their official interchange – a meaningful look or a brush with the back of her hand to let him know that she was there for him – he seemed to deliberately limit himself to treating her with the cold formality that he showed to everyone else. As she drove towards his house she wondered if his manner would be different now that the ceremony was over and Pansak was cremated.

His voice had given nothing away when he called her into his office to say:

'Please can you bring your grandmother to Baan Suan this evening? My father would like another treatment from her.'

She had greeted Khun Chai on his arrival at the temple on the first evening of the ceremony and walked with him to his seat in the *sala,* noting, to her surprise, that he was walking quite well and seemed more cheerful than he had been ever since his crisis nearly a year earlier. She had grown fond of him in the short time she had known him. He was always kind and polite to her.

'I thank your grandmother for this,' he'd told her. 'Where did she learn her skill? Not in a massage parlour, obviously,' he said with a wry laugh.

She told him that she didn't exactly know, but that when she was young, she had seen her cure people with her hands several times. She had heard that her grandmother had inherited the gift from her father.

'Ah, that means that you probably have it too.'

Joy smiled, shook her head and said: 'I don't think so.' Khun Chai looked at her for a moment before commenting:

'It's a precious gift.'

'I don't believe in that kind of thing,' she told him. 'Anyway, it scares me.'

'That's a pity. You shouldn't be scared…' Khun Chai said, and was about to continue when their exchange was interrupted by other people arriving whom she had to greet.

Then, on the Friday when she saw Sai wheel him into the *sala*, she wanted to go up to talk to him and make sure that he was all right, but there were too many things to attend to and more guests than usual, and it was the same for the next two days right up to the cremation.

As she now drove through the water clogged streets, she wondered if her grandmother was really capable of helping Khun Chai and, if so, what it was that she did. She remembered how, when she was about ten years old, a cleaner in the Mercy Centre had fallen and twisted her hip and they had gone to fetch Yai Li from her house. Being her granddaughter, she was allowed to be present when Yai Li treated the woman, who was in great pain. She saw how her bony hands glided over the injured part and then how her fingers gently made contact with specific points, and it was almost as if they actually penetrated right into that woman's body. She noticed how her grandmother had her head turned to one side as if she was listening to some sound like a bird, and then after a while she pulled her hands away, giving out a long silent sigh as she did so. Afterwards, the woman, who had been carried into the room, got up and hobbled away. From then on, Joy was often told of how Yai Li had helped people in Jetsip Rai who would otherwise be crippled or severely disabled. But Yai Li did not exploit her reputation in the neighbourhood. She accepted what they offered her and if she felt she could do nothing to help she would tell them directly, unlike others who claimed special powers.

As she grew older, Joy, aware of her grandmother's reputation, would sometimes say to her:

'But Yai. You could earn a lot of money with your gift. Why don't you just set yourself up? Lots of people will come to you.'

Yai Li would laugh.

'If I did it that way I'd soon lose any gift I had,' she would say. 'Besides, my knowledge is not complete.'

'Oh. Why is that Yai?'

'Because I had more to learn from my father and there wasn't time.'

'What do you mean?'

'He died before he could teach me what he knew.'

They were now approaching the gates of the mansion and Joy looked over once more to see that Yai Li had her eyes open.

'Have you been asleep all this time, Yai?' 'No. I've been preparing myself.'

'Why? Is Khun Chai difficult to treat?'

'No. Not particularly,' replied Yai Li. 'It's me. I'm getting tired.'

As they drove up the long winding driveway, past the huge pool and the tall tamarinds, Yai Li suddenly, for a moment, had the sensation of being in a foreign country, far not only from Klongtoey but the rest of Bangkok; a place suspended in time. Everything about it felt unreal. They parked behind the blue Mercedes and saw Sai waiting by the open door. He greeted them politely and indicated with his hand that he was waiting to drive someone out. For a moment Joy thought that it was Mitr and that once again she was not going to have a chance to speak to him. But at that moment Khun Arunee appeared at the top of the steps dressed in a long black gown, looking like an elegant queen of some cold northern land. As she glided past them and into the car waiting for her, she returned their greeting with barely a nod. They might as well not have been there, thought Joy. They were not worthy of her acknowledgment.

Khun Chai was waiting in the lobby reading a newspaper and immediately seemed pleased to see them. Mitr stood beside him and, without a word, wheeled his father into the bedroom, helped him onto the bed and then announced:

'We have some work to do. I will leave you to it.' With that he turned and left and, as he closed the door behind him, Yai Li could see her granddaughter waiting for him in the hallway with her briefcase held in front of her.

As soon as he had taken off his shirt and laid down on the bed, Khun Chai began talking excitedly.

'I've had a terrible week,' he said. 'I was all right for a few days after you did whatever you did to me. But it didn't last. Or maybe I needed more treatment. But that wasn't possible because of the funeral I had to attend, and the pains came back, and by last Friday I couldn't move at all without feeling the pain. It didn't help to have to sit there for hours in the *sala*. Those ceremonies just go on and on…'

He might have continued talking and complaining but Yai Li had placed both her hands on his back, one on his neck and the other at the base of his spine. This had the immediate effect of calming him, and he let out a long puff of breath. In a few moments his gentle snoring filled the room.

While the massage session was taking place, in Mitr's study on the other side of the lobby Joy and her boss sat opposite each other across the wide mahogany desk. He was handing over a document for her to put in her bag and study later at home.

'We've lost the rhythm,' he said with a look of annoyance. 'I know it couldn't be helped. But we have to speed things up a little now. Can you have this done by the day after tomorrow please?' His voice was terse and impatient.

'You know I will,' she said. She could see that he was upset. But she did not know how to change his mood. 'How have you been?'

'Awful,' he replied. 'I can't stand wasting time.' 'I understand,' she said.

'I mean, why a whole week? You know, with my grandmother the ceremony lasted for several weeks, apparently. Can you imagine?'

She laughed. He seemed a little more relaxed now.

'I've missed you.' At last, she could say it to him face to face.

'Yes. I've missed you too.' With that Mitr stood up and came to her side of the table, bent down to plant a kiss on her lips, then slipped his hand under her blouse to cup her breast. She could feel his desire for her rising. She knew that in a few minutes they would be on the chaise longue that was in the corner, as they had done countless times before during these extra working sessions. It was Mitr's favourite piece of furniture in that house, one that had been imported from Paris by his grandfather and had probably been the location of countless acts of sexual contact. But just as they were clumsily embracing, kissing and manoeuvring across the room over to their destination, the sound of the front door clanking open disturbed their amorous moment. And as they separated, footsteps approached the door which then swung open abruptly. They had just managed to disengage their bodies but were standing at an intimately close distance apart. Arunee, in her long silk gown, stood for a moment looking at one then the other. Her gaze remained on Joy. But her expression gave nothing away.

'I forgot something upstairs,' she said coldly, turning to her husband. 'You two are working again, I see. Documents? Contracts?' With that she turned and closed the door behind her.

Joy avoided Mitr's eyes. She felt both embarrassed and ashamed to have been caught in such an obviously explicit way. When she looked up again, she saw that Mitr did not seem nervous or even surprised. He merely shrugged his shoulders.

'She knows about us, doesn't she?' Joy asked the question that she had been wanting to ask for two years; not to know the answer but to have her suspicion confirmed.

'Yes.' Mitr replied.

'Since the beginning?'

Before he answered they could hear Arunee's high heeled footsteps coming down the stairs then crossing the lobby before exiting the front door.

'Yes.'

'You didn't tell me.' 'You didn't ask me.' 'And she is OK with it?'

'Yes, of course she is.' His look was a mixture of impatience and condescension, as though there had never been any doubt.

Before Joy could recover from this subtle blow, she found herself in his arms once more being steered towards the chaise longue.

In the room across the lobby, Yai Li, with her eyes closed was gliding the forefinger of her left hand over Khun Chai 's shoulder blade then down to the side of his rib cage as she had done in the first session. At some point she had heard the front door open and steps crossing the hallway, and then the sound of a female voice. But it all took place at a great distance and did not disturb what she was doing. As for Khun Chai, he was totally still until she reached the side of his neck. She felt him wince but this time he did not shout out. She continued her movements for a while longer before drawing away. Khun Chai did not move but lay still breathing deeply for a few minutes. Then slowly he pushed his forearms into the mattress, lifted his chest and began to slowly turn his head to the left and to the right as he had done on the previous occasion.

'It's better,' he said. 'But it still doesn't feel right yet.'

'No. There's a lot more to do. But with what you have we can't go too fast.' 'And what is it that I have?'

'Your nerve is sunk. I am trying to draw it up. But it needs more work.' 'And why do you think my nerve is sunk, as you put it?'

Yai Li shrugged: 'I'm not a doctor. There could be many reasons.' 'Name one.'

'Old age?'

Khun Chai laughed. 'I think you've hit the nail on the head,' he said. 'But there's something odd that happens when you do whatever it is that you do,' he went on. 'And I'm curious to know what it is.'

He was sitting up now with his legs slung over the side of the bed, and Yai Li was helping him put his left arm through the sleeve of his shirt.

'I had these visions the first time you were here, of me being a warrior in a battle. They were very vivid. I must have been fighting against the Burmese. I was wearing the clothes people wore in those days and I had a short sword in each hand.'

Yai Li said nothing in reply and did not tell him that she too had seen the same vision when she was touching him. She saw him slashing the air wildly against invisible enemies.

'I thought it was just my imagination. But today I had the same vision. Only this time I felt something else.'

Yai Li waited for him to continue. It was clear that he was trying to find the right word to describe his emotion.

'Terror. Yes. That was it. Terror. Of the violence, of war, of being harmed. Of harming. Of killing.' Suddenly his voice was breaking, and he seemed on the point of crying. But he immediately recovered his composure.

'I've been against war all my life, you know? It seems to me the most stupid thing about our species, this fighting and killing. I've always hated it. Do you think this has anything to do with it? I mean, is it because I've been through it all before and seen the horror of it?'

Yai Li remained silent.

'But how can my body have this memory?' Now she did speak: 'The body is memory.'

He looked at her for a moment with a puzzled expression.

'OK. I accept that the things that have happened to us somehow leave their trace in our bodies. But are you asking me to believe that our bodies also contain memories of our past lives?'

Yai Li opened both her hands to the ceiling.

'I can't answer that. But what did you experience? What did you feel?'

Before Khun Chai could answer, the door opened slowly and they turned to see Mitr standing there smiling at them.

'Have you two finished?' He asked. 'Joy should take you home now. I am sure you are tired, Khun Yai, and I know that Joy has work to do when she gets back tonight.'

As Yai Li got up, Khun Chai said:

'When can you come again?'

'Oh. Soon enough. I'll tell you when. You'll be better now. But I'll come back and do some more for you. Then you'll be all right.'

Chapter 9

During the following days, Khun Chai felt hardly any pain and was able to wander through the house and into the garden without any help from Sai. Still, he was impatient for Yai Li to return. Again, he had the sensation of being left dangling by her, which annoyed him. It seemed ironic that the person he had not trusted to help him was now the one he was depending on to do so. He found himself wondering about her more and more. There seemed to be an air of impenetrable mystery surrounding this woman whose beauty he was beginning to find attractive, which was strange to him, as he thought that he had long forgotten what this feeling was like. But who was this Yai Li? Where was she from? He could not place her accent. Upcountry for sure; Korat perhaps? But how could she be Joy's grandmother? He could not match them up in any way. They did not give him the impression of being close in any respect. The idea of them being relatives at all was surprising; Joy with her well-fed *loog kreung* looks, glowing with youth and confidence, Yai Li with her dark skin and thin, wiry body, timid as a bird. Where was the one in between them, the link, Joy's mother?

These questions continued to swirl around in his mind that whole week following her visit as he sat on the balcony in the late afternoon, smoking a cheroot and sipping his tea, watching the clouds forming, the lightning crash through the sky, the rain coming down and then the blazing sunlight that followed when the storm had passed. On the days when there was no rain, he would stroll slowly through the well-tended spaces in the half an hour of twilight that was his favourite time of the day, inspecting the trees and the flowers, listening to the birdsong, hoping to see a snake, or one of the monitor lizards that sometimes wandered into the garden from the nearby canal. During these quiet walks his mind would go back to that humble old woman who now seemed to have the key to his well-being. And he gradually realised that the one question that he needed to answer concerning her was how come she was reminiscent of someone he might have met before?

As he waited for a call from her, or a message sent through her granddaughter, he busied himself bringing the notebooks that were on the shelves in his upstairs bedroom down to where he was now living with Sai's assistance.

'Coals to Newcastle,' he told his helper. It was a saying that he had picked up from his schooldays in England, and whose meaning he tried to convey to Sai without much success.

'Well, Nai. If it's what you want to do,' said Sai with an indulgent smile.

The truth was that Khun Chai was not sure if it really was what he wanted to do. Most of the notebooks in the mountain that was piling up on his worktable, were of differing shapes and sizes, and contained thoughts hurriedly, carelessly, jotted down from different times over the past years. Newspaper articles that he had cut out and folded were also to be found in their pages, as well as photographs that he had taken of people and places. Khun Chai left them all untouched for a couple of days. Then gradually, almost reluctantly he began selecting some from the pile, leafing through them, picking out bits and pieces he found relevant to the drift of ideas that were beginning to form in his mind, and copying them into a brand new hardback notebook with an elaborate marbled cover that Mitr and Arunee had bought for him on their last trip to Paris. But there was no order or method to his activity. He did not know where he was going with the material, only a vague sense that something would eventually emerge from the chaos contained in those fragments.

'I don't believe it, Pa! You're writing again, aren't you? Wow. That's great.' said Mitr when he walked in one afternoon to find his father, pen in hand, frowning at an old newspaper clipping.

'Early days yet,' Khun Chai replied looking up at his son. 'I'm just pottering around for the moment. Scribbling. That's all.'

Mitr dismissed his father's remark with a wave of his hand. 'I remember you telling me some years back that you might have one last novel in you.'

'Did I really say that?' said Khun Chai. 'I don't remember.'

'Fibber. Of course, you do.'

Khun Chai shrugged at his son.

Afterwards, when he was alone, he recalled the conversation that took place between them five years earlier. He could not remember any mention of a last novel, only that Mitr had been insistent:

'But really, Pa. Why don't you write anymore? So many people like your books. I hear it all the time, from all sorts of people. When will your dad's next book be out?'

'I don't write anymore because I don't have to. You provide me with everything.' 'I don't understand. Why should you stop because of that?'

'You see, I don't have to struggle now. I don't have to make ends meet, like when I first started.'

'I don't believe that you started writing just to pay the bills. In any case, even if it were true, isn't it a good thing that you don't have to do it for the money? You don't have to worry about how many books you sell and all that. Now you can write without any pressure. Just for the joy of it.'

Those words echoed back to him when he was alone again. Hah! The joy of it, Mitr said. Had writing ever been a joyful occupation? He would be lying if he said no. The thrill of coming up with a good sentence that would never have to be changed. The satisfaction of finishing a book. The pleasure of seeing it in print. The appreciation from a reader he did not know personally. Yes. He had certainly known these 'joys', but they were intertwined with the hard grind over months and years; the wastepaper basket overflowing, the doubt and dissatisfaction, the days that produced one decent paragraph if he was lucky, squabbles with the editors. Did he want to go through any of that stuff again just to produce a piece of writing that would end up being read by a handful of people? And what would it contribute to a world already overwhelmed with books and literature and essays and articles – none of which seemed to have made much difference. Wars were still going on, bad governments were having a field day, the planet was on the point of collapse. What was the purpose of writing except to fulfil an urge to tell a story? And where did this urge come from?

As he picked his way through the old notebooks during the long hot afternoons Khun Chai recalled how he had started to write fiction.

'Whatever you do, don't give up your day job. You'll never earn enough from writing to make it worthwhile unless your book becomes a best seller, and even then. But if it's made into a movie that would be another matter.'

These were the cheerfully discouraging comments made by John Booth, his employer at the time, editor and owner of the *Bangkok Daily* where Khun Chai was working when he began his first novel. They were having dinner in a Japanese restaurant near the office in Pratunaam. It was to discuss a new project about the environment that John Booth wanted Khun Chai to tackle. But it turned into a personal conversation. The vast amount of sake they were getting through made both of them more forthright and expressive than usual. Khun Chai had just worked up enough courage to tell his boss that after ten years with the *Bangkok Daily* he was thinking of resigning his job on the newspaper to devote himself to a life of creativity.

'Anyway, why this great urge to write?' John Booth continued. 'Can't you just live life? Why do you have to add to it? What do you have to prove?'

Khun Chai had been in awe of his boss from the first day they met. His direct manner was evident to everyone in the office. But that evening his tone, although blunt, was not overbearing. It was, if anything, gentle and complicit.

'That I can be a writer,' muttered Khun Chai in reply. John Booth smiled at him and shrugged.

'But you're already doing that every day as a journalist, and you are becoming a pretty good one at that.'

They clinked glasses and downed some more warm sake.

'No. I mean a fiction writer, a storyteller. I have to prove it to my father.'

John Booth laughed, took off his thick glasses and began to wipe them with a napkin.

'But he's dead. He's been dead for quite a while.'

'That doesn't change things.'

'Phew! Sounds a bit Freudian to me. Do tell.'

Khun Chai, emboldened by the alcohol, told him of one afternoon about six months before he was sent over to London as a boy, to receive his privileged education and come back to Thailand fit to be a diplomat. He was sitting by himself writing at a table on the balcony in Baan Suan while his father and grandfather were standing nearby, staring out in silence at the garden. His grandfather came and stood over him and looked over his shoulder.

'Homework?' he asked.

'No,' Khun Chai replied. 'I'm writing a story.'

'For school? '

'No. Just for myself.'

The old man, clearly intrigued, patted him on the back.

'What is it about?' 'Oh. It's just a story.'

'Really? An adventure story, is it?'

'No. It's about growing up, and things like that.' he had answered seriously. 'So, you enjoy writing,' said his grandfather after an uncomfortable pause. 'Yes. I'd like to be a writer.'

His grandfather nodded. Again, silence.

'Well, you can write as a hobby once you have your career. It will help you relax, and take your mind off your work,' he said finally, and Khun Chai remembered thinking: this does not count as anything important to you.

At this point his father, who had been listening to their conversation, walked over and said:

'Do you think anyone will want to read stories you've made up? We're a society of gossipmongers. Mostly malicious stuff. Everyone tells a story. And people here don't read. Not like the *farangs*. It's too much effort. Too tiring for the brain. You won't make a cent. What are you going to live on? I'm afraid you'll have to think up a better profession.'

With that, both men had laughed. But whereas his grandfather's laughter was kind and understanding, his father's had the cruel, sarcastic ring of a bitter drunk, and from then on, he had continued to mock Khun Chai's ambition to be a writer constantly, up till the day they said goodbye.

'So, you're going to show him!' said John Booth when Khun Chai finished his reminiscing.

'Well, good luck to you, young man. You're going to need it.'

Three years later he was congratulating Khun Chai when they met at the book launch of the English edition of 'The Elusive City' at the Foreign Correspondents Club of Thailand.

'Well done. You made it!' he said hugging him. His joy at Khun Chai's success was genuine and effusive.

'Not really,' said Khun Chai. 'I've been serialised in a magazine. But the critics don't like the book.'

'Never mind the fucking critics. You've answered your father. Haven't you?'

It was true. But to have proved to his dead father that he could be a writer and get published, brought only a hollow sense of satisfaction and it did nothing to heal the memory of their problematic relationship as father and son. In fact, by the time he had finished this first piece of work and managed to convince a publisher to take it on he had already concluded that, with regard to writing, his father's advice, though given for the wrong reasons, was generally on the right track. Reading was not part of Thai culture; verbal story telling was, and going to the cinema was the modern *likay* show; and yes, gossip, particularly the malicious kind, was a prime source of entertainment. In this respect there was plenty of material to go round, not just about the family or people in the neighbourhood, but the dirt on politicians, monks, film stars, people in high places. Everyone was game and truth was never an obstacle. Bad reputations came out of this national pastime, and, even when unfounded, were never fully erased. His father was also correct in saying that there would be few people interested in the stories he made up. His Thai readership was minimal, and he made a pittance from the writing. But despite most of his father's predictions coming true, Khun Chai persisted with his career as a fiction writer. Over the years, by the time he was into his third novel, writing fiction had become a habit he found difficult to break. It was a way he could process his experiences and his feelings about his own life and those around him, and the chaotic city they inhabited.

This act of invention had become a compulsion, and he was no longer talking to his father's ghost.

Nevertheless, he felt fortunate to have heeded John Booth's advice about keeping a day job, and went on working for the *Bangkok Daily*. Otherwise, he would have been a penniless author. The income from writing fiction was insufficient to pay the rent. Even so, he held onto the dream of hitting the jackpot one day, and of having one of his novels or short stories transformed into a film script, the way other people's fiction had been. Then, perhaps, the money would flow in. This nearly happened several times during his writing career. A famous Taiwanese director was interested in one of his short stories. A French film maker wanted to turn one of his novels, *The Young Plane Tree* into a film script. But both projects fell through before they even got off the ground. It was only after *The Elusive City* was translated and published in Singapore that any serious income began to trickle in – but it was hardly enough to pay the bills or the rent on his house off Sukhumwit Road. By this time, he had come to accept that not only was he not going to make a proper income from writing, but also that he was not going to become famous either in his own country or abroad. A belated recognition had eventually come from Thai critics and readers and at home he was included in several low-key literary festivals in Bangkok. But he never felt that his writing was really appreciated by them or fully understood. He was convinced, though without any concrete proof, that this had something to do with his name and his family. The theme that ran through most of his plots was common enough; the clash between the traditional and the modern and the contradictions that it produced. Others had taken up the same sort of issues. But it seemed that the Thai critics did not like his approach, and he suspected, from what they said, that they presumed that he came from an elite background, which therefore disbarred him from knowing about the lives of ordinary Thai folk and what went on in the underbelly of Thai society. They did not spell it out, but they referred to him as a writer talking about things of which he could have no direct knowledge and whose style of writing was too self-consciously experimental, and therefore foreign for Thai taste. These critiques hurt him, but he consoled himself with the thought that perhaps the issues he dealt with were too close to home and that people did not want to be reminded of the confusing dismantling of their traditional cultural values in the name of modernity.

It was obvious from the kind of reviews and feedback that he received in the years following the translations of his books into English and other European languages, that the foreigners who read his books seemed to appreciate him more than his compatriots. He was invited twice to the Singapore Literary Festival and once to Oslo. These were entertaining trips and he enjoyed meeting other writers and sharing common ground. He was gratified that at last someone understood his central theme in a way that seemed to be lost on his local readers. But he would return home with a bittersweet feeling, a kind of sadness that he had never received the same respect from his Thai readers. He felt that the stories he told about the everyday struggles of ordinary working people, and the contradictions that they embodied in Thai society were worth telling because no other Thai writers were tackling the subjects in the way he did. The praise of foreigners was insufficient compensation for the disappointment he felt in having failed to inspire change in his own country. He realized that, in this respect, he had done better as a journalist writing about the transformation of Bangkok for the *Bangkok Daily* under John Booth's guidance.

When his last collection of short stories, *Unlikely Bonds*, was published he was in his late sixties, and he felt that he had done enough as far as fiction writing was concerned. By then he accepted that any ambition to bring about a higher consciousness in his readership was guided by his own vanity. Besides, he had run out of ideas, and he was getting tired in general: of growing physically weaker by the month; of his lapses of memory; of the politics of the land; of the endemic corruption of the system; of the apathy his compatriots regarding where the country was heading; and of his own cowardice in not telling the things that needed to be told but, instead, playing the self-censorship game to which everyone in his profession conformed because they were afraid of the consequences.

His financial needs were now all taken care of, thanks to his son. The debts had been paid, the house repaired, restored, extended and elevated to a place fit to entertain royalty as it once had a hundred years earlier. Mitr's success in the aggressive and lucrative world of real estate, at a time when Bangkok was booming, meant that Khun Chai could be totally comfortable in his retirement and not have any more worries as far as money was concerned. This was, of course, a great relief for him. But at the same time, it took away the motivation to carry on being creative. Mitr's generosity made it unnecessary for Khun Chai to maintain that fantasy anymore. It was time to give up writing.

Now, years later, he could not understand why he should be considering putting pen to paper again and still unsure whether he was really going to embark on a new project. The years of idleness had dulled his skills. He was not even clear about how to begin, let alone where he was going with the writing. But it felt different from before. He was in no rush, unlike when he was younger. Then there was an urgency to getting down to work every night, and the number of pages finished in a bout of writing were important. Getting published was the goal. This time, there was no desire to see his words in print. Now if he were to begin at all it would be approached differently without any agenda or endgame in mind; no ambition, no father to argue with, no reader or critic to convince. And he would try to be as honest as he could. This one, if it were to materialize, would be a labour of love. His last novel. Written joyfully. A closure.

Chapter 10

One afternoon, as he was thumbing through the notes and jottings, and rereading the articles he had kept, Khun Chai was inexplicably filled with a sense of anticipation, like that of approaching a fight in the days when he used to box as a schoolboy. He had the same feeling of walking up to the ring and parting the ropes to climb through them. The action was still to come, but the adrenaline rush was already coursing through his body. It was a similar sensation every time he was about to begin a new piece of work – a heady mix of excitement and anxiety. He knew that afternoon, that the juices were flowing once again and prayed that this time they would continue to do so, and he would have the strength to last the rounds. He was sure that Yai Li was the key. Her treatments would keep him physically mobile and positive.

That night there was no rain. The crescent of a new moon hung above the trees in the cloudless sky. The garden was alive with the sounds of birdcalls and the scratching of insects. As Khun Chai sat listening, flicking away the mosquitos at regular intervals, the idea that he had been looking for came to him like a beautiful snake sliding out from the thick undergrowth. It made him smile because he realized that what he wanted to write about was right there in front of him all the time.

A week later Yai Li returned to Baan Suan.

Khun Chai was at his desk when Sai showed her in. He looked up as she entered and nodded towards her without changing his serious expression, before turning back to what he was doing. She understood that she was to wait and so walked over to the tall windows that opened onto the balcony and stared out at the garden. Suddenly the call of a night owl pierced the air. It was a sound that she had not heard for a long time, and she always associated it with death. Involuntarily, she pulled back abruptly.

'Are you all right?' It was Khun Chai's voice. He had got up from the desk and was now walking towards his bed and undoing the buttons of his shirt as he did so.

'I am sorry. I didn't mean to be rude like that and keep you waiting. But just now I was finishing a paragraph and I couldn't break my concentration, because I forget things so easily these days.'

'It doesn't matter,' she answered him as she dragged the low stool towards his bedside.

'What did you catch out there that made you jump?' continued Khun Chai.

'Oh nothing,' said Yai Li, then added: 'Just an owl crying out.' 'An owl?'

'Yes,'

'I didn't hear it.'

When they were both in their usual positions, she on her low chair by the bed and Khun Chai lying face down, he said:

'As you can see, I've started writing again. It's thanks to you.'

Yai Li let out a laugh. 'What do you mean? What have I got to do with it?'

'No. It's true. I never thought I'd ever write again until you gave me that first treatment.' Yai Li, smiling, shook her head. 'It's nothing to do with me.'

'Oh, but it is,' he insisted cheerfully. 'And I want to know more about you. If you don't mind, that is. You are an inspiration to me. So, you must tell me things about yourself. Please will you do that?'

Yai Li was now holding a hand over her mouth. It was a gesture of shyness that made Khun Chai smile.

'There's not much to tell. My life isn't interesting.'

'Oh, but you have lots to tell. For a start you have a rare gift. You know you have. Joy told me that it runs in the family. I want to know where this gift comes from. Will you tell me?'

Yai Li felt embarrassed. But at the same time, she could not help feeling flattered. Nobody had been interested in her as far back as she could remember, not even her husband who wanted just one thing from her. Then there were people who wanted her to help them walk again, or sit up again, or be free from pain. But none of them really wanted to know her as a person. She was practically invisible, and she was used to being that way. Now here was a person she hardly knew, a minor royal at that, or at least one by name, who seemed to be genuinely interested in who she was. Or perhaps he merely needed information from her to put in his book.

He seemed to read her mind when he said:

'I know you might think I want to question you for my book. It's partly that. I admit it. But there's something else.'

He turned and looked at her with a serious expression.

'You see, I feel I know you, or that I have met you somewhere before. I am sure of it. How can that be? Is it to do with past lives again?'

They both continued to gaze at one another in silence. No, thought Yai Li. You can't get it out of me in this way. It is not about past lives, but this present one, and I am not going down that path. For in that moment there was no doubt in her mind that this Khun Chai was the young man she had met that autumn evening in London all those years before. But she said nothing and made a motion with both of her hands for him to lie down flat so that she could begin her treatment.

When the session was over, Khun Chai picked up from where he left off.

'Is it possible that we have met before, somewhere? Have you…?' He hesitated for a moment.

'Have you ever worked for any family that I might know?' Yai Li shook her head.

'I was a seamstress in a factory not far from here, Siam Garment.' It was not really an answer, and Khun Chai looked at her quizzically.

'Ah, yes. I know it.' He said. 'It's that big building just off the highway, about fifteen minutes from here. Been there a long time. So, you were working there. What? Since you were young?'

'Yes. I always worked there. Until I retired.'

'It was where they had that strike in 1974 during the students' movement, wasn't it?'

Yai Li nodded. She had taken part in the sit in and shouted the slogans along with her fellow workers.

'But I was there,' said Khun Chai excitedly. 'I covered the event for my newspaper. I interviewed some women about their working conditions and their pay. Maybe that's when we came across each other.'

Yai Li shook her head and waved her hand.

'No. I never met you there. You must have been talking to the leaders. I was just another worker in the crowd.'

'Did it change anything? The movement I mean, and the strikes. Did they make a difference?' Yai Li was silent for a while before answering.

'Yes. Of course, it did. But not enough.' 'No,' said Khun Chai as he nodded.

⚜ ⚜ ⚜

Later, when she was back home in Jetsip Rai, Yai Li felt confused. Should she have mentioned London? She did not like being dishonest. But at the same time, she felt resentful that with his insistent questioning Khun Chai had opened up a corner of her memory that she preferred to keep closed forever. What was she to do if she were to go on seeing him? There was no avoiding the issue.

That evening, she went to the chest of drawers that contained all her worldly possessions and took out a small wooden box. In it was a faded photograph of herself, seventeen years old, standing next to her auntie, taken in April 1963. She was wearing the dress that she would take with her to England in a week's time. Her aunt had it made for her by a friend who was a dressmaker.

'Wear it when there's a special occasion. You don't want to look like a peasant,' auntie had told her.

Her aunt could not quite hide the jealousy she felt that Li, as she was then, was chosen to go to England with the family, to be both nanny to the young child and to cook. After all, she had been in service to the family for nearly a decade, whereas her niece had been there for less than a year. Besides, it was she who had got the job for Li in the first place. But Khun Benjawan was insistent.

'You won't like it over there,' she told Li's auntie. 'It's cold and wet, and grey. We want you to stay here in Bangkok and take care of the house.'

In the photograph, Li's auntie is looking at her with a slightly disapproving expression, as though she did not trust that Li was the worthy owner of the dress. A few days later, when she helped her to pack, she told her:

'Listen. You haven't done this kind of work for very long. I've tried to help you not mess up. But in London it's going to be different. You are going to be on your own. Just remember to be polite all the time and to do your best to serve them. They are good, kind people who will treat you well. Do your work and when you get back here with them, you'll be treated differently, as someone experienced, who's been abroad, who's been to London.'

It was the dress that Li wore that evening of the dinner party, which took place six months after her arrival in London. Up till then there had been no occasion to take it out of the cupboard. There had been no entertaining at the apartment till that day. Khun Santi had been settling into his post at the embassy, where he was the new commercial attaché, and Khun Benjawan was busy decorating the apartment to her own liking and finding a school for her young son, Gan. Li had gone about doing her daily chores as if in a dream because London was so alien to anything she had known. They had arrived at the end of a cold, wet April. The skies seemed permanently overcast. There was no life in the streets. She could not understand anything that was happening even though Khun Benjawan tried to teach her some basic phrases every day. The boy she was meant to look after was a rude, spoilt brat. All of it made her depressed and homesick, but she was not going to let her auntie down and she tried her best to be grateful for having been taken abroad. And things did improve once she had made contact with some servants who had accompanied other Thai families. They would meet in the park on their free afternoons and exchange their experiences and the gossip they had picked up.

As for her employers, she had no cause to complain. Khun Benjawan was kind and considerate to her and would take her out with her when she went shopping and show her how to order food in the local stores. Her husband, Khun Santi, was at work all week at the embassy and even on weekends he was usually busy attending a conference, visiting a factory or showing guests from Thailand around London. At home he would spend time playing with his son. She did not feel as relaxed around him as she did with his wife, and once or twice during those months she had caught him looking at her in a peculiar way, but she thought nothing of it.

As the summer came, and with it the sunshine and the leaves on the trees, Li started to become more at home. On her days off she would meet with her new friends in the park near the apartment and exchange news and gossip. Then it was September, and the colours were changing again as the wind got colder and the days shorter. She remembered that on the day of the dinner party, a Sunday, it had been raining that morning. She was busy making the bed in the spare room for Khun Benjawan's mother, who was arriving at Heathrow late that night.

'Your mother won't like this weather,' Li had overheard Khun Santi saying this to his wife. 'I don't know why you invited her at all.'

She had not caught Khun Benjawan's answer.

Dinner had finished early, as usual. By nine all the guests were leaving. The ambassador had offered the use of his official car because it could be parked right in front of the exit gate at the terminal, and he had already told the driver to drop him and his wife off at the residence and then return to pick up Khun Benjawan to go to the airport.

Li was cleaning up the kitchen when the driver rang the bell.

'Thank you, Li. Great job this evening. The ambassador and his wife had a good time,' said Khun Benjawan as she put on her coat.

'Don't stay up for my mother. I'll see her to her room. You can meet her in the morning. She'll probably be up late because of the jet lag and change of time. You know what she likes for breakfast. '

With that she departed, and Li was tidying up the last details, putting the plates away in the cupboard, when Khun Santi poked his head round the kitchen door and said:

'Li. Can you bring me a cup of tea in my room, please? I am not feeling too well.'

'Of course, Nai.' she said, and immediately put on the kettle. A few minutes later she carried the cup of tea into their bedroom. She felt sorry that he was not well. Was it the food that evening? she wondered, and then felt relieved that she had not been responsible for it. On entering the room, she saw that Khun Santi had already taken his shoes off and was sprawled across the bed. He motioned for her to put the tea down on the bedside table. As she did so he suddenly grabbed her wrist and pulled her towards him.

'You are so young and beautiful,' he whispered, and she could smell the whiskey on his breath as he held her in both his arms and forced himself on top of her. 'You know you are.'

Li was too shocked to be able to speak. Her mind was racing, and she was afraid. She could feel his hands groping her breasts and then tugging at her dress, pulling it up towards her face as he tried to kiss her. She wanted to scream but nothing came out. Now he was undoing his trousers and she felt helpless to defend herself. He was much bigger and stronger than her, and he seemed to be filled with a furious desire that overwhelmed her. She closed her eyes tight ready to surrender. There was nothing else to do. Then she heard a woman's voice:

'Get up and get out of here!'

It was Khun Benjawan standing at the door. Her eyes were glaring at them like beams of fire. Li instinctively jumped off the bed, brushing down her dress, and rushed through the door past her. That night she did not sleep or rest. As she tossed and turned, she was consumed with feelings of shame. What had made him behave like that? She asked herself without coming to any answer. He was so mild and polite normally. She was sure that she had given him no cause to think that she was open to his advances. But what was Khun Benjawan going to say to her? Involuntarily her body kept cringing from the emotions she was going through. She thought that she heard their voices arguing and a door being slammed. She would recall it as the second worst night in her life.

The next morning at dawn, there was a knock on the door and then Khun Benjawan appeared looking tired and pale. Normally on a weekday, at seven o'clock, Li would be getting up to see that the boy was dressed, then prepare breakfast for everyone, grab a quick coffee herself, make sure the boy ate something while she prepared his snack box and then when all this was done, she would walk him to the school. But it was only six thirty. Khun Benjawan pointed a finger at her:

'Li. I want you to pack up your things. Don't worry about your work. I'll take care of everything. I don't have anything to do this morning. I don't want you to come out of your room, if you don't mind, until my husband and my son are out of the house. My mother is here, but she's not feeling well because of the long flight. She's taken some medicine and she's staying in bed. I don't want you to see her. I am going to try to get a ticket for you to go back to Thailand today.'

Li said nothing but the moment Khun Benjawan had closed the door behind her she immediately began to shake with fear. Her employer's tone was so angry that it made her feel guilty. On top of what had happened, was she going to be punished? Then, after a while, she calmed down and began to do as she had been ordered. She could hear Khun Benjawan's voice outside in the corridor saying to her son:

'Na Li's not well today. I'll be taking you to school.' The boy was protesting and saying:

'But why is she ill? What's wrong with her? I want to see her.' 'Well, you can't!' said his mother, firmly.

I am not even allowed to say goodbye, thought Li. She must think so badly of me.

In the taxi to the airport that afternoon they sat in tense silence for a long time. Then Khun Benjawan said:

'I don't believe in coincidences.'

Li was surprised by this remark. It was something her father had once said to her when she was a child when explaining to her how he would not have met her mother if she had not missed her train back to Bangkok. But Li could not figure out what Khun Benjawan was referring to and her employer did not seem to want to elaborate any further. Both were staring out of the window on their side of the seat. It was a dry, sunny day, and the leaves were red and golden.

'It was raining last night. I'd forgotten my umbrella. I had to go back to fetch it. Just in case we had to be standing out in it at the airport. I didn't want my mother to get wet.' Khun Benjawan's voice was flat. She seemed not angry now, but distracted, and exhausted.

So that's why she came back, thought Li.

'I know it's probably not your fault. But you can't stay with us now that it's happened. You understand, don't you?'

Li nodded silently. A man had assaulted her, and she was being sent home. It wasn't her fault. But she was to be punished for it as though it was.

For weeks after returning to Bangkok, Li felt frightened and depressed. She sensed that people shunned her because she was soiled, or she thought that they judged her for having done something bad. She found little sympathy from her auntie, to whom she recounted the whole incident.

'But what are you complaining about? He didn't actually do anything to you, did he? Worse things have happened to me.'

It was pointless to try to explain that what he managed to do was to make her feel like a worthless piece of meat.

'You can't stay here,' said her auntie. 'Not with all the talk in the household. They've already sent for another girl to take your place. I'll give you some money to get yourself a room in Jetsip Rai. I've got a friend there who can help. She cleans in one of those bars they have over there. Have you thought of doing something like that? I don't mean cleaning. You're young and quite good looking. You'd get a job easily working as a hostess. I hear you can earn good money.'

Li looked shocked at what her auntie was suggesting.

'Well, it's that or a factory,' said her aunt. 'I've got another friend who can probably get you a job in the clothing factory where she works. Do you know how to use a sewing machine?'

Li said no.

'Well, it's not that complicated. You don't have to have a fancy education to learn how to do it. My friend can teach you in a day.'

Yai Li could not blame Khun Chai for bringing up the memory of that night in London. Even now, in her mid-seventies, what happened still disgusted her and filled her with such shame that she had told no one apart from her auntie about it, not even her husband, or her daughter.

Only once in all the intervening years did she allow herself to revisit the incident. It was when, one day at the factory during a break, a woman in her group read out loud a story from the front page of that day's newspaper. It was about a society lady who had shot her husband dead when she found him in bed with a young prostitute. Yai Li, glancing over her friend's shoulder saw the photograph that accompanied the article. It showed Khun Benjawan, little changed from the time she had known her twenty years earlier, in a prisoner's outfit being led away from the courthouse. She was quoted as saying: 'He's always been a bad man. I have no regrets.' The article, under the heading 'A Family Tragedy', went on to talk about the death of her son from a drug overdose only a year previously. Yai Li had taken the newspaper home and reread it several times. It made her feel sorry for her former employer. But it did nothing to heal the wound that she bore in her heart and the sense of utter vulnerability as a woman who had been the victim of aggression.

As she examined the old photograph of herself as that young, innocent woman wearing the beautiful dress, she realised that she should be grateful to Khun Chai because he had unwittingly brought her back face to face with her darkness. She had always known that one day before she died, she would have to return to that painful place if she was to ever find peace in this lifetime.

Chapter 11

Not sure. Not sure at all.

After a strenuous search, Khun Chai found the notebook he was looking for. As he opened it and read these first words, his mind immediately plunged into the sea of memories that flowed in from all sides. The date that was written inside the cover was 2014 September 18th. It was his 70th birthday, when he moved back into Baan Suan from the rented house in the Sukhumvit area.

He had not expected to ever return there. Back in 2001 there had been a rumour, confirmed by many acquaintances, that Baan Suan was being sold by the family who had originally bought it off him, to an international conglomerate that owned the Jubilee chain of hotels worldwide. Their plan was to turn the property into the most luxurious City Spa in Asia. This did not bother Khun Chai one way or another. He had resigned himself to the fact that Baan Suan's future was out of his hands. He would have preferred it to be converted into a cultural centre, or perhaps a museum, or even a private retirement home. But a luxury Spa was fine with him, as long as the building was retained, and good luck to them. After all, several other properties had been converted into fine hotels in this way.

But then, overnight, the news changed. The conglomerate had pulled out of the deal and a group of Asian developers was set to buy the property and build a 64-floor super luxury condominium, complete with a heliport. This news upset Khun Chai who was now faced with the prospect that the beautiful house was going to be demolished and, in its place, yet another towering block of concrete was to be constructed. He felt a mixture of emotions when he heard about this possibility – sadness most of all, and anger close behind. But just as quickly as this news hit the headline of the business pages, he read that his son Mitr's company, Siam Estate, had somehow stepped in and bought the property from the family for a huge sum, with the aim of restoring it to its former glory. He had heard that after the floods in 2011, that hit that part of the city badly, the house was in need of serious repair. He presumed that his son was going to see to this and modernise the place before selling it on to someone who could afford it, and make a decent profit. This was his job, and he was the best at it.

Given all of this, he was totally surprised when Mitr announced during the birthday lunch by the river that the restoration of the house and grounds of Baan Suan was finally finished, and that he was giving the house to Khun Chai as his birthday gift. This announcement drew gasps from the guests around the table, followed by prolonged clapping. Khun Chai himself was lost for words.

'Happy Birthday, Pa,' Mitr said as he raised his glass. 'It's for all the sacrifices you've made for me. But, if you don't mind, Arunee and I want to move in on you,' he added, and everyone joined in with the laughter.

Finding himself back in the house where he was born and had spent his youth and seeing how impeccably it had been refurbished, Khun Chai was, naturally, filled with surprise and delight. When, as a young man, he had been forced to sell it he had never dreamed of setting foot in it ever again, and certainly not as its owner. For Mitr also insisted that it should be in Khun Chai's name and would not accept his protestations.

'I have many other properties, Pa,' he told him when they were alone together after the party.

Khun Chai could read between the lines. It was obviously more expedient to put the property in his name. Nevertheless, he was moved by Mitr's generosity and kindness and filial devotion – all admirable qualities that he could not remember transmitting to his son.

'How did you manage it?' he had asked him during their next weekly meal together.

'Oh, I made them an offer they couldn't refuse,' Mitr answered, and laughed. 'Besides, they could not afford to repair the place after those floods.'

Khun Chai sensed that there was more that his son was not telling him. He said: 'No. Really. What did you do?'

'Well, first I convinced them with your line. I told them how precious the house was as a historical monument and that it would be a shame to see it disappear. '

'And?'

'Well, they were suitably moved by that. But it was the money that won the day. No surprise. On top of the enormous amount I offered them, including cash, I also promised them a unit in the condo in Klongtoey.'

On hearing this, Khun Chai could not hide the urgency in his voice when he asked:

'What condo in Klongtoey?'

'The one we're building by the river, in the area they call Jetsip Rai.' said Mitr.

'So the rumour's true? Klongtoey is going to be developed?'

'Yes, Pa. It's going ahead. It's just a matter of timing.'

Khun Chai said nothing more because he did not want to turn what was otherwise a pleasant meeting into a possible argument, and he managed to hide his reaction to the news. But it upset him. For a number of years, while still a journalist, he had been a member of the small, vocal group of conservationists whose wide agenda was to push for a more ecologically friendly Bangkok. Their intention was to raise the consciousness of Bangkokians regarding the way their city was going: the traffic, the polluted canals, the permanent danger of an urban epidemic spreading; in other words, the chaos that was Bangkok, due to the lack of adequate town planning and to the fact that developers could do what they wanted without having to answer for their decisions. These were well worn issues that had been talked about for years without much real change happening. Politicians, governors, concerned businessmen had all expressed their desire and commitment to transform the city and make it better for its inhabitants, but the problems remained as glaring as ever.

The issue of Klongtoey came to a head a year before Taksin was ousted from office in 2006. The leaked plans for the development of the area stirred many people, including himself, to the conclusion that they had to be resisted by whatever means possible. It was a sensitive issue and touched a personal chord. His group had already been approached by community leaders from the slums, opposed to these plans to turn it into a completely modernised state-of-the-art urban conclave. It would mean evictions, and the rehousing of families who had lived there for several generations, albeit as squatters. He agreed with them that it was urgent to support the local residents, who were the poorest sector of the city, and the last in line to have their lives improved by better housing and social services. He had written about this in the newspaper with the intention of pressing for a more humane and equitable solution, even though he knew that there was no way to halt the project altogether and that outright physical resistance would end in bloodshed. But he and his friends were hoping, foolishly, that something would happen again to delay or altogether undermine the massive construction that was about to be initiated.

As if in answer to their prayers, political circumstances started to change rapidly. It was clear that there was a well-orchestrated movement to remove Taksin from government. The country came to be polarised into red and yellow shirts. There was political and economic uncertainty, and inevitably violence. Taksin's business partners from other Asian countries were watching which way the wind was blowing. Although Khun Chai was no fan of Taksin, whose self-serving populism he mistrusted, he did not want to see yet another coup take place and democracy postponed yet again, as it had been so many times during his lifetime.

Eventually, the conservative forces, with the backing of the army, prevailed. The only consolation for Khun Chai, as the country reverted to business as usual in the wake of Taksin's unceremonious departure to foreign shores, was that the plan to develop Klongtoey was postponed indefinitely, with nobody seemingly interested in reviving it.

But now, eight years later, he was hearing firsthand confirmation that the project had been revived and was going ahead. Mitr, aware of his father's opinion, added:

'Pa, it was never going to be forgotten for long.'

He was right. It was foolish of anyone to think that the developers would simply forget about that piece of prime estate forever and let the people who lived there continue with their daily lives. It was common knowledge that the construction companies had already begun to encroach on the edge of the district, and it was not long before the full-scale demolition of the area was going to be conducted. It was ironic that his own son was one of the key promoters of this latest piece of carnage.

'I respect your views. I really do,' Mitr had continued. 'I know you are against this. But it's going to happen, whatever you or your conservationist friends think about it. You have to come to terms with it, Pa. There's no way to stop it happening. You know that the city has got to grow. It can't stay as it is. There has to be development, for the general good. Otherwise, there is no progress. We'll do it the best way possible and try to benefit everyone.'

Khun Chai smiled at his son and said nothing. He was touched but not convinced by Mitr's attempt to soothe him. He did not say out loud that the kind of progress that Mitr was talking about appalled him. He had already watched as Bangkok had been turned gradually, district by district, into a dysfunctional urban mess with its jagged skyline of half empty buildings, the poor displaced and moved out of communities that were their lifeline into concrete cells, away from the gaze of those who wanted to see Bangkok as the gleaming, efficient place that Mitr envisaged.

During those first months after moving into Baan Suan, Khun Chai was wracked by feelings of guilt and ambiguity. He was moving back into his family home, now brightly restored and looking like a palace, while the people in the slums were about to be pulled out of theirs. He wanted to do something – write articles, join a protest movement, as he had done before – to try to redress this inequality.

'I hope that those people in the slums are not going to do anything foolish,' Mitr continued, as though he had sensed what was in his father's mind. 'There's no point in resistance. It would be useless.'

This was said for Khun Chai's sake, as a warning. But it was unnecessary. As a younger man he had written his articles and given voice to those opposing the development. He had stood firm with the people who protested and resisted. But this time the passion had gone. He knew that it was hopeless. He was aware, like everyone else, that the vision for Klongtoey had the financial backing of the Prime Minister and his business colleagues, so it was sure to go ahead. Mitr was right. There was no way to stop it. He could only resign himself to the inevitable. There was nothing he, nor anyone else could do to stop the monster from growing until it imploded on itself.

The conversation they had that day marked a shift in their relationship as father and son. The tension between them was never manifest. But from then on, they avoided the subject altogether whenever they were in each other's company. But it was like a shadow between them threatening to burst out of the corner. That his own son was the key player in the project that he was objecting to, produced in him a mixture of disappointment and sadness and he saw no way through their disagreement. Sooner or later, it had to reach a point where neither could avoid an outright clash of opinion.

Fortunately, he was wrong about the time scale. The threat to develop Klongtoey kept on being delayed year after year, because the new project was even more ambitious than the previous ones and involved even more investors from many other countries. It seemed that they could not be persuaded to reach an agreement on how large a chunk of the cake they were prepared to accept. So, the negotiations stretched on and on. Mitr, in the meantime, had many other development projects going on, not just in Bangkok but in Singapore, Taiwan, and India. Klongtoey was not his priority.

Until now. 2019. Mitr had at last managed to pull all the investors together, including new ones from mainland China who wanted to expand their business empire into Southeast Asia. The deals were concluded to every party's satisfaction, and the plans set in place for the bulldozers to start their engines. It was a triumph for Mitr, and the disaster that Khun Chai had been dreading for a decade and a half was about to come true. Another scar would soon be added to the already carved up city.

Not sure at all

As he began to thumb through the notebook, he started to think that he could at least make an attempt, with the little fire left in him, to have one last crack at preserving the memory of an area of the city that had been significant to him before it faded away altogether and appeared in coffee table books about 'Old Bangkok'. This was not just for himself but for anyone interested in knowing a time and a feeling in the city before Mitr's modern metropolis came into being. The fact that the woman whose talent, whatever it was, was giving him the energy to contemplate embarking on the project also lived in that district was, in his mind, an unmistakable sign. She would be his mouthpiece, and he would begin his story there in that extraordinary area of the city where he himself had known love for the first time in his life.

Chapter 12

'Can we just talk today?' asked Khun Chai as he led Yai Li past the bed and out to the balcony. She stood still in the doorway for a moment, unable to conceal her surprise.

'What about?' she said with a nervous giggle. Her mind immediately jumped to the question he had raised in their previous meeting.

'About Klongtoey,' he said, as he waved her to sit down by the table next to him.

'But don't you want me to work on your back first?'

'No. Thank you. I feel all right today. Really. I would rather talk to you. I know you live in Klongtoey, in the Jetsip Rai area. I just wanted to know a bit more about the district. I am sure you can help me.'

Yai Li felt uncomfortable, unsure of what this man expected of her.

'Yes,' he continued without waiting for her reply. 'I need your help. With the story, I mean.' Yai Li did not understand what he was talking about.

'I have decided to base the central part of my story in Klongtoey. Something important happened to me there when I was a young man.'

He stopped talking for a moment as if he were recalling something specific.

'It doesn't matter what it was. I am writing a story, not telling my life's history. Of course, I am inventing the person I was…'

At that point Khun Chai, who had been looking at the table covered with notebooks in front of him as he spoke, glanced up and saw that Yai Li's attention was not on him but on the shadowy figure making its way through the garden. Her eyes were following his movements, while Khun Chai's followed her gaze.

'Oh, don't worry. That's probably Ai Toh, Sai's son, out collecting crickets,' he told her. 'He's a strange boy. Doesn't talk at all. Mitr loves him. If he was home, they would be going around looking for insects together.'

Yai Li turned back.

'You were saying that you are writing about Klongtoey,' she said.

'Well, let's put it this way. I haven't actually begun yet. I am preparing myself to do so.' His laughter was self-deprecating.

'You see, Yai Li, writing is a funny process. I tried to be a writer in the past. But this time it feels different.'

He was about to explain to her why it was, but decided that it was better not to go off on a tangent. He continued:

'So when did you begin to live in Klongtoey, or were you born there?'

Yai Li looked uncomfortable at being interrogated in such a direct manner.

'No. I was born in Ayutthaya,' she said tersely. 'I didn't go to Klongtoey until I was twenty.' 'You moved there with your family?'

Yai Li shook her head. For a moment they sat in silence. Both seemed to have retreated into their private worlds.

'And you were working in the factory by that time?'

Yai Li stared at him. For a second, she was on the verge of spilling out the truth to him, about the circumstances that took her to Klongtoey after that terrible time in London, and the unpleasant events afterwards. But she kept quiet. Khun Chai noticed that her hands were fidgeting.

'What was it like back then? It must have been so different.' he said encouragingly.

Khun Chai regretted making such a banal statement, and he suddenly felt awkward at questioning her at all, and quickly added:

'What I really wanted to ask you about was the Mosquito Bar. Did you know it?'

Yai Li stared at him for a while before nodding her head, surprised that he mentioned the name at all. As she did so, it suddenly flashed through Khun Chai 's mind that perhaps she had worked there, and before he could stop himself, he said:

'Did you know a girl who worked in the bar called Pia?'

Yes, thought Yai Li, there was a Pia in the neighbourhood at around the time she moved to Klongtoey and who worked in the Mosquito Bar. If it was the same person that he was referring to, she was a pretty girl with long black hair who got dressed up and painted every evening to go to work.

'I know who you are talking about. But I didn't know her personally,' she said. 'Why are you asking me all this?'

'Do you know what happened to her?' There was a certain urgency to his voice.

'It was a long time ago. I can't remember. I think she moved away. But I am not sure what happened to her.'

'Would anyone know?'

Yai Li shrugged and turned away to stare across the garden. The shadow had disappeared. There were lots of people who would know, she thought, and who would still be found in Jetsip Rai. But I won't be asking them. No one wants to speak about the past there. It's too painful, or too shameful. Nobody wants to be reminded of those days. They would all rather forget what happened to them. As these thoughts came to her, she could feel a tension steadily rising in her chest until she could contain it no longer. When she finally turned back to him, she said quietly:

'We have met before, you and me. At least, I think we have. I should have told you when you asked. I am telling you now.'

Khun Chai was taken aback.

'When? Where?'

'In London. 1963.'

Khun Chai shook his head and frowned, trying to recall.

'The dinner party at…' She said softly.

Khun Chai kept on shaking his head. He had no recollection of meeting her. He had known no Thai girls when he was a student in London.

'It was when the ambassador...'

'With the ambassador! That was the day he told me that my father was ill.'

He looked at her now and, in that instant, recalled the beautiful young woman with whom he had exchanged that one brief glance at the door to the apartment.

Yai Li nodded.

'I was just beginning my university year,' said Khun Chai thoughtfully. 'The ambassador was my official guardian. He knew my father. They played cards together when they were young. They...' He might have gone on in the same vein but then he stopped in mid-sentence and, as if suddenly recalling a forgotten detail, he raised his forefinger, shook it and said:

'There was a scandal... Now I remember. Oh no! I am so sorry.'

'It doesn't matter,' said Yai Li. 'It was a long time ago.' Her voice was trembling when she said this.

They sat in silence for a while.

'But it wasn't your fault, was it?'

Yai Li remained silent. That phrase. She hadn't heard it applied to her since then.

'We all knew you were being treated unfairly at the time. It must have been so hard for you. That man had a terrible reputation with women. There were other scandals. Did you know that when his wife came out of prison, she committed suicide? It was a great tragedy all round.'

Yai Li gasped.

'I am sorry. You didn't know about that? I didn't want to...'

'It doesn't matter. But no. I did not know about Khun Benjawan.' As she said this, she put her two hands together and raised them above her head. 'I only knew that she had gone to prison.'

Their conversation ended soon after that with Khun Chai inviting her to come back at the end of the week.

'But only if you want to,' he added.

'And why wouldn't I?' she replied.

Then he said something that surprised her again.

'You know. You are a very special person. I really want to know your story.'

'But I've already told you. There's really nothing interesting about it.'

'There's something unique in everyone's life that we can all learn from. Please. I am serious. Why don't you write it down for me? Just what you remember. Jot it all down in a notebook.'

Yai Li laughed. 'I haven't written anything since I was at school,' she said.

'Well, who knows?' he replied. 'You might enjoy it.'

Chapter 13

Later, when she was home, Yai Li felt agitated as she went over what she had learned from Khun Chai. So many memories that she had kept well locked up in a far corner of her mind had already resurfaced since that first meeting with him. Now she thought of what he had told her about Khun Benjawan, and she could not help feeling a deep sadness. Despite the way she had been treated, she knew that Khun Benjawan must have endured so many dilemmas and collaborated in so many lies that, in the end, she was driven to take her own life. She remembered how many times during those first years in Klongtoey she too had felt like ending it all by taking a handful of pills or tying a gunny sack of rice around her midriff and jumping into the river.

What else had the poor woman's husband done to other women like herself? Khun Chai had told her that it was not her fault, just as Khun Benjawan had. She realised that people must have talked about what happened in London. But why did no one defend her? Why was it assumed that she was the seductress even though they all knew the truth? She had every right to feel angry. But instead, from the few things that he had said, and the way he had spoken, she felt a kind of vindication at last, and with it a sense of relief. There were people who did not blame her, after all. Perhaps it was time that those years of shame that had hung over her could now be left behind.

Then there was Khun Chai himself. This was the same person she'd met in London after all. But he had changed physically beyond recognition. How was is that their paths were crossing now, at this late point in their journey? There were no coincidences. It was what she believed. But what did it mean? Yai Li did not know what to make of him. He had the title of a minor royal. He lived in a mansion, the likes of which she had never seen before. But he did not behave at all like someone with wealth or power, not that she had known any, except for the ambassador in London, very briefly. That smooth-talking, well-dressed gentleman had treated her as though she was dust. But Khun Chai, who looked more like a country farmer than a princeling, seemed genuinely interested in her. There was an innocent sincerity about his curiosity that made her feel a trust that she had almost never felt before, certainly not for a man. But why did he need her to tell him about Klongtoey and Pia and the Mosquito Bar?

Then that bit about her being special and wanting to know her story. Did he really want to know how she landed up in Jetsip Rai married to a hopeless drunk?

She had never bothered to go back into her past in any systematic, deliberate way. Her history did not seem any more or any less interesting than anybody else's. In fact, her life had been marked by pain and loss. Why should she want to revisit all of that and recall the things she had been through and that she preferred to forget? And yet, the more she thought about it that night she began to feel an urge to 'tell her story' as Khun Chai had put it. She remembered how, when her daughter Nuan was dying in the hospice, she watched the volunteers there sitting next to the women in their beds, sometimes leaning in close to listen to them. When she asked one of them what he was doing, he told her: 'Oh just listening to her story.'

'Why?' Yai Li had asked.

'Well, sometimes it brings peace. We need to leave our stories to someone. Even the children. That's the way to go lightly.' She was puzzled by his words at the time. But now she sensed the truth in them.

The next morning, Yai Li went to the corner shop and bought a school notebook and a ballpoint pen. When she returned home, she sat at the table staring at the open page for a long time wondering where to begin. Khun Chai had told her that it wasn't necessary to put things in chronological order. She did not have to start with her birth. But then, where would she start?

Memories, images, conversations rise and fall in her like waves on the surface of the ocean. She realises that she has not written anything, apart from a few letters and filling in forms, since her father died, and she had to leave her studies. Suddenly, thinking of her father she picks up the pen intending to write. Now the waves are breaking, and the images and impressions begin to pour into the shores of her mind. Her pen hovers above the page.

She begins with the train from Ayutthaya to Bangkok. She can hear it starting up its engine. She recalls the scents on the station platform mingling together; the fried rice wrapped in banana leaves being handed up through the open windows of the carriages, the chicken and pork satay being grilled by the station office, the garlands of flowers, whose perfume mixed with the disinfectant from the public toilets, the oily smell of the train engine. She begins here because the station was her second home in her young years. Her father was one of the stationmasters. With his red flag tucked under his arm, his flat hat with the visor, and his whistle at the ready, he would stride up and down the platform in his ill-fitting khaki uniform and worn, scuffed leather shoes while she did her homework at the table in the small office and looked out every now and then at the crowds who were boarding to go to the capital or returning from there. And when the last train had come and gone, she would pack up her books into her canvas bag and together they would walk back to the rooms belonging to the railway company where they lived near the station, picking up their supper from the small market on the way.

Her father, called Ah Sem, was well known in Ayutthaya as a healer. But then there were many healers in those days, in the Buddhist and Muslim communities, and people went to whoever they trusted. Li's mother had died, soon after she was four, from cholera, and her father, still in his prime, never thought of remarrying. He was a well-built man with a thick head of curly hair, dark skin and a handsome, open face. On his days off there were women who constantly visited with their aches and pains for him to heal with his hands and his herbal concoctions, and among them good looking ones. Li remembered them all, and how some of them would try to flirt with him. But he never responded to their advances and seemed content to stay unattached. He was devoted to her and even though he was not educated, made sure that she could go to school as soon as she could and learn all the things that he had not had the opportunity to study. At the same time, he often made her watch him while he worked on his patients. Sometimes, as she grew up, she thought that this might have been to protect himself from the women. But she also realised that he was transmitting his gift to her and that it could not be done through a verbal explanation.

Usually, on a Sunday morning, when another stationmaster took over his shift, he would prepare for a visit by sitting still in front of a burning candle and a stick of incense for about an hour. He wore a pair of old shorts, with his top bare. His whole torso was covered in tattoos: squares and small circular diagrams and squiggly writings in ancient Khom that would move on his skin as he breathed deeply. This always fascinated her, and she once asked him, with the innocence of a young child:

'Were you born with those marks on you, Paw?' This made him laugh.

'No. My father made them.'

Seeing her puzzled, worried expression, he said:

'Yes. With a special knife and with ink. It was when he passed his power to me.' She must have looked frightened.

'Don't worry,' he laughed again. 'I won't tattoo you!'

It must have been around her puberty that one afternoon, as he was placing one hand on a woman's back and a finger on a point in her spine that Li understood what he was doing, in the sense that she could feel what was happening to the woman. At that moment he turned away from the woman and looked at her, then smiled and nodded before continuing with his work. From then on, he would ask her to lay her hands on his patients and guide them with his own until she learned to recognise what it was that she was feeling and what it was she had to do. Her father never asked people directly for money for his treatments, but there was a small wooden box by the door in which people put in what they felt like, or nothing at all if they were not satisfied or did not have anything to offer. He used this extra money to buy her the clothes, pens and books she needed for her school and told her that he was also saving up for her to eventually go to college, which was what he wanted more than anything for her.

Then one day in the cool season, when she was about sixteen, as she was nearing the station on her way from school, she saw that there was a commotion at the entrance. As she approached the crowd that had gathered, several of her father's friends came towards her and tried to stop her from going any further.

'Your father has been shot,' one of them said, in an almost matter-of-fact way.

'There's nothing more we can do,' said another, who looked shocked and upset. 'Come on. You shouldn't go in there. We'll take you home.'

She heard herself scream, but it is as if the voice was coming from someone else. She forgets what happens next. She was sitting in her house sobbing. The same men were by her, and some women too – his clients – whom she recognised. One of them, an older woman with teeth stained from betel nut, said:

'It was that old bastard, Ai Gaw, from the slaughterhouse. He got drunk. Went and accused your father of having an affair with his wife. You know, the pretty one who had the hip problem. Drew a gun and shot him in the head. Just like that. Your poor father. He didn't deserve this. He was a good man, a decent, proper man.'

So, if he was so good, why did he die like that? she kept thinking to herself in the days following her father's death – long, restless days that melted into one another like a bad dream ending with seeing his coffin slide into the burning furnace of the funeral oven while the monks chanted in the heat of the afternoon sun. Less than a week later, after packing up her few possessions, along with the box filled with donations, she turned for a last time to look round the room where she had spent her childhood knowing that she would never return there, and that from now on she had no one left to care for her except for a distant relative whom she hardly knew in Bangkok.

Then, after a couple years in Bangkok working in the fancy mansion off Sathorn road, still under the fog of grief that enveloped her, came London, and 'The Incident'. And after London, barely twenty years old, she landed in Klongtoey where through her auntie's friend she met her husband, Maitri. He worked for the Port Authority in the docks as a customs officer and he had all the connections. He helped her move into his sister's place and in those first weeks showed her the district. He made her feel welcome. He said he would take care of her. Whatever she needed he would be there to help. More than anything he made her feel secure, and less than a year after she moved into Klongtoey, he proposed to her, and she had no hesitation in accepting. They made their home in a small wooden building in the Jetsip Rai area in a narrow alleyway next to a vast expanse of wasteland, in the middle of which stood an enormous Prang tree where the locals would go to pray and make their offerings. This was before the whole area began to be built up and inhabited by immigrants from the north-east and the open land turned into an area where the ship containers were kept. But back then it felt like being in the countryside.

To Li, her husband seemed a decent man, not particularly good looking but with a certain charm and self-confidence. What was important was that he behaved decently towards her, and had not tried to take advantage of her. She had known no physical intimacy with any man up till then. What happened in London had made her afraid of men. She was a virgin when she married Maitri and still nervous about sex. But Maitri was kind and patient. Nevertheless, it took her a while before she would let herself be held and penetrated without feeling intense shame. It was about the time she found herself pregnant that she discovered that Maitri had a serious drinking problem. She knew that he liked to have a beer after work. But now he was staying out late and often had to be bundled back to the house, propped up on either side by his drinking buddies. By the time Nuan was born, Maitri was sometimes stumbling into the house in mid-afternoon, drunk and unable to hold himself together enough to even greet her or their child. Li tolerated his behaviour because she cared for him and because she had no other option. He had told her from the beginning that he did not want her to go out to work.

'I want you to cook for me and keep the place clean. I don't want to live in a pigsty like the others around here,' he'd say whenever he wanted to impress her that, unlike many men in the slums, he had a decent well-paid job. 'You have enough from what I give you. You don't have to go and work at the Mosquito Bar or the Venus Room.'

These were the two establishments that were not too far from where they lived, where her auntie had suggested she might look for a job, and where many of the local young women worked as hostesses and waitresses. They catered to the sailors from the merchant ships that docked in the port of Klongtoey, to the soldiers on leave from the war in Vietnam, as well as to local *farangs* looking for low-life amusement. There was easy money to be had working in those bars but a heavy price to pay in terms of the health of both the heart and the body. Many of the men in the district who let their wives or girlfriends work there enjoyed the extra income but resented the situation. At all times of the day and night, fights between couples would break out, sparked by jealousy and anger that sometimes spilled over into violence.

Li was grateful that Maitri earned enough to keep her at home although often she would feel trapped in that small house and in that narrow alleyway especially when the baby was born, and Maitri would hardly be around. Sometimes she would dream of leaving and returning to Ayutthaya, but she knew that she could not survive by herself. She had no choice but to accept her lot and give thanks that they had food to eat and a roof over their heads, and that her husband, for all his failings, was not a cruel man. For he was never once violent to her even when she told him incessantly that he should stop drinking. He would merely hold his head in his hands and start sobbing. She always felt that he was trying to escape from something, but she never found out what demon it was that drove him to push himself into that state of self-destruction time and time again.

His illness began on the day of Songraan, the water festival, and lasted a year. The doctor at the local clinic said there was nothing to be done. His liver had packed up. He was too weak to work, so after the first month he gave up his job and, as the sickness took hold, he just lay on the bed for most of the day, sweating and agitated, his belly bloated and painful, occasionally getting up to vomit. The flesh dropped from his body rapidly and his skin turned a strange shade of yellowy brown, like a dirty canal. Li watched her husband deteriorating daily while she nursed their two-year-old girl. A woman who lived a couple of houses away in the same alleyway provided them with a box that contained little balls of opium.

'You can smoke it or just chew it,' she told them. 'It will take away the pain and help him sleep.'

The opium was effective, but it also made him hallucinate, and when the effect wore off he would be trembling with fear. Li often wished that she had learned more about herbs from her father. But he had been killed before he finished teaching her the things he knew. She could only watch her husband suffer and pray that he would soon be released.

One afternoon while the child was asleep in her bed, he whispered to her as she wiped his feverish body with a damp cloth.

'I can't take it anymore. I want to die. Help me. Please.'

She stared at him, this man she hardly knew, the father of her child, someone who had been kind to her but for whom she had not felt any real human intimacy. His face was contorted in pain. The opium was not enough. Should she give him the rest that was in the box? she thought. Then she remembered something her father had shown her one day after a visitor had just left.

'If a person is suffering badly, you can do this,' he had told her. 'But you must never use it unless it becomes absolutely necessary.'

Then he showed her, by placing his thumb and forefinger on the front of her throat, barely touching her skin.

'Or you can do this.' Now he just put his forefinger to the side of her neck again with the gentlest touch. This time she could feel her body going numb. Immediately, laughing, he pulled his hand away.

'But you can't do that for too long,' he said.

'Why?' She asked.

'Because it can put them to sleep for good,' he said.

Yai Li had never used this knowledge she received from her father on anyone up till then. Now, with deep pity in her heart she reached over and gently put her the thumb and forefinger of her left hand on her husband's throat, hardly touching his skin. As she did so she felt a wave of energy run down her arm and through her fingers and into Maitri. Almost immediately, his face relaxed and the twitching in his legs stopped. She stayed in the same position until, gradually, his breathing slowed and finally ceased. Then she began to cry.

When they came to take his body away, the nurse from the clinic said to her.

'Oh, he's died from a heart attack. It's often the way with this kind of disease. It's better that he doesn't have to suffer any more.'

The notebook lay open on the first page. Yai Li held the pen above it. Her hand ached. She felt as if she had been under water holding her breath for too long. She was exhausted from the memories. Looking down at the page she saw that all she had written was: Ayutthaya. Father killed. Bangkok. London. Klongtoey. Married Maitri. Nuan born. Maitri died. Joy born. Nuan died.

As she closed it she said out loud: 'That's it with the writing.'

Chapter 14

Two days later they were both sitting by side with her open notebook in front of them on the table. She frowned when she showed him what she had managed to scribble down in her notebook.

'No. I couldn't do it,' she said. 'I can't write. It's impossible. This is all I'm going to do for you. You'll have to guess the rest.'

'But you can't give up that easily,' said Khun Chai as he finished reading out loud the words she had written in her schoolgirl's scrawl. 'This is just the bare bones. Not even. Where's the meat?'

Yai Li pointed to her head, then her heart, and lastly her belly.

'But you do remember what happened, don't you?' he persisted.

'Of course, I do. But it's one thing to remember and another to put it down.'

'Yes. That's true enough,' he replied, impressed by her remark. 'It's a long way from the head to the paper.'

'So how do you do it?' 'Oh, I make it up, mostly.' Yai Li looked bemused.

'So, the past is something you invent. It didn't really happen that way,' she said.

'Well, no… Not exactly…' 'I don't understand.'

'It's just that we don't remember anything correctly even just after it happened. We fill things in. We elaborate. We pick out the details we want.'

Yai Li shook her head disbelievingly at first. Then she shrugged in a gesture of reluctant agreement.

'And besides,' Khun Chai continued, 'With the distant past we remember things from how we are today, not as the person we were then. So, looking back now we might notice something from the past that we missed at the time.'

'It's too deep for me, Khun Chai,' she said. 'All I know is please don't ask me to write anymore.'

'All right then. I won't. We can do it another way. You can just tell me your story and I'll record you or make notes.'

Yai Li smiled at him.

'Are you really interested in my life?' She asked.

Khun Chai looked at her for a long while before replying.

'Yes,' he said finally. 'I really am.'

Later, when everyone had gone to bed and the house was quiet, Khun Chai pulled out a rectangular cardboard box from one of the cupboards where he kept his shoes. He had not opened it for a long time. He had brought it down with him when he moved to the ground floor. It contained stuff going back to when he was a boy; letters he had written to his father that he had rediscovered, albums with his old drawings, postcards written to him from friends over the years, articles and documents he had chosen to keep, and old photos. These were what he was looking for that evening, two in particular that he hoped were still there and not lost or thrown away by mistake. He found the first one easily, nestling between two postcards from Paris.

It was taken in 1965, the year he left London. It was April, Mac's birthday. Mac was his best friend. The faded photo showed Mac, longish hair slicked back, the jacket collar of his Italian suit turned up, his tie askew, laughing as he looked at the pigeon that had landed on his forearm. The girl next to him, who was French but whose name he cannot recall, is smiling at the camera. She has short, neatly cut hair, is dressed in a smart outfit and has a beige raincoat draped over her arm. They were in Trafalgar Square having just had lunch in a small restaurant in Chinatown. They are standing by the column, next to one of the lion statues. Mac had asked him to take their photo because it was a special occasion, his twenty-fourth birthday, his second round. The pigeon's arrival was not planned. Nor was the girl. Mac had met her at a party a week earlier. That night the three of them drank lots of wine, listened to Miles Davis, slept in the same bed in Mac's small flat in Shepherd's Bush. Halfway through the night he'd heard Mac begin to make love to the girl and turned away.

The second photo was taken by him two years later, in 1967 in Klongtoey, on a steamy hot, blindingly bright afternoon, by the entrance to a cheap noodle bar. The photo showed Pia, the girl he had mentioned to Yai Li, dressed in a pair of tight slacks, tee shirt and sandals and wearing dark glasses, her hair in a neat beehive, standing next to Mac. They had stopped there for breakfast. Mac was puffing on a cigarette and Pia was striking a pose.

Khun Chai cleared some space on his desk and put the two photographs side by side and looked from one to the other rapidly before picking them up and taking them out to the table on the balcony. The night was unusually still except for the constant buzzing of mosquitos that disturbed the deep quiet of the surroundings. Khun Chai sat with his elbows on the glass top and massaged his temple with the fingers of both hands while he scrutinised the two faded images in front of him. The session with Yai Li that evening had made him feel relaxed and peaceful and he had enjoyed her company and their exchange. He had meant it when he told her that he was interested in her. But it was only now, as he looked at the images he had taken half a century before and saw the connection between the two photographs that he realised that Yai Li was the link he had been looking for. She was leading him back to Klongtoey, and a particular corner of the district where he had not set foot since those days in the 1960s. Its significance to him was only now beginning to come to him with unexpected clarity, and it was all thanks to her.

Chapter 15

He'd met Mac in late 1963 at a meeting at the Thai Students' Office in London. There were many people of all ages at the gathering, both Thais and British. They were there to hear a talk given by the well-known monk from Chiang Rai who had been invited by a group of his followers to tour different countries in Europe before proceeding to the U.S. The aim of these meetings was to spread the teachings of the Dhamma. A letter had been sent out to the students requesting their presence and support on this important occasion. The conference room was crowded and Khun Chai, arriving late from a lecture at his college, squeezed into the back row where he found himself sitting next to a tall thin young man wearing a thick black coat and looking decidedly bored. The room was blanketed in an expectant hush.

The director of the Students' Office led the monk in through a side door, followed by several other middle-aged Thais and behind them a distinguished looking Englishman. They all sat facing the audience. After a short introductory speech by the director in both Thai and English, the monk stood up. He was a short, well-built, light skinned man and his face was open and kind. His eyes surveyed the room slowly and, adjusting his saffron robes, he seemed to enjoy taking his time to acknowledge everyone who was present. Then, in a high pitched, booming voice he began, in English:

'To-day is the twenty-pip centuree.' He dwelled on the last syllable as though he was making a point about the date. Then he looked round the room from side to side once more and smiled benevolently at his captive audience before continuing.

Khun Chai was expecting the talk to be given in Thai with simultaneous translation for the foreigners present, but the monk was obviously confident of his command of English. The combination of his sing-song accent along with his boundless self-confidence made all that he was saying virtually unintelligible, and Khun Chai wondered whether anybody else in the room felt the same. Suddenly he was holding one hand tightly over his lips and the other round his midriff in an attempt to disguise the uncontrollable fit of giggling that was racking his body. Turning to one side he saw that his neighbour was doing the same. They had not exchanged a word since taking their seats. But now in silent, spontaneous agreement they both slipped off their chairs and, bent over, made a quick exit through the back door. Once out of the building and on the pavement, they let out uncontrolled belly laughs to the surprise of the passers-by. They crossed the road still laughing and went into the park opposite where they stopped by a tree to recover their breath.

'Bloody hell! That's bad karma isn't it, what we did in there?' said Mac, the first to speak. This provoked a further short burst of shared amusement.

'I don't think the venerable teacher realised what he sounded like.'

'No. Obviously not. It was like one of our politicians in full fling performing for the foreign press.'

'We're going to be ticked off for this, you know. Don't think people didn't notice us leaving.

We'll probably be receiving a letter from the superintendent himself.'

'Well, too bad. It's worth it. I haven't laughed like that for ages.'

'Nor have I.'

It was only then that they introduced themselves to one another.

'So, you're royalty,' said Mac when he heard Khun Chai's name.

'No. Not really. My grandmother was some minor royal, I think. But I'm just a commoner. She gave me the name. It used to get me into fights at school. The boys would tease me about being a fraud. But it's just what I've been called since I was born. My mother insisted on it. Maybe I'll change it one day, so as not to confuse people.'

'Nah. Stick with it. It suits you. You have an aristocratic air about you. You were born to privilege.'

'And what about yourself? How did you get your name?' Mac looked sheepish for a moment.

'My father has always been a great admirer of the Americans. He seems to think they can do no wrong. He named me after General Douglas MacArthur, can you believe? '

'The one from World War II? Lucky he didn't send you to a military school,' said Khun Chai.

From the park they had gone to a nearby pub and for the next two hours, over pints of beer, talked as neither had done with anyone else in their lives. Khun Chai had been in England five years longer than Mac. He explained how his father had sent him to the boarding school in the Midlands where his grandfather had been and expected him to go to his old college at Oxford. But to his father's disappointment, Khun Chai had not done well in his exams and instead had got into The School of Oriental Studies where he was studying Development Economics and hating it. But at least, with a degree, he would be equipped to go into the Civil Service or the Foreign Office, which was what had been planned for him.

Mac, who was a few years older, came from a Thai/Mon family. His father part-owned a large paper mill in Nakhon Pathom. A self-made man who wanted his son to have the privilege of an education he did not have, he sent Mac to England to be schooled like the upper classes and come back to take over the family business and expand it to markets abroad. But after learning English in a crammer during his first two years in London, Mac had convinced his father to pay for him to study at the London School of Film Technique, his argument being that advertising was going to be the next huge industry in Thailand. His father reluctantly agreed. But Mac had no plans to have anything to do with advertising. His true interest was in making films and that afternoon he listed for Khun Chai all the ones that had inspired him and the directors he admired; names that Chai had never heard of. His passion was infectious and his knowledge impressive. When he had finished sharing his love of the cinema he said:

'And what about you? Are you honestly going to be a diplomat or whatever? I can't see it. How would you control your giggling when you met someone with a funny accent? You'd let the country down. You'd cause a diplomatic scandal. No, seriously, are you just going to please your old man? Is there something you really want to do?'

Khun Chai remembers being stunned by these remarks. They were delivered not as an attack or criticism but out of genuine interest, which made them all the more poignant. Unknowingly, Mac had exposed the doubts that had been troubling him since he began his university studies. He knew that neither his heart nor his mind was in what he was doing at the college. He had three years left before finishing his degree and then he would have to resign himself to his fate, and this filled him with a sense of helplessness. He felt that he did not have the right to question the path that had been mapped out for him.

'I don't really know,' he replied after a moment's hesitation.

'No. Well, why should you? But supposing there was no pressure at all, and you were free to follow your heart. What would you do?'

Khun Chai shrugged.

'Well, I read a lot. And I've dreamed of being a writer. But not seriously...'

'What do you mean, not seriously?' Mac put down his glass of beer and raised both hands to the ceiling. 'Listen, don't waste your time trying to please others and conforming. We Thais are such conformists! We don't like to break the mould. Come on! Get writing! Heaven knows we need good writers in our country. And hey, you know what? You can write scripts and I can make movies. How about that? I am serious.'

They laughed as they raised their glasses.

From that afternoon, and over the next two years, their friendship became sealed. During term time and in the holidays, they saw each other almost on a daily basis. Their colleges were close to one another, so they usually met at the end of the day in a pub, or in one of the cheap restaurants in Chinatown before going to see a movie. Khun Chai soon learned that Mac's taste was far from highbrow. They watched everything that was playing – the Hammer horrors, Spaghetti Westerns, the musicals. But it was the arthouse movies that were his inspiration. Sometimes they would finish off their evening by going on to the

Academy cinema in Oxford Street which was open all night to catch a rerun of old Japanese movies like Ugetsu Monogotari, which led to long discussions afterwards, or the Satyajit Ray films which inspired both of them, or the latest offering from the Italian directors he admired – Visconti, Fellini and his all-time hero, Pasolini. A game they often played was to challenge each other to come up with new versions of the plot, and it did not take long for Khun Chai to realise that this was how Mac was encouraging him to begin writing because he would insist on seeing the changes written out. This started right at the beginning of their friendship, after seeing Losey's 'The Servant', a film they both admired. Mac had challenged Khun Chai to come up with a Thai version of the ending and Khun Chai had made up a ridiculous version with the servant and his master running a gay club in Bangkok financed by the jilted fiancée.

'I told you,' said Mac, when he had read it. 'You've got a really vivid imagination, and a sense of humour. This is so good. Don't stop now.'

As the months went by, they became as close as two young men could get without having a physical relationship. London was their playground. The allowances they received from their families was enough to enjoy the riches that the city offered up. Bus and tube cost next to nothing, cinema tickets were cheap, as was eating out, and beer cost pennies. They went to parties that were taking place all through the week. On weekends they walked all over London as they talked and shared their ideas, discovering new areas of the city they had both come to feel at home in and enjoying the atmosphere of change and openness that was in the air. In the streets there were people with long hair and wearing bright clothes. In 1965 it seemed like this grey city was being given a fresh coat of colour. They were both infected by its new energy, most of all by the music that was being played everywhere. Apart from the late-night cinema at the Academy, they went to the Marquee where they listened to rhythm and blues, and to Ronnie Scott's in Gerrard Street to catch a visiting jazz musician from the U.S

June marked the highlight of that year for two reasons. One was the poetry reading at the Royal Albert Hall, where they squeezed into one of the boxes and sat next to a group of people who handed them pot to smoke. It was the first time either of them had tried it and it made the whole experience of sitting among the packed audience of the London counterculture listening to poets like Ginsberg and Corso an evening like no other. As they joined the crowd that spilled out of the Albert Hall, London felt like the best place in the world to be.

The next morning, when Khun Chai returned to the student hostel where he was staying, he found a telegram saying:

'Take the next flight back home. Your father very ill.'

It was sent by his 'aunt', who was really a first cousin of his father, an elderly spinster who lived a pious, simple life in the temple on the outskirts of Bangkok where she had ordained as a young woman and where she still lived as a lay supporter of the order. She and his father had never been close. It was with Khun Chai's mother that she had been friends, and she had always been concerned about his welfare, ever since his mother's death.

His return to Bangkok was a shock after the freewheeling year that he had spent in London. From the moment he landed, Khun Chai felt nothing but pressure. He spent every day of the next two weeks in the hospital with his father, who was on a life support machine to help him breathe. Sometimes the aunt would be by his side. But mostly he was alone in that small, sanitised space waiting for the inevitable to come. There was no communication between them until the last morning before Wigrom died, when they took him off the machine and he was briefly without his oxygen mask. The old man turned to look at his son with his bloodshot eyes and whispered:

'I am sorry.'

Those were his last words and Khun Chai did not understand their true meaning until after his father was cremated and he was sitting down in the lawyer's office with his aunt and discovered that not only had his father signed away all the lands to his foreman, Nai Samraan, who had been in charge of looking after them since Khun Chai was born, but he had left crippling debts as well. It seemed that Khun Sombat had made bad investments so that when he died he had nothing to leave to Wigrom, who quickly ran out of funds to maintain the estate. But by then he was too drunk to care. It was Samraan who had arranged substantial bank loans to cover the expenditure. During the years that Khun Chai had been absent, Samraan and his son, Nai Jit, had made themselves rich by selling off chunks of the land until there was nothing left to sell but Baan Suan itself. Meanwhile the banks were demanding repayment of the outstanding loans.

Khun Chai was shocked at the news. He remembered Nai Jit. They were practically the same age, and they had played together when they were young. Nai Jit's ambition was to become a Muay Thai champion and he had taught Khun Chai how to box. But there was never a strong friendship between them, and they had grown apart when Khun Chai started to go to his boarding school. Nevertheless, it was hard to learn that he had been betrayed by someone who had grown up in the household.

In any case, the situation that faced Khun Chai on his return from England was dire. Apart from the house and the garden there was nothing left. He could no longer depend on the fixed amount he had been receiving from his grandfather's trust as the capital had all but disappeared. His aunt was unable to help him, and he did not want to go begging to any of his father's old friends or the relatives that he hardly knew. He was twenty-one years old, with no qualifications and a totally uncertain future. From being someone considered by others as a rich, privileged young man, he was now penniless. There was no way he could go back to London after the summer. He had no choice but to put Baan Suan on the market, which he did with help of the family lawyer. His second task was to look for a job.

In both these pursuits he was lucky, or perhaps it was the prayers he offered up to the house spirit in Baan Suan. He would never know for sure, except that years later, when he had moved back there, he remembered standing in front of the shrine before leaving the property and saying to the house spirit:

'If it is at all possible, please bring me back here one day.'

After a few weeks of being on the market, Baan Suan was bought by a businessman for a sum that allowed Khun Chai to settle his father's outstanding debts and with the rest to rent a small house with a garden in one of the *sois* off Sukhumvit that would be his home for the next forty years. He also made sure he had enough to give to those in his father's household who wanted to either make their way back to their villages or to find work in Bangkok. In the end, only Mae Hom and her young family followed him to the new dwelling in Sukhumvit and it was there, years later, that Sai was born.

As far as finding employment was concerned, his first and only job offer seemed to come out of thin air. During his father's cremation ceremony, he met an American called John Booth who was the proprietor of one of the English-speaking newspapers, the *Bangkok Daily*. Mr. Booth had arrived in Thailand soon after the end of the Second World War and decided to stay. His wealth came from a generous inheritance and his background was in architecture. He was also a keen photographer. Not long after his arrival in Bangkok, Mr. Booth had been taken by a friend of Wigrom's to Pakret to visit Baan Suan. From time to time over the years he had visited and photographed the house that he considered the most beautiful in Bangkok.

After the funeral ceremony, he and Khun Chai were introduced and after a brief, polite exchange John Booth told him:

'If you need a job, come round and see me.'

Khun Chai was surprised by this invitation, and he did not consider the offer seriously. But one morning, after he had been to the lawyers to arrange for Baan Suan to be officially put up for sale, Khun Chai, depressed, walked down the street and into the building of the *Bangkok Daily* in Pratunaam. Within an hour he was shown to a small desk in the corner of the wide second floor office that would be his workspace for the next 20 years.

'What did you study?' asked his new employer as he showed Khun Chai around the building. It was supposed to be a formal interview but felt more like a chat with a schoolmaster. Mr. Booth was a dapper looking middle-aged man with a military haircut and wearing a bow tie.

'Um, Economics, at the School of Oriental and African Studies in London,' replied Khun Chai. 'But I never finished.' He was quick to add. 'I didn't get my degree. I had to come back before...'

'Not important. No one has a degree in this place. Me included. I never finished my architecture course. It was too long and too much work. But do you think you could write about it?'

'What?' 'Economics.'

Khun Chai looked embarrassed before replying candidly: 'No. Really. Please don't ask me to.'

Mr. Booth laughed.

'Ok. Ok. I got you. Well, what would you like to write about then? Can't just sit here doodling at the desk.'

'Culture. If that's possible.'

'Wow! That sounds ambitious. What do you mean? Culture in general or what's going on around here in Bangkok?'

'Yes. What's happening here. Films, literature, art, music.' Mr. Booth looked pensive.

'Are you going to take over where your grandfather left off?' he asked. Khun Chai was surprised that Mr. Booth knew anything about Luang Paiboon.

'Yes. I heard about him when I got to Bangkok many years ago, when there were still a few people around who remembered him. Quite a character, by the sounds of it. A patron of the arts and all that.' Mr. Booth continued. 'Anyway, do you have any background in that kind of thing?'

Khun Chai talked about the books that he had read and the films he had seen, and the music he'd listened to while Booth listened attentively.

'Well, you sound like you're into that world. And I'm aware there's a lot of changes going on in my own country and in Europe. But you're going to have a hard time here because there isn't much culture like that going on. But you seem to be keen. I'll let you give it a go.'

Khun Chai could not decide whether Mr. Booth was employing him because of his acquaintance with his father or whether he really needed someone to write about the arts in Thailand. In any case, he was grateful for the job and set about connecting to whatever was happening as best he could. But he found that the education that he had received abroad worked more as a handicap than any advantage it might have given him. He was seen as an outsider with *farang* manners, unacquainted with the local scene. Besides, he was writing in English, which marked him as an alien. All this was to change with time, once the sweat and grime of the Bangkok streets had overlaid the patina of his British education.

Chapter 16

Khun Chai and Mac met each other again in 1967. In the intervening years they had been corresponding regularly with postcards and short letters. Mac would write about the latest films he'd seen and add his comments. Khun Chai described the work he was doing, how he was trying without much success to get to know the Thai literary scene, how terrible the locally made movies were, and how impatient he was to start on the projects they had talked about once Mac returned home.

Mac was not meant to return until the following year when his studies were over. But his mother was taken seriously ill, and his father sent him a ticket to come back that summer.

'I can't face them yet,' he told Khun Chai, who had gone to Don Muang to fetch him the morning he arrived back in Bangkok. 'It's caught me off guard. I'll stay here with you for a few days before getting the train up north, if you don't mind. I need some time to adjust. It's all been too fast. My head's not right to deal with it just now.'

'Of course,' said Khun Chai, at a loss to respond adequately to Mac's obvious distress.

Apart from the unfamiliar look of sadness in his friend's eyes when he explained the reason for his return that summer – something he didn't do in the telegram he sent – Khun Chai was astonished at how different Mac now looked from when he had last seen him in London.

Gone were the Italian-style suits and pointed shoes. Now his hair was shoulder length and looked messy. His feet were clad in clumpy sandals and over his red bell-bottom sailor's trousers he wore a loose Mexican embroidered shirt. Khun Chai noticed how people turned to stare at him as they walked through the airport. He, dressed in his usual costume of short-sleeve shirt, khaki trousers and loafers, envied his friend's daring, colourful attire. Mac did not seem at all phased by other people's reaction to how he looked.

'By the way, I've got you a present,' said Mac as they got to the car and with that, he pulled out a record from his shoulder bag. It was The Incredible String Band's '5000 Layers of the Onion'. Khun Chai had never heard of them before.

'It only came out two weeks ago. I can't stop listening to it. They're the best. Much better than the Beatles.'

He was more cheerful now and as they left Don Muang he said:

'By the way. You haven't said anything about my new style. Don't say you haven't noticed.

'How do you like it?' Mac asked.

'Where does it come from?' asked Khun Chai. 'You don't look anything like the Beatles, or the Rolling Stones. Is it from the String Band, or whoever they are?'

This initiated a conversation that turned into a long, monologue from Mac lasting all the way to Khun Chai 's house. Mac did not want to talk about the clothes that he was wearing or his long hair, or the beads around his neck but about the new medicine – this was the word he used – that he had discovered.

'You remember that couple we sat next to in the Albert Hall at that poetry reading?' 'The ones who handed us the joint? Of course, I do,' said Khun Chai. 'Why?'

'Well, I bumped into them again last year in a bookshop on the Tottenham Court Road. Sarah and James. They are artists and into the music scene too. Great people. Anyway, I'm not going to bore you. I've been hanging out with them a lot since you left. One day in June I went round to their place in Bayswater, and James said: "Mac, do you want to try LSD?" I thought they were joking. What? Money? I said, and they laughed.'

'No, not pounds shillings and pence. It's this drug that helps you see things differently,' he told me.

'I thought, Why not? What's there to lose?'

Mac went on to describe his first acid trip with his friends in London. It was a sunny afternoon and soon after each had taken the drug – on sugar cubes – they had gone to Hyde Park and sat under an oak tree. Nothing happened for a while until two pigeons flew down in front of them and began making cooing sounds. Mac felt that they were staring at him and talking to him. He looked over at his friends and saw that the three of them were now nodding together in agreement. They rolled back on the grass laughing uncontrollably. After what seemed ages, all was quiet again. Mac lay with his eyes closed feeling the earth gently breathing beneath his body. It was a pleasant feeling of being held and sustained. At some point he opened his eyes again and, looking up saw beams of sunlight floating down through the leaves like glass tubes and at the same time he heard music that he had never known before. He reached his arms up. Then he felt James touching his shoulder.

'Are you OK, man?' The voice came from far away.

He couldn't answer but followed James's gaze as he turned towards Sarah, who was sitting with her hand stretched out, palm open to the sky. Mac could see the ball of light that she was holding. It was made up of patterns of colours that kept changing. From then on it was all colours and fractal patterns in the air, all over the surface of the grass. When they looked at each other, faces were coming through from the past and the future and Mac could see the aura shining around his friends.

At a certain point in his narrative, Mac suddenly stopped and went quiet and pensive. Khun Chai looked across and saw that his friend was smiling to himself.

'There's just no point in me trying to tell you about it. It's really impossible to put into words.' he said finally.

'Well, you're giving me a good idea. Sounds like an amazing drug.'

'It is not really a drug for me. It's something else,' said Mac thoughtfully. 'I've got some with me. I wanted to take a trip with you. I think it's important for you, for us. You'll never be the same again.'

By the time they reached Khun Chai's house, Mac, with the enthusiasm of a convert, and despite having said that words were inadequate, had talked a lot more about this wonder medicine that he had discovered. Without much difficulty he had persuaded Khun Chai to take it. But they decided to wait a day or two before doing so for Mac to get over his jet lag. In the meantime, as the String Band played on the record player, Khun Chai showed Mac the Bangkok noir screenplay that he had been working on. Mac was visibly enjoying himself as he read through it.

'It's good. But where have you got all these characters from?' he asked.

'Ah,' said Khun Chai pleased that his friend did not pull his work apart. 'I've been doing my research. You're not the only one to try new things. And I've got a surprise for you.'

When Khun Chai showed him the bamboo bong for smoking marijuana that he had obtained from a market stall in Sanaam Luang one Sunday, Mac whistled and laughed.

'I don't believe it,' he said. 'This is going to do my jet lag a world of good.'

That afternoon they prepared the marijuana and smoked together for the first time. After finishing the pipe, they lay on the floor watching the ceiling fan go round slowly while listening to the same songs until they were singing along to the words.

'You know the American soldiers call it Buddha grass,' Khun Chai told his friend.

'Why? Does it help them get enlightened?'

'Maybe. But I think it's going to stop them wanting to kill anyone.'

'Yeah. I can see how that could be. How could you even get on your feet after smoking this stuff?' said Mac.

That evening they went out to New Petchburi road where all the bars had sprung up to cater for the Rest and Recreation programme. Khun Chai wanted to show Mac the part of Bangkok that he had discovered. It was a honky tonk town, hastily constructed, consisting at that time of shabby two-story shop houses that were mostly catering to the entertainment industry. As part of his assignment to write on the city's nightlife, he had been able to access a world that he had not known before; the substrata of society that was giving rise to a new generation of Thais who were discovering their creativity. They were mostly musicians, but there were also artists and poets among them. All lived at the edge of society, earning their living using their talents. Money was flowing into Bangkok because of the R and R. The soldiers and sailors were blowing their dollars as fast as they could. The musicians played in the bars that had sprung up everywhere in the city, catering not just to the American soldiers on leave from the war in Vietnam but also to all the Thais and *farangs* who were now arriving in Bangkok to witness what was happening and to see if they could get a slice of the cake.

As they walked down the neon-lit road, past the garish billboards, they were both happy to be in each other's company. The effect of the marijuana made everything light and pleasurable. Khun Chai realised how much he had missed talking to someone who was on the same wavelength as himself. They made their way through the crowd, past the street stalls and the small restaurants with tables outside spilling over the pavement, and down one of the side streets till they reached the 'Peace Room'. This was a one-storey, long thin shack with a narrow wooden bar stretching down the whole side to a small stage at the end. Outside there were people dancing to the music of James Brown that was blasting from the speakers. Everything inside was bathed in a dim, soft shade of red. There were mostly GI's there with their girlfriends. All were moving to the music.

'Wow,' said Mac, impressed. 'Your newspaper pays you to come to these places and write about them? How did you convince them?'

Khun Chai led them to the end of the bar where they ordered beers from the barman who greeted him warmly.

'They're on in a minute,' he told Khun Chai.

When the James Brown number came to an end, there was a moment when all that could be heard was the sound of voices and laughter and clinking glasses. Then, suddenly, bright yellow lights shone onto the stage and an MC, looking like an Asian Elvis, dressed in gold lamé, appeared from behind a curtain and announced:

'Ladies and gentlemen, here's what we've all been waiting for tonight. The Rainstorms!'

After the energetic set finished, the lead singer leaned over to exchange a few words with Khun Chai who was standing in the front row. But the music was once again blaring from the speakers and there was no chance for him to introduce Mac. When they were out in the street again Mac said:

'Not bad. But did he know what he was singing?'

'No. He's learning English. I translate the songs for him, and I put the words in Thai so he can pronounce them.' Khun Chai replied.

'I thought as much. But he was better than the monk we saw in London. Remember?' They laughed.

'Let's go and get something to eat. I'm famished.'

They walked along the back street towards a small place that Khun Chai had often been to whenever he was in that area. On the way they passed a hotel called 'Alhambra', which was popular with the foreign travellers as well as with the GI's who took their bar girls there. People were standing around outside the neon lit entrance. The smell of marijuana hung in the night air. Suddenly they heard a scream. The glass door of the entrance was flung open and through it a young woman in a tight, short red satin dress, her long black hair flying behind her came practically jumping straight into Khun Chai's arms. They nearly both fell to the ground, but Mac was there to prop up their fall.

Breathlessly she said, 'Help me. Please. He's going to kill me.'

Without a word the three of them set off hurriedly down the street, Mac and Khun Chai looking back over their shoulders to see if anyone was in pursuit. But nobody was. Then they turned the corner into the busy main road where they hailed a taxi and got into the back seat.

'Where to?' said Khun Chai.

'Klongtoey,' said the girl addressing the driver.

They did not speak on the way. The girl was still catching her breath and kept looking into her small evening bag as though she had lost something. When they were getting out of the taxi, near the entrance to Jetsip Rai she reached over and paid the taxi driver. Then out on the pavement she said:

'I'm hungry. Are you?'

It was only when they were seated round the wooden table of a street food stall that they began to talk. The girl's name was Pia and she told them, as she wolfed down her bowl of noodles, that her boyfriend was a German tourist who was jealous because he didn't want her working in a bar anymore. It was he who was threatening to beat her up in the hotel.

'And who are you?' she asked them eventually. When they had introduced themselves, she said:

'Your eyes are red. You've been smoking grass. I can tell,' she said to Khun Chai. 'You, for sure,' she said pointing at Mac and smiling as she looked him up and down.

It was then that Khun Chai noticed how pretty she was. They exchanged glances.

'If you two like to smoke, why don't you meet me here tomorrow in the afternoon? It's my day off. I don't have to work till the evening. I'll take you somewhere you will like. I owe you a favour.'

Khun Chai and Mac looked at each other.

'Sure,' said Mac. 'We'll be here.'

'Good. See you then.' With that Pia got off her stool and turned to walk away down the road. Khun Chai on impulse got up and walked after her.

'Listen,' he said when he was by her side. 'Shouldn't we make sure you get back to your place safely? Just in case that guy turns up again.'

She smiled and then, to Khun Chai's surprise, reached out her hand and touched his cheek.

'You're a very kind person,' she said. 'But you don't have to worry about me. Anyway, he doesn't know where I live. I'll see you tomorrow. OK?'

With that they parted.

Later, back in Khun Chai's house, lying on the floor, again listening to the same record, they were still discussing their chance meeting with Pia, in the red satin dress and the long black hair going down to her waist.

'You're smitten by her, aren't you?' said Mac.

'Yes. I am,' Khun Chai admitted.

'Is this your first?'

'No. I had my first taste with one of the servant girls in my father's house. She was older than me. It wasn't romantic or anything. When I came back from England, she'd already left the household.'

'So, what exactly is it about this Pia that you find so attractive?'

'I don't know. Something about her I can't put my finger on. Her big white teeth? Her beautiful long hair? Her unavailability? I really can't tell you.'

The next day they woke up late.

'Well then? What about it?' said Mac. 'Shall we take the medicine today?'

Pia was already waiting for them at the food stall. She was wearing tee shirt and slacks and dark glasses, and her hair was piled on top of her head.

'Have you boys eaten?' she asked. 'Do you want to go to the place I was talking about? It's not far from here. We can walk.'

'We're thinking of taking this first,' said Mac who brought out a small phial with a dropper from his shoulder bag.

'And what's that?' Pia asked.

'It's LSD. It's medicine for the mind. We're going to take it. There's enough for you, if you want to join us.'

Pia shrugged.

'Sure. As long as it's not heroin. I hate that stuff. Yeah, sure. Why not? I need some medicine for my mind. And it's my free day.'

'Free from what?' asked Khun Chai. 'What else would you be doing on a Sunday morning?' Pia laughed. 'Free from fighting with my boyfriend, the GI.'

'I thought he was a German,' said Khun Chai.

'Oh, that's another one.' Pia replied without any hesitation, then shrugged. 'So, are we going to take this special medicine or not?'

Before they left the noodle shop, Khun Chai pulled out a cheap Kodak camera from his shoulder bag and took some photos of Pia and Mac. Afterwards they walked by the railway tracks towards the temple by the river, Wat Saphaan. On the way there Pia told them how she was only temporarily living in that district. She had moved there a year earlier from the north-east, Isaan, because a friend who was visiting from Bangkok told her there was lots of work and money to be made in the city. She said that she preferred to be back home, but it was a poor life up there and she didn't want to end up like her parents.

'Their backs are broken from the planting and their skin is burnt from the sun. No thanks,' she told them.

'So, what are you doing here in the city?' asked Khun Chai who already guessed the answer.

'Oh. This and that,' Pia replied. 'You know. Getting by.'

'And what about your boyfriend? Or boyfriends. Won't they mind you hanging out with us today?'

'Good heavens! You have a lot of questions, don't you? Well, the answer is no. I am a free person. I take care of myself. OK?'

They came to a row of wooden shacks that seemed to lean on one another to keep upright. Their stilt columns were sunk into a muddy green canal that was an offshoot of the Chao Phraya River. Thin canoes were moored to some of these columns. The place that was called Pi Lek's was at the end of the row. Narrow planks led from the road to the entrance. The girl who opened the door to them knew Pia and greeted her warmly. Coming in from the brightness of the street, it took a while for them to adjust to the dim light of the interior. Through a window on the far side streamed beams of dusty sunlight. But apart from that there was no other lighting. They could see an old, thin, dark-skinned man with long grey hair tied in a top knot, wearing a *pakama* cloth and a white tee shirt seated in the middle of the room. He looked up as they entered and waved the chopping knife he was holding in a sort of greeting before pointing it over to a corner where presumably they were meant to sit. No word was spoken.

Khun Chai and Mac saw that there were about a dozen others in that room, all seated on cushions on the floor. A few were Thai men and there were young *farangs* with cropped hair sitting next to Thai girls who looked relaxed and comfortable. Some of them were eating sticky rice and mangoes from plastic plates. These were obviously soldiers on their R and R. No one was talking, only watching. For a while there was only the sound of the man chopping the marijuana. Then suddenly he stopped and said:

'Ai Pia. Where did you pick up these handsome guys?' He laughed and Khun Chai noticed his gold teeth.

'They are from London.' said Pia and the man laughed even louder.

'Lon-dawn,' said the man and stared at them. 'Ah. Lon-dawn. I was there once.' Then he pointed the knife to his head. 'In here.'

When he had finished preparing the marijuana, he beckoned to one the young *farangs* to come closer. The young man crawled across the floor, then took the bong that was handed to him. When it was lit for him, he drew a long drag and then let out a long cloud of smoke from his mouth which was caught by the shaft of sunlight. This was followed by a bout of coughing and spluttering that went on endlessly. He sounded as if he were going to burst his lungs if he did not stop.

By this time, the acid that the three of them had taken was beginning to take effect. They were mesmerized at the spectacle of the young American soldier on leave having a coughing fit that seemed to last forever. They turned to one another and found themselves beginning to laugh softly at first, then uncontrollably. Pia struggled to control herself and managed a few words of apology before continuing to laugh even harder. This provoked an immediate reaction from the old man who lifted his chopping knife and said in an angry voice:

'I don't know what you're on. But you're messing with the energy in here. You'd better leave right now. Stupid kids!' With that he raised the chopping knife threateningly.

They quickly left the premises still trying to control themselves and did not look back until they had reached the end of the street where there was a small wooden landing pier that jutted over the canal. There they sat down with their legs dangling over the water until they were quiet once again.

Khun Chai stared into the muddy water and began to notice patterns forming on its surface, constantly changing, forming and reforming, and then he found he could see into the depths through the layers of liquid textures as though the canal were transparent and opaque at the same time. Mac had laid down flat on the wooden planks with his hands behind his head looking up at the clouds floating by in the white heat of the sky, watching these turn into dragons and angels and other creatures he had never seen before. Pia looked into the distance, her gaze following the curve of the canal past the rows of houses that bordered it, and she was no longer in Bangkok but in another land and another time when the modern city did not exist, only settlements on the water's edge, and she felt herself transported out into the wider river, and then further into the sea.

It was already afternoon when, they started to head back slowly towards Jetsip Rai, stopping regularly on their way to examine the details that caught their attention; a stray cat, a broken box, a flower rising from the muddy bank of the canal, a faded poster hanging off a wall, patterns of light and shadow. From the busy main road they finally turned into the entrance to the district and all at once they found themselves in a world of dazzling colours, bombarded by a barrage of sounds that seemed to be coming from all directions; the rhythms of upcountry folk music mingling with American R&B, voices bellowing out messages from invisible loudspeakers. They took their time manoeuvring through the crowded thoroughfare. Groups sitting outside the coffee stalls stared at them as they passed. Children playing barefoot in the dusty street pointed at them. Their faces were unknown to the people who lived in that quarter. Mac's appearance – the bright yellow shirt and the beads around his neck and the red sailor's trousers – was attracting attention. Someone shouted out:

'Are you Thai?' Another greeted Pia.

'Who are you bringing in here, little sister?'

As Khun Chai looked at the faces that he passed he saw their features changing, melting, showing their mistrust, and fear. The words directed at them made him feel threatened and suddenly he wanted to be far away from there. Pia sensed his mood.

'This way,' she said and deftly manoeuvred them down a narrow lane that led off from the main thoroughfare. Here they came across two women sitting on chairs in front of their shacks. One was fanning herself and the other was sewing a piece of cloth.

'Where have you been, Ee Pia?' asked the older of the two. 'Who are these boys you've brought here?'

'They're friends, Auntie. It's all right.' Pia answered in a voice that seemed to Khun Chai to come from far away. They rounded another corner and then came to a shack with a plywood door painted yellow. Pia pulled a key from her trousers and unlocked the latch.

Khun Chai felt relieved to be inside. He kicked off his shoes, walked directly to the large bed in the corner and tumbled backward onto it. By now he saw colourful shapes coming through the ceiling towards him, and sounds that he heard for the first time. Mac joined him on the bed, and he reached up to play with the transparent balls of light that were floating above him.

Pia slipped her sandals off and for a while stood watching the two young men she had brought into her home. It was the first time that she had brought anyone there in the two years she had been living in Jetsip Rai. The thought that they were not clients but total strangers and yet perfectly familiar made her laugh.

'Oh well. I'll join you then.'

With that she climbed onto the bed and for a while sat on the edge of the mattress between her two guests. Now she began to look around the room. Everything in that simple space was coming alive. She could see the rickety chair's humorous character. The cheap papier mâché box where she kept her earrings and trinkets became a thing of beauty. She saw the crystal dust of the multi-coloured light coming through the window. The fan overhead became a propeller lifting the room up into the sky. After a while she lay back on the bed and looked at her companions. Spontaneously, she stretched out her arms and slipped them under their shoulders. The men put their arms around her and around each other so that they were now one body. Waves of ecstatic energy flowed through them, and they enjoyed this union for what seemed like an eternity. Suddenly they are rolling in slow motion onto the floor. Their bodies separate and they are laughing and pointing at one another.

It was soon afterwards that Mac announced that he wanted to go out and explore the area. With that he rose from the bed, slung his bag over his shoulder and left through the door without even turning to say goodbye. It all happened so quickly that they had no time to dissuade him.

'He'll be all right, won't he?' Khun Chai asked after his friend had left.

'Of course,' said Pia with utter conviction. 'Didn't you want to go with him?' Khun Chai shook his head.

'So, what do you want to do?' she asked stretching out her hand to stroke his face tenderly, and he merely smiled as he reached for her.

Their lovemaking was unhurried. It seemed that the pleasure that coursed through their bodies was endless, and finally, afterwards they lay side by side staring up at the ceiling fan. After a second round they rested for a long time as they listened to love songs on the radio. Pia made tea and they shared a cigarette. The light in the room was changing. Evening was coming on. Khun Chai was getting less visual experiences now. But he could feel his whole body glowing with a sense of satisfaction that he had never known before; something verging on the spiritual. He turned towards Pia and put his hand on her belly. He was on the point of saying something, but Pia put a finger to his lips. Then she slipped from him and went to the corner and disappeared through a small door. He could hear the sound of water being poured, and he got up and followed her into the small bathroom that consisted of a squat toilet and a big clay tub out of which Pia was scooping water with a plastic bowl and washing herself. Khun Chai took the soap and washed her back and then her whole body.

No word passed between them until both were fully clothed again. Pia put on a yellow dress, of the same cut as the red one that she had worn the night they met. She had a small gold coloured handbag and shoes to match.

'You look so good,' said Khun Chai as he watched her combing her long hair.

'I have to go to work soon. I need to get something to eat before I do. I'm still a bit affected by the stuff we took. There's a place nearby we can go to.'

Khun Chai had already suspected what her work was. As they ate at the food stall, she told him that she was a hostess in the Mosquito Bar. He showed no emotion.

'But do you have to sleep with them?' Her answer was a shrug.

'I can give you money if that's what you need.' said Khun Chai. 'You don't have to sleep with them.'

Pia reached out to touch his arm.

'You're a nice guy. I appreciate what you're saying. But it's more complicated than that. You can't understand.'

'Try me,' he said. Pia shook her head.

'I don't want to go into it. Not now. Let's just enjoy this moment. That was an incredible day we've had.'

Khun Chai felt himself choking with emotion.

'I've fallen in love with you,' he said softly.

Again, Pia shook her head.

'Don't say that. You don't know me. It's just been a few hours.' 'But don't you feel anything at all for me?'

'Of course, I do. I'm human. But I don't want you to get hurt.' 'Let me be the judge of that,' he said.

That evening they took a taxi to the Mosquito Bar. It was a short ride, and they could have easily walked there but Pia insisted that she did not want to arrive hot and sweaty. When they were approaching the entrance, she told him to stay in the taxi.

'But when do I see you again?' he asked her.

'I have your number. I'll call you. Or you can call me.'

With that she closed the door, and he watched her walking up the wooden steps.

When he got back home, he found Mac lying on the floor, hands behind his head, eyes closed, listening to the same record. He seemed lost in the music and did not move even when Khun Chai reached down and tapped his shoulder gently. Finally, he opened his eyes and smiled broadly.

'Ah. You're back,' he said casually.

'I was worried about you. What were you doing walking off like that? I didn't know what happened.'

'You needn't have been worried. I had a great time. Just wandered around the market there. It was so colourful. And I met some young guys who bought me a beer at a stall and wanted to know what I was doing there in the district. They were friendly enough. I think they were stoned. After that I walked back here slowly.'

'But you don't know Bangkok. How did you not get lost?'

'I really don't know. Now I come to think of it. I can't remember how I got back. I walked. I was guided. I sensed my way back here. It doesn't matter, does it? I'm here!'

Khun Chai shook his head in disbelief.

'You don't trust, do you?' said Mac laughing. 'Anything. Anyone.'

It was not said as an accusation but from compassion and it struck a chord in Khun Chai. Nevertheless, he answered evasively:

'It's not a question of trust. I didn't want anything bad to happen to you, that's all.'

'Well, thank you for your concern. But you know, anything can happen. I could have been mugged and killed. Or got run over by one of those crazy Bangkok drivers. There so many possible endings to everything. And it's all right.'

Khun Chai smiled at his friend's words. They sat in silence looking at each other for a long time. Khun Chai felt the warmth of love and friendship welling up in his chest.

'Anyway, are you still feeling the effects?' asked Mac finally.

'Sure. But it's different. The visual stuff stopped ages ago. I'm just mellow now.'

'Ah. Mellow Yellow.' Mac said. 'Do you know that song? And what about Pia? Where is she by the way?'

Khun Chai shrugged and made a gesture with his hand to show that he did not want to talk about it. Then he said quietly:

'She's a hooker. She works in a place called the Mosquito Bar.'
'Oh, you poor sod!' said his friend.

'Well, we both guessed that, didn't we?' Mac just nodded.

They had a smoke together that night and then walked down the lane to the main road to a small bar where over a beer they exchanged their experiences of that day.

'It's a special medicine all right,' said Khun Chai. ' Phew! I don't think I'll ever be the same again. Like you said. Reality is not what it was. But I am not sure what difference it's going to make to my life. I still have to make a living, and pay the bills. I still have to get up tomorrow morning to go to work. I'm not going to start dressing like you. Or think of going to India to find a guru.'

They laughed.

'There you go. Playing it safe as always.'

'Don't blame me for that. I haven't got your courage.'

Neither spoke for a while.

'But I wish I didn't feel so sad about Pia,' said Khun Chai finally.

Mac reached over and patted his friend's back.

'If you're going to go on with her, take it as it comes. But don't torture yourself.'

Those were the last significant words that Khun Chai remembered Mac saying to him. There were more, of course as they said their goodbyes the next morning when Mac boarded the train to Lampang. But these were light-hearted pleasantries about promising to keep in touch and staying well – things said to mask the sadness of being separated yet again. Mac had already planned to fly back from Chiang Mai after seeing his parents and then take the plane the same day back to London. Maybe Khun Chai would be able to come to the airport. But it was unlikely. They would meet again the following year when Mac finished at the Film School. Then they would start the real work, as Mac put it. Neither of them was aware that this meeting, in the chaos of Hua Lampong station, with the passengers getting on with their luggage, the food vendors shouting out as they hawked their wares, and the announcements constantly blaring on the microphone, was to be the last time they would see one another.

Chapter 17

The word 'torture' that Mac had used kept coming into Khun Chai's head those following months, during which he tried his best to get closer to Pia. After work he would take a taxi to Jetsip Rai, arriving at around six. Or sometimes, with an excuse that he was on an assignment, he would take the afternoon off to be with her. Pia always welcomed him in a friendly way, but she did not let him make love to her every time he came by. They would often sit and talk like friends and sometimes smoke a small joint together and then she would bathe and prepare herself for work. She would let him take her to the Mosquito Bar but never let him go inside with her or wait after she finished working to fetch her, which was what he wanted to do.

'And don't sit outside spying on me. You must promise me. It will get me into trouble.' she said to him the first night that he left her at the entrance to the bar. Reluctantly he agreed. But it meant long sleepless nights working out how he could make things different for them. He did not want to be her friend. He wanted his love reciprocated. But even if they were to carry on just being friends, what bothered him was why she would not allow herself to receive his help. He was willing to spend everything that he was earning to look after her. It was not an enormous amount, but enough to get her out of that life and the shanty town where she lived. She could move in with him and find a decent job, as a waitress or a receptionist. Her good looks would be an advantage. But whenever he broached the subject, she would immediately cut the conversation short.

'I've told you. I don't want your money. Don't go there. OK?' And a flash of anger would cross her brow.

Rationally, he knew that he was in an absurd situation, on a ticket to nowhere. But an obsessive desire to become part of her life kept him repeating the same pointless routine day after day with nothing but suffering to show for it. He found the whole affair mysterious and unsettling. Even during his working hours, he had to deal with the demons that popped up with their dark scenarios as he imagined her being escorted by some *farang* to a hotel, and giving her body yet again to a stranger. He was consumed by jealousy and yet he could not pull himself away from her. Mac's words kept coming back to him.

One afternoon, a couple of months after their first meeting, he arrived to find her, not in jeans and tee shirt which was her usual way of dressing when not working, but in an expensive silk dressing gown embroidered with a dragon that he presumed was a gift from a generous client. She was fresh from bathing and smelled of expensive perfume. She made him tea. They had a joint and then she led him over to the bed.

'This is what you want, isn't it?' she whispered.

Their lovemaking was not like the first time when they had taken the acid, or any other time since then. It was passionate and carnal and afterwards Khun Chai was filled with a feeling of physical elation. That evening, when he took her to the Mosquito Bar he was glowing with love and lust for her. He was determined, come what may, that he would take her away from the terrible life she was living.

The following afternoon, he found that her door was firmly locked. There were no neighbours around to question about where she was. She had already told him that sometimes she would be obliged to spend the night with a client in some hotel, like the night they had met, but that she always came back to her place to change and get dressed. Khun Chai, worried and upset, took a tuk-tuk to Kasem Rat road and broke his promise to her by marching into the Mosquito Bar. The place was crowded with drinkers, mostly foreign, even though it was barely evening. There were people sitting on every seat at the bar. He walked past a table where tough looking merchant sailor types were downing beers and Mekong whiskey chasers and playing cards. At another there was a group of US soldiers on R. and R. with their Thai girlfriends, eating silently. There was no sign of Pia. He asked a young waiter where he could find her and received a quizzical look accompanied by a gesture pointing upwards.

He climbed the rickety stairs and came to a heavy door and pushed it open. Inside, the only lighting came from a small open window at the back. The place smell of stale smoke. There was broken glass, stubs and cigarette packets all over the floor. An elderly woman was sweeping between the tables in a corner. Around one of them sat four girls who were dressed in tightly cut short dresses. They were drinking beer and smoking. As Khun Chai approached, he saw that one of them was much older than the others and it was she who addressed him immediately.

'What are you doing here? We're not open for ages,' she said in a strong north-eastern accent.

'Go downstairs if you want a drink.' She stared at him with a fierce expression. 'Are you Thai?' 'I'm looking for Pia,' said Khun Chai.

They glanced quickly at one another.

'Ah. So, you're her hero,' the woman chuckled. 'We know about you.'

Khun Chai was annoyed by her tone and the thought that Pia had been talking about him to them.

'So where is she?' He persisted.

Once more they exchanged knowing looks.

'Listen. She's gone. She's not coming back to work here. That's what she told us yesterday.'

'But where did she go?' Khun Chai could hear the desperate, whining tone of his own voice. He was aware that he sounded like a man panicking.

The woman turned to the youngest looking of the four.

'Ee June. Did she tell you anything?'

The girl who was addressed took a sip from her glass and shrugged. 'She might have gone away with Frank. But she didn't tell me anything.' 'Who's Frank?' said Khun Chai. 'A soldier? A sailor? Where is he from?' The older woman spoke again.

'Frank is a bad man. We don't like him.' As she said this, she glanced round the table and elicited a nod of affirmation from each one of the girls.

Khun Chai looked crestfallen.

'Here. Sit down. Have a beer with us to drown your sorrow.' Her voice sounded compassionate now. But Khun Chai shook his head.

'Are you sure that she went off with this Frank?' he asked.

Ee June replied: 'No. Not really. To tell the truth we were all as surprised as you when she told us yesterday that she was quitting, especially the boss.'

'But where would she have gone with Frank?'

'Listen. I told you. I don't know. She didn't say. And for all I know she may have gone with someone else. Or by herself back home to the South.'

'Where exactly in the South did she come from?' Khun Chai insisted, remembering that Pia had told him that she came from the north-east.

'I don't know. Somewhere down there where they grow rubber.' Ee June giggled and so did the others.

Khun Chai turned to leave. The older woman said:

'We've all had our hearts broken, young hero. You're not the first. You won't be the last.'

Chapter 18

Khun Chai sat on the balcony holding the record, with its colourful psychedelic cover, in his hands and examining it carefully. Beside him on the tiled floor stood the bamboo bong. He had dug both these objects out that evening from a trunk in the cupboard of his upstairs bedroom and was now wiping off the dust from the record sleeve. He had not touched either of them since 1967. Looking at the image of the two long-haired young musicians on the cover he was reminded of the way Mac looked the last time they were together. On the back Mac had written some words.

'I want you to keep it,' Mac had told him the day he arrived in Bangkok. 'Look after it well. Don't scratch it too much. It's a work of genius.'

After Mac left to go up North to see his parents they talked just once more. Mac called from the airport while he was waiting to take the BOAC flight back to London. This was a week before he learned of Pia's disappearance.

'So, how's it going with the beauty?' he immediately asked.

'A disaster,' Khun Chai answered. 'She's just keeping me hanging on, giving me crumbs.' 'Well, break it off then.'

'Ha! It's not that easy.'

'Well, there's nothing to be done in that case. Keep enjoying your suffering like a good masochist,' said Mac and they had laughed. Then the conversation went onto what had happened with Mac's family and he said that all went well. His mother's cancer was being treated, and that they wanted him back as soon as he finished his course the following summer. They discussed what they could work on when Mac got back to Bangkok.

'Something on Jetsip Rai for sure,' said Mac enthusiastically. 'There's a lot of drama there. No shortage of plots. Look what's happening to you!'

There was an awkward moment before Mac hung up.

'I'm going to miss you, man. Stay well. See you in less than a year,' Khun Chai finally said.

While he carried on his hopeless affair with Pia, he received postcards from London with pictures of the city in the glory days of Flower Power and Mac's funny remarks on the back. The last card showed two girls in miniskirts outside the Bank of England walking past a man in a bowler hat, wearing a dark suit, staring after them disapprovingly.

The message that Mac scribbled on the back of the card said: 'Off to Paris for the weekend with one of the skirts! Lucky me. I'm no masochist.'

It was soon after receiving it, that Pia had disappeared from his life. His grief was alleviated by the thought that he would see his friend again in a matter of months. Then they would start on their adventure and set up a production company together. Khun Chai was already thinking of how he would turn Pia into a character in the screenplay that he would write when Mac returned. She would be the femme fatale who met with a bad end, or the slave of a cruel pimp who is eventually saved by an innocent student type. The plots kept flowing.

Then one morning he went into his office to find a telegram waiting on his desk. He had only received one other telegram in his life, from his aunt telling him to come home because his father was dying. He remembers holding this one in his hand for a long time while he nervously tried to guess its content. In his heart he knew that it was bad news.

It read simply:

'Mac killed in crash.'

These stark words sent his head reeling and he felt sick in the pit of his stomach. There was a telephone number at the bottom that he rang immediately. It was Mac's father. His voice choking with pain he told Khun Chai that Mac had been killed in London while riding pillion on the back of a friend's motorbike. They were hit by a car coming out from a side street. He, the father, had been informed by the secretary of the Thai Students Office who recalled that his son and Khun Chai were friends. He was sorry that it had taken him so long to get hold of Khun Chai's address, and he wanted him to know that they had held a ceremony at the temple for Mac.

Khun Chai could only utter some well-worn words in reply to all that he had just heard. After he put the phone down, he sank into his chair. That same afternoon when he got home, he pulled out of the cupboard the old, battered suitcase that he had brought back with him from England, one that he had used during all of his school years there. In it he put the String Band record together with the bong that he had shared with Mac, wrapped up in a blue silk cloth. He felt that these things already belonged to another time in his life that would never return. He did not feel sad so much as numb, as though a door had closed in his heart.

For the next couple of years, he threw himself into his work. Apart from covering all the cultural events of those years, he now began to turn his attention to the physical and social transformations that were happening to Bangkok as a result of the economic changes brought about by the war and by the influx of people from the north and south and from the money sent back by from the men and women who were going abroad to the Middle East and Europe. By the end of the sixties Bangkok was entering a chaotic boom time with new construction taking place at breakneck speed and new businesses initiated by ambitious entrepreneurs. Khun Chai observed and charted all these transformations diligently, offering his own undiluted critical opinion. The lack of adequate town planning meant that the city's infrastructure was fast collapsing. The canals where children living on its banks used to plunge in and play were now turning black. The air pollution was reaching dangerous levels. The horrendous daily traffic jams were becoming a way of life. His articles became popular with the readers of the *Bangkok Daily*. Khun Chai's voice was a mixture of cynicism and urgency. But whatever he wrote did little to persuade the politicians to change direction. Bangkok's hideous growth meant mega money to those who signed the permits. Progress, as it was called, seemed unstoppable.

Despite failing miserably in his efforts to change the minds of those who were responsible for deciding the city's direction and welfare, Khun Chai found satisfaction in his profession. The work was constantly challenging, and his enthusiasm was fed by the letters that he received from his *Bangkok Daily* readership. Meanwhile, his personal life was an endless routine of Bangkok events. Invitations arrived at his desk every day, and he could choose which ones to attend among those taking place around the city on any evening of the week. He accepted them because he did not enjoy being at home alone watching the TV or listening to music as he once did. With Mac's departure from his life, he was no longer interested in expanding his consciousness, although he would puff on the odd joint if it was offered. But generally, he now stuck to alcohol, which helped him to drop his natural shyness and reticence. There was no shortage of parties being held all over the city where he had many opportunities to make friendships. But he never allowed himself to let any of these develop into anything more than the superficial. It was the same with the few, occasional lovers he had during this stage in his life. None of them gave him the thrill that he had found in his brief time spent with Pia. At a gathering to celebrate Songraan he found himself attracted to a pretty girl called Ning who worked as a secretary in one of the foreign companies. They were married within six months and her pregnancy came soon after the wedding. Their son Mitr was born at the beginning of the following Chinese New Year, the Year of the Tiger, 1962.

Mitr's birth provided the two of them with a few months of shared common purpose. But it was obvious from the beginning that Ning did not enjoy motherhood. She would hand the baby over to the nurse they employed as often as possible. It was Khun Chai who delighted in having a son in his arms. As soon as she could, Ning went back to her work at the office and spent more and more time out of the house. Khun Chai might have been disappointed or hurt by her behaviour if he had felt any true affection for his wife. But he knew when he married Ning that it was not from love but from loneliness, and he felt that it was the same for her, although none of this was ever expressed between them. In fact, there was hardly any communication between them apart from basic, perfunctory exchange between two ill-suited human beings. He had shared more intimacy with Pia in one afternoon's conversation as he watched her dressing for her night's work, than in all the time that he was with Ning, who seemed to be permanently impatient with him. She made it obvious that she hated living in such a small house even though Khun Chai could now afford to have a cook and pay for a nurse to look after their son. On the rare occasions that she expressed her true feelings, Ning let him know that she felt that they deserved better.

'Why are you called Khun Chai when we live like paupers?' she would taunt him.

When Mitr was about two years old things began to get worse between them. Khun Chai knew by then that she was having an affair. He caught her talking to someone in English in excited whispers when she thought that he was not close by. But he also suspected that she did not care if he overheard her or not. She had also begun to drink heavily, and this made her cantankerous and ready to contradict him on every count, from his views on the pollution of the city to his taste in music. Their evenings at home often ended with a shouting match. Whenever they went out together, she would try to humiliate him in public.

'This can't go on,' he told her one morning when they woke up, both with a hangover from the excessive drinking at a party the night before. He was sitting on the bed with his feet dangling over the side, hunched over, nursing his aching head, his back to her.

'No,' she said quietly. 'I'm moving out.' 'Where to?' he said without turning round.

'Norway. Dag is going back there and has asked me to go with him.'

Khun Chai had met Dag, Ning's boss and taken an instant dislike to him. He was an arrogant, opinionated man who considered himself an expert on Thailand after living and working there for five years.

'And what about our son?' he asked. Now he was facing her. She looked away and buried her face in the pillow and began to cry.

Within two weeks Ning had gone from his life and he never heard from her again. It surprised him that she, as a mother, could abandon her son so easily. He could only conclude that she had never loved him. Not once after her departure did she make contact with him again to ask how Mitr was doing. Decades later, when Mitr had shown him how to use the internet and how to 'google', he put in her name in the search engine out of curiosity and her photo appeared immediately. It produced a strange sensation to see her now in middle age with a stout matronly figure. She was running a small business in Oslo. The two grown-up children standing by her side, whose father presumably was Dag, looked more Norwegian than Thai.

He was, by then, past the anger that he had felt when she had walked out on him and their son. In fact, he was relieved that they had not had to spend those years in perpetual conflict. Just as he himself had been brought up by Sai's grandmother, Mitr in turn was brought up very ably by Sai 's mother, Mae Hom.

The boy showed great intellectual promise from early on. He was a child who preferred reading to playing outside, forever asking questions about everything he did not understand, and whose main interest was numbers and figures. He would spend hours using an old wooden abacus that Khun Chai had inherited from his grandfather and kept as a piece of decoration to hang on his wall. Khun Chai, recognising his son's talents wanted the best education for him. By this time his modest income from the *Bangkok Daily* was being boosted by the money he was earning by freelancing for other publications. He was doing articles for magazines, brochures, hotels and airlines and some work for the advertising companies that were sprouting up in Bangkok, where tourism was taking off on a big scale. Still, it was not enough to cover the fees of the international school. It was John Booth, the paper's owner and editor who stepped in.

They were never close, but during the years they worked together a gentle friendship had been established between them founded on mutual respect. It was well known that John Booth was a homosexual whose young Thai lover had died from an overdose soon after he set up the newspaper. Since then, he had lived a solitary life and, whether due to the tragic loss of his friend or not, seemed uninterested in having any other close relationship. He seemed to Khun Chai to be asexual and perfectly content with it. Their friendship was based on a mutual appreciation of the peculiarities of Thai culture.

'You really get your own people, don't you,' he would remark to Khun Chai.

'Except that my own people don't think so.'

'Well, fuck'em!'

Booth was a rich and generous man and when, in a casual conversation, he heard of Khun Chai's wishes to send his son to the International School he offered to help pay for the fees.

'Listen. I'm a single guy. Got no family. I would like to help you, seeing as your son seems to be so gifted,' he told Khun Chai, who was both touched and surprised by this spontaneous offer.

'Please be generous and take my offer,' he had added and there was something about the way that he said this that made Khun Chai think that there was a sense of urgency behind the words.

This was the start of Mitr's brilliant academic career which took him eventually on a scholarship to the Harvard Business School. By this time John Booth, the angel who had given him employment and who had made his son's education possible, had died from liver cancer. But he had left a trust in his will that would cover the rest of Mitr's education. It was an act of kindness that was all the more powerful for coming with no expectations; no demand to be repaid, and whenever Khun Chai lapsed into cynicism towards the human race, as he did with more frequency as the years went by, the figure of John Booth would reappear in his mind to remind him that there was goodness and generosity in the hearts of men.

Khun Chai went back into his room and put the record on. The music transported him straight back to his youth and to his brief intense friendship with Mac.

'Gently tender falls the rain, wiping clean the slate again ...'

As the music played and the once-familiar words come back to him, he began swaying slowly and moving a step or two from side to side. His eyes filled with tears that began to flow down his cheeks. He had not cried when he left Baan Suan for England, nor when he learned of Na Cheua's death, nor when news reached him about his grandfather. He had looked silently at his father's corpse on the hospital bed. He had shed no tear when he finally accepted that Pia had gone away without a word and that he would never see her again. He gritted his teeth to control his emotions when he received the telegram telling him that the only true friend he ever knew had been killed. He felt numb with anger when his wife left him. He had sat unblinking by John Booth's bedside as the old man lay dying. It was only now that he understood the depth of the grief that he had carried for so many years hidden away, well disguised, and wondered why it had taken him so long to allow himself to express it in this simple way.

As he carried on dancing and crying, he realised that losing all these people had shaped the direction that his life had taken and created the person he had became.

Chapter 19

Yai Li was so surprised to see Khun Chai standing in her doorway leaning on his walking stick that all she could do was to put a hand up to her mouth. It was not just the unexpectedness of his visit, but the bright flowery shirt that he was wearing over his Thai fisherman's trousers and the wide brimmed Panama hat that covered his head. He bent forward with a formal gesture of greeting as he took off his hat and said:

'I'm sorry I did not call to tell you I was coming. I was afraid you might not have let me.'

'And why wouldn't I?' she replied. 'But how did you find my place anyway?'

'It was easy. I had Sai park the car outside near the archway and I asked people where you lived. A kind young man brought me to the entrance to your alley and pointed out your house.'

'Well, you'd better come in then,' she said pushing the door open for him to enter and noticing Mae Da sitting in her chair by her own doorway staring in disbelief at the whole scenario.

'Have you come for a treatment?' she enquired when they were inside. 'I thought I was meant to see you next weekend.'

'No.' he replied. 'I don't need anything from you. I just wanted to see where you lived. That's all. I haven't been in this area for forty-two years.'

They were seated now, he on the sofa with his stick next to him and she on a cushion on the floor. For a while neither of them said a word, and the only sound in the room was the whirring of the fan on the side table. Yai Li could see him now as a dapper looking young man, the one she had met in London. He looked totally relaxed in these surroundings that were a world away from the opulence of Baan Suan.

'And what were you doing here, exactly, apart from wanting to see where I live?' she asked, but she had already guessed. 'Is it because of that Pia that you mentioned?'

Khun Chai nodded.

'Still looking for her?'

'Yes. I think I am.'

'Where did she live?'

'Near the old mosque.'

'Ah. Yes. That area was burned down years ago. It was a bad fire. Lucky more buildings weren't destroyed.'

Khun Chai nodded.

'And they tore down the Mosquito Bar at around the same time. Or so I heard.'

Yes. Yai Li remembered walking past as the bulldozer demolished the site. There was a crowd of people, some of whom she recognised, standing watching in silence. The same thing was happening all over Bangkok in those few short years when familiar landmarks ceased to exist.

'Tell me. Why was this Pia so special to you? Was she a real beauty or something?' Yai Li felt surprised at her own directness, but she felt that he had come to talk to her about this. Why else was he there?'

Khun Chai laughed.

'Do you know? I can't really tell you. No, she wasn't particularly beautiful. In fact, I can't remember anything special about her except the way she wore those tight, short dresses.' He paused and smiled. 'Maybe it was just because I could never be with her. That made me want her even more. Do you understand?'

'Not really,' said Yai Li. 'I have never been able to work out what makes people do what they do. And the older I get, the less I understand about their capacity for pain.'

Khun Chai laughed, then looked at his watch.

'Listen. It's a little early. But can I invite you out to dinner? There's a place nearby, off Rama IV.'

'I can't go dressed like this,' said Yai Li pointing to her sarong.

'Well. Look at me! We can be the odd couple going out on a date.' Khun Chai replied.

At the restaurant the waitress eyed them with amusement as she took their orders. Khun Chai suggested sharing a bottle of beer. Then they began to talk and did not finish their meal until more than two hours and three bottles later. Yai Li was surprised at how easily Khun Chai made it for her to tell him things that she had not shared with anyone for many years, and never with such honesty. She told him about her early life in Ayutthaya, her move to Bangkok, her marriage, her daughter's death, her granddaughter Joy. She even revisited the incident in London. For his part, he listened attentively absorbing all the details like the journalist he had once been. What she told him came from a world he knew little about. Even during the time that he was hanging out with the artists and the musicians, he had not met someone who could give him the insights that Yai Li offered up of what it was like to be a member of the underprivileged majority of the land. He was pleased that she trusted him with her narrative. He only interrupted her to check on the timeline of events. There seemed to be a remarkable synchronicity to many of the key moments of their lives. It was as though their parallel paths had come together at this point in time for some reason that he could not yet fathom. It was not a bad basis for a short story, he thought wistfully to himself.

When Sai dropped Yai Li at the entrance to Jetsip Rai, she and Khun Chai said goodbye to each other like two old friends after an evening out. But later when she was lying on her bed, still tipsy from the alcohol, she shivered with embarrassment. How could she have talked so much? Why did she tell him about Maitri's drinking, and about Nuan's illness? She still hardly knew him. Why did she trust him with all that information when she wouldn't even share it with Mae Da her neighbour? But there was nothing she could do about it now. Before she finally turned off the light, she raised her two hands towards the Buddharupa that was on the shelf at the side of her bed.

For she knew that in spite of everything she had enjoyed herself that evening – something that she had not expected to happen, and for that she gave thanks.

As he sat watching the lights of the city flash by through the car window Khun Chai began to enter that in-between state where the rational mind gives way to other dimensions. Certain colours, like the pink and green from the neon lights took him back to memories, or rather impressions and vague recollections of events that had occurred throughout his life in the city; the images overlapped in no specific chronological order and the emotions washed over him like rainwater. Then, at an intersection where they had stopped at the lights behind a long line of cars, Khun Chai found that he was feeling a sense of elation.

A moment later as he looked up to an old billboard advertising a massage parlour, with a badly painted, scantily dressed young woman smiling down with her inviting, and yet innocent look, he began to laugh.

Sai glanced in the rear mirror and said:

'Nai. Are you OK?'

Khun Chai did not answer his driver immediately. How could he tell him what was going on inside him?

'There's nowhere in the world like Bangkok, is there, Sai? It's such a crazy, ugly, poetic place.

'I've always hated it, and loved it at the same time,' he finally said. Sai nodded patiently into the rear mirror.

Chapter 20

'Do you think they are falling in love?' Mitr asked the question without looking up from his computer.

His words took Joy by surprise, and she almost made a mess of the toenail that she was painting with pink varnish.

'I mean, he's taken her out five times in the past three weeks, if I remember right. I can't recall a time when he ever took anyone out to dinner or lunch except for me.' Mitr said. 'And they seem to be getting on very well. I don't know what they get up to in those treatment sessions.'

Joy was giggling. 'Stop it. That's a terrible thought! They're too old for that kind of thing.'

'Unlike us,' said Mitr, who then turned to her, got up and walked over to the bed and slid off the dressing gown he was wearing. She put the nail varnish on the side table and then slipped the tee shirt she was wearing over her head.

An hour earlier, in the fierce heat of the afternoon they had driven up the long driveway. The sea in the distance beyond the stretch of white sand was shimmering like a sheet of metal. The manager came out to greet them warmly.

'Everything is in order,' he told them.

The beachside property was one of Mitr's latest acquisitions that came with the investment company that he had recently taken over. It was all but finished, and needed only the final touches to the swimming pools, the gardens and the tennis courts. It was to be the most luxurious property in Cha-am. The sale of the units had started and already three had been sold. The penthouse that Mitr kept for himself had been refurbished to suit his taste, under the guidance of Joy who had overseen the final details. She chose the furniture and the paintings that hung from the walls and the Buddharupas and statues that were dotted around the wide, airy space with its magnificent view of the sea. This was the first time that they were going to spend a night in this new place, and she could not help but feel a sense of triumph. He liked what she had done and praised her good taste. But more importantly she had managed to provide an opportunity for him to be there with her. It was to be the last inspection before the official opening at the end of the month with a member of the royal family attending, the monks giving their blessings and the important officials of the district sitting around to receive the thanks and the gifts for their help in facilitating what needed to be done. This would, of course be an occasion for Mitr and Arunee to be pictured together as the shining couple of Thai society. But for now Joy was glad that he was there to spend the night with her.

The sun was beginning to set by the time they climbed off the bed. Joy felt the afterglow of satisfying, unrushed sex. It was rare for her. All the tension that she had felt during the past weeks melted away, and she sensed that the same was true with Mitr. The funeral and the subsequent ceremonies with the ashes was well behind him. The deal with the Chinese company had come through. His father seemed relatively well and happy. There was cause for celebration, and here they were in the most beautiful apartment waiting for the night to fall before dressing and going to their favourite restaurant in Hua Hin.

'Champagne?' Mitr said as he put his gown back on.

'I'll get it.' She replied.

Mitr was standing on the balcony with his hands on the railing, admiring the view, when she brought out the tray with the ice bucket and the bowl of snacks and put it on the marble table. He turned when he heard the cork pop and smiled broadly at Joy.

They raised and clinked their glasses.

'You really do your job well, don't you?' he said. 'Here's to us!'

'Here's to the crumbs that come my way,' Joy replied cheerily before draining her glass.

'Hey, steady. You'll be drunk before we get to the restaurant.'

'No. I won't. Don't worry about me. Anyway, I want to celebrate a bit tonight. I think I deserve it.'

The restaurant was crowded. It was a Friday and Bangkokians who had houses or apartments in Hua Hin and Cha-am were down for the long weekend. There was no one in the crowd who they knew directly but one or two people turned to stare at them as they were shown to their table. Joy did not care if they were recognised. She was having dinner with her boss. It was as simple as that. Besides, that evening, after the bottle of Moet that they had finished she was too high to care. Nevertheless, as always, she managed to keep up a discrete appearance, despite the desire to reach over and hold Mitr's hands across the table or touch his leg with her foot. Over the meal they talked again about Mitr's father and her grandmother.

'But he's so cultured and sophisticated, and she's totally uneducated. She can hardly write.' Joy told him. 'What on earth do they have to talk about?'

Mitr shrugged and laughed.

'Beats me. But, you know, my father always identified with the underprivileged. He grew up with the servants. He felt closer to them than to his own parents. He told me that many times as I was growing up. He told me he didn't want me to be a snob.'

'And you're obviously not one, since you're with me, and I'm a slum kid.'

They had never talked like that together and Joy felt an intimacy with Mitr that she had not known before. They left the restaurant in a good mood and Joy looked forward to the rest of that night. When they got back to the penthouse, Mitr said that he wanted a nightcap, so they moved to the balcony with a bottle of cognac and two glasses. The moon had risen and cast a soft silvery glow over the surface of the sea. A slight breeze was blowing and carried the scent of seaweed and frangipani. The temperature was comfortable. It was the end to a perfect day. Joy put on the Brazilian jazz that Mitr liked. They sat sipping their drinks, watching the beautiful scene in front of them. Time was suspended. Then Mitr's mobile started whirring. He took it out of his pocket and glanced at it, then made a hand signal to Joy that he was going to go inside to answer it.

As Joy waited for him to rejoin her, she became more and more agitated. She knew that it was Arunee. Who else could it be? Otherwise, he would either not have accepted the call or answered it in front of her. Suddenly she felt that the evening had been ruined.

It was almost ten minutes before he came back out to the balcony and the relaxed expression had disappeared from his face.

'So, what did she say?' asked Joy curtly when he sat down and took up his glass once more. He looked at her with an expression of annoyance.

'You don't need to know,' he snapped.

Joy finished her cognac in one gulp, then poured herself another large shot and drank it down. Then yet another tumbler full.

'Don't do that. Please. It's not necessary and it won't do you any good,' said Mitr.

'I'll do whatever I want,' said Joy, fiercely. 'I am a grown woman. I have no rights over you and neither do you over me. You don't own me.'

'Now you're talking nonsense and you're behaving like a child,' he said impatiently.

Joy got up with the glass in her hand and found that she was unsteady on her feet as she headed for the living room. Mitr shook his head.

'You're drunk. I hate seeing a woman drunk.'

Joy was about to enter through the sliding doors, but she stopped and turned around. Suddenly all the anger that she had kept tightly curled in her up till then rose into her chest.

'And I hate your wife!' she spat out the words. 'She has you round her little finger. And you're not man enough to admit it. You who think you're so clever and powerful, you're just another frightened little worm.'

With that she smashed her glass onto the floor. Its contents splash all over the tiles. By now Mitr was on his feet.

'What are you doing? Don't speak to me like that! How dare you? You little tart.'

Joy came towards him with her eyes flashing, her hair wild, and her face flushed. When she was in front of him, she began to pummel her fists on his chest. He put up his hands to protect himself as he kept drawing alway from her.

'You would never think of leaving her because you're nothing but a coward. Yes, you're a coward who's afraid of his wife,' she screamed as he backed away from her till he was against the railing. Then suddenly his feet slid from beneath him and she saw him flip backwards over the side. Later she remembered it as if in slow motion. The slippers he was wearing practically brushed her cheeks. His body was in a jack knife position, the way high divers jump backwards before they straighten again. Both his arms were stretched up to the air. His neck was craned towards her, and his hands reached skyward as if by so doing he could keep from falling. The glasses slipped off his head and his eyes showed absolute terror.

Chapter 21

MONK EXPELLED FROM TEMPLE FOR TAKING YAA BAH PILLS

Writer: Maliwan Sakdee

Sri Saket: A police team raided a temple, Wat Dhammadathu, in Bua Gaew district of this Northeastern province on Sunday and arrested a monk for selling methamphetamine pills. The raid, carried out by a team led by a senior assistant district chief, followed a tip off from informants after there had been complaints from those who frequented the temple that the monk, Phra Jetana, aged 76, had been selling meth pills to young people who came to the temple.

Phra Jetana denied the accusation, police said. But the team recovered a box containing 150 meth pills from under his bed. When confronted with the evidence, Phra Jetana told the investigating officer that it belonged to a man who frequented the temple and who had been supplying him with the pills over the previous six months. Police are still searching for the whereabouts of this man, who was known as Loong Mon to Phra Jetana, but so far with no success in locating the dealer.

During the interrogation of the monk a urine test was carried out and it confirmed that Phra Jetana had taken the drug before he was arrested. It was subsequently confirmed that he was addicted to Yaa Bah.

His denial that he was a seller was later confirmed by other monks and members of the community who frequently went to the temple. Never had anyone purchased Yaa Bah from Phra Jetana. But Loong Mon, the dealer, was well known to them. It was not clear why Phra Jetana agreed to keep the box of drugs in his kuti. Nevertheless, because he had broken one of the main vows and had been complicit with a criminal, he was immediately stripped of the monkhood by the abbot of the monastery

It was an article on the third page of *Thai Rath*, the newspaper that was delivered to Baan Suan every morning. The photograph with the monk being interviewed in the police station only showed the face at an angle from behind, so that the features were impossible to distinguish. But it was the name that drew Khun Chai's attention and made him reread the article carefully. Ten years earlier, he had heard from one of the servants who had worked for his father that Nai Jit, the foreman's son who had helped his father to take advantage of Wigrom's drunkenness to sell off chunks of the property, had become a monk in the Northeast. Having set up a tourist guide business from the proceeds of the sale of the land around Baan Suan, as well as the pieces of furniture that Wigrom, in his daily stupor, was not even aware were missing, he had run into financial difficulties in his wheeling and dealing and incurred a massive debt. In order to escape being harmed by his debtors, or going to prison, he had become a monk, henceforth known as Phra Jetana.

Could this monk, he wondered, be the same person? Was this Nai Jit he was reading about? If so, it seemed that Phra Jetana's demise was a neat example of karma, the kind that his old nurse Na Cheua would have enjoyed telling him about to show the truth of Buddhist teaching – punishment for bad action.

As he held the newspaper in front of him and kept staring at the photo, still intrigued by the whole affair, Sai came rushing out to the balcony. By the startled look on his face Khun Chai could tell that there was something wrong.

The young man seemed so upset that he just stood in silence trembling for a while, on the verge of tears.

'Take your time, Sai. There's no hurry. What's this about? What's wrong?' asked Khun Chai gently.

'It's your son, Nai.'

Part 2

Chapter 22

Khun Chai flicked on the four light switches, then pushed open the heavy doors. As he stepped into the vast room, he looked up at the chandeliers that his grandfather imported from Paris when the house was built, and he remembered feeling, as he was growing up, that they were an unnecessary, bombastic display of wealth. What they illuminate now looked like a range of gigantic mountains of broken meringues. White sheets, changed monthly, covered the teak furniture from Myanmar, chosen by Arunee's interior designer – tables and chairs, benches and stools and lamps that have been piled up in irregular sets. Khun Chai was glad that all this was under wraps because, apart from his disapproval of the wood being illegally imported, the furniture's modern design was not to his taste, nor did it fit with what was now the so-called ballroom, where no balls had ever taken place. It was the least used space in the whole house and Khun Chai could not understand why such effort had been made to refurbish it in this fashion.

It was over two years since he had stepped foot in it. The last time was for his birthday party, organised by Arunee, an affair he would have preferred to have avoided. He did not need another reminder of his age. But, as always, it was difficult to refuse the gesture without upsetting his son and daughter-in-law. So he had complied with their wishes to make it a special occasion for him, and got dressed up in a suit, which he hated, and then spent an uncomfortable, embarrassing evening talking politely to people he would rather not have seen, including Arunee's father Pansak who, thankfully, was not in good health and lacked the energy to sustain his usual monologue.

That evening, three days after he heard of Mitr's death, still in shock, he had wandered down the dark corridor from the dining room as if he were sleepwalking, with a vague purpose in mind. It was as though he was being led to the room that had once been central to the life of Baan Suan. Two photographs, one on either side of the main door bore witness to this. They had been obtained by the interior designer who had researched the history of the house, and like a good detective had found these images and had them restored. The one that hung on the wall to the left of the door was taken from the far end of the room. The date at the bottom right-hand corner says November 12th, 1918. News of the end of World War 1 had reached them the day before. The men are all dressed in formal Western evening attire; dinner jackets and bow ties. Four of them are standing by the snooker table, cues in their hands. The rest, including Khun Chai's grandfather, Khun Luang Paiboon, are sitting by the long bar raising their glasses to the camera. Khun Chai, who had never scrutinised the photograph with such care before, noticed that all of them are wearing sombre expressions, as befitting a formal meeting, but not a celebration.

He walked over and turned his attention to the other photograph hanging to the right of the door. It had been taken at an angle from what had previously been the bar towards the French windows leading out to the garden. In this one it was late afternoon. The chandeliers have not yet been switched on. The nearer group consisted of men sitting at card tables. They were all wearing light-coloured suits. At the largest table sat Wigrom, his father, looking young and dapper. He was holding a thumb up at the camera, presumably to denote his success at the table and he was smiling. In the background, a group of elegantly dressed women stood talking to one another. There was no date on the photograph, but Khun Chai knew that it was taken in early 1932, the year that his father apparently could not lose a game. For a moment he felt the urge to pull one of the sheets off the furniture but decided against it, knowing that it would reveal nothing he is not already familiar with. He suddenly remembered why he was there.

Since Mitr's death he had not left his downstairs room and the balcony outside it. Sai had been bringing him his meals, delivering them in silence at the exact times and then returning to take away the barely touched plates an hour later. He respected his master's wish not to be disturbed even though he could not fathom what was going on in his mind. For Khun Chai had stopped talking from the moment that Sai had delivered the news about Mitr to him. On hearing it, he dropped the newspaper he was reading and gave out an audible gasp of pain, as though his heart had received a terrible blow; a few moments later, tears had streamed down his face. But when Sai began to say something comforting, Khun Chai had put up his hand to discourage any further interchange and then turned his back on him. Since then, he had been silent.

His grief was complicated. The first blow on learning of Mitr's death, and the way that he understood what Sai told him, produced an immediate reaction of anger towards Joy.

'The police said that she pushed him over the balcony,' Sai kept repeating.

But the visceral wish for vengeance and justice that immediately consumed him became suffused with more subtle emotions the next day when he read in *Thai Rath* that Joy was insisting that it had been an accident. He had carefully weighed up the testimony that she offered. It was meticulously reported, and he could hear her voice as he read and reread the words. Her description of what had taken place seemed to be sincere, and although it did not make the sorrow of losing his only son any the less, or take away the desire to blame someone for this loss, her testimony planted the seed of doubt in his mind as to what had precisely happened to Mitr.

Nevertheless, the realisation that he would never again have his only son in his life was strange and appalling to Khun Chai. It inevitably brought up the memories he held in his heart. When Ning, Mitr's mother left Baan Suan for good, Khun Chai had asked Sai's mother, Mae Hom to help him look after the infant. This she did with the same care and kindness that Na Cheua had shown when she had looked after him when his mother had died. But as Mitr grew, Khun Chai did not feel adequate as a single parent and he could not help the feeling that he should never have married Ning in the first place, let alone have a child with her. He thought of remarrying, so that his son would have a mother, but just as quickly dismissed this idea. He did not want to make the same mistake of committing to someone he did not love, and he knew he was much better as a bachelor. In any case, he watched Mitr grow up as a happy boy, content to be in his own world of numbers and facts, precocious and self-contained, who did not seem to need any advice or guidance from him. From the age of about nine, Mitr began to show that he was the more decisive and clear thinking of the two of them, and Khun Chai found himself complying with his son's wishes rather than dictating his own. This was to be the nature of their relationship from then on, and over the years, as Mitr became even more proficient intellectually, he would often find himself annoyed by his son's utter self-confidence and his superior way of treating everyone around him, including his own father, as people who were not quite up to his mental level.

Nevertheless, he also came to acknowledge that his son was the only person with whom he communicated with any intimacy. Apart from their divergent views on practically every subject, from politics to aesthetics, Mitr was the person he talked to, although, in recent years less so, due to Mitr's intense workload and frequent absences from Baan Suan. The issue of the Klongtoey development project had of late also started to provoke tensions between them once more. But none of this touched the essential love and respect each bore the other. As father and son, he and Mitr had enjoyed a relationship that Khun Chai could not have imagined possible, given what had happened with Wigrom, his own father.

He had gone to the ballroom that evening in order to come to a decision about Baan Suan, which in all but name was Mitr and Arunee's property. His signature on the title deeds was a mere formality. The bills and all the expenses for the upkeep, including the servants' wages were taken care of by Mitr. From the beginning he had felt like a permanent guest there. This anomaly had weighed on him ever since he had moved back to the family home. But Mitr's death had accentuated the sense of absurdity surrounding his ownership of such a grand property. He was now toying with the idea of getting rid of it altogether. It was not that he had no attachment to it. But any feelings of nostalgia were overshadowed by the pain that was part of the history of Baan Suan and once again part of his own history. Why would he want to go on living in that enormous place, sharing it with his son's widow, when everything reminded him of his terrible loss and the absence of his son? In that vast room he confronted, yet again, the sense of injustice at being the owner of a house that had a ballroom, an observatory and a swimming pool, in a time when people were living in shacks across the city, without electricity or running water. He wanted to convince himself of his decision – half taken already – to sell Baan Suan. Of course, that depended on what Arunee wanted. But he suspected that she would have no objections.

'It's more trouble than it's worth,' he had overheard her saying to a friend one day when she was walking in the garden unaware of his presence on a bench behind the frangipani bush.

'Mitr bought it just to please his father. It's much too big for us. We have no family. There are so many better things to do with it.'

He remembered being surprised at these words because he had presumed that she was just as acquisitive as her father, and enjoyed being the mistress of this great mansion.

He looked across the enormous, lifeless space for one last time.

'I hope I never have to set foot in here ever again,' he whispered to himself before leaving the room.

Chapter 23

It was one in the morning when Yai Li saw that it was Joy calling her on her mobile.

'Yai. Please. You've got to come. I have no one else.'

Within ten minutes of coming off the call, in which Joy explained in a tearful and barely intelligible voice what had happened, Yai Li was out of her door and heading for the shacks that were in a lane near the side entrance to Jetsip Rai, where the pickups and taxis usually parked. She was hoping that Loong Pan and Pa Wong were still awake. She did not know how she was going to ask for his help at this late hour. But Pa Wong owed the fact that she was still on her feet to the treatments that she received from her three years earlier, for which Yai Li had not asked for a penny.

As she neared the parking lot, a pink taxi came round the corner, slowed down and stopped by her. Then the driver rolled down his window.

'Yai Li. What are doing out so late? Where have you been?'

It was Loong Pan, coming home from his long shift. Yai Li felt this was a good sign. He was not already snoring in his bed or having a row with his wife.

'I have a favour to ask. And I wouldn't be asking it if I wasn't desperate.'

Loong Pan clicked his teeth, already suspecting what the favour was going to be.

'I need a ride to Cha-am. I'll pay you of course. But we have to leave right now.' Loong Pan shook his head slowly and blew an exhausted puff of air out of his mouth. 'Are you sure it's that urgent?' he said weakly.

'I wouldn't be standing here asking you, if it wasn't,' she replied. He paused for a moment.

'It's going to cost you.'

Yai Li shrugged.

'All right. Wait here. I'll have to tell Ee Wong first. Otherwise, she'll think I'm seeing my little mistress. I won't be long.' He laughed, climbed out of the car and walked over to the lane nearby.

Yai Li took advantage of his absence to call Joy's number. There was no reply.

The scene that confronted her in the police station in Cha-am made her nervous. She wished that she had someone by her side to accompany her. But Loong Pan refused to go in with her. 'I'll wait in the car, if you don't mind,' he said. 'I don't much care for police stations. And besides, I need to get some sleep. Otherwise, I won't have the strength to drive you all the way back to the city, and then start my shift. You'll be all right.'

Knowing that it was absurd to even think of it, she wished, as she went through the entrance, that Khun Chai was with her. She guessed that he must have heard the news by now and wondered what must be going through his mind at that moment.

The waiting area was filled with people who immediately looked up at her. A young woman got up from her chair and approached her.

'Are you the grandmother?' she asked Yai Li, without introducing herself.

Yai Li nodded in reply. A man standing nearby held up his mobile phone and took a picture. A powerfully built female police officer then came round from behind the reception desk and, practically pushing the two aside, told her:

'Follow me please.'

She was led down a long corridor into a neon lit room where Joy was seated at a table, head in her hands between two other stern looking policewomen. She looked up at Yai Li, reached her arms out towards her grandmother and began to cry.

'They don't believe me, Yai,' she kept repeating between her sobbing. Yai Li sat down and stretched her hands across the table and held her granddaughter's. She did not know what to say. She wanted to be comforting, and reassuring to Joy. But no words came, not even meaningless ones. Only when she arrived home just as dawn was breaking and fell on her bed exhausted from the ordeal, did she let out a long wail of grief.

The following day the memory of the previous evening in the police station kept coming back to disturb her. It was as though she and Joy were locked into a nightmare. No, she kept thinking. Khun Chai was wrong to have told her that we don't remember things clearly, that we distort our experience, because she retained every detail about the journey down to Cha-am; Loong Pan driving at breakneck speed like a madman through the dark roads, then the painful meeting with Joy and her own catatonic presence at the police station, even the old love songs on Loong Pan's radio as they drove back to Bangkok from Cha-am that night. It had all been overwhelming and she wished none of it had happened. She felt ashamed of her own impotence.

The news was all over the front pages of the papers. There were lurid images of the bloodstained tiles where Mitr had fallen to his death. A headline screamed: 'Billionaire tycoon crashes to earth in suspicious circumstances.' Every stall and corner shop in Jetsip Rai sold out their newspapers by mid-morning. Everyone in the district felt involved. Joy had grown up there, and there was a sense of shared kudos among its inhabitants. She had made herself famous, albeit for all the wrong reasons.

On the face of it there was no reason why Joy's version of events should not have been accepted. In one interview after another, her description of the events of that fateful evening was consistent and coherent, and the combination of shock and tears she displayed seemed totally genuine. She faltered only once, when asked if she was in love with her lover. She had hesitated before saying: 'I don't know', and this seemed to be significant to the investigators, and even more so to the journalists who got wind of this.

But the real doubt that was cast on the veracity of her testimony emerged from what the police who arrived on the scene learned when they interrogated the other guests and residents in the condo. Given that the property had only been recently put on the market it was natural that there was still a low occupancy. On the evening of the incident, there were only two other units being used. One was rented to a retired Swedish couple who planned to spend one half of the year in Cha-am and the other back in Stockholm. They had gone to bed early, as they always did, and had heard nothing. But they were deeply upset that a death had taken place on the property and were thinking of moving out. The other occupants were a gay couple who, although awake at the time of the incident, also heard nothing as they were watching a series on Netflix with windows closed and the air conditioning full on. They too were shocked to hear of what had happened. The only other person to be interviewed was the manager, a bachelor whose apartment was on the ground floor, with a door leading out to the swimming pool area. At around eleven thirty he had gone out to have a smoke and walk around the pool before going to bed. This had become his regular routine since he took up the job.

He told the police that he heard voices raised in anger from the direction of the balcony where Joy and Mitr were staying. This was in the courtyard adjacent to the swimming pool area, separated by a tall hedge of bamboo. He had no doubt that it was them because there was no one else on that side of the building, and he had himself taken them up to their room that afternoon when they arrived. It was clear that they were having an argument. Then he caught the sound of breaking glass followed by more loud voices. But he could not hear what they were saying. Next, he heard what he took to be a long scream followed by a distinct thump like a heavy sack hitting the ground. This was his exact description as he explained to the investigating officer that he was still in the swimming pool area, round the corner from the wing where the incident took place. He quickened his steps as he heard more screaming, and it was then that he saw the figure of Khun Mitr lying on the terrace. Looking up, he also saw the face of Khun Joy who was yelling down to him for help. It was he who called the police station.

On the strength of the manager's testimony, the police were insistent that further investigation was needed and were recommending that the case be forwarded to the Public Prosecutor. By the next afternoon Joy had been transferred to the Remand Prison in Bangkok. Television crews had filmed her leaving the police station in Cha-am and were now in front of the gates to catch her arrival at the prison. The next morning her first appearance in the courts received the same coverage. For Yai Li, it was heart breaking to see Joy in prison uniform. The images were broadcast throughout the week by all the TV channels. Overnight, the death of the director of Siam Estate – was it an accident, murder or manslaughter? – had replaced every other scandal in the country as prime viewing. In Jetsip Rai there were people already making bets on the outcome. Generally, it was odds on that Joy would eventually be prosecuted for the murder of her lover, although the motivation was unclear.

Yai Li found her life turned upside down by what was happening. She could not step out of her front door without someone making a sympathetic, yet unsolicited comment. She could not walk through Jetsip Rai without seeing people bent over their mobile phones to catch the latest details of the investigation from the social media. She knew they were doing this because if they happened to lift their heads and notice her, they would nod politely yet pointedly in her direction. Every now and then, an old acquaintance would come up and say to her: 'We are praying for your granddaughter'. But nobody's kind words could take away the feelings of deep anxiety that Yai Li was now feeling. And the worst of it was that there was no one to talk to and share her worries. She longed for someone like Khun Chai to give her wise advice and to calm her fears.

When she went to the Remand Prison to visit Joy, they stood behind bars, separated from each other by a thin corridor. On either side were other families holding onto the bars and shouting out as loud as they could, trying to make themselves heard. Joy and Yai Li merely stood staring at each other for a long time, while the voices around them rose to a crescendo. Then, when the voices did die down for a second, Yai Li thought she could make out the words 'Khun Chai' being spoken by Joy, so she did the same without making a sound; Joy seemed to understand and nodded.

When Yai Li got home that evening, she felt drained by the intensity of the visit. Hardly had she taken her shoes off and lain on her bed when there was a loud knocking on her door.

'Yai Li, Yai Li,' It was unmistakably the raspy voice of Mae Da, her neighbour.

'Go away. Please. I'm really tired,' said Yai Li , filled with annoyance.

'No,' said Mae Da through the door. 'Open up. This is important. I swear.'

Reluctantly, Yai Li pulled herself off the bed and went to open her door. At once, Mae Da spoke, excitedly.

'That *farang* father who runs the Mercy Centre said that their lawyer can get Joy out on bail and that they will pay for it. He's been telling everyone that Joy is one of the family and a child of Jetsip Rai. They won't abandon her, whatever she's done.'

The priest was true to his word. By the end of that day, thanks to the vigorous efforts of the lawyer from the Mercy Centre, Yai Li and her granddaughter were reunited and sitting opposite one another in Joy's apartment in Bang Na, knees touching, hands clasped, looking at each other with tears in their eyes.

'I swear I didn't do it, Yai,' said Joy finally. 'You believe me, don't you?'

Chapter 24

Khun Chai had been waiting for over half an hour after ringing the bell for Sai to come before impatiently opening his bedroom door into the lobby. He wanted Sai to go upstairs and fetch him the file in which he kept all his official documents. He needed the number of a legal firm he had once used and whom he trusted. But when Sai did not appear, he decided that even though his legs were hurting that afternoon, he would go slowly up the stairs to his old bedroom and find the file himself. He had just crossed the hallway and reached the bottom of the stairs when he heard the familiar, firm footsteps in the corridor above. It was too late to retreat back into his room and, besides, he had not the strength or the agility necessary to do so with any speed. So he stood holding on to the balustrade and waited for Arunee to make her way towards him down the stairs.

They had not seen one another since both learned of Mitr's death. Khun Chai had been so involved with his own shock and pain that he had not asked how his daughter-in-law had taken the news, and he could only presume that Sai had informed her of his wish to be left alone. Now, as watched her walking down towards him, he regretted not having made at least some effort to communicate with her before. It was impolite and unkind. But it was too late.

She paused in front of him with a mixture of mild bewilderment and pleasure at seeing him there, which surprised him, and put her hands together to bow to him. It was a formal gesture that she had been told by Mitr to stop doing after they were married.

'And do call him Pa, not Khun Paw, please.' he had said.

Spontaneously, Khun Chai reached out both his arms and gently touched the sides of hers. For a moment, he could see that she was on the point of tears. But she checked herself.

'Should we talk?' he said.

'Yes. I would appreciate that,' Arunee replied. 'But not now, if you don't mind. I've got to go somewhere.' Aware that her words might have sounded offensive in the circumstances, she quickly added. 'I am going to see Joy.'

Khun Chai could not disguise his bewilderment on hearing this. Her intention seemed incongruous to him. He raised his eyebrows then screwed them into a frown. He did not have anything to say in reply.

'I want to make sure for myself if she actually killed him or not.' She explained.

Khun Chai took a few moments to take this in.

'And how will you do that?' he said.

'Oh, by asking her outright. I trust in my instincts. Don't forget that I was trained as a criminal psychologist.'

Khun Chai had totally forgotten this.

'And what if you come to the conclusion that she's guilty?'

'Then I'd do everything in my power to make sure she gets everything that's due to her. You can bet on it.'

Khun Chai had no doubt of this in his mind. As she turned to leave Arunee said:

'Let's have dinner together this evening.'

This was the first time that she had spoken to him with such unforced naturalness.

'Yes. I'd like that,' he said. 'There's something that we need to talk about urgently.'

They both knew that he meant the funeral ceremony for Mitr. His body had been kept in a morgue in Hua Hin, to where it had been transported after the autopsy. The funeral parlour still had not received any instructions as to where it was meant to be taken.

'Yes, I know, Pa,' said Arunee.

Khun Chai was glad that she addressed him by that familiar term that Mitr had always used. He bared his hands, inviting her to make a suggestion.

'I'm onto it. I'll talk to you about it when I get back. Alright?'

Later, after she had left and he was alone on the balcony, he found himself thinking about his daughter-in-law, now a widow, and wondered what was going on with her. Why this need to meet Joy in person? Was it because of her training as a psychologist? What if she concluded that Joy had killed her husband? Would she exact a brutal revenge? And if not, could she forgive her? As these thoughts played out in his mind, reflecting what he himself had been thinking over those days, he realised how little he knew of Arunee. Even on the car rides that they had shared when she accompanied him to the clinics and hospitals for his appointments with the specialists, they never ventured beyond small talk if they discussed anything other than the condition of his bones and nerves. The truth was that he had never bothered to get to know her. It was partly because he did not want anyone to come between him and his son, not that she made any effort to do so. Yet he had not been prepared for her presence in the household. But more than this feeling of intrusion, it was that he could not separate her from her father in his mind. So even though he respected his son's choice of partner, he found the association to Pansak that came with it distasteful.

Mitr told him several times about the work that Arunee did for the women who had been beaten up and battered. With her wealth she had set up a foundation that ran a Centre in the Phra Pradaeng area that was a safe house as well as the centre of operations for the foundation. It was called the Mudita House and had once been featured in a newspaper article. It was well known in Bangkok high society that Arunee was on her way to being formally given a title for her humanitarian efforts. Mitr was proud of her work. But Khun Chai made it obvious every time his son spoke of it that he was not interested in learning more about it. This was not because he did not believe in the work that her centre was doing or that he questioned his daughter-in-law's motives. He accepted that her wish to help was sincere, and that the foundation work was a full-time occupation for her, not just a hobby to fill in the days. Nevertheless, he could not bring himself to show the respect and appreciation she clearly deserved. He knew that this was mean spirited of him, but it made no difference. He could not help associating the funds that were used to maintain the foundation with the ill-gotten gains accumulated by her father.

⊱ ⊱ ⊱

That afternoon Sai drove Arunee that afternoon to Joy's apartment on the other side of city. There was a lot of traffic and the silence between them grew heavy. After half an hour Arunee said:

'How's your son taken it?'

'Ai Toh?' Sai hesitated before answering her. 'Very badly, I think.' he said. 'He doesn't understand what has happened and he's hearing all sorts of things from the others which they shouldn't be talking about. I am worried about him, to tell you the truth.'

Arunee made no further comment for a while but gazed out of the window. She remembered Mitr's fondness for the boy, who was now 15 years old. In fact, she often felt that he treated Toh as the son he never had. In any case, with Toh, Mitr showed a playful side to his nature that was not evident in any of his other relationships. Moreover, it seemed to come naturally to him. On the days that he was home he would often play with Toh in the swimming pool, teaching the boy how to swim and dive off the springboard. They would sometimes walk round the garden together and Mitr would point out the insects to the boy and tell him their names. He was both patient and compassionate to Toh, who was considered mentally subnormal by everyone in the household including his own parents. But Arunee knew from the moment he was introduced to her that he was autistic, and when she moved into Baan Suan one of the first things she did was to see that her suspicions were officially confirmed by tests done in Baamrungraaj hospital and paid for by her. She would have sent him to a school for special needs children if she could, but Sai and his wife insisted that he stay home with them, and she respected their wishes. At any rate, the remoteness that came with his condition made him shy away from everyone except for Mitr whom he seemed to trust and cling to with a fierce loyalty.

'He knows something bad has happened,' Sai continued. 'He knows that Khun Mitr did not go on holiday or away on business. He can sense that something is wrong. But we don't know how to tell him,' Sai said, his voice cracking with emotion. 'We're not sure he'll understand.' Arunee nodded.

'Yes. It's difficult. Let me think about it,' she muttered confidently, for Sai's sake. But she did not really see how it was going to work out given the intense attachment Toh had for Mitr.

Joy's condo was a five-storey block that stood deep down a narrow lane. On one side there was a stretch of wasteland, strewn with rubbish, waiting to be sold and developed; on the other, a bungalow that looked in need of repair. The parking lot in front was empty except for an old pickup van, and a small blue Toyota that she recognised as Joy's. Arunee was thankful that no media were there. She had already made up her mind to tell Sai to turn back if any journalists or television crews were hanging around the front. Relieved, she climbed out of the Mercedes and stood for a while looking up at the nondescript building, knowing that this was where her husband had often driven before heading to the office in the early morning after mumbling some feeble excuse and kissing her on the forehead.

It was Yai Li who answered the door and who almost jumped back on seeing her. Arunee said gently:

'I am sorry. I should have given you a warning.'

At that moment Joy appeared behind her grandmother and she too looked stunned by Arunee's presence.

'May I come in?' asked Arunee.

They both stood aside wordlessly, as though they had no choice but to accept her presence. Still without saying a word, Joy showed her guest to a seat by the window and Yai Li immediately went into the kitchen to make tea.

The two women sat for a long time looking out of the window at the cheaply built dwellings behind the condo and the tall trees dotted between them. The tension in the room was palpable. It was broken by Joy who suddenly began to sob into both her hands.

Arunee kept looking out as though she were unaffected by this show of emotion.

'You hate me,' Joy blurted when she finally stopped crying. 'And you have every right to.' Arunee now turned to stare at her for a while like a bird watching its prey. Then she spoke. 'I have come here to ask you one question. I have to know. Did you kill him?'

Their eyes were locked now. Joy slowly shook her head from side to side. Arunee continued to watch her intensely before saying:

'Then tell me exactly what happened.'

Yai Li decided not to disturb the two women. It was better to give them time to be alone together. Joy would call her when they finished their conversation. She could hear their muffled voices through the door but could only guess at what was passing between them. As she sat in the kitchen gazing out at the jagged skyline in the distance, she wondered why Arunee had come to see her granddaughter at all. She thought, at first, that it was to do her harm, to hit her or slap her, or worse. But it was obvious that she was wrong. She recognised no aggression in Arunee when she opened the door to her. She guessed that she was grieving for her husband and was looking for answers. But it seemed odd, nevertheless. What would this visit resolve? Perhaps Khun Chai had a hand in it. She thought of what he was going through after the loss of his son. Did he believe that Joy killed him? Was that why he had sent his daughter-in-law over? Should she herself try to see him and explain? Would he even want to see her at all? Did the friendship that they shared before Mitr's death count for anything? Or was it just a few weeks of contentment that she would never know again?

All these questions and uncertainties spiralled into her mind like dust whipped up by the wind. She did not try to come to any conclusions. All she knew was that she believed in her granddaughter and her version of what had taken place. This was all that mattered.

When Joy finally opened the kitchen door Yai Li was surprised to see that she was smiling.

'Khun Arunee is leaving now, Yai,' she said. 'She wanted to say goodbye to you.'

Yai Li said nothing but looked past Joy at Arunee still seated in the same position by the window. She felt that the energy had changed in that room. Something had lifted. It was the same sensation as when she felt a release in one of her patient's bodies.

Arunee got up and bowed to her respectfully with both hands.

'Thank you for helping my father-in-law,' she said. 'You have made a lot of difference to him, in more ways than one.'

These generous words touched Yai Li who bowed back at her. She was about to ask after Khun Chai but kept quiet.

'I am sure he misses you,' Arunee added. 'Perhaps we can arrange for you to come to see him again soon, to give him another treatment.'

After she left Joy turned to her grandmother and said simply:

'She believes me!'

Chapter 25

During the next two days, Yai Li was in a constant state of confusion and nervousness. When they were alone again Joy had explained to her grandmother everything that had passed between her and Arunee. She told her finally that Arunee wanted them to move into Baan Suan.

'What?! Are you serious?' She cupped both hands over her mouth after she cried out those words. It was a childhood habit.

'I know, Yai. I thought the same thing. It took me totally by surprise as well. She just said: 'You can't stay here. They won't leave you alone. They will make your life hell. Come to our house. You'll be better off there, and your grandmother can carry on giving treatments to Khun Chai.' Joy had told her about the journalists and TV crews being there every morning waiting to ask the same questions.

'We can't go anywhere. We have to depend on one of my neighbours to do the shopping for us. Luckily, she's on our side. By the afternoon they're gone. The news people, I mean. It's probably because they have to cover another scandal. Or they just get bored.'

They had both laughed at this and it was then, out of the blue, that Arunee had made the offer.

'Of course, it depends on Khun Chai,' she'd added. 'I will have to speak to him first about this. But I am sure he will agree.'

When Joy could still find no adequate response, Arunee went on.

'Just until the hearing's over and done with, and then you can come back here and get back to your own lives. It'll all be behind you before you know it. People's memories are short around here.'

When Joy finished recounting this to her grandmother she said:

'Well, Yai? What do you think? She seems sincere. It's just weird that's all. I mean, I would never have imagined her even thinking of being kind to us. She always seemed so cold and snobbish. In fact, I always thought she hated me.'

'Do you really think she really believed you?'

Joy looked at Yai Li with her expression of impatience.

'Well, Yai, that's what she said. I can only take her at her word. Why are you doubting that? What are you suspicious about? Do you think she wants to get us to Baan Suan and then lock us up there, and punish us in a dungeon? I'm sure they must have one there.'

Joy found her own words amusing.

'No,' said Yai Li. 'I just don't understand why she's doing this. That's all. I have never understood people.'

'So, would you come? '

Yai Li scratched her head. What she wanted to say to Joy was that she wished the whole mess were over so that she could go back to her shack in Jetsip Rai and take up her old life again.

'I will come because I want to make sure you are all right,' was what she actually said. 'And don't you want to see your friend again?' asked Joy.

'Which friend?' said Yai Li.

Joy rolled her eyes to the ceiling.

'Which friend?'

Yai Li's friend, as it turned out, was equally puzzled when he heard his daughter-in-law's proposal when they dined together that same evening. It had come at the end of the meal that had begun well enough as they sat opposite each other across the round marble table. Normally Mitr sat between them. Khun Chai had insisted on his place being laid and on bringing out the bottle of Veuve Clicquot La Grande Dame that they had brought back for him on their last trip to Paris.

'Well, who else am I going to drink this with?' he said to Arunee as they were sitting down.

'We might as well raise a glass to him since nothing will get him back.'

His voice broke as he spoke these last words, and Arunee walked round the table to put her arms round his shoulders.

When Samnieng, the serving girl, had scooped the rice onto their plates and put the dishes on the Lazy Susan, Khun Chai took the bottle out of the ice bucket, popped the cork and filled their glasses.

'He would have enjoyed this,' he said, after raising and clinking his glass with Arunee's and taking the first sip.

'Yes. I am sure he would,' she replied softly.

'Well? Is Joy innocent? Or do we make sure she gets a life sentence?'

Arunee took her time explaining to him what had happened in Joy's apartment that afternoon, and the conclusion she came to. He did not interrupt her but listened attentively until she had finished.

'But at what point were you convinced?'

'It wasn't anything specific that she said. It was the way she spoke. She was full of remorse about what happened. But she did not falter in the details. She was honest and open. She is not a criminal. I'm certain of that. There was nothing premeditated, and I would be the first to want to pin this on Joy if I had the least suspicion that she had planned to murder him.'

She paused for a long while, suddenly aware of the reality of Mitr's absence from the table, and from her life. She then said:

'A terrible accident has occurred, Pa. We've both lost someone we love. I know how much you must be grieving. But it was not her fault. Believe me.'

Khun Chai poured himself another glass and sipped it slowly before speaking.

'The prosecutor is saying that she pushed him. Apparently, they have new evidence. At least that's what the papers say. So, at the very least they are going for a charge of wilful manslaughter.'

'Poor Joy,' said Arunee with a sigh. 'She's already suffering. She does not deserve to go to jail.' This expression of empathy puzzled Khun Chai who took time to respond.

'I have to admit I am surprised by what you're telling me. Do you mean that you didn't mind?' 'That she was his mistress? Well, he didn't hide it from me. He never hid anything from me.' 'Were there others before her?'

'Oh, of course, quite a few over the years. But he dropped them very quickly. He got bored. I think he was genuinely fond of Joy. She was a cut above the others. I could see that. Well, he liked her efficiency, anyway.'

'I didn't think you were so modern in your thinking.'

Arunee laughed ironically.

'I think you mean traditional, Pa. Thai men have always felt an entitlement, haven't they? I remember hearing how Mitr's grandfather had a harem of young men and women. I just preferred it to be up front and not sneaky. No. What did annoy me were the excuses for going off to see her and spending time with her. I don't understand why he bothered. I guess it was out of politeness. But I told him from the beginning that it was up to him what he did, as long as he didn't make her pregnant.'

Khun Chai was on the point of asking why she and Mitr had decided not to have children, but he checked himself, feeling that this would have been prying into a corner he was not meant to enter. The year after they were married, Mitr had announced to him: 'Arunee doesn't want children,' with his usual finality. There was no explanation and he let be known by his expression and body language that there would be none forthcoming.

It was at this point that Arunee chose to tell her father-in-law about her idea of bringing Joy and Yai Li to stay in Baan Suan.

'What?! Are you serious?' exclaimed Khun Chai with the same words that Yai Li had used, spilling some of his champagne onto the front of his shirt.

'Yes, Pa. I am,' said Arunee. Khun Chai frowned.

'But how did you ever come to think of this? Have you asked them? And what did they say?' Arunee put up her hand to calm her father-in-law.

'I've just suggested it to Joy, that's all. Maybe I should have discussed it with you first. Of course, I should have. I am sorry. But I did not know how I was going to react to what Joy told me. When I'd heard her explanation, it just felt right. And they have said nothing. I told them it would depend on you, of course. And perhaps they won't want to come at all.'

'But…but…' was all Khun Chai could manage in response.

'It doesn't matter. You don't have to make any decisions now. No pressure to say yes or no. I just wanted to be open with you.'

Khun Chai took a long gulp of champagne.

'Well, I appreciate your frankness even if I don't quite understand your decision.' He paused and shifted in his chair before continuing. 'Now, since we're in the business of being open to each other I have something to tell you too.'

'Oh. What's that, Pa?'

'I am thinking of selling Baan Suan.'

If Arunee was surprised by this announcement she showed no sign of it. She raised her glass to her lips and took a small sip from it before saying softly:

'But Pa. Where would you go?'

Chapter 26

The media were there in full strength that morning outside the courthouse. In the days leading up to the hearing, attention had shifted from the main story, namely the circumstances surrounding the death of the director of Siam Estate to the fact that his mistress, the accused, was now apparently under the patronage of the deceased man's wife and living in their house. This new development caught them all off guard. The reason that they got wind of it was because of Joy's neighbour who, on being cornered on her way out of the condo one morning and asked as to how the accused and her grandmother were doing, replied offhandedly:

'How would I know? They left here two nights ago.' 'Where did they go?'

'They told me they were going to a place called Baan Suan. I don't know where that is, and I didn't ask. So please leave me alone.'

The journalist who posed the questions did not know where it was either. But when she returned to her office, one of her senior colleagues said:

'Wait a moment. That's the name of that old mansion belonging to Mitr's family. I'm sure it is. Up in the Pakret area.'

From then on, during the next week, the press corps had camped out in front of the main gates of Baan Suan but had no luck in obtaining any more information as there was no movement in or out of the mansion until the morning of the hearing.

Arunee's decision to accompany Joy to the court hearing was the result of a conversation between the four of them at dawn that morning. At first, all of them were going to attend. But Khun Chai's condition had worsened over the days before the hearing was to take place. Having become convinced of Joy's innocence, he was now stubbornly determined to see justice done.

'I don't care. I want to be there,' he kept repeating. But it was obvious that if he did attend, he would need to be wheeled into the courtroom.

It was Yai Li who intervened and said:

'You are in no fit state to do anything. I will stay here with you and give you a treatment.'

'But don't you want to be there yourself?' he asked.

'Of course, I do,' she said. 'But I know that Joy will be in good hands and that we will see her back here this afternoon.'

She was referring to what Arunee had told them the previous evening after a lengthy phone call with a cousin of her father who was a high court judge. He had nothing directly to do with the case. But he knew the officials who were going to preside at the hearing, and he assured her that the result would be favourable to Joy.

'Ha! Well done, Arunee. Corruption again. It's our Thai way, isn't it?' cried Khun Chai when he heard the news.

'Yes. You are right, Pa.' Arunee concurred. 'But sometimes corruption for the right reasons is better than injustice for all the wrong ones.'

'Well said. Very pragmatic.'

Yai Li did not follow the dialogue that followed, about laws and ethics and historical precedents. She was merely relieved to hear that there was a 99 per cent chance that her granddaughter would not have to be put on trial by jury and that within a day she could be officially declared innocent of any crime. This was why she felt no difficulty in sacrificing the opportunity to be there at the hearing with Joy.

As to Joy herself, she was still nervous even after hearing the reassuring news.

'But what happens if…?' she had begun to say when Arunee put a hand lightly on her arm.

'It's going to be fine. There's nothing to worry about.'

'But I've read that the prosecutor is bringing in that forensic expert.'

'Precisely,' said Arunee with a nod. 'That's why they will see that you are innocent.'

⊶❧ ⊶❧ ⊶❧

As soon as they climbed out of the car they were confronted with a chaotic scene. The crowd surged forward from all sides. Joy could hear her name being called out from behind by young voices and turned round to catch a group of schoolgirls in uniform standing with her old friend Nong Maew, holding up a banner on which was painted:

'We are with you, Pi Joy.'

She knew that they had been sent from the Mercy Centre to give her support. She held up a hand and waved to them. When she turned back, she saw that reporters and others were swarming over Arunee. One young man was shouting:

'Are you really protecting your husband's killer?'

The police were trying to hold everyone off but without much success. For a moment it looked like someone was going to be crushed. Joy glanced into the Mercedes and saw that Sai was sitting rigid and expressionless at the steering wheel. Fortunately, they were only a few steps from the entrance to the courthouse, and now Joy could see the lawyer from the centre coming out to greet them and pushing aside several people who were shooting a video.

She had already met with him twice, once at the remand centre where he had arranged for bail and another time in her apartment. He seemed a good, kind man but out of his depth in this public situation. He was more at home in the juvenile courts where he went regularly in his work for the Mercy Centre. She was glad that she had Arunee's solid presence by her side. In recent days her admiration and respect for this woman, who she had previously despised and been jealous of, and who had every right to be her enemy rather than her friend, had been growing in an unexpected way. She admired the effortless way that she achieved her goals. The confidence she exuded, curiously, reminded her of Mitr.

In the end, the whole court process took less than half an hour. It was pronounced that Mitr Thammawong, the CEO of Siam Estate, had died in an accident; death by misadventure as a result of his foothold slipping on the spilled alcohol on the terrace floor. This was the conclusion of the forensics expert. The notion presented by the prosecutor that he had been pushed violently against the railing was dismissed as speculation because there would have been contusions on his lower back as he hit the metal. But there were none. When the official verdict was finally pronounced, Joy and Arunee exchanged a meaningful glance across the crowded room.

⸺᪥, ⸺᪥, ⸺᪥,

Yai Li had given Khun Chai a treatment as soon as the others were out of the house. This had become the daily routine since her arrival at Baan Suan; once in the morning and another in the evening. Usually, the morning session was much later, when Khun Chai had finished his breakfast. But today was a special day and he had got only a few hours' sleep. The aches too were more acute that morning.

'It must be the stress that I am feeling,' he commented when they began the session.

She did not answer him because she felt that it was something other than just stress that was the cause of the pains that he was suffering. She had already noticed that in the intervening weeks when they had not seen one another, he had lost considerable weight. From the outside this suited him as it made him look a little more handsome but on the other hand, the first time that she touched his skin again she knew that something was wrong with his internal energy, his *lom*. Her father had taught her how to listen to this wind (*fang lom*) and to recognise the signs of heat and cold and damp. She had said nothing to him, but she knew that she would have to, eventually.

That morning, after their session, they had watched Arunee and Joy arriving at the courthouse on the television set that Sai had set up for them in the bedroom. There was no coverage of what went on inside, only the comments of the woman journalist standing outside with the crowd, reporting the event. After listening to a few of her comments, Khun Chai decided to mute the sound.

'I don't want to hear how they are going to try to milk this. It's bad enough losing my son.' He choked on his words as he said this and Yai Li spontaneously reached over and touched his hand.

'I am so glad you are here.' he told her after a while. 'I needed you near me. But I didn't know if we could ever meet again after what's happened. But Arunee was right to invite you and Joy here.'

'Will you ever really forgive her?'

'Your granddaughter? Yes. Even though I wanted, and still want to blame someone for Mitr's death. That's how we are. We can deal with our grief better if we can point a finger away from our pain. But I accept that it was an accident, and I hope they do too.'

Yai Li looked at him and smiled.

'You're a decent man.' She kept her hand on his. 'But you've been sad all your life.'

Khun Chai bowed his head and stared down at his feet. He looked like a little boy whose secret has been discovered. Then slowly he looked up.

'You too. You carry such pain. I think that's why we get on so well.'

Yai Li now withdrew her hand from his.

'I have often wanted to feel healed, and to be at peace.'

Khun Chai chuckled.

'Well, it's too late now. Seems like we're two old, sad people who have found one another.'

They both laughed.

When the image on the television began to show the journalist stepping back into the crowd to allow the camera a clearer view of the entrance to the building Khun Chai unmuted the sound. When they saw Arunee and Joy emerging through the door with smiles on their faces, they turned to each other and nodded quietly.

'*Sathu*,' said Yai Li as she raised her hands up to the sky.

'Let's not go straight home,' said Arunee when they were driving away from the courthouse.

'They'll be waiting for us at the gates. They are not going to let us off the hook this easily.'

'Whatever you like,' said Joy. 'I am just so relieved not to be wearing handcuffs and led to a cell.'

Arunee told Sai to take them across the river to the Phra Pradaeng district. Then, turning to Joy:

'There's a place I want to show you. And we can do a little ceremony of thanks there. Would you like that?'

After over an hour's drive through heavy traffic they crossed the Chao Phraya, swollen after the heavy monsoon rains, its greeny brown water glinting in the blistering sunshine like the back of a water snake. It was an area of Bangkok that Joy had never been to, and it looked as though it belonged to another age, forgotten by the developers. There was more greenery here than in the rest of the city and an absence of high-rise blocks. They turned down a dusty road and reached a simple two-storey house surrounded by a small, leafy garden. At the entrance there was a sign painted in bright colours saying: Mudita House.

Joy could see that there was a group of about a dozen women waiting to greet them as they turned into the carpark, and guessed that Arunee had texted them that they were coming. Most of the women were young, around her age, but there were several who must have been in their fifties or even older. They held their hands together in greeting when Joy and Arunee stepped out of the car.

'I'll introduce them later,' said Arunee. 'Let's go and say our thanks first.'

It seemed to Joy that everything had been carefully prepared, as though the outcome of her case was already a foregone conclusion for Arunee, and this was the final act to complete the successful process she had just executed. A gardener led them and the group in silence into the back garden where, in front of the elaborate wooden house spirit shrine, there were flowers in a vase, incense burning, candles lit, and a pig's head on a silver tray surrounded by small dishes of cooked food and fruits.

Joy, who had grown up in the Mercy Centre run by Catholics, had never seen such a spectacle before. Once or twice, she and her companions had been taken to the local temple, Wat Saphaan to learn how to meditate with the abbot. The Catholic father, who was broad minded and considered a maverick by the other Catholic priests in

Thailand thought that this would help them cope with all the traumas they had known in their young lives. In his opinion it was better than psychotherapy, and he held no prejudices against the Buddhists apart from the fact that they did not believe in Jesus Christ or Mary the Mother of God. His tolerance extended to the point of not minding that the abbot insisted on the students bowing to the Buddha statue before beginning the meditation session. In any case, this would be compensated by their attendance of Mass the following Sunday. But despite this exposure to Buddhism, the more exotic, eclectic aspects of the religion were practically unknown to her. Naturally, she had seen the house spirits dotted all over the city, in the entrances outside the big skyscrapers and hotels, in people's gardens, including Baan Suan where there was an old one tucked away in a far corner by the swimming pool. It was visited only by the older servants who would light a candle or a stick of incense from time to time. She knew it was part of the culture, although she could never relate it to the dry practice that she learned from the abbot of Wat Saphaan. Mitr himself had made a point of not having one built in the Cha-am condo. 'I can't stand all that superstition,' he'd told her on more than one occasion. 'People waste so much time and money on that mumbo jumbo in our country.'

His words came back to her now as she saw Arunee approaching the shrine, and putting her hands together before touching the tray on which the pig's head stood, as a gesture of offering. She wondered if this had ever been a point of contention between her and her husband. After she bowed, Arunee turned to Joy and motioned her to do the same, which Joy did, as she presumed this was the act of gratitude that Arunee had mentioned earlier. Later, when they were in the house being served soft drinks, Arunee told her:

'This is a very powerful site, and the house spirit here is well known. It's not just me coming to ask for a good outcome. Others do so too. But you must always fulfil what you promise, as well as making an offering.'

'And what did you promise?' asked Joy.

Arunee smiled.

'That's between me and the house spirit. But the offering, of course was so that you would be free. Today. So, aren't you happy?'

Arunee introduced Joy to the women who were being housed there in the centre. They were from different walks of life, all of them from the bottom end of the social strata. Half of them had been sex workers. They had all suffered violent abuse. The house mother, a big strong woman in her fifties the women called Pi Matana, explained to Joy how they were usually contacted by the police, or a neighbour of the victim, or a social worker.

'It's all really by word of mouth. The ones who land up here are lucky. There's a lot of violence out there. Men are crazy these days and the drugs they take are getting weirder every year.' Joy could see for herself how damaged some of the women were. Having known violence herself, she felt an immediate empathy with them.

'Sometimes when they get here, they are so hurt that they can't talk for weeks or months.'

She explained that they had a team of psychologists to help.

'But loving kindness is the best medicine in the end,' she said. 'And Khun Arunee is amazing in that respect.'

Later, in the car on the way back to Baan Suan, Joy found herself in a state of turmoil. It was such an intense day. Only that morning she was still uncertain about what was going to happen to her. Now after the visit to Mudita House what she had just seen and heard still remained with her, reminding her of her childhood at the Mercy Centre, and the girls there who had suffered abuse and had miraculously been rescued or escaped from their tormentors. The most deeply wounded ones never really recovered. Some would fly into fits of rage for no reason and try to hurt whoever was nearby. Compared to them she had nothing to complain about except that her mother was dying from Aids and her grandmother could not take care of her. These were things that she had buried in her heart never thinking that she would ever have to go back there. But the visit to Mudita House had stirred up all these unpleasant memories.

They were on the big bridge again crossing over from Thonburi. She stared out of the window and tried to make her mind blank. At that moment she felt the back of her hand being gently touched. Quickly pulling it away she turned round in surprise.

'Sorry,' said Arunee. 'I didn't mean to disturb your thoughts. You were far away. Are you OK?' The look in Arunee's eyes was friendly, inviting conversation. But for Joy it was still too strange to be sitting by the side of the wife of her ex-lover. Although a part of her felt that she could trust Arunee, Joy still held back from opening to her completely. She did not want to talk about what was upsetting her. She smiled and said:

'Tell me about the pig's head.'

Chapter 27

In the end they decided on a small intimate ceremony for Mitr to be held in a modest temple near Don Muang, called by the locals Wat Dok, where, before she died Khun Chai's grandmother had built a row of *kutis* to house the monks. No one in either the family circles or the business environment in which Mitr had many acquaintances was informed. This was Khun Chai's wish.

'I don't want it to be a circus,' he said firmly. 'Only us and the people in the house.'

So, on that swelteringly hot afternoon in late October, in contrast to the elaborate affair at Pansak's ceremony, there were just two rows of white plastic chairs in the courtyard of the *sala* where the simple wooden coffin stood. Arunee had arranged for Mitr's corpse to be transferred to the temple in secrecy so that the press would not try to attend the ceremony. Even though the case was officially closed there was still interest in the story. It seemed that neither the public nor some of the journalists were satisfied with the outcome. Their appetite for a good scandal had been aroused but not yet sated. Interest was now focused on the relationship between Arunee and Joy, with some of the tabloids hinting at their possible complicity in Mitr's demise. At any rate, the truth no longer mattered. The Press wanted to pursue the story to its most lurid conclusion, which was why the family had decided that a quick, simple ceremony was the best option.

The seats in the front were occupied by Khun Chai, Arunee, Yai Li and Joy. Behind them sat Sai, his wife, Pao with her arm around their son Toh, who was visibly disturbed, Mae Hom, Samnieng, and the rest of the servants. There were twelve people attending in all. The space around them was empty except for the mangy looking dogs trying to shelter from the fierce sunlight and a lottery seller resting under a mimosa in the far corner near the entrance where the cars were parked.

Just as the monks were beginning their chanting, the figure of a man appeared at the front gates. He stood for a while peering in before walking slowly past the lottery seller towards where they were sitting. He wore a loose checked shirt, his trousers looked threadbare, and his sandals worn down. A plain shoulder bag was slung over his right arm. When he got closer, he looked around him, found a chair from the side, drew it over and sat behind the servants. At this point only Arunee, among those in the front row, had caught sight of him, and she wondered who he was and what he was doing there uninvited. She also noticed that there was some movement behind her when he sat down, and she caught some of them looking round at this stranger in their midst with bemused expressions.

After the monks finished their chanting, they all walked up to the coffin. Khun Chai, Arunee and Joy were wiping tears from their eyes. Yai Li was holding Khun Chai's arm, supporting his unsteady steps, when she heard someone crying behind her. It was Toh, Sai's son whom she had only seen at a distance as he had not come near her since she arrived at Baan Suan. Now, close up, she saw that he was a muscular boy with the figure of an athlete. He was crying softly at first but soon he began to wail like a wounded animal and the sound of his distress found response in the temple dogs that started howling in unison at that moment. Sai was quick to put his arms round his son and lead him away towards the parked cars.

The lay helpers in the temple did their work efficiently in sliding the coffin into the furnace and everyone went back to their seats while the monks continued to chant. Soon they could see the smoke rising from the chimney of the temple roof.

'Is that all we are?' muttered Khun Chai continuing to dab his eyes.

At that point, the stranger who had arrived at the ceremony stepped forward. Khun Chai had not noticed his presence till now and he was taken aback. Before he had time to say anything the man went down on his knees and, putting his hands together, prostrated himself, bowing his head onto the ground in front of Khun Chai. When he straightened up, he said:

'I am sorry for the loss of your son who I never had the chance to meet. I have come to beg your forgiveness, Khun Chai. I was brought up by your father who looked after my own father and mother. I repaid you with my bad Karma. I have done you and your family wrong, and I would like to make amends. I say this before the corpse of your son who is being cremated in that coffin behind me.'

Khun Chai at first found no words to respond to this obviously rehearsed speech. He could only sit staring into the sad, tired eyes of this man he had once known but would not have recognised if he passed him in the street. Now he saw that it was Nai Jit, the foreman's son who had played with him when he was a small boy and taught him how to do Muay Thai and kick the soft young banana trees in order to strengthen his shins – the same Nai Jit who later helped to cheat his father and who ended up as the monk Phra Jetana whom he had read about a few weeks earlier. This same person, who had once been strong and wiry, now had short cropped grey hair and a face so lined it looked like the shrivelled skin of a persimmon that had been left to dry in the sun. Finally, Khun Chai said:

'Are you here to ask for my help?'

The man, still with his hands together, looked down at the ground before raising his gaze once more to meet Khun Chai's. 'I am.'

There was really no need to have another servant in Baan Suan. The house, the grounds, the washing and cleaning, the cooking and the serving were all taken care of and there were two chauffeurs to drive the cars.

'But are you sure you want to take him in, Pa, after all that he's done?' asked Arunee when they were back in Baan Suan.

Khun Chai shrugged his shoulders in a gesture of resignation.

'He seems to be genuinely contrite, and he looks like a broken man. And he did this in front of my son's coffin. How can I not help him?'

'Well, I don't know about that. But he certainly has nowhere else to go and no one else to turn to. He told you as much, didn't he?'

'Yes. He said that after they kicked him out of the temple no charges were pressed. The police accepted his version. He went to stay with some old relatives in Korat. But they didn't want him to be there more than a few weeks. Nobody he knew before wants to have anything to do with him now. It's pitiful. He's brought it on himself.'

'And you who lost the most, want to help him,' said Arunee with a laugh. 'Mitr always told me that he thought you were either the most compassionate person he knew, or a complete and utter sucker.'

'Or both,' said Khun Chai now laughing too.

'It's your decision, Pa. I leave it up to you.'

This was how Khun Chai decided that Nai Jit, as he would now once again be called, be given the job of guardian, which meant that he was responsible, both day and night, for vetting the people entering and leaving Baan Suan, including all the employees and tradesmen. In fact, they had been thinking of hiring someone to do this ever since the press had tried to invade the property during the whole court process. There were still some who tried to get into the property with the intention of taking pictures or interviewing members of the staff. Nai Jit's job was to prevent this happening. He was given the old shack where the porter lived, in the days when he would open the gates to the carriages, and the same salary as the others in the household. But before formally telling Nai Jit all of this, he called him to the balcony once more and asked him:

'Are you still taking drugs? Because if you are, you can't stay here.'

Nai Jit swore that when he was expelled from the temple, he gave up taking Yaa Ba for good. 'It's an evil drug,' he said. 'I thought it would help to keep me young. I was wrong. It destroys so many lives. It has destroyed mine.'

Khun Chai saw no reason not to believe him. He saw his decision to accept Nai Jit back into Baan Suan as an act of homage to his old nurse Na Cheua who was forever going on about forgiveness being the most important and difficult to attain of all our human qualities. It was also a good way to 'tamboon', to do a good deed and transfer the merit to his late son, Mitr. He was unaware that his act of kindness would be repaid in a way neither he nor Nai Jit could have foreseen.

Chapter 28

The funeral ceremony at Wat Dok was like a truce offered by the press out of respect to the family of the dead man. It was the only day they did not have to navigate their way through a phalanx of reporters camped out in front of the entrance to the house. But as soon as it was over, it, was business as usual, although there were now visibly fewer of them. Even after Joy was officially absolved from all criminal charges the interest in the story lingered on. It seemed that the tabloids were not going to let their readers be satisfied with the outcome of the investigation and the official closure of the case. There had been several articles in the more popular tabloids hinting that Arunee and Joy had planned Mitr's demise together, and the court's verdict did nothing to end this speculation.

The original plan was for Yai Li to return to Klongtoey and Joy to her apartment in Bang Na when the dust had settled, and the court case was behind them. But Yai Li heard from Mae Da and other acquaintances that there were journalists continually hanging around Jetsip Rai asking questions about her and even pestering the girls at the Mercy Centre to give them any information on Joy. Meanwhile, they also learned through Joy's neighbour that there were cars parked permanently outside the condo in Bang Na with journalists waiting to catch a glimpse of Joy and interview her. In the lane outside the gates of Baan Suan, apart from the reporters there were strangers lurking throughout the day on the off chance of taking a photo of anyone coming in and out of the property, including the people who worked there. Even a simple shopping trip to the local market by the cook and one of the servants was like running the gauntlet.

They decided that the best tactic was to stay as quiet as possible.

'Don't worry. They will soon have had enough,' said Khun Chai. 'I've seen it before. It's our national pastime. We're a nation of hungry ghosts. The important thing is to give them nothing to chew on. They will just get tired and eventually move on.'

In spite of these words, Khun Chai himself was not counting on them being left alone for some time. There were factors that made their situation a little more interesting to the public than usual; Mitr's high profile when he was alive as a businessman and would-be politician, the fact that Arunee was the daughter of the late public figure, Pansak, and his own name, which still had significance for those who had read his books and articles over the years. But most important of all was what a well-known female journalist was focusing on in her spicy articles: the relationship between the wife and the mistress. She had an enormous following on her social media and this was what was keeping the whole story lubricated.

There was, unsurprisingly, a siege atmosphere in Baan Suan. If it had not been for the size of the house and garden, which meant that they had all the space to themselves that they needed, the sense of claustrophobia might have been intolerable. After the first unsuccessful attempts by Sai to drive Arunee to her work without being noticed, they decided to explore other options. It was Sai who came up with an idea that impressed them for its creativity.

Behind the house there was a wide canal that wound its way through that whole area and eventually joined with the river in Pakret. In former times it had been a conduit used by the local farmers to take their produce to the market and to trade with other country people, which meant a constant stream of small boats laden with fruit and vegetables going up and down the *klong* every day from morning till dusk. But gradually the transport by pickup and motorcycles became more convenient and as the years went by there was less and less traffic on the canal. Meanwhile, with the increasing pollution due to a lack of ecological planning and the rapid development of the city, the waters of the canal had become black and acidic. The local children no longer dived in from the rickety wooden piers. The monitor lizards and the snakes no longer appeared on its banks with the same regularity as before. The locals avoided using the path that skirted it because of the toxic stench that frequently exuded from the surface. The family that had bought Baan Suan off Khun Chai had built a high concrete wall along the whole side of the property that bordered the canal, to stop people using the canal path and peering into Baan Suan. But because some of the servants liked to use the path to go out to the local village nearby, they had a small discreet wooden door built into the wall. During the intervening years the wall became covered in thick bougainvillea, wild vines and morning glory that intertwined to make it a thick layer of greenery in which all kinds of creatures made their homes. Apart from cutting the grass patch in front Nai Wang, the gardener left this thick wall alone, his reasoning being that it discouraged any would-be robbers from trying to come over.

'They wouldn't get through the thorns,' he was fond of saying. 'Anyway, a snake or a scorpion would sting them before they were halfway over.'

The door, unused for so long, was now hidden under all this thick growth.

It was Sai, who suggested that they reclaim it. So, with his help, Nai Wang hacked down the plants until, after the long years of neglect, the gnarled wooden door was revealed again. There was still a lock on it, but it had rusted over the years, and besides no one could remember where the key was kept. With great care, using crowbars, they finally managed to heave it open without causing too much damage.

Another part of Sai's solution to the problem of how to leave Baan Suan unnoticed involved opening the old boat house, which had also been left abandoned in a far corner of the garden next to the back wall. A long, hand-crafted boat specially used to ferry important guests to and from the pier in Pakret in Khun Luang Paiboon's time and later the card players in Wigrom's was still lying on the teak wooden slats.

'They really knew what they were doing in those days,' said Sai as they dragged the boat out into the sunlight for the first time in years.

'They must have used special varnish on everything. Look. Only some woodworm here and there. Nai Wang and I can easily fix that.' His idea was that if Khun Chai or Arunee, Joy or her grandmother needed to get out of Baan Suan unnoticed they could be taken across the canal in the boat and picked up in the lane beyond the patch of wasteland on the other side.

'But they would see you leaving the front gates,' Khun Chai objected when he had heard Sai's plan.

'Of course, they would see me driving, Nai. But Samnieng or one of the others would be with me. It would look like we were going to the supermarket or something. They're not interested in us. We're just the servants. I would drop them off and then fetch you or Khun Arunee.'

'Well. It's worth a try,' said Khun Chai, surprised and pleased at Sai's ingenuity.

This was how Arunee managed to be smuggled out without being pestered by the vultures at the gates of Baan Suan and driven over to Mudita House in Phra Pradaeng. The first trial run, as they called it, went off without a hitch. It was before her second journey out that Joy came up to her and asked if she could join her.

'I am getting a little stir crazy in here,' she said. 'I'd like to do something a bit more useful than sitting around watching television all day.'

'Of course,' Arunee replied. 'I was going to invite you. But I wasn't sure you'd want to come.'

Over the following weeks a routine was established. At around seven in the morning the two women would leave by the back gate. Fad, Sai's cousin and Samnieng's husband, would take them to the other side in the boat and leave it moored to the small pier that he had repaired on the day Sai and the gardener cleaned and mended the boat. Sai, having taken either the cook or Samnieng to the market, would be waiting with the blue Mercedes to drive them to Phra Pradaeng.

Usually, at that early hour when he left the front gates, Sai would notice that the lane in front of Baan Suan was practically empty. The journalists and their teams tended to arrive a little later. He constantly wondered out loud to Mae Hom, his mother, why they felt so motivated to do this day in day out when there was no story that he could think of worth telling. But then his wife, Pao, who read the newspapers and heard the gossip in the market would remind him that it was the relationship between Khun Arunee and Khun Joy that everyone was talking about. Could they be guilty of plotting Khun Mitr's death? This, she told him, was what everyone was talking about.

Sai was indignant when he heard this for the first time and angry with his wife for even contemplating it. Nevertheless, during the car journeys to Phra Pradaeng he would look into the rear mirror more frequently than usual, in order to catch any signs of complicity between the two women sitting close to one another in the back seat, and he would try his best to listen in to their conversation, although the antiquated, noisy air conditioning system of the old car made this difficult. After he returned home with them in the afternoon, his wife would turn to him and say:

'Well?' with a look of expectation in her eyes.

But Sai would shrug and reply: 'Nothing special. They went to work and came back. That's all.'

After the first week he grew tired of this kind of conversation and impatient with his wife.

'I don't want to hear any more of this nonsense,' he said firmly.' 'You've got it all wrong. You can enjoy the gossip with your mates in the market if you want. But don't get me to join in with you. I am not going to play that game.'

In fact, Pao did not get it entirely wrong.

The journeys to and from Mudita House were life changing for both women, who always sat in the same place; Joy directly behind Sai, and Arunee behind the empty front seat. On the first drive back to Baan Suan, Joy, looking at the back of Sai's head, said:

'I will never be able to express my gratitude to you enough. Today I felt good for the first time in a very long time.'

She did not say what she really meant, which was that she had never in her life felt a sense of well-being like that. Not that anything special had happened that day. They had enjoyed crossing the canal in the morning and had arrived at Mudita House still giggling about how Sai's strategy had worked so seamlessly, and they had escaped the attentions of the hungry crowd at the gates of Baan Suan. Then, while Arunee went to the office to take care of the paperwork for the Foundation,

Joy wandered around talking to the women and helping in the kitchen until it was time to leave in the early afternoon. She had done exactly what Arunee had suggested:

'Just hang out with them. Make friends. There's nothing more than that to do around here.' It all reminded her of her childhood in the Mercy Centre in Jetsip Rai. That's what they used to do; hang out and talk. But those days did not hold good memories. They were too intense for her, not just because her mother was lying in a bed nearby, dying from Aids, but because she found no way of fitting in with anyone. The others talked to her but never in the relaxed way that they did with each other. She herself could never relax. Part of it was the attention she received by being a *loog kreung*, and pretty, and the pressure of having to live up to this special status she had. She wanted to be accepted and to be the same as everyone else, but she remained constantly on the outside, and this led her to reject most of her companions and to focus on trying to get out of there as soon as she could. Her academic success had been motivated by this desire to escape as soon as possible from that environment.

But there in Mudita House it felt as though she was being given a second chance to feel part of a community, to belong, to be of use, and to be accepted just for who she was. This all happened on that first day.

At her remark Arunee merely nodded before saying softly:

'I know.'

By the third trip to Mudita House, they were already discussing what more Joy could do to help some of the women who had been so badly hurt that they found it hard to communicate with the others.

'I know them from my childhood. I have lived with them. They feel worthless, soiled. They need to regain respect for themselves. Loving care is not enough.'

She told Arunee how at the Mercy Centre she had taken part in the dance and music sessions every weekend. A generous Irish donor paid for young professionals to go there and teach the kids how to play both traditional and modern instruments and dancers to teach them how to do both classical dance and hip hop.

'This is what is needed at Mudita House,' she told Arunee excitedly. 'You see, they have to interact with others, and they also need to discover their creativity. The more they interact and the more they learn, the quicker they will regain their self-confidence.'

Arunee agreed.

'We will do something like that. Straightaway. You are amazing, Joy.'

As she said this she had reached across the seat and placed her hand on Joy's. This time Joy did not pull away but flipped it over and held Arunee's. Long afterwards, they would remind each other that this was the beginning.

Sai had no inkling that all this was going on literally behind his back. There was nothing particularly interesting in their exchange that he could detect. Apart from the fact that he found it confusing at the beginning to be driving his ex-boss's wife and his mistress, and to see that there was no animosity between them, he found that their behaviour was perfectly normal and irreproachable.

'They are polite to one another,' he would explain to his wife. 'They talk about the work in Mudita House. That's all they do.'

He could not have guessed that, by some unspoken agreement, the two women had decided that whatever passed between them would not give rise to any further speculation. They were both already aware of what was being written about them in a growing number of newspapers. Some of these articles were direct comments on the official verdict being influenced by extraneous factors – a coded way of saying that it was a case of corruption. Others that alluded to the strange relationship between ex-wife and ex-mistress even included cartoon illustrations. As a result, at home in Baan Suan, they kept their distance with one another except at mealtimes when they would exchange polite conversation. Even in Mudita House, they treated one another like working colleagues, and often Joy was reminded of the way that she and Mitr had behaved in public. It was only in the back of the Mercedes, when they were being driven to and from Mudita House that they permitted any intimate verbal interchange to take place, and even then, they both maintained a stiff, almost blank expression as they shared increasingly personal details, and, as if by instinct they always kept the tone of their voice at a pitch that was drowned by the whirr of the air conditioning, so that Sai was never able to pick up any significant detail that was exchanged between them.

It was on one such ride, coming home that Arunee said:

'Did you love my husband?'

They had been talking about people who professed to be in love and yet were capable of being cruel and violent to the supposed object of their love, the way that some of the women's partners had been.

'No,' said Joy spontaneously, then took her time to add: 'I was in love with what he represented, I think. Power.'

Arunee nodded in silence as she digested Joy's answer. She thought that some of her father's mistresses would have said the same thing.

'Did *you* love your husband?' Joy then said.

Arunee turned and flashed a look that made Joy unsure if it expressed anger or merely surprise. She immediately shook her head and muttered:

'Forgive me. I had no right to ask you that.'

'Oh, but you have every right,' said Arunee having recovered her composure and directing her gaze through the front window once more. 'And the honest answer to your question is: yes and no.'

'What do you mean?'

'I mean that I was never in love with him. It was him who kept coming after me, when I was a student. I still don't really understand why. There were so many others to choose from. Perhaps it had something to do with my being a powerful man's daughter, or something like that. I'll never know. Anyway, he was so insistent. He would not be denied. He just had to win me. In the end I gave in. But love? I suppose when you spend so many years sharing a life with someone there's a connection that you can call love.'

Joy wanted to ask more, but she was unsure of how far she could go. She decided that it was better not to pursue any further. She did not want to offend. It was Arunee who continued to speak, in the same low dispassionate voice, without turning to her companion.

'We were not suited at all. At the beginning of our marriage, he told me he wanted children. But I could not have any. We considered adopting. We even thought of doing an IVF treatment. I wanted to make him happy. But soon I realised that the idea of not having a child was not really an issue for him. His work always came before anything else. He was an ambitious man. You must have seen that. He had big dreams. To make more and more money. To turn Bangkok into the best city in Southeast Asia. I think he was aiming to run the country one day.'

'He might have been brilliant at it,' Joy could not help interjecting, remembering how much she had admired his decisiveness and clarity in his business dealings.

'Or a complete disaster,' said Arunee with a chuckle. 'He would have governed us like a CEO. And we've seen where that has led before.'

By now they had reached their destination. Joy was glad that their conversation had ended on that light-hearted note. But there were still so many more questions that she wanted to put to Arunee about the man with whom both had been involved.

Chapter 29

Yai Li was worried about the way Khun Chai was deteriorating. His weight loss was starting to be perceptible. His eyes were often yellow and liverish. He himself insisted that he had never been better in a long time. It was true that since he began receiving regular treatment from her, he was moving with more ease and complained less about his aches and pains. But her hands told her another story. When she touched him, she sensed that his energy, his *lom*, was weakening. Once or twice during a session he had fallen into a deep slumber and woken up without knowing where he was, until she gently reminded him. Often, while she held her hand over his kidney area, she could see the colour of his skin changing to a dullish grey. These were all signs that her father had taught her to look out for.

She shared none of this with him, even when he pressed her:

'Well. How do you find me?' He would often ask anxiously when they finished. She would shrug and answer evasively:

'How do you feel?'

At this he would wag a finger at her, and say with a smile:

'You're a crafty one.'

The friendship that had been established between them before Mitr's death had not only been restored since Yai Li and Joy came to stay in Baan Suan, but bloomed gently and steadily like a flower during the weeks that they were in daily proximity. The sense of shared confinement added to the feeling of complicity between them. The treatments took place every couple of days and normally in the morning, after Khun Chai's breakfast and lasted for no more than an hour. Usually, Yai Li would have a long rest afterwards and leave Khun Chai to do his scribbling or read his thick book. They would then meet for a late light lunch before spending the afternoon together on the balcony. During the first weeks after Yai Li and Joy's arrival in Baan Suan these meetings were often silent, with Yai Li doing her crochet work – something she had learned in the community centre at Jetsip Rai – and Khun Chai reading the newspaper or his Chekov short stories. They were a picture of calm contentment. On finding them like this one afternoon when she returned from Mudita House, Joy had remarked:

'Why, you look like a couple who have been married for years, if you don't mind me saying so.'

Gradually they began to talk about things that Khun Chai brought up. For it was he who always initiated the conversation as though, at a certain point the silence became uncomfortable for him. And he would often begin the exchange by saying:

'Do you think…?'

The first time this occurred Yai Li quickly interrupted him:

'I've told you before. I am not a thinker, unlike you. I haven't been educated. You can do the thinking.' And he laughed.

'But you have opinions, don't you? You can't deny it. I want to hear them. All of them.'

They began to talk about everything; subjects ranging from the state of the economy to the ecological disasters to ghosts and UFOs. The television that Sai had installed for them to follow the news of the court case had been left in Khun Chai's room and what they watched on it became the source of many of their discussions; they found that they concurred more often than disagreed, which surprised them both.

Once, out of the blue, he asked her:

'Have you ever taken drugs?'

She giggled and shook her head vigorously.

'I have,' he told her. 'I used to smoke ganja when I was young. I still have the bong. And I once took LSD, a very long time ago.'

Yai Li shrugged. She had never heard of it.

'I took it with my friend Mac, and with Pia, that girl who I told you about.' 'And what happened?'

'Well, I learned that we only see and hear and sense in a partial way. We miss so much that's going on. We're too stuck in our rational minds. The drug opened up a new dimension for me. I saw that reality is not what it seems. It's far richer than what we think we know.'

He smiled now at his recollection of that day in Klongtoey.

'I could have told you that without taking anything,' said Yai Li. Khun Chai nodded.

'Yes. But you see, I didn't have, and won't ever have, your wisdom.'

Over those long afternoons, waiting for the two women to return from their work, they eventually got round to talking about their past once more. It was a continuation of the previous conversations during the dinners at restaurants and meals shared before Mitr's death. But now it was as if they were exploring these issues in depth, like archaeologists taking time to brush away the dust and examine the details of their find. They opened up to one another like old friends making a last stab at understanding the journeys they had been through. Yai Li started shyly at first, but she felt she could trust him completely, and seeing that she had an eager listener who was genuinely interested and who gave her all the time in the world to tell her stories, she shared with him the pain and unhappiness that she had known, the worries and the disappointments, the grief and regrets, in a way that she had never expressed to another human before. To finally have the opportunity to put these recollections into words gave her a sense of liberation, like ice melting from her heart.

Khun Chai, for his part, reciprocated her openness and honesty by telling her in detail of his own past, from his through childhood in Baan Suan with an alcoholic father, through the strangeness of being in a boarding school in England with all its codes, to his tortuous journey up to the present. He, too, found that this sharing of his life story brought about a sense of relief, a lightness that he could feel in body and mind. It was more than unburdening. As he took her back with him in time, he was discovering a kind of direct insight into his past. Patterns were revealing themselves that he had not discerned before.

Once, a journalist who had read all his novels and short stories had asked him what the underlying theme of his writing was, and he had told her:

'To get to the truth.'

'By making up the past?'

'It's the only way I know,' he'd said at the time, and it was an honest reply.

But he saw now that there was another way and that was to verbally recount his experiences as truthfully as possible to someone who would truly listen without judgement – not a professional listener like a therapist who would analyse his words, but a friend who would simply be present to receive them. In Yai Li he had finally found that person. She was becoming the guardian of his life's story, as he was of hers.

On one occasion, during another of these intimate conversations, he had remarked:

'It's strange, isn't it? If my friend Mac hadn't been killed in an accident, my life would have been completely different. I'd have been writing film scripts and making films with him.'

'But you can't think like that. There's no "might have been" or "could have been". Things happen the way they happened,' Yai Li replied.

'Of course, you are right. We can't change the past.' He paused. 'Do you think it's all destined then?'

'You mean do I think it's all mapped out for us? I don't know. Sometimes I do, sometimes I don't. But I have always felt that I had little choice. My father, for instance. Or what happened in London. Or my husband, or daughter. No, none of it. Not this either. Otherwise, how would we be sitting here talking to one another?'

'So, if it's all beyond us then we might as well surrender.'

'No. I think there's one thing that's in our power.'

'And what is that?'

'We can choose how we live through what happens to us.' Khun

Chai sat thoughtfully, digesting her words for a long while. 'So, we both chose to be sad,' he said finally.

She held his challenging gaze.

'I am learning not to be sad anymore.' Khun Chai nodded gently. 'So am I.' he replied.

One morning at five o'clock, Khun Chai made his way from his side of the house, through the ballroom and into the corridor on the other side of it. He was headed for the three bedrooms there; tastefully decorated, all of them with their own ensuite bathrooms that were kept for house guests. Over the years, Mitr and Arunee had people from abroad staying from time to time. These were old friends they had known since their student days, or families who had looked after them or befriended them when they studied abroad and who were on a visit to Bangkok. But gradually they stopped inviting them to Baan Suan, since neither of them had the time or inclination to entertain. Instead, they would arrange for these old acquaintances to stay in a hotel in town on the river. As a result, the rooms had been empty for years.

When Joy and Yai Li moved into Baan Suan, Arunee insisted that they should occupy them, and Khun Chai had made no objections.

'At last, someone's going to use them again,' he said.

Khun Chai stood still for a while. At the end of the corridor the French windows led out to the west side of the house, where there was a patch of lawn and beyond that the servants' quarters. A faint light was appearing through the glass, enough for him to see several pairs of shoes placed outside the door of one of the rooms. He thought that he could make out the shiny patent leather slip-ons that Yai Li had worn to their first meeting all those months back. He approached the door hesitantly, still uncertain if he was going to make the final step of entering through it.

The previous evening, at the dinner table, they had talked of how nearly all the journalists who had been camped outside the front gate had disappeared. The newspapers that morning had featured on their front pages the story of the teenage son of one of the politicians in the ruling party accused of killing his gay lover. The young man subsequently went into hiding before he could be apprehended. Overnight, this had replaced all the other ongoing scandals.

'I think that, possibly, we can begin to relax,' said Arunee. 'They might leave us alone now.'

'And about time,' Joy added. 'What do you think, Yai?'

Yai Li finished her mouthful and said:

'Does this mean I can go back to Jetsip Rai?'

It was this last, casual remark that kept playing on Khun Chai's mind long after the others had gone to bed. No one had answered Yai Li or continued the conversation, because at that moment Sai had come to announce that the police were at the front gates.

'It's nothing to do with what has happened here,' he was quick to say waving his hand towards Arunee and Joy to reassure them. 'It's Nai Jit. They found him drunk in the market, and he started a fight. The police have brought him back here.'

The whole process of handing Nai Jit over to them took just over half an hour and involved Arunee passing a white envelope to the policemen. Meanwhile, Sai and his cousin Fad between them managed to carry Nai Jit into his shack and put him to bed. During this meeting, Joy and Yai Li had discreetly removed themselves from the dining room and did not return even after the policemen had left.

Later, when all was calm again and he had said goodnight to Arunee, Khun Chai sat on the balcony thinking about the conversation at the dinner table. As Yai Li's words echoed back to him, he began to panic. It was a feeling of slight anxiety at first, like a knot in the pit of his stomach. Then his heart started to thump and race, and he thought for a moment that he was about to have a heart attack. His chest felt heavy and blocked. The palms of his hands felt clammy with sweat. He tried to steady himself by drinking the cup of lemon grass tea that Samnieng had made for him earlier and he felt a little better, at least physically. Mentally, however, he was stuck in the same desperate territory. The prospect that Yai Li was going to leave Baan Suan and return to Jetsip Rai filled him with existential dread. He could understand intellectually why this should distress him. He had become dependent on her for his well-being. But more than that, he realised how attached to her emotionally he was. She was now someone he could talk to in a way he had never done before to anyone else. In psychological terms he had made her into his sister, his confessor, his mother figure all rolled into one. But none of this understanding helped him. The thought that this connection to her was now to be cut pushed him to go beyond the limits set by a lifetime of discretion and good behaviour.

After staring down at the shoes neatly placed in front of the door, Khun Chai slowly turned the carved wooden handle and stepped in. Dawn light suffused the room and he saw Yai Li lying on her back on the huge double bed with one arm slung across her face as though she were shielding her eyes from the sun. She was wearing a faded red pah-sin sarong and a white tee shirt on top. She looked beautiful to him, in repose. Khun Chai noticed that instead of having the air conditioning turned on, she had opened all the windows, with just the wire screens to prevent the mosquitos from coming in. He stood for a long time at the end of her bed watching her breathing steadily, and was on the point of turning round to leave her when, letting out a soft groan, Yai Li stirred, pulled her arm from her face and opened her eyes. Then with a start she sat up. But there was no look of fright on her face. She calmly said:

'Aren't you feeling well, Khun Chai?' He shook his head.

'I'm OK,' he said softly.

'Then what are you doing here?' she asked gently, thinking that perhaps he was sleep walking, and she did not want to wake him up too abruptly.

'I wanted to talk to you,' he said.

Yai Li stared at him without answering.

'I needed to talk to you,' he continued. 'I …'

'What? At this hour. It's not even light yet. Have you been to bed?'

Again, he shook his head.

'Please forgive me. I just wanted to say…' He hesitated. ' I wanted to say that if you left Baan Suan, I would die.'

He had not wanted to sound melodramatic. But there was no other way to express how he felt.

It was Yai Li's turn now to shake her head and click her teeth.

'No, you wouldn't. Anyway, even if I did leave, it wouldn't mean we wouldn't be seeing each other again. I'd come to visit and to give you treatments. Nothing will change. What are you scared of?'

'Of losing you,' he replied.

'Oh. Like you lost that Pia.' Yai Li chuckled. This time he nodded.

'You see, I think I am in love with you. No. That's wrong. I am definitely in love with you.'

Yai Li first put up both her hands, then a forefinger to her mouth, to stop him saying anything more.

'I think you'd better go back to your room and get some rest now,' she told him, and like a child obeying his mother he dutifully turned on his heels and quietly left the room.

After Khun Chai had gone, Yai Li lay back onto the bed and took up the same position with one arm crossing over her eyes. Her lips were smiling.

'Has he gone mad?' she said out loud to herself and her smile broadened.

⚜ ⚜ ⚜

'But don't you see? This is not my home. I can't stay here in this palace. You may be some sort of Khun Chai, but I am certainly not a Khun Ying and never will be. I feel awkward all the time being served on. I haven't known anything like this in my life. I am only used to serving. You've been kind to us, and Sai and the rest of them too. But it's impossible. I don't belong here. It's as simple as that,' said Yai Li in a mildly exasperated tone.

This was later the same day, after Khun Chai had woken up from his short sleep. They were sharing a late breakfast of rice gruel and coffee. Khun Chai, revitalized from his rest, and far from being embarrassed by what had taken place just hours before, had insisted on explaining to Yai Li at length that he could not live without her presence in his life. She was now the most important part of it, he told her. He spoke with the innocence of a young lover, confident that his beloved would be won over by the sincerity of his words. There was no shyness or self-censorship in his expressions of appreciation and love. He talked like someone with nothing to lose, and Yai Li, unprepared for these ardent confessions, was nevertheless touched and tried as hard as she could to keep level-headed, although she knew that she too had feelings for him that were new and surprising to her.

'Well then,' he said. 'We can find somewhere else to live. Anywhere. We don't need to have servants. We can look after each other.'

Yai Li laughed.

'Would you cook for me? Would you do the cleaning and the washing?'

'Ah. You may well joke. But remember that I had to look after myself all those years I was a student in England. I cooked and cleaned and washed my own clothes.' He replied good – naturedly.

'But that was a thousand years ago. Anyway, you are a Khun Chai, a little prince. I could never allow you to do the cooking, or anything else. I would have to look after you.'

They went on with this light-hearted, flirtatious banter for a while and then suddenly Khun Chai's amused expression changed. Frowning, he said:

'I don't know how long I have left in this world. I mean it. I want to spend the rest of my time with you by my side.'

He paused, cleared his throat then went on:

'Will you consider marrying me?' Yai Li gulped audibly.

'What?! At our age? Don't be ridiculous,' she said finally. 'What on earth for? Are you thinking of having children?'

This brought a smile back to his face.

'Well, why not? We could adopt a little one if we wanted to. Or lots of them.' 'Now I know you're joking.'

'Seriously. I mean it. And please don't avoid my question. Will you marry me?'

Yai Li panicked and muttered:

'Khun Chai, Khun Chai. Are you sure of this?'

She was playing for time. He kept silent and stayed gazing at her.

'And what if I said yes? Crazy as it would be.' She went on. 'I would still insist that we can't live here. And you certainly won't feel at home in Jetsip Rai after all this.'

She gestured to the domed observatory above them, to the long balcony, the leafy garden and the swimming pool in the distance. He was about to protest, but she stopped him.

'Be honest.'

'All right. I will admit that I live like a spoiled gentleman. But I can change. I am willing to try anything if it means we are together. Not here. Not Jetsip Rai. Somewhere we both like. This is a vast country.'

Yai Li found no words to reply to this.

'But you still haven't answered my question,' said Khun Chai.

Chapter 30

It was obvious to Arunee and Joy that something unusual was going on in Baan Suan. Whereas in the beginning, when they came back from their day at Mudita House, they would find Khun Chai and Yai Li sitting on the balcony enjoying each other's company in a sedate, polite fashion, they now often returned to the sound of laughter and joyful chatter. The way the two of them related to each other was now so relaxed and playful that the two women felt infected by it.

'I've never seen Khun Chai like this,' said Arunee one day in the car. 'I've always known him as a rather grumpy person, unsmiling, permanently complaining about something, cross with the world. I don't blame him, of course, with the pain that he has been going through. But he never seemed to enjoy anything. I wasn't even sure he was really happy to be back in Baan Suan, to tell the truth. Really, to see him smile and laugh is quite a change.'

'Well, I would never have dreamed of seeing my granny like this either.' Joy replied. 'She's not usually a talkative person. Now she's like a little girl giggling away.'

'Long may it last. I don't know what he'll do when you've left.' Arunee turned and gazed through the window at the river below.

'I don't know what I'll do either.' These last words were half whispered, as if she were speaking to herself. But Joy heard her and reaching across the leather seat, held her companion's hand lightly in hers.

The friendship between the two women did not go unnoticed by Khun Chai and Yai Li. Unconsciously echoing the remarks made about them, Khun Chai said:

'Your granddaughter looks so much better these days since she's been here.'

'Yes, I know,' said Yai Li. 'She's like a new person. She was always so wound up and so impatient with me. Now she has stopped treating me like an ignorant peasant. Something extraordinary has happened to her.'

'Talking of which, I've never seen my daughter-in-law look so well either. She's even stopped all that fiddling around, re-arranging the of chairs and glasses and cutlery. So obsessive. It used to drive me mad.'

'Yes,' said Yai Li with a slight chuckle. She too had noticed Arunee's peculiarities from the moment they had first met. Her father had told her once, after treating someone with the same sort of behaviour, that it came from fear of losing everything, but he did not explain any more to her and she had not really understood his meaning until now.

'She's not nervous anymore, is she? She's happy,' she said. Khun Chai nodded in agreement.

'Well, that means she wasn't happy when Mitr was alive.' he muttered.

Mentioning his son made Khun Chai wince with pain for a moment. They had hardly talked about Mitr's death. On the first evening of their arrival at Baan Suan, Khun Chai had announced quietly:

'I have come to accept that my son died from an unfortunate accident. I want you, Joy, to know that I do not blame you. And I also would like you not to speak of the matter anymore, if you all don't mind. It will help me make peace with my loss.'

Once or twice during a session Yai Li would say:

'Don't keep the tears in your chest, Khun Chai. You'll explode one day if you do so.'

But she never went further. She respected his wishes, which was why his remark took her by surprise that afternoon.

'I still can't believe he's dead,' he continued. 'You know, it's very odd. But I forget about what's happened sometimes. How can that be? And then it sort of crashes back into my heart like a car out of control.'

He was close to tears as he spoke, but he locked his jaw tightly to control his emotions.

'Grief is like that,' said Yai Li. 'It steals up on you like a thief, sometimes when you least expect it. I still miss my father. I still cry for him. And he died over sixty years ago.'

Saying this she reached over and touched his arm, and he responded by patting her hand and saying:

'You see. This is what I mean. What am I going to do without you?'

⊱⊰, ⊱⊰, ⊱⊰,

It was now the end of the first week of November. The rains had stopped. The air was already cooler. The city was drying out after the watery onslaught that had lasted longer than other years. The Loy Kratong ceremony was almost upon them. When Mitr was alive, their table by the river at the Oriental Hotel would already have been booked. He was not a man who enjoyed the rituals and ceremonies that dotted the year and avoided them as much as possible. But the exception was Loy Kratong. When he was a young boy Khun Chai would take him to Lumpini Park where they floated their *kratongs*, that they had made themselves, on the lake and watch them float off among all the others, marvelling at the beauty of the lights bobbing up and down in the water while an orchestra played nearby; then they would go to have a meal in Chinatown. Later, as Mitr was growing up, they would be invited to Loy Kratong parties all over the city and, at one of these, as a teenager, he had drunk his first glass of champagne. Since then, this ceremony became an important marker for him. It was the only time that he truly seemed to allow himself to relax and have a good time, and it was at a Loy Kratong party in Thonburi that he had met Arunee.

For Khun Chai too, Loy Kratong was a special occasion. His favourite season was always this time of year and as a child he enjoyed watching the servants make the little *kratongs* from banana leaves and put flowers and a candle in each one. When he worked as a journalist the ceremony took on a different aspect for him. He saw the whole ritual as an important way of showing gratitude to the river and the waterways and one of the few remaining ways to keep city people in touch with their ecology. On a personal level it had always been a moment of celebration. Particularly, in recent times, it was an opportunity to let go of whatever tensions had arisen between him and Mitr that year and to rediscover their bond as father and son. They would raise their glasses of champagne and let everything float away down the river.

'No. I don't want to go back to the Oriental,' he said when Arunee suggested that they had better reserve a table before they were all taken.

Arunee was then about to say: Not even in honour of your son? But she saw his determined expression.

'Don't you want to celebrate it at all, this year, Pa? We could go somewhere else if you like.' Khun Chai shook his head and hesitated for moment before saying:

'Yes, I do. Of course, I want to celebrate Loy Kratong. Wouldn't miss it for the world. But why can't we do it here in the house? Those awful journalists will be at the Oriental and anywhere we went, even though we're not hot news anymore. I would rather not risk spoiling a nice evening by having to thwack someone with my walking stick.'

They all laughed knowing that he would never do any such thing.

'Besides, I don't know if I have enough strength to go all the way into town and back. And I don't see why we can't enjoy ourselves here. Us and the servants. Sai and Mae Hom can get them to prepare everything beautifully. And you can invite the women from Mudita House, if you like, Arunee. Why not? I've never met them. We can have the party by the swimming pool. We've never done that before. Always a first time.'

He looked around at their astonished expressions.

'Everybody in agreement?'

Chapter 31

Two days before the Loy Kratong ceremony, Khun Chai was unable to move from his bed. Sai found him curled up in pain. His breathing was rapid and shallow.

'Yai Li. Yai Li,' was all he could mutter.

When she was brought to him, she sat holding his clammy hands and looking into his eyes for a long while before speaking.

'I can help you. But maybe you should think of seeing a good doctor. What you've got is beyond my capabilities,' she said softly.

Khun Chai did not take his eyes off her but said:

'I know that's something is very wrong. I can feel it in my guts. But I am not going to see any doctor. I know what they'll do. Lots of expensive tests. Then they'll probably cut me up. Just so long as you can help to keep me moving, I'll be all right.'

The treatment that morning took over an hour. She used all her skill, and while she passed her fingers over his spine, he felt as though they were penetrating his skin and muscle and unraveling the nerves that were knotted in his back. At one point he seemed to lose consciousness and when he came round, he turned to see her on the chair beside the bed, again staring at him.

'What did you see, Khun Chai?' she asked.

As if suddenly remembering a detail from a dream he said:

'It was the same scene again. The battlefield. Only this time someone cut me, right here,' he said, pointing to an area below his chest.

Yai Li did not react to this but merely nodded.

'Can you move now? Try sitting up.'

To his surprise, Khun Chai maneuvered his body into a sitting position with no pain, then carefully hauled himself off the bed and onto his feet. He then put both his hands on her shoulders.

'I keep telling you. I can't do anything without you.' Yai Li smiled, knowing what was coming next.

'And you still haven't given me an answer to my question.'

'I will tell you after Loy Kratong. I promise.'

The drama just before Loy Kratong took place on the 10th, and nearly prevented it going ahead. That morning when Sai and his wife Pao got up, they found the floor to their room littered with squashed insects of all shapes and sizes, and among them three dead birds that Ai Toh must have caught and killed. He himself was lying in his bed in the corner with his eyes wide open.

'What have you done, Ai Toh?' asked his mother going over to him. 'What's all this madness about?'

But Ai Toh continued to gaze in silence at the ceiling. She knew there was no point trying to get him to explain.

'Well. You have to clear up this mess. We're too busy preparing for Loy Kratong tomorrow. There's still a lot to be done with all the guests coming. So you'd better help out.'

Without a word Toh jumped off his bed, grabbed a broom from the corner and aggressively began to sweep up the insects and the birds into a pile in the middle of the floor. Then, when he finished, he spat on it and walked out of the room. They could not find him that morning and presumed he was in the garden. They called for him when it was mealtime but there was no response. The day was filled with chores. The lawn was mowed, the swimming pool cleaned, tables and chairs had to be moved to the poolside, lamps set up, banana leaves cut down to make the *kratongs*, for it was Khun Chai's wish that they were homemade, like when he was young, rather than bought from the market. Nobody could remember seeing Toh until in the late afternoon when Nai Jit, coming out of his room saw Ai Toh go to the small side door to the entrance gate, turn the lock and head out into the street. He presumed that the boy had been sent out on an errand and thought nothing of it. But as night fell, Sai and Pao began to worry, and Sai went out on his moped to the market and asked people there if anyone had seen his son. But no one had. By midnight both he and his wife were so worried that they went to the police station. But there was no report of anyone of his description. They were desperate now and spent the long hours praying that nothing had happened to Ai Toh and that he would reappear in front of them some time in the night.

'He's been behaving strangely since Yai Li and Khun Joy's arrival in Baan Suan,' said Sai to his wife.

'Well, he took Khun Mitr's death very badly. Did you see how much he cried at the funeral?'

'We're all sad about it. But I don't understand those temper tantrums he's been having for no good reason. I don't know what's going on in his mind.'

'I feel like giving him a good clout,' said Pao. 'But it wouldn't help, would it? He's never done this before. What has come over him? Where can he be?'

'He's never been out of Baan Suan, except with us. And he has no friends. He must be lost.

'Tomorrow I am going to look everywhere till I find him.'

After that sleepless night, Sai got up at first light and went to the balcony on the other side of the house to see if Khun Chai might be still awake, and sure enough he found his master sitting alone puffing on his cheroot and gazing out at the garden.

'Nai,' he said. 'My son Toh's missing. I am going out to find him. I am not coming back till I do.' 'Well. I hope you do,' said Khun Chai. 'Because remember that you have to pick up those women from Mudita House in the afternoon. There'll be a lot of traffic today. Don't leave it too late.'

'I can't promise you I'll be back in time, Nai.'

It was the first time in his life he had ever hinted at disobeying Khun Chai's wishes. The older man was taken aback for a second, but he could tell from Sai's expression that he would not be dissuaded.

'All right then. Get your cousin, Fad to drive the van.'

'He can't. He's working all day at that hotel on the river. He won't be back till late.' 'Well, that does it then,' said Khun Chai with childish petulance.

'Go on. Go and find your son. I'll have to ask Arunee and Joy to drive the van, and if they can't I'll drive the damn thing myself. Or we cancel the whole thing!'

But in the end, it was not canceled. At six the sky began to turn into the deep turquoise of twilight. By now everything in the house had been prepared. The *kratongs*, beautifully made by Mae Hom and Samnieng were laid out on a low round wooden table at one end of the pool. Along the far side there was a long buffet to serve the food. Scattered around the lawn were the seats that had been taken out of the ballroom for the occasion. Khun Chai's wicker chair, a small side table and a sofa were placed by a frangipani bush. A small dais had been set up under one of the tamarind trees for the musicians who were coming to play for them that evening. This had been Arunee's idea and had won Khun Chai's delighted approval.

'It will be like the old days,' he said, satisfied with this detail, and impressed that she had thought of it.

Arunee and Joy stood on the balcony of the first floor and watched the lamps being lit all round the garden. A gentle breeze was blowing, bringing with it all the fragrance of the flowering bushes.

'This is my favourite light,' said Joy. 'Mine too.'

'It's so beautiful,' said Joy. 'Everything. It's like a dream.'

'Yes. It is. And do you know? We've never done this kind of Loy Kratong before in Baan Suan,' Arunee replied. 'Mitr didn't...' she stopped herself. Then:

'It's because you're here.'

The improbable friendship between the two of them still amazed and confounded Joy. At the beginning, when Arunee had come to see her at her apartment and invited them to stay in Baan Suan, it had crossed her mind that there might have been some ulterior motive to Arunee's kindness towards her, in spite of having criticized her grandmother for being suspicious. Her own cynical nature invented scenarios such as: she's setting me up, she wants to punish me for Mitr's death and she's going to do it when I am absolutely under her control. But during the weeks that she spent at Baan Suan and the whole time they were subsequently together she saw, to her shame, that her paranoia was unfounded. Arunee's kindness seemed totally genuine. Still, it was difficult to stop the dark thoughts that kept coming in her thoughts from time to time. Was Arunee grooming her as some object of desire? This projection too found nothing to support it. It was true their hands had touched several times and once or twice Arunee's words, such as the ones she was hearing that evening, were open to interpretation. But there had been no declarations of love or desire, no hint that Arunee wanted anything else from her other than friendship. Yet the question remained: why her? There must have been so many people in her society that she could relate to and be friends with. Why should she choose, of all people, the person who had been her husband's mistress, and who had been accused of causing his death?

As she stood there, in the light green silk shirt that Arunee had recently given her – the colour suits your eyes, she had said – Joy found herself recalling friendships she had witnessed while she lived in the Mercy Centre, and the crushes that were directed towards her during those years. She had never gone further than holding hands with some of the girls who had declared their affection for her. Now she found herself thinking:

What if I were now to turn and reach out and hold Arunee and kiss her? Would she respond? It was the first time that any such idea had come to her, and she found herself surprised by it.

As if she could hear her friend's thought, Arunee drew herself away in a swift movement and walked to the far side of the balcony.

'Samnieng,' she shouted down. 'Those chairs are all over the place. It looks really messy. Can't you put them in order? Please?'

There was no annoyance or impatience in her voice when normally there might have been. She turned back to Joy.

'I'm like that. I like things in their place,' she said and smiled. 'Can't help it.' 'I've noticed.'

'But I am getting better.'

⋙ ⋙ ⋙

The evening started well. A van was hired to bring the women from Mudita House. They were all dressed for the occasion, and, on their arrival, they were totally surprised to find themselves in such opulent surroundings. Shy at first, they remained huddled in a bunch. But Arunee and Joy made them feel welcomed straightaway by walking with them round the garden and by introducing them to the household. That evening, those who looked after Baan Suan were included in the celebrations, not as servants but as participants in the ritual to come. All were in their best clothes, even Khun Chai who wore a blue silk shirt over his white linen trousers.

The unexpected bonus to the meeting came in the form of Khun Sumanee, the director of Mudita House. She was a tough, kindly, bespectacled trained nurse and social worker in her fifties whom Arunee had found when she was establishing the Foundation and whom had been with her ever since. When she introduced her to Khun Chai, Khun Sumanee said:

'It is such an honour to meet you, Khun Chai. I never thought I ever would. I used to read all your articles in the *Bangkok Daily*. And when you started writing fiction, I bought every one of your books. Please consider me a fan!'

It had been a long time since Khun Chai received such a compliment from a total stranger and he could feel the old thrill of knowing that he had touched someone with his writing and won their admiration. Even though he had often told himself that at his age he no longer needed his ego boosted, he knew that he still enjoyed the fix. Beaming at her, he said:

'Come and sit down with me.'

While they sipped cold white wine together, they talked non-stop, to the slight annoyance of Yai Li, who decided to leave them and help in the kitchen.

'And are you working on anything nowadays?' asked Sumanee at one point, inevitably. 'Well. Yes and no,' replied Khun Chai. 'I am trying to begin. I've been making notes. I even have a rough outline. But so much has been happening that my efforts have been slightly derailed.'

Sumanee laughed.

'And what is the outline, if I may be so bold as to ask? I know some writers don't like to talk about their work until they've finished it, and I will not be offended if you don't want to tell me.'

'Well,' said Khun Chai. 'I am not one of those writers. In fact, I find that talking about it helps me get more ideas.'

Sumanee waited for him to go on. But Khun Chai hesitated as his eyes looked across the garden around him and drifted up to the house itself.

'This place for a start. It has to feature in it. This way of life that is about to disappear forever.'

Sumanee nodded.

'And will you regret it?'

'No. Not at all. I am surprised to still be part of any of it. But very soon only the very wealthy will live like this, and I am certainly not one of them, or want to be. I want to see everyone share in the wealth of the country.'

Sumanee raised her eyebrows. Noticing this, Khun added:

'I'd have been called a commie for talking like this back in the day. In fact, I was, many times. But I was never a communist. More of an anarchist. Not that they would have known the difference. Anyway, the term is meaningless nowadays, isn't it, with the Chinese turning into arch capitalists.'

Sumanee looked intrigued by what she was hearing.

'So, you were an anarchist. Really? I have never met an anarchist before. And are you still one?'

'I am, I suppose.'

'Which means that you don't like authority.' 'Certainly not the type we have here.'

'And I presume you approve of the demonstrations that are going on.'

'If I were young, I would try to join every one of them. I never really did when I was young. But I was another person then. There has to be change. It will come from the young.' he said.

Their conversation might have continued but at that moment the musicians had started to play and soon the sound of the *ranaad* wooden xylophone, the *kluy* flute, the *ching* cymbals, the two stringed *saw-oo* and the *thon* drums drowned out the conversations that had been taking place all over that beautiful setting. The listeners sat entranced by the ancient music that evoked another time. And as they listened the full moon shone above them in a clear cloudless sky, casting a silvery glow over the whole spectacle.

It was after the main courses had been cleared away and the fruit and sweets were being served, that it happened. By now the musicians had left to go to play in one of the big hotels in town. Several of the women from Mudita House were making their way over to the wooden table to light the candles in their *kratongs* after Arunee had announced:

'Let us begin the ceremony. Please, go ahead. Any time you feel like it.'

They were kneeling down, saying their prayers, making their wishes before putting their *kratongs* onto the water. The black marble pool, lit from below, gave an impression of great depth. When the first two *kratongs* were launched everyone clapped. 'Ah. I wish Mitr were here,' whispered Khun Chai to Yai Li who was now back by his side. 'He would have enjoyed this so much.'

She touched his arm lightly.

What happened next would be remembered for years to come by all those who were present in Baan Suan that night.

Nai Jit, in the smart clothes that Khun Chai had given him, was serving coffee from a large silver tray. He was about to approach Arunee and Joy who were sitting together by the poolside, waiting for their turn to float their kratongs, enjoying each other's company. Joy was saying once again how beautiful Baan Suan looked that evening, and how special the party was. Suddenly, there was the sound of a woman shouting out:

'Dai Laew! Good God!' It was her high-pitched voice that made them all look round. At first all eyes were fixed on her. She was one of the younger ones from Mudita House who was now standing with her shoulders hunched up, with both hands covering her mouth in a gesture of extreme fear. Her face was turned, and she was looking across the garden, in the direction of the front gates. At first no one could make out what she was seeing, what it was that had made her shout out. Then from behind one of the tamarind trees the figure of Ai Toh emerged.

His hair was wild and unkempt, his shirt dirty, and he was carrying a machete whose blade glinted in the moonlight. For a moment he stood still, his eyes scanning the guests gathered there, who remained frozen as if suspended in time. It was as if he were surprised to see so many faces that he did not recognize. Then, suddenly, he saw Arunee and Joy sitting together. With his mouth open as though he were giving out a silent scream, he walked towards them holding the machete in the air like a warrior going into battle. His intention was clear. As he approached them, he quickened his step. Then, when he slashed the machete down, Nai Jit held up the tray to protect the two women. The cups and saucers and everything on the tray flew in all directions. There was a loud clang as the steel blade caught the edge of the silver tray and then sliced through Nai Jit's forearm. Blood spurted into the air. As Ai Toh raised to strike again, Nai Jit, having yelled out in pain and dropped the tray, held the boy's arm with his undamaged hand and, twisting his body, pulled them both into the water. At this point they all saw another figure race towards the pool and dive in. It was Sai, Toh's father. In a flash, Nai Wang, the gardener, was also in the water, and now all of them seem to be like one body, thrashing and shouting while streams of blood spread out and engulfed the kratongs that were bobbing up and down on the churning surface.

Nai Jit was hauled out of the water bleeding profusely. Fortunately, Khun Sumanee, with her nurse's training at once applied a tourniquet and bandaged the wound.

'We must get him to a hospital straightaway. Is there one nearby?'

It was Joy, accompanied by Samnieng, who drove Nai Jit to the Central General Hospital, stayed with him in the emergency ward and made sure that he was admitted to a private room to receive urgent surgery on his arm. As she left, she asked the night nurse who was in charge if he was going to be all right.

'Oh. He'll be fine. He's lost a lot of blood. But we're replacing that now.'

'And will his arm be all right?'

'Now that's another matter. The surgeon will do his best. But I've seen worse. And he's lucky it's his arm.'

Joy did not understand her.

'What do you mean?' she asked.

The nursed looked round and then made a gesture with her left hand over her lower abdomen, cutting the air.

'Oh. I see, said Joy.' Do you have many cases like that?' The nurse nodded.

'Women are angry,' she said darkly.

Chapter 32

In Baan Suan the chaos continued for over an hour. After Nai Jit had been taken out of the water, Sai and Nai Wang managed to hold tightly onto Ai Toh and steer him to the steps. The boy did not struggle outwardly, but his expression showed that he was suffering some sort of internal seizure and his head kept shaking violently from side to side.

'Don't worry. He's not going to do any more harm,' Sai shouted out as they bundled him away towards the servants' quarter, followed by his tearful mother and Yai Li. Those words did little to calm the frenzied atmosphere in the wake of what had happened. One of the young women from Mudita House was crying uncontrollably.

Khun Sumanee was saying to Arunee in an anxious voice:

'Are you calling the police?'

'No! I don't want the police anywhere near here,' Khun Chai interjected. 'We can sort this out by ourselves.'

'But he could have killed someone,' Sumanee insisted.

'True. But he didn't. He's unwell. The police will just beat him up and throw him in a cell. That would finish him off. Ai Toh's part of our family. We'll take care of him.'

Khun Sumanee, looking bemused, could find no answer to this.

There was relief all round when the hired van finally arrived at the gates. Hurried, awkward goodbyes were exchanged, with Khun Chai promising to visit Mudita House one day. The guests, still looking like they were in shock put their hands together and bowed through the windows of the van.

After they left, Khun Chai sat in his wicker chair and blew a long sigh of relief before finishing off the wine that was in his glass.

'Well. Maybe it wasn't such a good idea to do it here,' he said to Arunee who had taken a seat next to him. But his words found no response except for a slight smile.

They were now the only ones by the poolside. The air, so agitated before, was calm again. The gentle cool breeze felt soothing. They could hear the insects and the call of a night jar. After a while he said:

'Any news from Joy?'

'She texted me. They will operate first thing in the morning to save his arm.'

'It was good of her to take him. She's a decent person. I have grown fond of her. I never thought I would.'

'Me neither,' said Arunee. 'She's helped the Foundation so much recently. I wish that she would…'

Khun Chai did not let her finish.

'Why don't you ask her to be part of your team? I've been thinking about it. They have ruined her reputation with what they've written about her. All the bad things will stick. That's what it's like in our country. It will be hard for her to find a decent job now and she will always be having to deal with the gossip. She's efficient, she's…'

This time it was Arunee who cut him short.

'I'll think about it, Pa. But thank you for your advice.'

At that moment they saw Sai and Yai Li walking up to them side by side.

Yai Li sat down next to Khun Chai, while Sai remained standing as he told them:

'Khun Yai has calmed him down completely. I don't know how she did it. She put her hands on his head and stomach. He's fast asleep now.'

'He's all right, 'said Yai Li. 'But he will take time to recover. He's been poisoned.'

Sai explained to them how he had spent the day going round the markets and the shopping malls many times, and to two police stations without any luck. Nobody had any recollection of him. Then in the evening, just when he was about to give up his search, he rode down a side street and saw one of Samnieng's cousins at a noodle stall with some friends. Taking a chance, he approached him and asked him whether he had seen Ai Toh.

'I saw him near the river with that crowd in Pakret, the ones who hang out near Wat Bo.' The young man told him.

Full of hope, Sai went there and saw three teenagers he vaguely recognized in a parking lot standing by their motorbikes smoking cigarettes. But there was no sign of his son. He walked up to them and said:

'Have you seen Ai Toh?'

One of them laughed in his face.

'Is that what his name is? You mean the deaf mute?'

Sai, incensed, closed on the boy and punched him in the stomach. The boy doubled up in pain and Sai prepared to defend himself from the others. But they did not react as he was expecting them to. Instead, one of them put his arms round his friend who had just received the blow and said, in a whining voice:

'Why did you have to go and do that? We've done nothing to you.'

'He insulted my son. You know he's not a deaf mute. You know he's not well. I'll ask you again.

'Did you see him today?'

'Yeah, we saw him this afternoon. He looked lost, like he'd been sleeping rough. We've been there ourselves. We bought him a snack and water. See? We even helped your son.' 'Then what?'

'Nothing. We hung out with him by the river.' 'And what else?'

The boy shrugged.

'We smoked.' 'Ganja?'

'No. The other stuff.'

It was dark by now. He rode round the streets for another couple of hours, still unable to find his son. That was when he decided to return to Baan Suan.

When Sai finished recounting his tale, Khun Chai said:

'So what was he smoking if it wasn't ganja?'

Arunee answered him.

'It's that synthetic cannabis, Pa. They call it spice in America. It's dirt cheap and easy to get.

It's sold all over the slums. It drives people crazy.'

'What, even crazier than *yaa baah*? And where did he get the machete?'

'Oh, he just went into the tool shed when he got back just before me,' said Sai. 'But I don't know why he wanted to do anyone harm.'

'It was the poison. His demons became a reality,' said Yai Li. 'We must all try to forgive him.' 'That's all very well,' said Arunee heaving a long sigh. 'But don't forget that it was me he wanted to kill. Me and Joy.'

It was nearly one o'clock by the time they all went to bed. Khun Chai, left alone, sat in his wicker chair by the poolside looking down into the water for a long time. He insisted that he did not want to be on the balcony that night and had asked to have another bottle of white wine brought out to him. He would have liked to have a drinking companion. But after the drama no one wanted to stay up half the night with him. Sai had offered to empty the pool and clean everything up, including retrieving the machete from the bottom of the pool where it was still lying. But Khun Chai, seeing that he was exhausted, told him to get the rest he needed and to be with his son and his wife.

At some point, Joy had returned from taking Ni Jit to the hospital and after explaining to him briefly, why, because of the traffic, she had taken so long, she begged to be excused and rushed to her bedroom.

Now he had only the insects and the reptiles to keep him company. The lamps in the garden were out. The house was dark. The full moon's light shone on the trees and the bushes and the wide lawn, covering everything with a silvery veil. Its reflection in the water was so clear, that it looked as if it were floating on the surface. For a moment, as he sipped his wine, he was reminded of Li Bai's poem about the moon, that he had read when he was a young man, and the way that he had been touched by the legend of how the poet had drowned. But then he remembered what had just happened. He could still see the strands of blood covering the water like burst veins. And all the *kratongs* were still floating there, silent reminders of that dreadful evening that could well have ended in tragedy.

Looking up at the house, his eyes searched for the window to Yai Li's room. There was no light on. He thought of how she had promised to answer his proposal of marriage after Loy Kratong. When the festivities began, he had been excited about this, and when the musicians had struck up their repetitive, hypnotic melodies, bringing on an other-worldly atmosphere, he was sure that she would say something positive to him. But she didn't and what happened later in the evening had shaken him up.

As he sat alone, staring once more into the pool, getting a little more drunk with each glass of wine, he began to have doubts. Had he done the right thing by proposing to her? Was it just a mad whim on his part? Was he really ready to share his life with someone with whom he had so little in common? There was not even the beguiling force of desire to motivate this wish to be with her.

If he had read about their relationship in a novel or short story, he would have found it far fetched, or, at least, unlikely. But then as a writer he had learned a long time ago that reality, on all levels, was often stranger than anything invented in fiction. When in the past he was accused of distorting the political complexities of the country in his writings he would answer:

'Well, nothing I invent can beat the 18 coups and 8 constitutions that we've had since 1932.' Or, when one critic said that the corrupt characters in his books were the product of an overly active imagination, he sent him back a list of the scandals that he had collected from the tabloids over the years that involved monks, businessmen, politicians, and even those whom nobody was allowed to mention directly.

So, in the end, why not him and Yai Li? Two old incompatible people from different sides of the railway track. Perhaps it could even work. There were so many possible endings.

'Anyway, it's too late. Like always, it's too late. I've gone and asked her,' he muttered out loud as he poured himself another glass. Then raising it to the moon in the sky and to the moon in the pool he said:

'To Li Bai.'

꧁ ꧁ ꧁

That same night, in the west wing of the house, Arunee made her way down the stairs in the moonlight that was streaming in through the tall windows. The wood creaked and although she knew that there was no point in hiding her footsteps, she, nevertheless, trod carefully, placing her feet where she knew they would make less noise. When she was outside Joy's door, she held up her forefinger to tap softly on the wood, but instead gently turned the doorknob and entered the room.

'Joy,' she whispered.

As though she had been waiting for this visit Joy, still awake, said immediately:

'Don't turn the light on. It's bright enough in here with the moonlight.'

Arunee approached the bed and stood at the end. She looked down at the figure on the bed who was in an oversized blue tee shirt with her wild hair spread all over the pillow.

Joy's heart started to beat in anticipation. But Arunee did not move.

'I couldn't sleep,' she said. 'I had to talk to you.' 'I couldn't sleep either.'

'I saw you come in earlier and I wanted to go down and talk to you then. But I thought you were tired. You must be. Was it terrible?'

'No. Not really. Nai Jit was in a lot of pain. He nearly passed out on the way to the hospital. Samnieng had to hold him tightly. I was happy to be able to help. But it was tiring. Yes.' Arunee looked around her and found a chair to drag to Joy's bedside. Joy, still on her side kept looking at Arunee, remembering what she had thought the previous evening when they were standing together on the balcony. In the moonlight, Arunee was a picture of beauty. She was wearing a white satin dressing gown and her hair was bunched on top of her head. She resembled a statue of Kuan Yin that Joy had once seen in a museum in Singapore that she had been taken to by Mitr. It struck her now that Arunee had the remoteness of that goddess.

'I am still in shock about what happened. I am afraid of him now.' 'Of Ai Toh?'

'Yes.'

'Khun Chai told me that he's going to be kept here to be looked after. Do you think that's wise?'

'No, I don't.' said Arunee shaking her head. 'I lay in bed thinking of the best thing to do. I am convinced he has to have good professional help. I've always thought that. But now perhaps they'll listen to me. It's not just that I am afraid he'll do it again but…'

'I understand, and you are right,' said Joy interrupting her. 'But we'll sort it out. He doesn't have to stay here in Baan Suan.'

'There's something else that disturbs me, and you are the only person I can share it with.' Joy waited. For a while Arunee said nothing, as though she needed time to compose her thoughts.

'When that boy, Ai Toh, looked at me, looked at us, it was as though he was accusing us. I could feel what he was thinking. He saw us as evil people. I know that he thought that we were responsible for Mitr's death.' As she said this Arunee began to cry.

'The terrible thing,' she continued between her sobs. 'Is that he saw right through me. Ai Toh saw the truth.'

'What do you mean? You had nothing to do with your husband's death. It was my fault.'

'You see. That's precisely where you're wrong. I have been wishing it for years, secretly, in my heart.'

On hearing this, Joy involuntarily put a hand to her mouth.

'I don't mean I wanted to kill him, or that I got anyone to cast a spell or anything like that, though I know wives who have done that and gone to a spirit doctor to get their husbands cursed. And I certainly wasn't expecting it to happen the way it did. But I can't help thinking that my wishes somehow were part of his death.'

Arunee hung her head and continued to sob.

Joy was moved as much by what she heard as by the fact that Arunee had confessed this to her. She understood now why Arunee felt such an urgency to visit the apartment and to meet her personally. It was to see if she were the agent of her malicious wish for her husband to die. As these thoughts were going through her mind, from nowhere she heard her mother's last words to her, uttered a few days before she died at the Mercy hospice.

'Be careful what you wish for, little one.'

'But why would you have wanted him dead?' she asked when Arunee was calmer. 'What did he do to you? Did he hurt you?'

Arunee shrugged and then shook her head vigourously.

'That's the point. Nothing. He treated me with respect. He supported everything I did. The Foundation, Mudita House. He was generous…'

'Was it because of me?'

'No! No! You mustn't think that. It has nothing to do with it. I didn't mind that. Honestly, I didn't.'

'What then?'

Arunee looked away before speaking.

'It's simple. I couldn't stand to be touched by him. I wanted to die every time when he held me, when we made love. It made me feel unclean.' As she said this, she wrung her hands together as though she were washing them.

'But you were married to him for years. Was it always like this? '

'Yes. Right from the beginning.'

'And he knew?'

'I am sure he did. How could he not? He must have felt that I didn't enjoy having him put his hands on me and penetrate me. But no. I never told him outright. We didn't talk about it. I used to fantasize at first that he would run off with someone else and leave me alone, particularly when he found out I could not have children. But he stayed and stayed. And these past couple of years I thought that the only way my nightmare could end was if he were to die. And now he has.'

Joy sat up and swung her legs over the side of the bed then raised herself to a standing position in front of Arunee. Then she reached down and tenderly put her arms round her friend's shoulders.

'Your nightmare is over now,' she said.

'Then why do I feel so guilty?'

'Well, that I don't know. Maybe you need to go to a temple and have a cleansing ceremony with holy water. I think that's how people do it. But I don't know much about these things.' Arunee reached round and put her own arms round Joy's legs and rested her head against Joy's belly.

'There's so much more I want to tell you,' she whispered.

'Shush. Not now,' said Joy as she held her friend's head to her body, realizing that it was the first time in her life that she was consoling another human being. And as she continued to stroke Arunee's silky hair, she felt a wave of compassion flowing from her heart.

Chapter 33

By the time Khun Chai came out of his room the next day the pool had been drained and its walls scrubbed clean. When Sai brought him his breakfast, he was still feeling the heaviness from having drunk the whole bottle of wine by himself until dawn. The bright sunlight hurt his eyes, and his head was heavy and filled with questions.

'Where is everybody?' he asked Sai impatiently.

'Khun Arunee and Khun Joy have gone to Mudita House by themselves. It seems one of the girls there was so shocked by what happened last night that she's having some sort of crisis and it's affecting the others. That's what I heard.'

'It must have triggered something bad she experienced. It happens,' said Khun Chai. 'And what about Nai Jit? Any news?'

'It's all OK. They saved his arm. He'll be back here tomorrow.' 'And Yai Li? Where is she this morning?'

'Yai has gone to fetch a monk she knows from Wat Saphaan in Jetsip Rai. She told me that this place needs to be cleansed of the violence it has seen. This monk can do this for us.'

Khun Chai was about to say: why didn't she ask my permission first? But instead:

'And your son. How is he now?'

'I don't think he remembers much. It's always hard to tell with him. But he's still not right. We don't know what to do. Maybe he needs another treatment from Yai.' 'Hmm,' was all Khun Chai said in reply.

Yai Li did not want Sai to drive her to Jetsip Rai that morning even though he offered. Instead, she went part of the way with her granddaughter and Arunee and then took the bus from Phya Thai. It was the first time that she was going back to her neighbourhood for over a month. Her departure from her home had been hurried. She had packed her clothes and shoes in an old overnight bag and left for Joy's apartment when Joy was released from the remand prison. She had left behind the few things that she really cared for, including the box containing the old photographs. She had been worrying about this box from time to time, reassuring herself that it would be worthless to any thief.

As she crossed the railway track and stepped through the arched entrance to Jetsip Rai, she noticed nothing different from when she had left. The dusty main drag was crowded with motorbikes weaving between the pickup trucks. Children were running around playing in the lanes. The gaming hall was full of teenagers. Music blared out from the market. It was all as she had left it, as though time had stood still while she was away. But as she walked towards her shack, she could also sense eyes turning towards her with looks that were usually reserved for strangers to the district, a mixture of curiosity and distrust. Nobody greeted her until she walked past the stall where *somtam* salad and fried chicken was sold.

'How are you doing, Yai Li?' shouted the fat woman who was vigorously pounding the ingredients in her mortar. 'Did you miss my *somtam*? Is this why you're back?'

Her question was accompanied by a broad smile.

'Of course, it is,' replied Yai Li. 'No one makes *somtam* like you.'

When she finally turned into her narrow lane, she could see the familiar figure of Mae Da on her low wooden seat, smoking her cigarette. It was as though her neighbour had not moved from there the whole time she had been away.

'Well, well,' cackled the old lady. 'Had enough of the high life? Back to Klongtoey fried chicken?'

Yai Li could not help but laugh.

'And yourself. Still smoking, Mae Da? You know it's not good for you. When are you going to give up?'

'When do you think? When they throw me into that furnace and I go up in smoke, of course,' she replied.

As Yai Li turned the key to her front door she remarked to Mae Da: 'Nothing's changed at all around here.'

'Of course not. We're older, we're sicker. We're poorer. That's all. Apart from that…There's one thing, though. We've all been given notices that they are going to move us. Yours will be under the door.'

Yai Li read the piece of paper that had been slid into her shack while she was away. As usual Mae Da had misinterpreted what was written, which was that given the fact that the development of the district was now entering its second stage the Port Authority, on whose land Jetsip Rai stood, wanted to explain the options regarding the rehousing of the inhabitants. A public meeting was being convened at the main offices for the 30th November.

That was in just over two weeks.

Yai Li folded up the piece of paper and put it into her shoulder bag. She did not think that there was any point in attending the meeting. This was simply a gesture to show the people of the district that they were not going to be completely ignored. It was obvious that decisions had already been made. She thought of what Joy had said to her on more than one occasion: that she, like her neighbours, just wanted to bury her head in the sand and pretend that the change was not going to come. But her granddaughter was wrong. Yai Li had for years thought of the day when she and the others around her would have to move from their homes. But what options did any of them have, without the means to choose where they were going? They were all at the mercy of those in power, as always. She had already seen how, years earlier, when they had torn down a part of the district in order to widen the road, the people who lived in the shacks there were shunted into the concrete blocks where each family was given a cubby hole to live in. It was where there was the most crime in the whole area. But the authorities congratulated themselves on having done their job of rehousing. She did not want to end her days in one of those blocks anywhere in the city.

Khun Chai's offer of marriage gave her an option that she would never have imagined possible. Not that she could contemplate the idea of moving into that mansion. But he already told her that he was willing to move. Still, his proposal struck her as so absurd that every time she thought about it, she would smile to herself. It was not that she did not like him or enjoy his company. He was a cultured, amusing, interesting person, and the first man with whom she ever felt relaxed. But the idea of getting married at her age, and to someone from such a different background, was too embarrassing to contemplate.

As she went around the room, collecting little things that she found and taking those she wanted out of the wooden box and transferring them into her shoulder bag, she kept wondering whether she should call someone in Baan Suan to see if Khun Chai was all right but decided not to. She would be back there in a couple of hours. She had seen the empty wine bottle in the morning when she went out into the garden to help Sai and Nai Wang clean the pool. It had been such an intense evening. The treatment that she had to give to Ai Toh to calm him down had taken her to her limit. When she touched him, she felt that she was dealing with a dark, destructive force that had invaded his vulnerable young heart. It was the drug that he had taken, but it was not only the drug. It was all the poison of the city that had taken him over.

Wat Saphaan was a short walk from her shack. After finishing what she went to do in Jetsip Rai, she made her way there in the fierce heat of the morning sun. She had told Sai that she was going to the temple to see Phra Sobhon and invite him to Baan Suan to clean the bad energy of the previous evening. She also mentioned that she was also going there to ask the monk to take away the darkness in Ai Toh, because that was something that was beyond her powers. It needed someone who had deeper *samadhi*, deeper concentration than she had. Sai had gratefully agreed to this.

Before ordaining, Phra Sobhon had worked with Yai Li's husband Maitri, for the port authority. They belonged to the same group of friends who went out drinking together. He always struck her as different from the others, always shy and sensitive and caring. He had helped carry Maitri home many times from a bar binge. Then one day, to general disbelief, he announced that he was going to ordain as a monk. They heard that he went to a Forest Monastery in the Northeast. Then, after no news for several years, one day he was back in the district in Wat Saphaan, the poor man's temple. When Maitri died, he had chanted over the corpse. Over the years he built up a reputation of being gifted with the power of exorcism. If there was a place that was haunted because some violent murder had taken place, or if someone was suffering from possession Phra Sobhon would be the monk they invited. Everyone in Jetsip Rai was convinced that he had the gift to do this kind of work. Yai Li herself saw him in action on two occasions. Once a woman who lived near her became possessed by the spirit of a well-known gangster who had dabbled with magic before he was shot. She began to speak with a man's voice threatening her family. Another time Phra Sobhon was invited to a derelict building where a man, high on drugs, had killed a child who was the daughter of someone Yai Li knew well. While the monk performed the ritual in one of the rooms, all of them who were standing outside saw smoke coming out of the windows as if there was a fire burning inside, and heard what sounded like a long sigh of relief.

She found him in his *kuti* lying on his bed with his eyes closed, his hands crossed over his heart. His attendant, a young man wearing a *pakama* and a tee shirt, showed her in but put a finger to his lips to tell her to be quiet. He was unaware that they knew one another. The small room smelled of dead flowers and candle wax. Apart from the altar with the Buddharupa that stood to the right of the low bed and a meditation cushion in the corner, the room was distinctly bare. Yai Li sat by him, her legs tucked under her, not knowing whether or not to disturb him. She looked at him, wondering if he were ill. It was a strange time to be lying down. He was much thinner than when she had last seen him, which was two years earlier at a funeral. His skin was sallow, and he had black spots on his face – the same as the ones she saw on Khun Chai's back. His assistant, who was sitting in the corner staring at her, coughed gently, as though to let Phra Sobhon know that he had a visitor.

'Oh. It's you, Yai Li,' said the monk without opening his eyes. 'I am sorry I am not sitting up. My body is not well.'

Yai Li held up both her hands in a gesture of respect and said:

'How did you know it was me, Ajarn?'

'Nobody has your vibration, Yai Li. Only you.' he said. 'But you've changed. Something has happened to you. You are not so old.'

Yai Li laughed.

'Ajarn,' she said. 'I am ancient, like you.'

Now he too chuckled.

'What have you come for?'

Yai Li explained to him what had happened in Baan Suan the previous evening. But seeing him prone on his bed, and after what he had said, she did not make the request for him to leave the temple and go all the way across the city to do the ceremony. It was he who said:

'So, you've come to ask for my help. But you think that I am too ill to travel.' He paused. 'Well. Don't worry about me. My aches and pains come and go. I may be all right tomorrow, in which case I'll be there. It will be in the morning. Just leave the directions with Ai Nok. Now leave me. I need to rest.'

When Yai Li returned to Baan Suan that afternoon she reported everything that had happened to Khun Chai.

'Well, if he can come, I suppose it won't do any harm,' said Khun Chai. 'Anyway, I am curious to meet your famous monk. If you say that he knew you were there without opening his eyes, then he must have something special. That or he peaked.'

Khun Chai was amused by his own remark, but Yai Li did not share his cynicism.

'You intellectuals don't believe in anything, do you?' she chided him.

'You're wrong. I have seen things too. I know there are things that can't be explained. It's just that there is so much fakery in our country. Difficult to tell the true from the false.'

'Well, you needn't worry. He's the real thing. Take my word for it.' She said this firmly and looked cross, making Khun Chai smile.

'By the way, 'she continued. 'I found this in my house.'

She took put the piece of paper from her shoulder bag and handed it to him to read, and when he had finished reading it, she said:

'Are you serious?'

'What do you mean?' he asked, confused by her question.

'Are you really serious?' she repeated her question as she stared at him. But now she was smiling, and suddenly he understood what she meant.

'Of course, I am.'

'If you are, then I accept your proposal. I have no choice now.'

Khun Chai took her hand, squeezed it, then got up from his chair without a word, and walked into his room. When he returned, he was carrying a small blue velvet box that contained a thick gold ring with a deep red Burmese ruby surrounded by a crown of diamonds. It was so beautiful that it made Yai Li draw her breath and open her eyes wide.

'This was my grandmother's. It's the only valuable thing I have. I've kept it all these years. I thought of giving it to my wife, Mitr's mother, when we were married. But I didn't because I didn't love her. I am glad I didn't give it to anyone else. I want you to have it.'

Chapter 34

They had parted wordlessly when Arunee's tears finally subsided, and she had regained her calm. She got up from the chair, brushed down her satin dressing gown and squeezed Joy's hands as she looked into her eyes, gave a slight nod and turned to go. Afterwards, Joy lay for a long time feeling a mix of different emotions until, exhausted, she went into a deep sleep. When she saw Arunee again in the dining room the next morning, she could feel her heart beating faster as she realized that all that she wanted to do was to walk up and hug her. But she controlled this urge because Mae Hom was standing by listening to what she was saying. Arunee looked up and smiled at Joy when she entered, but did not stop talking:

'Listen, Mae Hom. The point is, I think that Ai Toh needs help. I can't see any other way. But, of course, like I said long ago, it's your decision. You, Sai and Pao must agree about this. There are places that Toh can go to and be well cared for. I can arrange this, and I will cover the cost. It will be my gift to you.'

Joy, not wanting to disturb this conversation took her coffee out to the terrace. While she sat there alone Sai came up to her and said:

'Khun Joy. They have rung from Mudita House. One of the women there is having a crisis. They are asking for you and Khun Arunee to go. Could you please take her? I don't want to leave Ai Toh yet, and my cousin is still asleep. He only got back this morning from work.'

It was when they were in the car and through the gates of Baan Suan that Arunee turned and said:

'Thank you for last night.'

She reached her hand across and touched Joy's, who held it for a second and then drew it to her lips and kissed it briefly. It was a spontaneous gesture that did not seem to surprise Arunee, although Joy noticed that from then on, until they reached Mudita, Arunee held her hands clenched tightly together in her lap. And if she was expecting an intimate discussion to follow her act of tenderness, she was met with a long prosaic monologue on the problems of autism and how the condition was being treated in Thailand, and what institutions she was going to contact where Toh could be cared for. Arunee's intentions regarding the boy's well-being were obviously sincere. But it was as though she deliberately wanted to steer clear from any intimate verbal exchange between them. Joy was disappointed but listened attentively to her friend.

Their whole morning in Mudita House, was spent dealing with the situation that had arisen when the women had returned from Baan Suan the night before. One of them, called Nong Daeng, the twenty-five-year-old who had cried by the poolside, was in such a state of distress that she could not stop trembling violently, as though she were going to have an epileptic seizure. Khun Sumanee had given her a sleeping pill. But in the morning, when she woke up, she was still disturbed, barely articulate and threatening to kill herself. Her hysterical condition was scaring the others, and the atmosphere in the house was becoming unstable. Sumanee did not know whether or not to take the young woman to the hospital.

When Arunee and Joy arrived at Mudita House, the women came rushing up to them even before they were out of the car.

'Nong Daeng's gone mad,' one of them said immediately 'She wants to hurt us.'

Arunee put her arm round her and gently said:

'What happened yesterday was very upsetting for everyone, including me, and Pi Joy. Now let's see what we can do to help Nong Daeng.'

Up till then, Joy had not seen Arunee in action before. She had noticed how poised she was whenever she was dealing with people on an individual basis, like with Mae Hom over breakfast, but never before with a group of people, and certainly not women who were highly agitated. She observed closely as Arunee gathered them all into the main area of Mudita House, which was a covered terrace that overlooked the garden. She insisted that Nong Daeng was also present and made her sit next to Khun Sumanee. She then asked all of them, one by one to take their time recounting what they remembered of the evening and what it brought up for them. One by one they spoke.

Joy was reminded of the same type of group sessions they held in the Mercy Centre when she was growing up there. But at that time, those meetings, held on a regular basis and led by a professional psychologist who volunteered at the Centre, did not seem to her to achieve anything. The girls would fidget and look embarrassed. None wanted to talk about what had happened to them. The young psychologist was kind and well meaning, but she always gave the impression of trying too hard and having some goal she was working towards. In the end, nothing really happened in those meetings that convinced Joy that they were worth attending.

In comparison, the way that Arunee coaxed the words out of the young women seemed effortless. There were even moments when she injected a sense of humour and soon the change of energy among them was palpable. It was as if a storm cloud was evaporating and allowing the sunlight to shine through. Nong Daeng was the last person to speak. She found it difficult at first to say anything that made sense. Partly this was because she was still under the influence of the tranquilizer. But it was also obvious that something that happened in Baan Suan had been overwhelming for her. It was with the utmost patience that Arunee finally persuaded Nong Daeng to tell her story. This is what she shared.

She grew up with her mother, father and elder brother in the slums in Laad Prao. They were poor but they had enough because both of her parents were employed. Her mother worked in the kitchen of a shopping mall food court. Her father was a guard in the parking lot. There was a seven-year gap between her and her older brother whom she adored and who often had to look after her until the parents returned from their long hours at work. He was a handsome, caring, clever boy who liked Muay Thai. But he fell in with the wrong crowd and, when he was sixteen, he was given Yah Baah by a friend. When their father found out, he beat him and made him promise never to touch the stuff again. One day he disappeared, and they were all worried sick about him. He returned almost a week later, one evening when the parents had come home. He kicked open the door and stood there for ages with a machete in his hand and a wild look in his eyes.

'Ai hiah! You bastard!' her father, a fierce, strong man, shouted out.' What the hell do you think you're doing. I am going to beat the shit out of you.'

But her brother ran towards him and cut him down with one terrible blow, then turned to her mother who put up both hands to plead with him. But he slashed her neck and killed her too. Then he came towards her, and she was too frightened to utter a sound. She knew at that moment that she was going to die. She closed her eyes tight and braced herself for the blow. She heard the swish of the machete and then she felt his body falling on top of hers. He had cut his own throat. His blood spilled over her.

When Nong Daeng finished her story, they all sat with their heads hanging down. Some of them were crying. Slowly, Arunee told them all to stand up and gathered them one by one until the whole group was surrounding Nong Daeng. And then she got them to put their arms round each other with her in the middle and just stay there. Joy herself was crying too by now. Then she could hear Arunee say:

'Nong Daeng, how are you? Do you feel safe?'

At first there was no reply. Then Nong Daeng said in a soft voice:

'I do. It's the first time in my life I have ever told anyone this story. It has haunted me since I was a girl. Other bad things happened to me. But that's the one that's hurt me most. And last night everything came back. It was like it was happening all over again.'

'But you see, nobody was hurt in the end. I am still here,' said Arunee. 'And Pi Joy is still here.'

By the time they dispersed the change in Nong Daeng was visible.

'Just keep a good eye on her,' Arunee told Sumanee and Mae Matana when they were leaving.

'She will be all right.'

The meeting had been so intense and demanding that she had suggested to Joy that, instead of staying to eat with the women in Mudita House, which was what they usually did, they should go to a restaurant on the river.

'I think we deserve it, don't you?' she said, and Joy was happy to agree.

They made their way to 'La Riva', an Italian restaurant that was the latest fashionable place to eat in Bangkok.

'It's lunchtime. We'll get a table easily. The beautiful people usually go there at night,' she added.

On the way there they did not talk. Arunee needed time to recuperate and Joy too wanted to digest what she had witnessed and felt.

When they were seated at their table by the wide smokey glass overlooking the broad expanse of river and sipping their Prosecco, Joy immediately began:

'Where did you learn how to do that? Or did it just come naturally? That was brilliant what you did in there!'

Arunee looked embarrassed.

'It wasn't that great.'

'No? Well, I thought so. You were so confident. Were you trained in therapy or something?'

Arunee took in a long in breath before replying:

'I was in therapy. When I was in America. And yes, I did group therapy too.' 'Really?'

'Yes. And you're the only person who knows this. I didn't even tell Mitr about it.'

Again, Joy was not entirely sure whether she should push further or allow Arunee to decide to open up to her or not. Before she could check herself, she said:

'I hope it wasn't anything like that awful story that Nong Daeng told us.' They both laughed. But then Arunee's face darkened.

'It wasn't. There was no physical violence. But…'

Joy reached across the table to hold her friend's hand. 'You don't have to go back there if you don't want to.' 'Well, if Nong Daeng can, I don't see why I can't.'

So it was that during the elaborate meal, Arunee told Joy how when she was a young girl, her father's only daughter, his treasure as he called her, he would like to make her watch as he made love to his numerous girlfriends, who were mostly professionals.

'He never abused them. Not as far as I remember anyway. But I know some of them were really upset that I was there at all. Of course. Who wouldn't be? That's a form of abuse, isn't it? Anyway, I found it all repellent. I used to stand there clenching my hands and clenching my teeth. It was a cruel, painful experience for me. I still don't know what he got from my being there. He was so perverted. As for me, it put me off sex for good. Do you understand now?'

'But it did end.' said Joy weakly when she had heard the story, and she reached over to stroke her friend's cheek. Arunee kept her hand there for a few moments as they exchanged expressions filled with tenderness.

'Oh sure. I just refused to go along one day when I was in my teens. But the damage was done. That's why I needed therapy. I didn't think it would do me much good. But I have to admit that it helped me. I could have ended up doing bad things to myself without it.'

Joy was at a loss to find any words of comfort except to keep muttering:

'I am so sorry.'

'He tried to make it up by throwing his wealth at me. But, as I say, it was too late, and nothing could compensate for the harm he had done. Sometimes, when I was older, I felt like killing him. The therapy helped me. I learned eventually to forgive him, whatever that means. But it's the work of the Foundation that has saved me.'

As they were leaving La Riva that afternoon Arunee turned to Joy and said:

'You are turning out to be a good friend. Thank you.' And then three words that remained with her long after they were uttered:

'Give me time.'

Chapter 35

Sai went over to fetch Phra Sobhon and his assistant Nok from Wat Saphaan the following morning. Nok had called saying that the monk felt well enough to leave the temple, but insisted that they must not expect too much from him as his health was delicate. Khun Chai, who got up earlier than usual and put on his smart clothes, decided that the Phra should be served his food on the balcony. A small altar was set up, with fresh flowers, candles and incense prepared and beside it the wooden dais where the monk would sit. There was an air of expectancy as they all waited for his arrival. Yai Li had told them of his powers. Everyone was standing huddled by the covered entrance to the house, shading themselves from the fierce sunlight. Nai Jit, discharged from the hospital, had been brought back to Baan Suan the previous evening. Only Pao and Ai Toh were missing.

When the Mercedes came up the driveway and drew up on the gravel in front of the steps, a frail, short, pale-skinned monk wearing a brown knitted woolen hat emerged from the far side of the car helped by his assistant. As Sai went to park, Khun Chai felt the same pang of disappointment that he had felt when Yai Li arrived at Baan Suan for the first time. The Phra he saw in front of him looked hardly able to stand without his assistant to hold his arm and he did not exude any obvious supernatural powers. He seemed an old man, like himself, only in a worse state of health. But then, remembering how wrong he had been when he first met Yai Li, he smiled as he bowed with his hands together, along with the others.

Phra Sobhon's movements were so deliberate and careful that it seemed to take him ages to straighten up and turn around to acknowledge their greetings. He took time to look from one to the other with a steady, kindly gaze. Then, shielding his eyes from the sunlight, he looked up towards the dome. Then he turned back to the garden and scanned it from one side to the other. Silently, he lifted his hand and after pointing in the direction of the pool, whispered a few words to his assistant.

All this took place at such a slow pace that it seemed to produce a soporific, settled atmosphere that was in stark contrast to the hectic rhythm of the city beyond the walls of the house. Nok left his teacher for a moment, approached Khun Chai and said:

'Ajarn needs a bowl of rainwater, if you have any, and a bunch of fresh flowers. But please make sure there are no thorns on the stems.'

Nai Wang, the gardener was duly dispatched to the side of the house where the enormous clay water container, dating back to the Ayutthaya period, stood. It had been put there when the house was built to collect the rainwater from the roof. He came back carrying a porcelain bowl filled to the brim. Arunee herself went around the balcony cutting flowers from the ceramic pots and trimming off the leaves before handing the bunch to Nok.

In silence they all made their way step by step behind the Phra and his assistant to the swimming pool, which was now full again and looking every bit like the symbol of wealth that it was meant to be. Phra Sobhon stood still for a while and looked down into the water. Then, raising his head he started to nod as though he were acknowledging something that the rest of them could neither see nor understand. Nok handed him the bunch of flowers and then took the bowl of rainwater from Nai Wang and held it out for his teacher, who now began to chant in a low voice a prayer that none of them had heard before or recognized. As he did so, with eyes half closed, the old monk dipped the flowers into the bowl and then, with economical movements of his arms, flicked the rainwater onto the surface of the pool and continued to do so until the prayer was finished. Handing the bunch of flowers back to Nok, he headed back towards the house.

Apart from the prayer that he had uttered at the poolside and the standard ones to give blessings after he had been served his food, which he barely touched, Phra Sobhon said nothing until tea was served to him. Khun Chai, who found the silence uncomfortable tried to initiate a conversation by saying:

'So, Luang Paw. Why is the rainwater important?'

The monk looked at him and smiled as he made a gesture with his fingers, of rain falling from the sky.

'Ah yes. Because it comes down and cleanses,' said Khun Chai answering himself, and the monk nodded.

'So that means the area by the pool is now clean.' The monk now shook his head.

'Yes. But this house isn't.'

This was the first time that Phra Sobhon was speaking, and his voice was so low that they all had to lean forward to catch what he was saying.

'This whole place needs to be cleansed. There's a lot of darkness and pain. All the rooms.' he continued. 'But I have not got the strength to do it. Otherwise, it should be changed.'

'What do you mean, Luang Paw?' asked Khun Chai. 'The house should be changed?'

Phra Sobhon looked at him for a long time before answering.

'Its past is full of suffering. It has been used for the wrong reason.' Khun Chai was surprised to hear this, but said:

'I think I understand,' he said. He wanted the Phra to elaborate but at that moment Yai Li interrupted their exchange by saying:

'There's the other matter, Ajarn.'

'I haven't forgotten, Yai Li,' said Phra Sobhon with a laugh. 'But from what I see, most of you here could do with cleansing.' He looked pointedly at Arunee then at Joy as he said this. 'You have shadows hanging over you.'

None of them needed any further invitation. Wordlessly, they lined up behind one another on the balcony and took turns to kneel before the Phra who, while he chanted his prayer, kept dipping the bunch of flowers into the bowl and then sprinkling the water onto their heads. Even Khun Chai with his painful knees managed to go down onto the floor in front of the old monk and receive his blessing. The ritual seemed to take forever, and when it was over at last, they were all sitting on the floor of the balcony drenched in rainwater. Phra Sobhon paused to sip his tea when he had finished and said:

'Now where's the boy?'

Pao and her son were fetched from their room. It was the first time that Toh had appeared since the evening of Loy Kratong. He looked confused and frightened, as though he was ready to turn and run away and his eyes darted from one person to another. But when they made contact with the Phra's gaze he seemed to immediately calm down.

With his hand the monk bade the youth to come closer and sit in front of him. Then the two of them sat looking at one another for a long while until the boy slowly bent his head and lowered his eyes. Now, Phra Sobhon, instead of sprinkling the water over him as he had done with all the others, merely held the drenched flowers on Toh's head as he chanted, and soon the boy's tears mingled with the water that was pouring down his face and over his shirt.

Last to do the ritual was Pao, and when she was done, she pointed to her son and asked the old monk:

'Will he be all right now, Luang Paw? Will he be well again?'

'He's a special being. He can see more than most of us. But he's vulnerable. He's been invaded by the darkness. Many young people have been these days. He's all right for now. The poison's been cleansed from his system. But you should think of getting him ordained. In the Northeast there are still good monasteries where he will be well taken care of and where his gifts can be developed. But you must take him far from the city. This is a bad place for him to be.'

Toh was listening to this with his eyes still looking down. But those sitting near him could see that he was smiling.

'Well, what's the verdict?' said Khun Chai after the Phra had left Baan Suan and the four of them were having lunch together. They all knew what he meant. But nobody wanted to answer him. He continued:

'I don't know about you. But I didn't feel anything. I know everyone's calmer now, and that's a good thing. What I mean is that I did not feel he had any special powers. Not like you,' he said looking at Yai Li who immediately put a hand to her mouth and giggled.

'Stop it, Khun Chai! Don't say such things! I am just an old masseuse. He's a great teacher and healer.'

'I saw a Taoist priestess do what he did once in Singapore,' said Arunee. 'What did you see?' asked Khun Chai.

'She moved around this old house chanting and kind of dancing, and she cleaned the darkness out of a building. It felt like that, anyway.'

'Oh. Is that what Phra Sobhon wants us to do here? Will Baan Suan then be entirely a ghost free zone?'

His sarcastic remark was ignored by them.

'But how do you feel, Khun Chai?' asked Joy. 'Are you better? You seem to be in a very good mood.'

He turned and smiled at her.

'It's true. I have to admit that I do feel better after that sprinkling of rainwater. Fresher than I have been for a long while. But maybe it's just that I am glad that we're here together, and no harm was done that evening. Nai Jit has not lost his arm entirely. Ai Toh seems back to his normal self, although I agree with what Phra Sobhon said. Perhaps it would be good for him to go and be ordained. There's that monastery near Ubon that people say is a good place to go to.'

'Well, what more do you want, Pa?' asked Arunee pleasantly.

'I want to be happy,' he answered her, smiling even more broadly. She laughed at his unexpectedly innocent remark.

'And what would make you happy?'

He stroked his chin for a moment with a thoughtful expression on his face, then reached over to touch Yai Li's hand.

'Since Loy Kratong is behind us now, and since you are both here with us, I want you to know, Joy, that your grandmother has agreed to marry me. And if Phra Sobhon is still alive by then, I hope we will get some more rainwater sprinkled on us at our wedding.'

Chapter 36

It was after lunch. Since they were taking the day off from going to Mudita House, Joy and Arunee decided to spend the afternoon by the swimming pool in the shade of the tamarind tree. They were both in their swimsuits but neither had dared so far to go into the water even after the Phra's exorcism.

'Well, well, well,' said Arunee when they had settled into their deck chairs. 'Who'd have thought? The two old lovebirds. I didn't have a clue. Did you?'

Joy laughed.

'None at all. I mean, I knew they were fond of one another. They do make a strange couple, though.'

'They certainly do,' said Arunee with a serious expression. 'But are you ok with it, really? I mean them actually getting married.'

'Why not? It seems anything goes these days. Anyway, I don't think I have a choice. They seem to have made up their minds. What about you?'

Arunee shrugged her shoulders, as though she was unconvinced.

'It's just that it's all happening so fast. Mitr's death, and then…'

Her tired voice trailed off and she sat hugging her knees. Joy reached over to touch her on the shoulder.

'You're thinking about the house.'

Arunee turned to look at her for a moment and nodded:

'How can you read me so well?' she said. 'Yes, to my shame I am thinking about Baan Suan and its future.'

'You don't want it to go to my grandmother in case Khun Chai dies first. Is that it? Are you already thinking along those lines? You are, aren't you? And then if she dies it will come to me.'

Joy realized even as she was speaking that she would not have dared to say these things a week earlier, not with such candour. She had seen so many things that she had not allowed herself to express, but she now felt the confidence to be truthful. She also saw that she had accessed a side to Arunee's personality that was new to her.

'How funny that would be! The thought that you might one day be living in my house. Does that make you feel insecure?'

She saw that her friend did not share her amusement.

'Well, you don't have to worry. I have no ambitions to own this place. It would be such a burden to be responsible for all this. I wouldn't know what to do with it. I prefer my nice little condo in Bang Na, frankly.'

Arunee still kept silent.

'What do you think that monk meant about changing the house?' asked Joy. 'I'm not sure, 'said Arunee.

At that moment they heard the sound of a 'ping' coming from Arunee's leather shoulder bag.

'Your phone,' said Joy who reached over for it and passed it over to her friend.

'It may be Sumanee. I told her to keep us updated on that girl, Nong Daeng.I hope she's not freaking out again.'

As she read the message Arunee's face clouded over immediately. She slid her finger over the screen and her eyes widened with surprise.

'What's happened?' asked Joy, alarmed at her companion's expression. Arunee turned the screen round for both of them to see.

'Sumanee told me she'd received this just now, and that I should be prepared.'

They watched a short video clip posted on Facebook that showed the two of them sitting at the table in La Riva two days earlier. Their hands were intertwined, and their faces were close as they talked. It looked as though they were either about to kiss or had just done so.

Then Joy reaches out to touch Arunee's cheek. There was no mistaking the intimacy. There had been only a few other tables occupied in the restaurant that afternoon and none had been close by. They concluded that it must have been one of the waiters or waitresses who had pointed the camera. In any case the video, probably sent to a friend, had been subsequently posted and gone viral.

The comments ranged from the smutty to the accusatory. The one that seemed to provoke the most responses was:

'The lovebirds are celebrating. They are guilty as hell!'

It was obvious that they were still very much a source of heavy gossip across the social media and the social strata.

Arunee flicked her mobile off angrily.

'Why can't they just leave us alone?'

With that she walked to the pool side and plunged into the black water.

⚓ ⚓ ⚓

'I would like to say that it will pass quickly, like all gossip in this country. That's been my experience in the past. People get bored and find something else to entertain them. It's part of our culture, as my late father used to say. But honestly, I am not sure anymore.'

It was Khun Chai, commenting on what he had just heard from Arunee. They were all having tea on the balcony.

'Social media has changed everything. Not that I know much about it. But it's all so much more aggressive these days.'

'They can still get bored quickly,' Yai Li added.

'True, Yai, 'said Joy. 'But you don't understand the power of Facebook and Instagram and the rest of it, because you have never used any of them. There are millions of people out there now following this, both those we know and those we don't, and among them journalists saying that they did not think justice was done. They are pushing for the police to re-open the case.' They sat in gloomy silence for a long while.

'So, what can we do?' said Arunee angrily. 'This is unacceptable. It's vile. We've got to answer them.'

Joy: 'All of them? How can we?'

Khun Chai: 'You can argue with them all you like. But you probably won't change their opinion. The narrative is out there now, beyond anybody's control. Besides, it's the video I am worried about.'

When he was being shown the video clip, he could not help thinking that he was watching two women in love. There was no reason why others would not come to the same conclusion.

Khun Chai: 'There's only one solution. You two must leave.'

Joy: 'Leave here? But what good would that do?'

Khun Chai: 'No. I don't mean leave the house. I mean leave the country. It's probably best to do so separately and stay away for a while. Go and do something pleasant together. Take some time off from this crazy place. Have the rest that you deserve. Have some fun. Take no notice of any of this stuff. If it were me, I would close your Facebook and Instagram and all the other accounts. Give them nothing to bite on for a while.'

Both Arunee and Joy took a moment to mull over his suggestion.

'But I suppose that you have to get visas first,' he continued. 'That will take time.'

'No, Pa. That's no problem, at least for me. Mitr made sure we both had diplomatic passports. He used his influence. Something to do with being commercial adviser to the honorary consul of Estonia.'

'And I have two passports, 'said Joy. 'Khun Mitr helped me to get a British passport because of my father, and I have a Thai one. It made it easier for me to travel with him.'

'You have them with you?' 'I have them in my briefcase.'

Khun Chai held up both his thumbs in approval.

'But how long should we stay away? And what about my work with the Foundation? I can't just leave it, 'said Arunee.

'Well, you will have to. You can trust Khun Sumanee to hold the fort while you are gone. I have met her, and I think she's solid enough to take care of things. She's compassionate and intelligent – a good combination. Mudita will be fine in her hands.'

After listening to Khun Chai, Arunee and Joy kept glancing at each other as though they were communicating in telepathy. It was Joy who finally spoke.

'I think you are right, Khun Chai. There's no other way. I am grateful for your advice. If we take it, I think we should go as soon as we can.'

Arunee got up from her chair, walked round the table and put her arms round her father-in-law's shoulders before putting her hands together.

'Yes. Thank you, Pa, for thinking of our well-being. You are a wise man. I think we should start packing right now.'

Chapter 37

Joy was used to dealing with the logistics of travel. As Mitr's secretary, whenever they went abroad, she had taken care of all the arrangements down to the minutest detail, so that her boss would have no cause to complain. Now she was doing the same thing for herself and his wife. That afternoon, she used all her experience to see that their plan was carried out as efficiently and seamlessly as possible. It took her an hour and a half of concentration on the internet. Arunee was to leave earlier for London and stay overnight there in a hotel near Heathrow Airport. She herself would take a flight to Madrid with a connection two hours later to Paris. In Paris they were booked into the Hotel Lutecia for three nights in two adjoining rooms. They would decide whether to stay there or move to other accommodation.

Joy, who did not have any clothes that were suitable for autumn in Europe, packed a small overnight case.

'Never mind,' said Arunee. 'I will take you shopping in Paris. That's what I always did with Mitr when I went there. I want to see you looking Parisian and elegant. We'll have a good time. Pa's orders!'

Their flights out of Bangkok were three hours apart, but Joy did not want to stay in Baan Suan alone with Khun Chai and Yai Li. She preferred to wait at the airport. That evening, after a light supper and saying their farewells, the two women were driven separately to the airport. Sai took Arunee in the Mercedes and his brother drove Joy in the van. The decision to stay apart until they were both in Paris was not their preferred one. When they first discussed it, they did not see that it was necessary.

'I think Khun Chai is being a little paranoid,' said Arunee.' It won't make any difference if we arrive there in the same car.'

'Perhaps not. But you never know. These oldies are sometimes right.'

In the end, they were glad that they had listened to his cautious warning. For as soon as she had finished checking in at the counter, Arunee turned to face a young, pretty, well-dressed woman standing next to the queue who smiled at her and said:

'You are Khun Arunee Thammawong, aren't you?'

Arunee was immediately on her guard, and merely nodded in reply before walking brusquely towards the entrance to passport control. The airport was crowded. She trailed her overnight case behind her as she weaved in between the people, feeling flustered and annoyed. The young woman kept in step with her.

'Can I ask you a few questions?' Arunee shook her head.

'But where is your friend? Aren't you traveling together?'

There were other questions that were fired at her, but Arunee chose to ignore them all. As she handed her boarding pass to the airline official and went through, she turned slightly and caught the young woman holding her smartphone to take a picture. By the time she reached the business class lounge she was still trembling. She then did something that Mitr always did whenever they were waiting for a flight, which was to pour herself a tall glass of whisky. Then she texted her friend.

From a distance, Joy had seen Arunee being pursued by the person she presumed was a reporter and wondered how she had discovered the details of the flight. She guessed that it must have been someone on the check-in desk who recognized the name. She prayed that Arunee was not going to react and cause a scene out of anger and frustration. She wished she were by her side to protect her. With a sense of relief, she saw her go through to passport control and disappear round the corner while the young woman began messaging on her phone. Khun Chai had been right.

Unlike Arunee, who had chosen to wear a smart dark blue trouser suit, Joy was in a grey nondescript sports outfit complete with trainers and a baseball cap. She had also taken the extra precaution of putting on the glasses that she usually only wore when driving.

'You're going in for the full disguise, I see,' Arunee had said before they left Baan Suan.

'Just in case. Yes. Do I look very plain?' 'You could never look plain.'

Now she was glad that she had dressed down. From what she saw happening to Arunee she knew that she should try to stay as invisible as possible. The check-in for her flight was still not open, so she took the elevator and went two floors up to where the food courts and restaurants were and found a place that was crowded with tourists. She chose a corner table at the back, took a book out from her shoulder bag, and ordered a plate of fried rice that she did not touch. From that position she bided her time watching the diners come and go. There were only two or three moments when she felt nervous, and they were when a Thai man or woman came into the restaurant without carrying or trailing any baggage, and peered around them. As a precaution she pulled her cap down and raised the book that she was pretending to read to her eye level. But her fears were ungrounded and when it came time to check in, she made her way calmly to the airline desk.

Less than an hour later she was sitting in the window seat of the Thai Airways flight to Madrid, waiting for the plane to take off. Her bag was under the seat in front of her, her cap and glasses were off. She stretched her legs. She could relax at last. As the flight attendant leaned across the empty seat next to her to hand her the complimentary glass of champagne she whispered:

'It's Khun Joy, isn't it? I was sure it was you.'

Joy, in her panic almost spilled the drink. But she saw that the stewardess was smiling at her in a kindly way.

'Don't worry. All of us are with you. We all think you are innocent,' she said. 'Are you going for a holiday, to escape all the fuss?'

Joy nodded.

'Yes. A holiday,' she said. 'To escape.'

When, a day and a half later, they were reunited in the Hotel Lutetia, Arunee and Joy hugged each other like long lost friends. They had already talked by phone when they landed in their respective destinations. Joy had explained what happened on the flight to Madrid.

'It was like a having a fan club, or something. They treated me really well. Kept giving me drinks. Hung around me like hens. I thought they were going to ask for my autograph at one point.'

'Oh, I don't trust them a bit,' said Arunee. 'I wouldn't be surprised if they took a photo of you while you were asleep, and it's posted on Facebook or Instagram by now.'

'You may be right. But do you know?' Joy replied. 'I don't give a shit! We're out of there.'

⚜ ⚜ ⚜

Paris, as Khun Chai had predicted, was the welcome rest that both needed. On sunny days they walked down the avenues and through the parks enjoying the autumnal colours and the gentle light coming through the trees. When it rained, which it often did, they would sit in a café talking or reading magazines or visit a museum or gallery. Joy was enchanted by everything she saw. It was her first time in Europe, and she had not expected it to be so different from Asia, particularly from Bangkok where she could not remember going for a stroll just for pleasure. She had not imagined she could be so moved by simply getting to know the beauty of a place by walking down its streets. Arunee, for her part was glad to be able to initiate her friend to the city where she felt inspired and revitalized, and she enjoyed surprising Joy by taking her to the hidden corners off the tourist routes; small, squares and side streets that looked as though they had been untouched for centuries.

'How come you know it so well?' asked Joy.

'As a little girl I used to come here with my mother. Just the two of us. She had been brought up here. She was the daughter of a diplomat. She knew Paris inside out. We came here the year she died. I was ten. I remember how we walked and walked till my feet got sore. It was as though she wanted to leave me with her love of this city, like a legacy.'

'Is that why you kept coming back? To be reconnected to her?''

'There you go again. How well you know me. You are very special.'

Sometimes they would walk hand in hand, or arm in arm, through the streets humming a song that both liked.

'This would get them going on Facebook,' said Joy.

'Yes. Why don't we post it ourselves?'

The crossover from being friends to being lovers took place after they left the hotel and found a serviced apartment off the Rue St. Germain des Prés. It was spacious and comfortable, with two bedrooms, one single and one double, a bathroom to share, a living room, and a kitchenette. The windows overlooked a quiet treelined street. They were so pleased with their find that they decided to take it for a month. By now, Joy had seen how, unlike other people, Arunee had no financial obstacles.

'We can always leave earlier if we need to, if something happens to either of them, or if there's a crisis at Mudita House,' said Arunee.

'Or we could stay here forever,' said Joy. 'You are used to doing anything you want, aren't you?'

'Does that bother you?'

'If I am honest, I have to admit that it makes me jealous.' 'But it's also a burden, you know and…'

'Money can't buy you love. Is that what you're saying?'

The first night that they spent at the apartment it was raining outside and a cold wind was blowing. They had spent the afternoon at the Musée de Montmartre and eaten in a Senegalese restaurant. Their exhilarated conversation was about the paintings, sculptures and objects that had impressed them in the museum.

'I still can't believe it, 'said Joy. 'That we're here so far away from all that madness of Bangkok. I don't know how to thank you.'

'You don't have to thank me. I am grateful to you for being here with me.'

No word was exchanged when they climbed into the double bed together, no questions, or declarations of love or desire. It was as though everything that had gone on before between them had inevitably led them to this intimate embrace. As the rain pelted the tall windows of their room, they both discovered for the first time the quality that had been missing from both their lives.

Chapter 38

'Do you want a fancy wedding?' Khun Chai asked Yai Li, who burst out laughing.

'Of course, I do! In one of those expensive hotels, so that I can invite all my friends from Jetsip Rai. And I'll get a long dress made and buy myself a new handbag, and I'll go to the hairdressers and have my hair dyed. What on earth are you thinking of?'

'But why not?' he said with a slight impatience. Yai Li shrugged.

'When I got married to Maitri we went to Wat Saphaan and got a blessing, then to the local registry office. After that he disappeared to go off with his friends and wasn't back till the next morning. What about you?'

'Oh, when I got married, I was so sad I got drunk at the reception and thought of throwing myself into the river,' said Khun Chai.

'Why were you sad?'

'Because I didn't love her, and I felt desperate and stupid for doing something that I knew was such a mistake.'

'Well, make sure you are not making the same one this time.' Khun Chai looked at his bride to be with a serious expression. 'You know, I had my doubts.'

'So why are we doing it?' She flashed him a look of annoyance. 'At our age. It's not necessary. You have my company. I'm with you every day. I'm not going to abandon you. If it's just to help me out because you think I am going to be homeless, then I would rather we just remain friends.'

Khun Chai held his hands up to calm her.

'But you don't understand. This is important to me. I told you I had doubts because I wanted to be honest with you. I have always had them. I can't remember doing anything in my life that I didn't doubt first. That's how I am. But I am certain that I want to marry you. And I may well insist that we do it in style, in the ballroom of a grand hotel, with a huge cake, and a band, and you can invite anyone you want.'

'No. Please don't. It would be too much for me. Don't forget how different our backgrounds are. I would have to invite all that crowd from Jetsip Rai. They'd probably steal the furniture and fittings. They would not be up to your people's standards.'

Khun Chai frowned.

'I hate all that bullshit,' he said. 'Nobody is better than anybody else. My grandfather was a degenerate. My father was a gambler and a drunk. Yours was a healer who helped a lot of people. Who's the noble one among them?'

Yai Li reached across the table and stroked his hand.

'Would you have married that Pia if you could?' she asked him, her eyes twinkling.

'Oh. Like a shot,' he replied.

It was now over two weeks since Arunee and Joy's departure from Baan Suan. Before leaving, Joy had shown them how to use WhatsApp on their mobile phones and thanks to her instructions they now received short, texted messages from time to time saying: 'we're okay' or 'enjoying Paris immensely', and they would reply in the same vein. The house felt different without their presence. In the evenings, Khun Chai and Yai Li would now sit on the terrace instead of in the dining room and share a simple supper. Recently, Khun Chai seemed to be losing his appetite; a detail that did not go unnoticed by Yai Li who refrained from commenting, as anything she said regarding his health – even a casual remark – was always rejected by him.

'Don't fuss,' he would say. 'I really can't stand that.'

Nevertheless, he allowed himself to complain about his various aches and pains and continued to ask for her to give him treatments. She knew that her touch comforted him. Lately, after a session he would sometimes accompany his words of gratitude with a long hug and a kiss on her cheek.

The first time that he did this he said:

'You don't mind, do you? We're going to be husband and wife after all.' 'I don't mind if you're not going any further,' was her reply.

Her words amused him.

'I'd have to get some of that medicine if I was going to.' 'Oh. You can forget the medicine.'

Their friendship was now at a stage that they could talk with ease about these things. After Yai Li had told him about what happened in London, she was able to share with him the way that she had always mistrusted men, including her husband, Maitri, who was the only person who had ever made love to her. Others had tried to win her affection after he died, but she was never interested. Khun Chai was the first man with whom she spent any time, and she could still not understand what it was that put them together.

Khun Chai, for his part, talked to her freely about his past.

'Sexually I was a lightweight. I had a few girlfriends. But I didn't go around chasing women, and the ones I was attracted to didn't give me a second glance. I think I channeled the energy of desire into my work.'

This made Yai Li laugh in disbelief.

'Oh. You're being clever again. I don't understand any of that. I bet you went elsewhere to channel your desire – like all Thai men.'

'I didn't, you know. Just the thought that I was with someone who didn't want to be with me and paying her for it…After knowing Pia I just couldn't do that.'

'Oh no! Not that Pia again. One day we should go looking for her all over the country till we find her. Then maybe she'll stop haunting you.'

These exchanges were the first time that either Khun Chai or Yai Li had spoken with such freedom and openness to another human being, and as the days went by the trust and intimacy between them deepened and fulfilled them in a way that was more powerful than any carnal gratification of desire.

┉┉ ┉┉ ┉┉

One morning, Yai Li was surprised to find Khun Chai already up and dressed.

'I went to bed early last night. I'm going to train myself to do so from now on. If we're going to share the same bedroom, it's not going to be pleasant for either of us if we keep different hours.'

'But what about your writing?'

'What writing?' he said. 'I'll get back to it, if I do at all, after we're married. There's plenty of time. I'll establish a new routine. Now please get yourself ready.' 'Why? Where are we going?'

'We're going to Ayutthaya. I want to see where you came from.'

The drive took no more than an hour along the new highway. During it, Yai Li sat nervously in the back seat holding his hand. Sai kept looking in the rear mirror and smiling at them.

'I don't know why you want to do this'. she said. 'I haven't been back since I left all those years ago.'

'That's why we're going.'

Their first destination was the railway station.

'I don't remember it like this at all,' Yai Li said immediately when they parked outside. 'They've made everything look so new and shiny.'

Then she turned her head to a corner of the carpark and her gaze remained there for a while. 'Was that the spot?' asked Khun Chai gently and she nodded. The memory of that hot dusty afternoon came back to her like a blow to the stomach.

'Why did you make me come here?' she asked. 'You never said goodbye properly, did you?' She shook her head.

'No. That's true. It was all such a rush. They made me pack. They put me on a train. I don't even remember him being cremated. Or if he was, I didn't take part in it.' 'That's what we're here to do.'

Khun Chai asked if she wanted to go back to the house where she had lived with her father.

'No. It's not necessary. Besides it's probably gone by now. It used to be over there, in a street between here and the pier,' she said pointing in the direction of the river. 'But please don't make me go there.'

'Was there any temple your father went to around here?'

'He wasn't a religious man. He had his own path,' she said, recalling how her father had told her that his powers had nothing to do with bowing to Buddha statues.

'But on Makha Bucha we would go and do the Wien Tien ceremony at a temple nearby. I think it was called Wat Bodhiram. We used to walk there. So, it can't be far.'

'That is where we are headed.'

Khun Chai had been to the city many times in his life. He was fond of Ayutthaya. Whenever he had guests from abroad – a journalist or a visiting writer – he would take them there and hire a boat to visit the ruined temples on the river that had been given the status of World Heritage sites; deservedly so, in his eyes, after the careful restoration they had received from the Fine Arts Department. He was always sure that his guests would be impressed. He often wished that the same care had been applied to restoring and preserving the old monuments of Bangkok. He had never been to this particular one, Wat Bodhiram. It was also on the river, but it was not one he would have taken anyone to see.

As soon as they got out of the car, he looked around and realized that it was one of those *wats* that was everything that he found off-putting about Thai temples. An imposing black marble plaque in front of the entrance with gold lettering explained the history of the place, which he read with interest, learning that it was seven hundred years old and had been burned down several times by invading Burmese armies and subsequently restored. But there was nothing about its modern appearance that provided a clue as to how it might have looked. All around him Khun Chai saw the mess that exemplified Thai Buddhism in the twenty-first century. Several courtyards were cluttered with the paraphernalia of superstition and folkloric belief. In a corner, stood a stone Buddharupa covered with pasted squares of gold leaf, where people went to ask for lottery numbers. Along the wall of the covered walkway, a row of statues depicting the Buddha in different postures were made of shiny bronze coloured resin. In another courtyard, a glass-fronted shop sold amulets and replicas of past abbots. In front of it there was a huge depiction of Mount Meru, made from plastic, and next to that a murky fishpond with a fountain in the middle topped by a white Buddha. There was nowhere that he looked that was not, in his eyes, imbued with bad taste – so much so that he found it amusing.

Yai Li, recognizing the tone of his laughter, said:

'It's not up to your standards, is it?'

'I don't mind,' he replied. 'Really, I don't. It's a gem in its own way. Very quaint.' 'Oh, what a liar you are!'

There were several people about, going in and out of the main hall of the temple to pray and bow to the huge golden statue that stood surounded by elaborate frescos painted in bright, garish colours.

Khun Chai sent Sai off in search of the abbot whom he was going to ask to perform the ceremony. But, after a long while, Sai came back and told them that the monks had all been invited to bless a new supermarket that was opening in the centre of the city.

'There's no one here, only an old nun. She's sitting under a tree in the back courtyard.' 'Let's go then. We don't need to bother her,' said Yai Li quickly.

'No. We're here now,' Khun Chai insisted. 'Let's pay our respects to her. There's no harm in that.'

The nun was sitting crossed legged on the circular seat that surrounded a huge Pikul tree that looked older than the whole temple complex. She did not seem to notice them approaching, nor when they pulled up the white plastic chairs in front of her. It was obvious that she was either partially or wholly blind. But, on hearing them, she looked up and said:

'Please excuse me. My sight has almost completely failed. They say they can restore it with operations. But I said, No. Why? At my age I've seen enough anyway. Have you come to visit the temple? Or to see the abbot? I'm afraid he and the other monks have gone to bless a shop – one of those big ones that are opening. They won't be back till this afternoon. I am not normally here. I live in another temple. But sometimes I visit because I always used to come here when I was young.'

She smiled, showing a row of rotting teeth.

Khun Chai and Yai Li glanced at one another. It was as though Khun Chai were seeing if she recognized this old nun from her childhood. But Yai Li shook her head.

'Sister. Do you remember a healer who lived near the station when you were young?' asked Khun Chai spontaneously.

'A healer, you say? There was only one around this district. Lots in Ayutthaya. But only one who lived around here. That was Ah Sem. Of course, I remember. We all knew him. He treated my aunt. She couldn't walk and he helped her walk. He treated lots of people, anyone who wasn't well. He was a good man, a kind man. We all respected him.'

Then why did he have to die like that? thought Yai Li, yet again. As though she heard the question, the nun continued:

'Why did he have to go in that terrible way, shot by a drunk?' she sighed. 'There's no answer to these things.'

Khun Chai was about to tell the nun that Yai Li, the healer's daughter, was right there beside him but Yai Li put a hand on his forearm and shook her head.

The nun went on reminiscing about her youth and recounted how she had decided to ordain when her husband died, until she began to tire of her own monologue.

Afterwards, when they had said their goodbyes and were walking away, Khun Chai turned and said:

'But why didn't you want me to tell her who you are?'

Knowing what he was referring to, Yai Li replied:

'Because I did not want to talk about the past. We'd have been here all day. Did you see how talkative she was?' 'Yes but…'

'But nothing!' It was the first time she had raised her voice at him. 'You want me to make peace with what happened to my father. I appreciate your good wishes. But I'll never be at peace with it. Not totally. How can I? He died for no good reason. A stupid, jealous drunk shot him when he was in his prime. Cut short his life. It broke my heart. Do you think doing a ceremony would make it better? Nothing can take my grief away. It's with me and will be through this lifetime. I have accepted it. It's you who wanted to come here and do this. Not me.'

Khun Chai was stunned by her forceful words.

'I am so sorry,' he said and held her in his arms as she sobbed.

They went out by the side entrance to the courtyard where they had met the nun. To reach the carpark they had to walk through an area called 'The Historic Garden'. It was again full of gaudy, coloured resin statues, all life sized, depicting various battle scenes. In between groups of figures, a plaque on the ground described the battles fought between the Siamese and Burmese warriors prior to the fall of the Ayutthaya kingdom in the 18th century. As they weaved their way past these frozen scenes of warfare, Khun Chai suddenly stopped. In front of him there was a warrior in Siamese costume, with an elaborate helmet, holding a short sword in both hands, surrounded by three Burmese warriors dressed in their traditional garments who were pointing their spears menacingly at him.

For a moment he closed his eyes and looked as though his knees were going to give way. Sai and Yai Li quickly held his arms from either side to prop him up.

Later, when they were in the car, Yai Li said:

'You remembered, didn't you?'

He nodded.

'I was there. I died on that battlefield.'

'That's why we came here.'

Chapter 39

Even though they had promised that they would not check their social media accounts while they were away, they did receive messages on WhatsApp keeping them up to date on what was happening back home. From Sumanee, the director, Arunee heard that all was calm in Mudita House. One of the trustees, a well-connected businessman and ex-colleague of Mitr's had decided to resign from the Foundation and had sent a formal posted letter to Mudita House saying that he could no longer be associated with Arunee given the news that was circulating about her in business circles. He also added, for good measure, that he found her behaviour unworthy of her late husband. It was a message meant to wound and it did; Arunee had considered him to be a personal friend, not just a business colleague, and a man with liberal values.

Joy had received a WhatsApp from her old friend Nong Maew at the Mercy Centre asking where she was, as no one had heard from her for a while. She also said that the posts on social media about her and Arunee had all but disappeared. She ended by saying:

'You can come out of hiding now, Pi Joy. It's all good.'

It was this message that influenced Arunee and Joy's decision to cut short their stay and return to Bangkok in late December. But there were other reasons, the most obvious being the weather. Late autumn in Paris had been a mixture of pleasant sunny days and cool, damp ones that grew cooler and damper as the weeks went by, until finally, the raincoats they were wearing could no longer keep out the cold. The daylight hours were getting shorter, and this brought with it a sense of melancholy that affected them 60th.

'No wonder there was so much literature and poetry written in these countries,' commented Joy.

They were also beginning to miss Bangkok. After taking in all the culture and the beauty of Paris, they realized that there were things they could not find in those well-tended, elegant, ancient surroundings. They even had fun making a list of what these were, starting with what they both disliked about their city: the traffic jams, the flooded lanes during the rainy season, the carpark attendants' shrill whistles, the polluted, stinking canals, the Christmas decoration under the boiling sun, the massage parlours. When they came to what they liked they toyed with the food, the temples in the old part of the city, the river, Phra Pradaeng, but in the end Joy suggested that it was simply the people.

'They are so cold to each other here, and rude.'

'Well, not all of them. Anyway, thats's just the Parisian style,' said Arunee. 'Even the French from other parts of the country comment on it.'

'Yes. But still. Why live in such a beautiful place and be so grumpy? People at home are really friendly, even the poor ones who have nothing. All the tourists comment on it.'

'Ah. That's because we know how to please,' said Arunee.

'But it's not all put on, is it? Don't you think any of it is genuine?'

'No. I think there's a lot of real kindness and care. That's true. Maybe Buddhism has a lot to do with it. But what I don't understand is why you think the people in Bangkok are so great after what they've done to you, and to us?'

Joy shrugged her shoulders.

'It's what Khun Chai said: gossip is our national pastime. They can't help it. A juicy scandal comes along and immediately, bang, everyone's dining out on it.' 'I don't see how you can be so flippant about it.'

'I guess it's a lesson in humility for me. And being here with you has made me stronger. I feel I can take it on now. It won't affect me. I am ready to answer them.'

Saying this Joy put her arms round her friend and kissed her.

'Let's go back and face the music.'

Their last meal in Paris was in a small brasserie near where they were staying. It was pouring with rain that evening. They were seated in their usual corner by the window watching the people hurry by with their umbrellas held low over them. They had spent the day in the apartment slowly packing up their things. Now they sat quietly sipping their glasses of wine and picking at their plates. Neither felt hungry. Both were nervous at the thought of returning to a city where they had already been judged and condemned. The bravado that Joy had felt lately seemed hollow that evening.

'Will we ever do this again?' she asked.

'Oh. I hope so,' said Arunee. 'Many times!' 'But what happens when we get home?'

'I don't understand.'

'Will we still be together? Or will we keep up pretenses?'

'It depends on how brave we are.'

'I am not brave. But I can't bear not to be with you.'

'I am not brave either. I have always cared too much what people say. Even if they have stopped all the nonsense on social media, it can all start up again any moment. And it's not just Facebook or Instagram. It's when we go anywhere together. The tongues will be wagging. The question is: Do we let them take away what we have?'

They held each other's hands and stayed silent for a long time.

'We've had no one even look at us while we've been here. We can hold hands. We can walk through the streets arm in arm. We can kiss,' said Joy. 'I shall miss this freedom. Why is it that everybody is so hypocritical in our country?'

Arunee shrugged.

'They like the theatre. They like the masks. They go for displays of piety, and propriety. Everything is dressed up for show. That's how it is.'

'Well, as the song says, they can't take any of this away from me.'

They clinked their glasses and asked for the bill.

Chapter 40

December 14th, the day before Arunee and Joy were due back from Paris, a big demonstration was planned to protest the government's banning of the Future Forward party. It was announced at short notice, although there had been rumours that it was going to be the biggest one for over five years. When he read about it in *Thai Rath*, Khun Chai was immediately determined to join in. The evening before it was to take place, he and Yai Li had been arguing about his wish to participate.

'How can you even be thinking of it?' asked Yai Li, when she first heard of his intentions, not conveyed to her but to Sai.

'Think of where it will be best to park,' he was saying when she came in on their conversation. Sai, remembering the exchange he had with her the first time they met, was smiling.

'Are you going in the wheelchair or are you using the walking stick?' she continued. She too could not help smiling. 'Do you think your presence is going to make a difference? It's not as though they have invited you to make a speech.'

'Oh. Now you're making fun of me. But our country's future is at stake. We can't just sit around being bullied yet again.'

'But what will it achieve, this demonstration of yours? What good have they ever done? I went on those marches in 1973 and 74…'

'Well, I didn't, I am ashamed to say. I just stood on the sidelines and watched. I remember you told me that conditions improved because of those marches.'

'It's true. There was a tiny change. But I also said that it was not enough.'

'Well, that's how change comes in this country. Drop by drop. We can't give up.'

'It's all very well, talking your fighting talk. But I don't see you up to running round the streets avoiding the water cannons or the police trying to beat you up.'

Khun Chai laughed.

'I wasn't planning to be in the front lines. Just adding my bit. Showing that old farts like me haven't lost hope in the young ones.'

'And you think this is important?' Khun Chai nodded.

'Well then,' said Yai Li with a look of resignation. 'I suppose I'll have to keep you company in that case. I'm certainly not letting you go there alone. But I never imagined I'd be going to another demonstration again in my life.'

In the end they did not join the protesters. On the morning of the demonstration Khun Chai woke up with the pains in his back that did not allow him to move with ease, and Yai Li had to give him a long session before he could do so once more.

They had to be content with watching the events of the day unfolding on the television screen. Yai Li was secretly relieved, not only because Khun Chai was unable to go, but because the demonstration turned out to be a peaceful one, with both the protesters and the police showing restraint.

'It's only the beginning,' said Khun Chai as he watched the images on the screen. 'There will be more in the future. The young have had enough. You can sense it, can't you?'

Yai Li had to agree. Seeing how many people there were, mostly young, and the eager looks of hope on their faces she was reminded of their group from the Siam Garment factory walking arm in arm down Rachdamnoen Avenue towards Sanaam Luang, singing and chanting slogans that demanded justice and equity.

⚜ ⚜ ⚜

Arunee and Joy guessed that it might have been the fact that Bangkokians were too involved in the demonstration and in its aftermath to tweet, post or text about anything else. Or perhaps it was simply that the two of them had ceased to be a source of entertainment, or fodder for those who wanted to spit out their ire and envy. At any rate, they arrived back in the country and breezed through the airport without anyone paying them any attention or glancing their way.

In the car, Sai filled them in with news of Baan Suan. He told them how he and Pao had taken their son up to the Forest Monastery near Ubon, as Phra Sobhon had suggested. Pao was still there making sure that Toh was being well cared for. The abbot had told her that for the moment they were taking him in as a helper, but if he wanted to, he could ordain as a novice the next rainy season.

'And what about Khun Chai?' asked Arunee. 'Has he been well?'

'On and off. He gets tired easily these days. And he goes on losing weight. But he refuses to see a doctor.' Sai replied and told them of the trip to Ayutthaya and how he had to be helped back to the car.

'He wanted to go to the demonstration yesterday, Khun. Can you imagine? But his body wasn't up to it.'

'And any idea when the wedding is going to be?' asked Joy.

Sai: 'None at all. They haven't told me anything.'

Joy: 'But it's still going ahead, isn't it?'

Sai: 'The last I heard.'

Arunee: 'And what do you think about it?' Sai's face broke into a broad grin.

'You mean them getting married. What can I say, Khun? They seem to be in love, and they get on well. I have never seen Khun Chai so happy. These days, people do all sorts of things, don't they?'

Arunee looked at one another and reached for each other's hand across the leather seat. That evening, the four of them had dinner together on the balcony. The air was cool and the sky clear and starry. Arunee and Joy had rested from their journey and enjoyed a late afternoon swim in the pool. Cold, rainy Paris felt a long way away. During the meal they told Khun Chai of the places they had visited and the walks they had taken, with such enthusiasm that Khun Chai, at one point, addressing Arunee, said:

'But I never heard you talking like this this after your trips there with Mitr.'

'That's because we didn't do these things,' Arunee replied. 'I would go out by myself while he stayed in the hotel, most of the time in the business centre, on the computer, getting things done over here.'

'That sounds like Mitr,' said Khun Chai. Then, looking at Joy, 'Well, I am glad you had someone to share Paris with this time, and you both seem to have benefited from being there.'

'It was your suggestion. Thank you again.'

Arunee reached over and gently touched Khun Chai's arm, something she had never done. 'Listen, Pa. We have something to tell you both.' She glanced over quickly at Joy, whose eyes showed surprise.

'I don't know how you will take this. But we don't want to go around hiding the truth from you, tiptoeing around pretending. I have fallen in love with Joy, and I think she has with me. It's the first time either of us have felt this way towards anybody.'

She looked across at Joy, who nodded and smiled.

There was a long silence. Yai Li looked down at her hands. Her face revealed nothing. Khun Chai displayed no outward reaction either but waited patiently for his daughter-in-law to continue.

'It happened in Paris. It wasn't planned. We were content to just be friends. At least, I was.' 'No wonder it's called the city of love,' said Khun Chai.

Arunee, who had been uncertain how he was going to take the news, sat back in her chair and gave out a sigh.

'So, you could say that we're a couple now. Like you two,' she said.

Now it was Yai Li who spoke.

'I saw it coming. From that first time I saw you together in Joy's condo. Your vibrations were harmonious, I thought to myself, although I couldn't understand how, given what had happened, and I was still nervous about why you were there at all. But this is good news. You have my blessing. It may be hard for other people to accept it. But you two being together is not as strange as me being with Khun Chai.'

All four of them laughed.

'Are you thinking of getting married too?' she went on.

'Oh, Yai. I wish we could,' said Joy. 'But it's not legal here. In France, yes. But not over here.' 'Not yet. But it will happen. You'll see. One day soon.' said Khun Chai cheerfully.

Arunee and Joy's disclosure of their relationship brought a sense of satisfaction as well as amusement to Khun Chai. He did not feel that it was in any way a betrayal of the love he bore for Mitr to think that his son's widow had at last found the love she was looking for in such a short time after his death. Whatever anyone else wished to read into this was up to them. But for him it was the first time that he saw Arunee joyful and bright. He had always seen her as a heavy, obsessive and controlling person. This change was an unexpected gift. The idiosyncrasies and the ticks, he noticed, were still there but without such intensity as before. The fact that she was in love with a woman did not seem to him any more improbable than his old friend and mentor John Booth's love for men. He was glad that she was able to take the risk of openly declaring her preference instead of carrying on pretending and upholding the precarious norm set by a hypocritical society. And he was impressed that Joy was turning out to be such a dependable and loving companion for her. He had been struck by her strong character from the beginning when she was Mitr's secretary but in the months that he had come to know her better he had seen her grow into a fuller, more confident person. He wondered if this would have happened if she had not been subjected to the challenges she had had to face following Mitr's death.

It was not lost on him that what happened to all of them had to do with Mitr. His son had been the catalyst for all these changes in Baan Suan, including his own affection for Yai Li. And, along with the grief and sense of loss that made itself felt from time to time in his heart, when he thought of Mitr, he would also smile at the imagined conversation that they might be having in one of their weekly lunches by the river.

'Do you know that your wife and your secretary are in love? Do you know that my masseuse and I are getting married? It's all thanks to you.'

Khun Chai's decision to celebrate New Year's Eve at the Hotel Siamois was made after the conversation with Arunee and Joy.

'Since we are all in the business of coming out, we must do it in style,' he said the next day, when he asked Joy to make the reservation for them. It was one of the properties that Mitr's company had acquired and refurbished that year and was already described as the most luxurious place to stay in Bangkok.

'It will be crowded. We should book in good time. Make sure it's the best table with a view of the river,' he told her.

'I'd rather stay here and have *somtam* and grilled chicken,' said Yai Li when she heard of the plan.

But in the end Khun Chai persuaded her by saying that it was going to be their engagement party. She reluctantly allowed Joy to go through Arunee's wardrobe and choose an outfit for her to wear for the occasion; a cream Armani trouser suit, brown slip-ons and a gold evening bag. Khun Chai also insisted that she wear the ruby ring he had given her.

'I am going to look like a proper Khunying now,' she told her granddaughter.

'But of course, Yai. You are marrying a Khun Chai after all.'

When she appeared on the front steps of Baan Suan that evening, she could have been taken for an old aristocratic lady or an aging film star. Khun Chai, in his best dark blue suit and striped tie was also the picture of elegance.

'What a handsome couple you two make,' said Arunee.

Joy had sent word forward to the maître d' that they were coming. She knew him from the time that the hotel was still being redecorated and the new staff chosen. At the re-opening this handsome, competent young man had been particularly attentive to her. She knew that this was because she was Mitr's secretary. She wondered if he were going to be just as polite when he saw her with Arunee. But any fears she harboured were immediately dispelled when he welcomed them warmly and personally led them through the dining room to their table by the tall window that looked out on the Chao Phraya. He pulled a chair back for Yai Li first, then Arunee, then Joy and finally when he stood by Khun Chai he said:

'Khun Chai, krup. We are all sorry for your loss. Your son was a great man.'

When they were seated, Khun Chai looked around him. People were still arriving, and the place was filling up. At the table next to them there was an elderly couple. The man was a farang wearing a light grey suit. His head was bald except for the strands of white hair that were pasted across the round, tanned pate. He had dark rings under his eyes and wore a sour expression. He had the look of someone who was sickly. The stout woman beside him could have been from anywhere in Southeast Asia. Her grey hair was tied back in a neat bun. She wore a light blue, high-collared silk dress and dangling from her neck was a gold cross. Khun Chai took in all these details because as he sat down, he noticed that they both turned to look at him pointedly, and he had returned their gaze with a slight, polite bow. But he saw that, whereas the man immediately turned back to the menu that he was reading, the woman's eyes remained on him for a while longer.

The meal was excellent, as was to be expected, and they were content to take their time between courses listening to the pianist whose repertoire of songs seemed inexhaustible. It was still a long way till midnight.

'I don't know if I am going to last till then,' said Yai Li. 'I am a little drunk already.'

'Well, then don't drink any more, Yai,' Joy chided her jokingly. 'Otherwise, you might get up and dance.'

'Yes,'replied Yai Li. 'And I wouldn't want to do that!'

'You can do whatever you please,' said Khun Chai. 'Have you seen how many admiring looks you've received this evening?'

Yai Li laughed.

'I feel as if I am in some kind of a dream tonight. It's all so unreal, this luxury. I feel I have arrived in the deva realm.'

'Now you do sound drunk,' said Joy.

Since their arrival Arunee had been discreetly looking around the room to see if their presence was noticed. The foreigners who were dining there that night were paying them no particular attention apart from looking up now and then to check out who their fellow diners were. Among the Thais she had noticed glances directed their way and looks of recognition. But the faces were not familiar, and she felt so relaxed that even the sense that people were whispering about them did not upset her.

'You're right again, Pa,' she said. 'Tonight is our coming out party as well as your engagement.

Doesn't it feel good?'

It was now almost eleven thirty. There would be fireworks over the river soon. When the three women went off to the rest room Khun Chai decided to walk out to the terrace to smoke his cheroot. He had no pains that evening. The night was cool. A pleasant breeze was blowing. The boats ferrying diners were going by in both directions, lit up with fairy lights and crowded with party goers. Music blared out from them. Khun Chai lit up and leaned on the railing. It had been a good evening, probably the last time he would do something like it, and he was glad to have been able to show this lifestyle to Yai Li. Why should there be any class differences at all? Why couldn't everyone enjoy an excellent meal? These and other vague thoughts, fueled by the considerable amount of red wine that he had consumed, and the thudding sound of the dance music being played on the boats going by, combined to distract him from noticing the presence of the woman who had followed him out to the terrace and was now standing next to him. It was only when the boats had passed, and the music faded into the distance that he heard his name being uttered.

He turned to see the woman who had been sitting at the next table with the old *farang* gentleman.

'Khun Chai,' she said again, and he nodded, although he was puzzled. His mind raced to try to recall if he recognized her.

'I heard the maître d' say your name when he was seating you, and I wondered if you were the same Khun Chai I knew years ago. I wouldn't have recognized you, I must admit, and I am sure you haven't a clue who I am. But there was something about you that hasn't changed.'

He could not match her face, her voice, or her rather stiff manner to anyone he could remember. Then it suddenly struck him like a thunderbolt.

'Pia!' he blurted out.

She smiled. He remembered the smile. In a flash he saw her as she once was, not this neatly dressed, prim, grey-haired lady in front of him.

'Is that your wife, with you?' she asked. 'She's very beautiful. Are the other two your daughters?'

Without replying to her question, he said: 'But what are you doing here? I mean in Bangkok. I thought you'd left…' The words were spoken before he could stop himself. She now looked slightly annoyed. It was another expression he remembered.

'I am here with Khun Hans, my husband. We are on holiday from Heidelberg in Germany where we live. It's my first time back for a very long time.'

She turned her head as she said this and looked back into the dining room. The worry showed on her face.

'I am sorry. I must go now. Khun Hans has not been well. He's waiting for me. It's good to see you again.'

With that, she put her hands together and bowed and he did the same. Then she turned away from him, and he watched her make her way back quickly to their table and lean down to take her husband's arm, help him to stand, then guide him towards the exit door. She did not look back.

It was like seeing a ghost appear and disappear again in the space of a few minutes, and he knew that this time she had gone for good.

He remained for a while smoking his cheroot, watching the river and listening to the water lapping against the concrete edge of the terrace. The memories rose and fell in quick succession along with images half recollected from another lifetime. But what was surprising was that there was no charge to them. He felt no emotion, no agitation in his heart. This chance meeting with the person who he thought had been so important in his life had stirred up neither excitement, nostalgia, nor regret. What's more, there was no urge to see her again, no curiosity as to what had happened to her in the intervening years, whom Khun Hans was, whether she had enjoyed her life, had a family or anything like that. She was a stranger who had greeted him by the river. That was all.

As he looked at the lights from the hotel on the other side reflected in the dark waters, he flicked his cheroot into the water and said out loud: 'Jawohl, Frau Pia' and laughed.

They left soon after the fireworks were finished, all of them tired, full and tipsy. Arunee and Joy sat in the front of the Mercedes with Sai who had come back to fetch them. Khun Chai, unconcerned by Sai's constant glance in the rear mirror, had his arms round Yai Li in the back seat as she leaned her head on his shoulder. He spoke to her in a low voice so the others could not hear:

'I met Pia this evening. She was the woman at the table next to us sitting with the *farang*. When I went out to the terrace, she followed me.' Yai Li remained silent for a while before saying:

'And are you planning to meet her again?'

'No,' he said. 'Never. That chapter has finally finished for me. It's closed for good.'

When they arrived back in Baan Suan they hugged and said goodnight. But when Yai Li turned to go to her room Khun Chai took her hand and said:

'Please stay with me tonight. I would be grateful.'

'I thought you'd never ask me,' she replied.

Chapter 41

For once the term New Year was living up to its promise. In the weeks following the celebration at the Hotel Siamois, the mood in Baan Suan was calm and peaceful and there was a sense of renewal. It was as if the dramas that they had been through in the previous months belonged to a time that had now passed into a dimension that none of them cared to revisit. Arunee and Joy were pleased to no longer have to deal with the stress of social media. The gossip surrounding them had evaporated like a cloud into the blue sky. They continued to go every day to Mudita House, where they did not try to hide their feelings for one another, and their joyful combination seemed to have a positive effect on the young women there, several of whom were in their own relationships. At home, they were now sharing Arunee's room on the first floor, and no one in the household seemed surprised or offended by their new-found intimacy.

Meanwhile, Pao returned from Ubon and reported to them that Ai Toh had settled down well in the temple and that the monks were taking good care of him. Even though he was only a helper, he was already joining in all the routine of the monastery, going on alms rounds, carrying the monks' begging bowl, and attending chanting and meditation sessions. She and Sai planned to make a visit there during the Songraan holidays.

As for Khun Chai and Yai Li, they continued the gentle rhythm of their life. Although they continued in separate rooms, they now got up and had their breakfast at the same time and after that they would begin their daily activity in a leisurely way. If Khun Chai needed a treatment, she would give this to him in the late morning, and sometimes another in the early evening before dinner. Even before Arunee and Joy's return to Baan Suan, they had also begun to spend an hour each day swimming or just sitting by the poolside.

After the new year, Khun Chai began at last to work on his novel and sometimes he would be writing for most of the afternoon until dinner time, while Yai Li, sitting at his side would be quietly doing her crochet or reading the book that he had given her, *Four Reigns* by Kukrit Pramoj.

'You'll enjoy it,' he told her. 'Take your time. It's a classic. I met Khun Kukrit once. A really interesting man. And I knew the person who translated the book into English. She encouraged me to keep writing at a point I was thinking of giving up.'

'And you? What are you writing about?' she had asked him when he handed it to her. 'Oh, I'm writing about us,' he replied.

She put a hand to her mouth.

'Who is going to want to read a book about two old people like us?'

'Ha-ha! You may be right. But you know. I don't care. I am writing this for me, and for you.' 'And how is it going to end?'

'Well, I haven't got there yet. It depends on us.'

She never asked him again about his writing but was content to watch him out of the corner of her eye and see the thoughtful expression on his face as he held the pen unmoving over the notebook, or the joyful abandonment that was written over it whenever he was flowing.

During that month of January, it seemed that the sense of well-being that emanated from Baan Suan would last forever. Khun Chai seemed stronger than he had been in previous months. He was putting on a bit of weight and his aches came with less frequency. The two women joked that it was the medicine of love that was giving him this renewed energy. In this buoyant atmosphere, plans for the wedding were discussed and it was decided that it would take place after Sai and Pao's trip to the Northeast to visit their son, Toh.

'You must make a list of the people you want to invite,' said Joy.

'Shall we hold it at the Hotel Siamois? You enjoyed it there, didn't you, Pa?' added Arunee.

'I don't want it to be a big affair,' said Khun Chai. 'Besides, most of the people I've known are either dead or incontinent. And I can't stand most of the members of my family. No. I prefer just us and the people in the house. Like on Loy Kratong, but without the drama. Good food and good wine.'

'That suits me,' said Yai Li. 'I don't want to pretend to be a Khunying like that again.'

The four of them were enjoying such an easy-going, warm relationship with each other that they felt protected from the world outside. It was as though nothing that was happening beyond the walls of Baan Suan could harm them. Even when Khun Chai read them an article about a new virus coming out of China which threatened to become a pandemic, it seemed to refer to something that was so remote that it provoked no special reaction in any of them except for Khun Chai himself who said:

'If it's anything like the "Spanish Flu" in the last century, it's going to be devastating.'

But none of them knew what he was referring to and he had to explain the history of that pandemic.

'But surely that can't happen, Pa. Can it?' asked Arunee. 'I mean, we're in the twenty-first century.'

'Have you forgotten Aids?' was his terse answer.

In mid-January the Ministry of Health confirmed the first case of Coronavirus infection in Thailand. A Chinese woman from Wuhan had been detected at the airport and hospitalized. By the end of the month a total of 19 cases had been reported. Khun Chai seemed deeply affected by the news.

'But that's nothing, Pa,' said Arunee. 'More people get the 'flu all the time. Anyway, if we're careful I don't see how we'd get it. We're not traveling anywhere, and certainly not to China.' But her words, far from being reassuring, seemed to annoy him. She could see from the way that he read each article and now followed the local and foreign news religiously every evening, how obsessive her father-in-law was becoming. Gradually the calm of Baan Suan that they had enjoyed after the New Year was undermined by Khun Chai's pessimism about the virus and its consequences.

At dinner time he would not only update them with the latest news and the figures, but would insist on sharing his own increasingly negative comments, such as:

'The Chinese are lying to everybody. The virus didn't start with the animals in the market. It was a mistake in the lab, just like the Aids virus.'

At first, no one felt like contradicting him, or arguing with his views. But as the days went by his outbursts became more vitriolic.

'Our government are covering up the numbers. They are lying through their teeth. Can't you see? They're afraid of losing the tourists,' he insisted. As he absorbed more news, he said: 'They'll be wanting to dish out vaccines next. Mark my words. And they'll be useless. It's just another way for the pharmaceuticals to get richer…'

It was Yai Li who finally expressed her impatience with him.

'Khun Chai,' she said gently one evening at the dinner table. 'You've got to stop talking like this. You are so negative about everything. You're going to make yourself sick if you go on in this way.'

He looked at her with the same fierce expression that he had worn the first evening they met. For a moment he looked as though he were going to reply rudely to her. Then his face relaxed. 'Maybe you are right,' was all he said in reply.

From then on, he kept his views concerning what was happening with the Coronavirus situation to himself. But it was obvious to them that he could not stop his worries from growing, and his mood became darker by the day.

Whether it was this constant state of anxiety that contributed directly to his illness will never be established. But Yai Li's words were remembered by all of them. By the end of February, Khun Chai was beginning to have night fevers and the pain in his back had worsened again, to such an extent that Yai Li's treatments could do nothing to alleviate them. Apart from this, he was also now suffering abdominal seizures and his skin was taking on a yellowish tinge while his appetite had all but disappeared. But despite the considerable discomfort that he was obviously going through on a daily basis, Khun Chai refused to even discuss going to the hospital to see a specialist when it was suggested by Arunee.

'None of them helped me before, and I don't see how they can help me this time,' he told her with the stubbornness that was by now familiar to them.

In the end, it was only when Yai Li, crying, told him that she was going back to Jetsip Rai if he did not let himself be examined, that he allowed them to take him to the Bangkok Nursing Home. There, with Yai Li in a small bed by his side, he was kept overnight while they did a whole range of tests on him, including the ultrasound, which was to demonstrate graphically, beyond any doubt, that he had Stage 4 pancreatic cancer.

'How long does he have?' Arunee put the inevitable question to the specialist, a balding, sullen oncologist trained in America, whose cold, offhand manner reminded her of Mitr when he was in a bad mood. He explained that only one per cent of those with stage 4 could expect to live for up to five years. The rest would probably die within two months to a year, depending on whether there was metastasis and how deeply this had taken root in the system. In Khun Chai's case, it had already invaded his lungs and liver, hence the jaundiced tinge of his skin.

'So, we are talking months,' she said.

'You can never tell,' he replied without changing his expression. 'Chemotherapy and radiotherapy and the drugs we can give him may help to prolong his life quite a bit.'

'But there's no possible cure, doctor.' The doctor shook his head. 'None, I'm afraid.'

When they returned to Baan Suan that afternoon, Khun Chai was wheeled by Sai into his bedroom where he rested till the evening, and when he appeared for dinner he seemed, to everyone's surprise, to be in the same good mood as he had been before the news of Covid hit the headlines. It was as if the heaviness that had been plaguing him had lifted, leaving him bright and cheerful once more. They had not talked in the van coming back from the hospital. Now he told them, as he sipped his white wine, that while Arunee was sorting out the payment at the desk and Joy and her grandmother were waiting in the lobby, the oncologist had come to say goodbye to him.

'Yes. I saw that, Khun Chai,' said Joy. 'And I noticed that he didn't look very pleased when he came away from you. He walked straight by us without saying a word.'

Khun Chai replied: 'I told him: 'Doctor, you have been very kind and you have all treated me well, and I am impressed by the technology and know-how you have applied to my body. You have my gratitude. But please know that I will not be back for any more treatment here.' I think he was a bit shocked. I said that all I needed was a prescription for some good drugs to help control the pain. He didn't seem to like that. But I don't mind. I can get Sai to get me anything I need anyway, from those dealers down the road.'

'You mean you have decided not to take any of the treatments they are offering you, Pa?' said Arunee in consternation.

'What's the point?' Khun Chai shrugged. 'I mean, there's no cure, and they know it. So why should I submit myself to those things when all it's for is so that they can convince themselves they are doing something, instead of admitting there's nothing to be done? That and taking more money off us.'

'But Pa, you don't know that!' said Arunee, who was now visibly upset.

'I am sorry. But I do. I have known for ages that I have been ill. I have been going into the internet to see what it could be. Trawling. That's the word, isn't it? You see, Mitr's gift did come in useful after all. The symptoms have not been bad all the time, just coming and going, steadily increasing. But it started to really worry me about the same time that Covid started. Now these tests have confirmed what I already found out from my research. Maybe I should have done them earlier. But I was scared. Anyway, I hope you understand why I have been so ill-tempered lately. I apologize to all of you if I have been a pain in the arse. But at least it's not Covid! And by the way, I think I might have been wrong on quite a few things I said about the disease.'

He laughed but they did not join in. He reached over to Yai Li who was shielding her tearful eyes from him.

'I need your help. I need all your help. I am trying to accept that I am incurably ill, and what that means. It's not easy. Please be strong for me. I want to prepare myself.'

Chapter 42

The first thing that Khun Chai wanted to do to prepare himself, as he put it, was to bring the wedding day forward. Yai Li and Sai duly went to visit Phra Sobhon once again in his *kuti* in Wat Saphaan. The monk laughed when he heard what Yai Li had come to ask of him.

'If I was the best astrologer, I would never have guessed this was why you came,' he joked. 'I should really tell that Khun Chai of yours not to bother, that it will not help him to get married. It will only add to his attachment when what he needs to do now is to let go of everything. But we are old friends, Yai Li, and I can tell that this is important for you too.'

'It is, Luang Paw,' she said. 'Though I don't understand exactly why. I only know that I have found love with this man.'

'Ah. Well, that is a good enough reason.'

Two days later, on a beautiful clear, cool morning, Phra Sobhon arrived by taxi with Nok, his assistant, and performed a simple ceremony for Khun Chai and Yai Li in the presence of Arunee and Joy and the rest of the household. Khun Chai sat in the wheelchair with Yai Li on the ground next to him. Both were dressed in traditional costumes, which made them look like characters from another century. They put their hands together and bowed their heads, and as the birds sang in the trees, the Phra chanted and sprinkled holy water on them, and then on everyone present before announcing, with as much enthusiasm as he could muster:

'There now. You are man and wife. May you be happy together!'

When they served him his meal after the ceremony, he told them:

'It's lucky you invited me now. I don't think I will be leaving the temple again. At least not in the near future. There are rumours that soon we might not even be allowed to leave the monastery at all because of this terrible disease. What is it called?'

'Covid,' said Khun Chai. 'Yes. I have heard he same thing, and I think that soon we will all have to be wearing masks if we go out. How do you think it will end, Luang Paw?'

The old monk opened both his hands. Then in his quiet voice he said slowly:

'It's difficult to tell. It may go on and on for a long time. This disease is a symptom. It's a manifestation of a deeper sickness in the world. Look what has been done to Nature. Look at how people live these days. The darkness has to play out until the healing can take place. It's Vipakha-Kamma.'

It was a term Khun Chai had not heard since he was a boy listening to his nurse Na Cheua's version of the Buddha's teachings. Soon after uttering these words, the Phra asked to be taken back to his monastery. It was clear that he had little energy left. Before he climbed into the taxi, he turned to them and smiled:

'Whatever else is happening in the world, be at peace. Be well!' he said as he waved.

It was the last time any of them would see him again. He died later the same year from the Covid virus, said to have been brought into the temple by a homeless man.

That night, Khun Chai and Yai Li lay in each other's arms as man and wife and felt the mingling of their love. It was not the ecstatic sensation that he had known when he had been with Pia as a young man. There were no shifting patterns of light, no rainbow colours, no overwhelming rushes of pleasurable energy. But instead, a deep current of contentment flowed between them as they touched and embraced like the two old lovers that they were.

⚜ ⚜ ⚜

In March the Covid situation had worsened globally. But in Thailand the figures of those becoming infected, at least according to the official calculations, remained among the lowest in the world. Nevertheless, strict precautions were being put in place. Testing booths were set up all over the country. Those found to be infected were isolated. People arriving in the country were put into quarantine. As Khun Chai predicted, masks became obligatory. Vaccines were yet to come. His own condition was deteriorating too, although the decline was subtle rather than dramatic. There were days when he felt no symptoms at all, just a low level of energy. Then he would ask Sai to wheel him out to the balcony where he would sit reading or just gazing out at the garden he knew so well. On others, the pain was only bearable when he was lying down.

It was towards the end of the month when he started to feel that he was approaching another phase of his illness. By now he was taking the morphine that a local doctor he knew prescribed for him to control the pain, and while it worked up to a point, he found that it did not agree with him. It was as though he was pulling away from his surroundings and feeling that he was no longer connected to what was going on around him. This was how he explained it to Yai Li. For her part, whenever he was lying there in his bed she would sit by him quietly, doing her crochet or reading *Four Reigns* carefully, slowly turning the pages of the thick book. If he wanted to talk, she would respond. But he did not have much energy to do so. In any case, she kept their conversations to a minimum because she did not want to exhaust him. Whenever he asked her to, she would touch him with her loving hands, and this seemed to bring some relief to his body. But it did not last, and she knew that her skills were not enough to make him better. She sometimes found it hard to hide her sadness as she watched him suffer and so she would leave the bedroom and walk around the garden until she recovered her equanimity.

Joy and Arunee found solace in each other and in their work at Mudita House, where more women were arriving every week. It seemed that the level of domestic violence had risen along with the collapse of the economy and the confinement that was now the established policy. Fortunately, up till now they did not have to deal with the problem of Covid infections among those who found refuge there. The day-to-day demands kept them busier than before. Baan Suan used to offer a respite from the intensity of Mudita House. But now, coming back home in the afternoons, they could not help but feel infected by the melancholy atmosphere that spread through the house like a blue cloud. In the evenings after dinner, they would go to bed early and watch television, and on weekends they would slip away to the beach in Rayong.

Of the two, it was Arunee who was suffering more. Being used to finding solutions and putting things in order, she felt impotent in the face of what was happening to her father-in-law, and this disturbed her profoundly.

'Why doesn't he let me take him back to the Bangkok Nursing Home?' she constantly asked Joy. 'The specialists know what they are doing. Why is he so pig-headed? I can't stand to see him wasting away like this.'

Eventually her frustration spilled over. When they returned home from Mudita House one afternoon and found Khun Chai sitting on his wicker chair on the balcony, she marched up to him and declared:

'Pa. I am calling the oncologist this evening to make an appointment for you this week. You can't go on like this.'

Khun Chai looked at her with a kind expression and smiled.

'We've been through this, Arunee.' he said. 'I appreciate your concern. But please respect my wishes.'

'No. Pa. I won't. You can't just give up like this.' She was almost shouting now.

'But I'm not giving up. This is my choice.' His voice remained calm.

'But why?' Why won't you let them help you?' The tears were running down her face. He put his hand on her shoulder.

'I am not interested in prolonging my life with their modern medicines…' 'But why not?' she protested.

'Because I am tired, my dear. I have lived enough.'

'But what about being with Yai Li, the woman you have just married. Don't you want to live longer so that you can be with her?'

Khun Chai looked at her with the compassion that came with the intuitive understanding of why she was so motivated to keep him alive.

'I would have liked more time, of course. No doubt about that. But I don't have to live longer to be with her,' he said gently. When he saw her puzzled expression, he continued:

'I am with her. I will always be with her. Time and distance cannot separate love.'

These words struck such a deep chord in Arunee that she immediately stopped her crying. She looked up and stared at him for a long time. It was as though in that moment she realized something that no books, or intellectual study, or religious sermon could have ever given her. When she walked away from him that afternoon and back into the house, she knew that something fundamental had changed in her from the brief exchange that was to remain in her heart in the years to come. After that day she never again pestered him about going back to the hospital but dedicated herself to looking after him as best she could.

The transformation in her was obvious to Joy who questioned what it was that had brought it about. In answer Arunee said:

'Khun Chai is the only man who has been truly kind to me, without expecting anything in return. His sickness disturbed me deeply. It was something I could not and cannot control. I thought that I was afraid that I was not doing enough for him, and I felt guilty, and at the same time angry that he wouldn't let me help him. But I realized that what I was really afraid of was my own mortality. Do you understand?'

Joy nodded although she did not completely follow her friend's meaning. But she did remember that, when, as a child she was taken to see her mother who was dying in the hospice, she knew that she would never see anything so intense again in her life because suddenly it was all there, living and dying, Life and Death, not separate but intimately entwined. And she guessed that this was what her friend was getting at.

'And he is showing me how to confront it, instead of avoiding it,' Arunee continued. 'I am learning that in doing so everything changes. I don't have to be in control anymore. I, too, can begin to let go.'

Chapter 43

In early April the pains in Khun Chai's abdomen and back were getting steadily worse even with the morphine. Lying down sometimes aggravated them, so he preferred to sit up in his wheelchair during most of the daytime. Arunee had taken the step of employing a private nurse to be permanently in the house and to administer the drug that he was now taking intravenously at various stretches of the day. At first her presence was resented by Yai Li. But very quickly she saw that this was the right course of action, because she alone was unable to cater to Khun Chai's bodily needs. Besides, the nurse, called Khun Chada, a thin, middle aged and kind person, was sensitive enough to understand the situation and what was needed of her, remaining discreetly in the background until her help was called for, and allowing Yai Li to act as the principal carer.

Despite his condition, Khun Chai's mood remained relatively calm when the pains did not consume him. He spent his time looking out into the garden or addressing a few words to Yai Li. In the evening he would often allow Joy to read to him from the collection of Chekhov's short stories that he had been reading since before his illness. He now found it impossible to hold the book in his hands or focus his eyesight on the typed script, and he could only listen for a while to a few paragraphs before tiredness overcame him. But hearing the stories brought him immense pleasure. As for Joy, who had never read anything that was not to do with her academic studies, she was discovering a new world during these sessions. She had never imagined that literature could reveal so many layers of emotion, or that something written so long ago could reflect things that were so relevant to her life.

When Joy came to the story that was called 'The Death of a Government Clerk', she at first resisted, being put off by the title.

'But it sounds so morbid, Khun Chai,' she protested. 'Do you really want me to read this to you?' It was obvious what she was implying. But Khun Chai smiled.

'Please. If you don't mind,' he said. 'Don't be afraid of the title, Joy. I read it when I was a young man. It made a strong impression on me then. I'd like to see if it is still as meaningful as it once was.'

When, a day later, she finished it, Khun Chai asked her:

'Did you enjoy it?'

She shrugged. 'I found it strange. Absurd. Almost comical. But sad too. Why did that man Chervyakov die like that? I don't quite understand. Was it shame? Can shame kill you?'

'You're right,' he said slowly. 'It was shame. But more than that. I think it was breaking the norms of politeness. Remember that he was a mere clerk, not from high society, and he did something that went against the accepted code of behaviour. That was the real killer.'

'I think I'd like to read more of his stories,' she said pensively, and he nodded his approval.

'You can read my books too, if you like. And when you've read them, you can have a go at continuing the book I am writing because I certainly won't be finishing it now. In fact, I've hardly started it.' He laughed gently.

Joy looked baffled at his words.

'But I've never written anything before,' she said.

'Well, why not give it a go? You might enjoy yourself.'

Khun Chai could not know that the seed he planted that night would one day bear fruit.

⊱≼, ⊱≼, ⊱≼

The last conversation that the four of them had together took place on April 13th over dinner to celebrate the Songraan festival. That year, because of the Covid situation, the festivities that were normally held in the streets of Bangkok were banned. Instead of the usual frantic, almost hysterical activity that marked those days of constant partying, the city looked like a ghost town where only the mangy dogs and the homeless addicts roamed. Since travel was restricted, Sai and Pao had to postpone their trip to the Northeast to visit their son. But they had heard from a lay member of the community that Toh was doing well and everyone there was pleased with the way that he had integrated into the life of the monastery. As a result, the whole household was present, and a blessing was planned to take place by the pool after dinner.

During the meal Khun Chai sat silently, but towards the end of it he raised a finger as a sign that he wanted to speak. Then, making a great effort and in between fits of coughing, he began:

'I haven't much strength. So, listen carefully. I have spoken about this to Yai Li, and we are in complete agreement. This house is beautiful. We all know that. But it's much too big for one family. It should not be enjoyed just by us. We must find a better use for it. I want everyone who is living here to be able to stay if they want to. Those who want to leave should receive help in setting up home elsewhere. Yai Li does not want to be the owner and she wants to be in a modest place. So officially I am leaving Baan Suan to you, Arunee. I have told the lawyer already and signed the papers. After all, it should be yours. Mitr paid for it. But I leave it to you trusting that you will carry out my wishes in the way you think fit.'

With that short speech, that sounded rehearsed and yet incomplete, he sank back exhausted into his chair.

Later, when they wheeled him to the swimming pool where everyone lined up to receive the blessing that, according to custom, the senior member of the household bestowed on them, he seemed to be only partly present to what was happening around him. Yai Li had to help him pour the water from the bowl onto the hands that received it and, instead of the usual words that he might have uttered, he merely smiled at each one and gently nodded his head. When they were in bed together that night, Arunee said to Joy:

'I don't think he has much time left. It's obvious, isn't it?'

'Yes. But he seems to be accepting it very well,' Joy replied. 'Perhaps it's the morphine he's taking.'

'I am sure that it is. But it's more than that.' 'Yes. I think it is too.'

'Your grandmother's love. That's what has made the difference.'

While Arunee and Joy were talking in their bedroom, Khun Chai, the drip tube attached to his arm, lay next to Yai Li. In the far corner stood a small night lamp with a cloth covering it. Khun Chai preferred having this dim light to the thick darkness, because when he woke up in the night he could remember where he was, rather than thinking that he might already have died. This was what he had told Yai Li and the nurse, Khun Chada, jokingly, when the tube was first inserted into his arm.

That night, after the dinner and the water blessing ceremony, he could not sleep even though he felt deeply exhausted and despite the effect of the morphine that was now entering his system drop by drop. He remained still, looking up at the ceiling, watching the shadows turning into shapes of trees and animals and dancing figures. It reminded him of the trips to the local fair in Pakret when he was a child, taken there on the shoulders of the gardener, his nurse's husband. Usually there would be a few other servants with them, which was just as well because, some time in the course of the evening, the gardener, Nai Noon, Na Cheua's husband, would disappear to go drinking with his friends and not return till the next morning. It would be one of the other servants who would later have to carry him back to Baan Suan. When they arrived at the fair, which was an explosion of lights and colour and music, they would immediately head to the corner where it was quieter, where the Shadow Theatre, *Nang Yai*, was being performed. Khun Chai would sit in the front row along with the other children, enchanted by the spectacle of the *Ramakien* story which he barely understood but which was full of excitement and drama.

'Can't you sleep?'

Yai Li had her back to him on the bed as she spoke. Now she adjusted her position to face him.

'Are you all right? Do you need anything?'

Khun Chai shook his head.

'Just enjoying the shadows', he said, pointing a finger up to the ceiling. 'They remind me of my friend, Mac. He wanted to make films.'

'Yes. You told me.'

'But he died. So young. I loved him, you know?' Khun Chai paused and closed his eyes.

'Do you think I will meet him again? I mean...'

'I ask myself the same thing about my father. Sometimes I feel completely certain that I will meet him again, that he is waiting for me.'

'And do you think we will meet again?' 'Do you want to?'

'Yes. And this time sooner rather than later, I hope.'

They lay for a long time in silence with their hands intertwined, each lost in thought and in memory. Over the past months they had come to know one another like two people who had spent a lifetime by each other's side. There was no more need to tell stories or reminisce, or even to verbalize what was in their hearts. As sleep finally came to him, Khun Chai muttered: 'Will you help me when the time comes?'

The time that Khun Chai was referring to came three days later, at 5.30 in the afternoon, just after Arunee and Joy had arrived back from Mudita House. It had been raining heavily. The sound of the bullfrogs could be heard through the open window. That morning the nurse had insisted that she could wait no longer to insert the nasal cannula into Khun Chai's nostrils and connect him to the oxygen bottle that had been standing in the corner since her arrival at the house to take up her duties. She had wanted to do this for over a week when she saw that his breathing was becoming laboured and his energy level was steadily decreasing. But Khun Chai kept refusing with a firmness that bordered on anger. Even now he protested. It was only when she told him that she could be accused of dereliction of her duties that he surrendered.

'Well, we can't have you getting into trouble. So go ahead with what you have to do,' he said. But by the afternoon he was regretting his compliance.

'It doesn't help at all,' he told Arunee and Joy when they came in to see him. They were wearing their masks and had washed their hands carefully as they did every day on returning to the house. They sat side by side looking down at him, lost for words as they saw his chest, which now seemed so bony and fleshless beneath the thin cotton top he was wearing rise and fall, and heard the strange gurgling sound that accompanied his breathing. He motioned for them to take their masks off.

'Covid won't make any difference to me now,' he said, and Joy's eyes filled with tears. 'I'd like to see your faces once more.'

Slowly, he held out his right hand towards them and when they both put theirs on his, he reached over with his left and gently laid it on top.

'If you have found love and friendship, hold onto each other. There's nothing more precious,' he said, before closing his eyes. They stayed like that for ten minutes before pulling their hands away, bowing respectfully, and then leaving him to sleep.

When they were gone, the nurse, Khun Chada, came in to check his heart rate, to see that the drip was functioning as it should and that the nasal canula was still in place. He was aware of her presence but kept his eyes closed as he did not want to interact with her or have to answer any of her questions. But when Yai Li entered the room, he sensed her presence and immediately opened them again. They looked at one another without uttering a word, but the communication that flowed through their eyes was clearer than any verbal expression could have provided.

Khun Chai lifted his hand to his face and carefully pulled the contraption out from his nostrils and laid it on the pillow beside him. It took a few anxious seconds for him to adjust to the loss of the oxygen, but eventually he recovered his calm, even though his breathing was now faint.

Then he nodded at Yai Li, who first put her hands together in prayer and closed her eyes for a moment. When she opened them again, she reached over and barely touching his skin, laid her forefinger on the side of his neck, the same way that she had done for Maitri her former husband; only this time it was not pity that she felt, but a love so deep that she felt her whole being filled with its radiance. Khun Chai looked at her for one last time and then closed his eyes forever. The crackling sound in his throat ceased. A stillness came over his body. There was the faint hint of a smile around his lips. Yai Li stayed for a while, silently taking in the features that she had come to know so well in such a short time. Then she replaced the contraption, bent over to kiss his brow, bowed with her hands together, and left the room to call the nurse.

Chapter 44

Given the situation that was worsening by the day, strict restrictions were now in place regarding all social activities and gatherings, and this included the ceremonies held in the temples throughout the country. Khun Chai had already told them that he did not want anything but the simplest cremation and they complied with his wishes by taking his body to the old *wat* on the river in nearby Pakret. There, with everyone masked and the disinfectant get splashed round liberally, they watched his coffin slide into the furnace and the smoke rise into the cloudless, blazing hot April sky. The next day Arunee and Joy fetched the ashes and the remaining fragments of his bones that had withstood the flames.

In Baan Suan, the sense of grief and loss were palpable during the following weeks. It was somehow enhanced by the collective depression that was now beginning to blanket the city. The servants went about their work in a daze. Even though during the months previous to his death Khun Chai had hardly spoken to any of them, his absence was now felt keenly by each one of them. With the master of the house gone, a sense of uncertainty about the future pervaded.

Arunee put off the inevitable meeting that she knew had to be held because the loss of her father-in-law, however much it had been expected, produced a sadness whose intensity she was not prepared for, and this made it hard for her to feel motivated to perform any of her duties. It was fortunate that Joy could allow her the time and space to grieve without putting any pressure on her. Eventually, it was Arunee who one afternoon said:

'We have to tell everyone what's going to happen. I think I am ready now.'

They had talked about the issues between themselves after that evening when Khun Chai had announced his wishes for the house. Arunee had already invited Joy to become a trustee and member of the board of her Foundation. Her task would be primarily to fundraise and to ensure that the finances of the organization remained healthy.

'It's just up your street,' she told her friend, and Joy accepted gratefully. In the months since she had been working at Mudita House, she had discovered a sense of fulfillment that she had not known working in the private sector. She was certain now that she could never return to that world of corporate finance, real estate and the wheeling and dealing that she had witnessed. Working for the Foundation was like the calling she had been expecting.

They had discussed what Khun Chai had said about Baan Suan and neither of them found it easy to decipher his vague words. Did he mean that he wanted the house and grounds to be turned into a public space that would be shared with the public, like a museum, or a cultural centre? But then he had stipulated that he wanted everyone who was living there to be able to remain there should they wish to. How would this work? Did he have a specific project in mind along the lines of what Phra Sobhon had suggested with his similarly equivocal pronouncement that was equally open to interpretation:

'The house should be changed…It has been used for the wrong reason.'

They remembered the words well enough. But then how should it be changed, and what would be the right reason?

After endless conversations they came to the conclusion that Baan Suan should be turned into an educational establishment for women, with an emphasis on educating those who were underprivileged. Arunee was excited by Joy's suggestion that they should try to reach the sex workers who wanted to change their lives and do something better. All of it was challenging, but the more they had discussed the idea the more certain they were that this was the vision they shared, and the one they wanted to aim for.

Money was no obstacle. Arunee's father, Khun Pansak, so despised by Khun Chai, had left her with vast wealth that included property all over the city, investments, and a box of precious gemstones from all over the world that was sitting in the vaults of the main branch of Bangkok Bank on Silom Road.

'I shall get rid of all of it to pay for our school,' said Arunee. 'I have been wanting to do this since he died. But I did not know what I would do with all the money. I will do it now and attone for all the bad things that he did in his life, to his women, and to me.'

Joy had to laugh at her friend's newfound determination.

'Does it work like that?' she asked. 'I'll make sure it does,' said Arunee.

So it was that the plan for the reinvention of Baan Suan was drawn up. They were aware that the only obstacle was the pandemic.

'We will have to be patient,' said Joy. 'Nothing is possible right now. But it has to change soon, doesn't it?'

⟶❦, ⟶❦, ⟶❦,

Ten days after Khun Chai's cremation, the household was gathered together in the late afternoon. Arunee explained to them the decision that she and her companion had come to regarding Baan Suan, and when she had finished, she asked for their comments. At first there was a hushed silence. If they had been surprised by what they had heard, their faces showed nothing but mild amusement. For a while, each waited for someone else to speak. It was Sai who spoke first:

'It sounds like a fine idea to me, Khun Arunee, krup,' he said. 'I am sure Khun Chai would have been pleased. He was always complaining how the place was too big. But what I want to know...seeing as Mae Pao and I are still planning to go to the temple in the Northeast to see our son when we can. So, what I want to know is that if Ai Toh wanted to come back here...I am not saying he does. But if he wanted to, could he come back?'

'Of course, he can,' said Arunee. 'The past is the past. I hold nothing against him, and neither does Khun Joy. But I think, Nai Jit, you should have a say in this seeing as it was you who was injured by him.'

Nai Jit put his hands together.

'I myself have been forgiven by Khun Chai, and I am grateful to have been taken back into this house. I have forgiven Ai Toh in my heart.'

Arunee beamed at him.

'But, Khun,' he went on. 'Is it going to be residential? Are people going to be staying here?'

'We haven't decided on that yet. But I expect that we will be offering accommodation to those without a home.'

'If there's going to be a load more people here, they'll need feeding,' said Mae Hom, and Samnieng nodded in agreement. 'We're going to need more help in the kitchen, and with the cleaning.'

'Of course, you will. And you shall have it.'

The comments and the questions went on until the light faded from the sky and it seemed that everyone was satisfied with what they had learned. There was no one among them who wanted to move from Baan Suan.

'Where else would we go, Khun?' asked Nai Wang the gardener. 'You're stuck with us whatever plans you have for this house. They won't even let us out of the front gate,' he added, and they all laughed.

In the end, the only person who wanted to leave was Yai Li.

'But why, Yai?' asked Joy with the familiar tone of frustration and impatience that had been absent for so long that it made Yai Li smile to hear it again. They were sitting on the balcony, Yai Li in the wicker chair where Khun Chai had always sat, with Joy beside her.

'It's because this is not my home. It never was and it never will be. I came here because of you. Remember?'

'Yes. But you married Khun Chai, so Baan Suan became your home.'

Yai Li shook her head and made a gesture with her hand.

'No. No. You can't persuade me to stay whatever you say. I talked about it with Khun Chai, and you heard what he said that evening. I could never even dream of inheriting this place from him. It's the most ridiculous thing I can think of.'

'Yes. But why can't you stay, all the same? To be with me, Yai. To help me.'

'Well, it's sweet of you to say all this. But the truth is that you've always done very well without my help. And now you have Khun Arunee, who, I have to say, I have come to like and admire although I had my reservations at the beginning. But she's a good person. I can see that. Maybe it's partly thanks to you. And you are a better person, and I am sure it's a great deal to do with her. No. You will both be fine here. Anyway, it's not as if I am going to disappear. I will still be around, and I will visit from time to time.'

By the end of the week, Yai Li had packed her small suitcase, slung her cloth bag across her shoulder and bid them all goodbye. As Sai drove her down the winding driveway she turned to look back at the house and her eyes caught sight of the domed observatory. It was the only place that Khun Chai had not shown her in the whole building. This was not because he did not want to. Often, he would tell her of the hours he had spent during his childhood alone there, while his father was drinking himself into a stupor on the balcony below, and how with the help of a book which he still kept, he had learned the names of the stars and constellations.

'By looking up I could get another perspective on what was below,' he'd told her. 'And I could feel far away from my cares.'

The reason they never visited his refuge, as he called the observatory, was simple. The stairway leading up to it was narrow and steep. Neither of them had the strength in their legs to either go up nor down. But now, as the house receded into the background, she imagined Khun Chai up there, looking down at her and waving goodbye.

They arrived at the entrance to Jetsip Rai in the afternoon and Sai left her in exactly the same spot where he had parked a year earlier. They had not said a word to one another on the whole journey, but now as he took her suitcase out of the boot for her, he bowed low and with a quivering voice said:

'Khun Yai, thank you for what you did for Khun Chai. You are more of a Khunying than any of the others I have ever met. Just call me whenever you want me to come and fetch you.'

The streets that were normally so full of life were practically empty. There was music coming out of some of the windows she passed, and occasionally the sound of loud voices. But as Yai Li slowly made her way towards her shack, dragging her suitcase behind her over the rough surface, she had the impression that all the life of the district had been drained away. The few people she passed, like herself, were wearing masks, and this added to the strange, unreal atmosphere. Nobody greeted her and she recognized no one until, rounding a corner, she saw a familiar figure walking towards her. It was the tall, bald Irish priest who was the director of the Mercy Centre, known as Khun Paw by the locals. Even with a mask on there was no mistaking who he was in his black shirt and black trousers. He was alone and striding at a rapid pace. But he immediately stopped when he approached her.

'It's Yai Li, isn't it?' he said with only a hint of a twang in his Thai accent. She nodded and put her hands together in greeting.

'Yes. They told me you'd been away. Are you back now?'

Again, she nodded. 'Ka, Khun Paw. I am back.'

'Well, that's good to hear. Listen, I am in a bit of a hurry. I wish I could stay and chat with you, but I have just had a call from over in the slaughterhouse from one of our people. His mother has gone down with Covid. She may die. They've asked me to go over to pray with them. So, I must leave you.'

As he said this, he was already moving away from her. Then, turning, he said over his shoulder: 'Don't be a stranger. Come and see us in the Centre. Come and help if you have time. Just be with the children. They need your wisdom and your love. For your daughter. For Joy.'

With that he hastened his step and was gone.

Five minutes later, she was in the narrow lane and the sight that struck her made her smile. It was Mae Da sitting on her low wooden seat, smoking her cigarette and looking as if she had not moved from that position since Yai Li left Jetsip Rai the last time. The only detail that had changed was that she had a thin light blue mask pushed up on her forehead. She showed no surprise on turning to see Yai Li again but let out a throaty laugh.

'Had enough of life in the palace then, have you?' she said as Yai Li drew near. 'Or did they kick you out?'

Yai Li took off her mask.

'How have you been, Mae Da?'

'Well, I'm not dead yet, and the Covid or whatever they call it hasn't got me so far.'

'Have many people been sick from it around here?'

'More than they're letting on. But then that's natural, isn't it? We don't count. We are poor and invisible.'

She drew on her cigarette and coughed as she let the smoke out. Yai Li refrained from making a comment. She felt glad to see her neighbour again.

'So, are you here to pick up some more things or are you staying this time?' asked Mae Da.

Later, after she had finished cleaning and dusting the place, and unpacking her suitcase, Yai Li turned the fan on and lay down to rest. She reached into her shoulder bag and took out the copy of *Four Reigns* and placed it on her bedside table. She still found it hard going. But she was determined to go on reading it in honour of Khun Chai. Then she found the small, decorated porcelain urn given to her by Arunee, that contained some of Khun Chai's ashes. She had decided to put it under the Buddharupa so that it would always be near her. Now she held it up to the light and as she contemplated it, she knew that it was not a matter of having someone's ashes, or relics, or an object they had owned. These were symbols, reminders of the past. What mattered was the connection of the heart, and this was ever present. She could feel him living on in her and accessible to her any time that she needed to converse with him or share a joke. All she needed to do was to picture him and hear the distinct sound of his voice, or the ironic laughter that accompanied the comments he made about what he saw in the world around him.

As she lay there, back in her own shack in Jetsip Rai, with the familiar pungent smell of the drains wafting through her open back window, the clanking of cooking pots from a shack a few doors away, the mangy dogs barking in the distance, the world of Baan Suan seemed like a story that someone had invented, with her as a figure who was included to add another dimension to the plot. She could not have stayed there, as she constantly told him. The luxury that he took for granted made her uncomfortable. She tried, without success to explain this many times to him; that it wasn't that she did not enjoy the clean, crisp sheets to sleep on, a bathroom with a toilet that worked without readjusting the valve each time, the meals offered up as if by magic, and, to top it all, an enormous black marble pool to swim in. He had tried, in his own way, several times, to help her to overcome her resistance to all of this.

'Is it that you feel guilty that you have this when there are so many who have next to nothing? If so, I am with you,' he would tell her.

But that wasn't it, she would tell him impatiently. She did not suffer from the kind of tortured social conscience that he did. She felt no guilt. It was altogether something more physical for her. She told him that just as some people cannot bear to be touched and massaged, her body could not stand so much pampering. But he did not really understand what she was talking about.

Often, when they were together, she wondered how things would have been in reverse. Could he have relaxed into the lifestyle she offered him in Jetsip Rai? Could he ever feel at home there, with all his refined sensitivities, eating the spicy street food, putting up with the noise and the music of the streets, dealing with those who would not begin to understand the things that he was referring to in his conversations? It was obvious to her, watching how he treated people, that he was no snob, but prided himself on being a person who could communicate with the common people. Still, she doubted that he would have been happy there in her tiny shack.

In the end, there were so many things that she could not explain to him, nor he to her, and even if he had not died, she was not sure whether they would ever have totally understood one another. But it made no difference. All she knew was that for the first time in her life she had met someone who respected her and loved her for who she was, and this was all that mattered. His love had healed her wounds. Now he was gone, and she needed to return to her roots to continue with her life. Otherwise, she would have remained trapped in his, with all the nostalgia and melancholy of that enormous mansion to deal with. She also felt that she wanted to be in Jetsip Rai till she was forced to move out, to show solidarity with her neighbours and the people she knew there. She did not discount what Joy had told her, and she knew that if it were not for Covid the bulldozers might already have been beginning their destructive work. But, for the moment, the prayers at the sacred tree seemed to have worked yet again. She would keep going there with her friends and continue to make offerings.

But what was she going to do now with the rest of her time? There were no more financial worries. Khun Chai had taken care of that by opening a bank account for her and depositing all his savings in it just before the illness prevented him from leaving Baan Suan. He had also given her an amount of cash that he had squirreled away over the years and kept in his drawer for a rainy day. This alone was enough to pay her rent for the foreseeable future. There was also the ruby ring which she had taken off and now kept in its little box. She could probably buy a small house in Ayutthaya with it if ever she had to find somewhere else to live.

Remembering the brief meeting with the priest, she now felt ashamed that she had not thanked him for what he had done for her granddaughter. And then there was the lawyer from the centre, sent by the father, who had played a significant role in the whole affair, whose reassuring presence provided the support that both she and Joy needed to maintain confidence that justice would be done. She had not had time to thank him personally because she had not seen him again after the ordeal. Now she would make an effort to do so. The Irish father's words, uttered in haste, also rekindled in her thoughts that she had entertained over the years, of doing something for the community. She had never properly returned the generosity shown by the priest and the people at the centre to her daughter when she was dying, and to Joy when she was growing up. She always promised herself to do so one day. But time passed by, and she did not have the energy to make any contribution. Now that she was free and provided for, she thought that being with the children at the centre who had been wounded and abandoned was something she could try, and that the gift that she had could, perhaps, be channeled into healing them. She would do this not only from gratitude, but also in homage to Khun Chai and the extraordinary, short-lived, wonderful time that they had shared.

She remembered the last conversation they had together before Arunee and Joy returned from Paris. They had been watching the news one evening and it seemed that everything was in collapse, not just in Thailand but in the world; the political debate that had become so intense, the economic uncertainties, the climate change that was producing so much suffering, the wars that were going on, the violence, the drugs…

'There doesn't seem to be any solution to any of it. That's why I don't watch the news,' she told him. 'It's just too depressing.'

'But it's better to keep being informed than pretending that everything is ok,' he said.

'I don't see why. We can't do anything about it. So what's the point of knowing? We just become more and more upset.'

He had shrugged and kept quiet although she knew that he disagreed with her.

'Well, what's your answer then?' she insisted with genuine curiosity.

'I honestly have none,' he told her. 'I've given up pretending I have any answers. All I know is that goodness and loving kindness will take us through. That's all.'

His words now echoed back to her as she reached over and lay the urn carefully on the table next to the copy of *Four Reigns*.

Even though her grandmother's decision to return to Jetsip Rai continued to puzzle her, Joy felt that it was the right thing to do. She could not imagine her Yai sitting around on the balcony all day long, being waited on as she knitted a crochet blanket and pining after her dead husband. Nor did she see her helping with the cooking and cleaning. After all that had happened, she could not have demoted herself and become a member of the household, especially after her marriage to Khun Chai and the change in her status. It was right that she should want to leave. Still, as someone who had spent the years of her childhood trying to find ways of getting out of the slums, it was hard to accept that anyone would want to return there if given the choice. But her grandmother had always been a mystery to her and she had come to learn not to try to understand why she did certain things. Besides, they had promised to call each other and speak on zoom at least once a week.

The months after Khun Chai's death were busy ones for Joy. Arunee had insisted that she follow up her inspired suggestion about introducing music and theatre into Mudita House, and Joy had set about finding the funding for these projects as well as the appropriate musicians and actors. This meant meetings and interviews that had to be arranged under the limitations of the Covid situation. In the meantime, she and Arunee were beginning to work on the educational project for Baan Suan that they had discussed. Their aim was to come up with an in-depth proposal that would meet with the approval of the Ministry of Education and other relevant government departments; they knew that they needed this to have the project taken seriously, especially in a time when the work of NGOs was viewed with suspicion, if not downright rejection. This involved inviting experts and advisers to meet with them face to face, which was a challenge in itself. The job of physically converting Baan Suan into a place serving a radically different purpose from the past, was next on their list. But it could not go ahead until they had received some sort of positive official response to their proposal. Nevertheless, a team of young architects who had previously done work for Mitr's company, Siam Estate, were called in to do a preliminary survey. This included finding a way of using sustainable energy on the property and converting the existing physical spaces to fit the project. It was their suggestion that the room that had been Khun Chai's downstairs bedroom be used as the central working space of the future college. It would be converted into a library and conference room. This met with Arunee and Joy's enthusiastic approval. But again, hanging over all the discussions was the shadow of Covid. No one could predict when it would end, or whether things would even worsen. The building works in the city had already slowed down drastically. The number of infections and deaths was rising. In this climate it was hard to extract any commitment from anyone in the building industry.

'Well, then,' said Joy after the departure of the architects. 'we will just go about things patiently, as we said we would. In the meantime, I will be responsible for sorting out the books in Khun Chai's collection, so that when the library is built, they will be ready to be put on the shelves.'

This was how Joy came to spend her afternoons and evenings after coming back from Mudita House, in the space that Khun Chai had occupied during the last year of his life. There were hundreds of books that had been placed haphazardly on his shelves and it took her long hours arranging them according to their different genres. She was surprised by their range. Besides the novels and the poetry, there were books on spirituality, ecology, science that she had not expected to find in his collection, as well as stacks of magazines and obscure publications. While he was alive, she had never gone further into that room than the doorway where she would leave her grandmother. Now she became familiar with the particular chaos that seemed to contain a private sense of order, as though a piece of notepaper, or an article cut out from a newspaper had been placed deliberately where it was with a specific purpose. It amused her to think how this contrasted with, and complemented so perfectly, Arunee's neat working space where not one sheet of paper or pencil was out of place.

All of it was challenging. Apart from arranging Khun Chai's collection of books, Joy had to put his papers in order, which meant going through the notebooks that covered over four decades and trying to place them in some sort of chronological order. When she began her task, she could feel his presence. It felt to her like a slight resistance – a disturbance in the air – that made her uncomfortable. It did not scare her because she thought that even if it were his ghostly presence, it would not be a malevolent one. He had never been anything but kind towards her. She figured that he was probably annoyed to have someone putting order to his mess. Then one afternoon, as she began to tidy a small desk in the corner that was piled high with books and papers, she saw a small red moleskin notebook fly off the table onto the floor. There was no window open, no wind in the room, and nothing that could have moved it from its position, which was nowhere close to the edge of the table. Instinctively she put her hands together and said out loud:

'Khun Chai. I'm sorry. I should have asked your permission first and to tell you why I am doing this.' She then proceeded to light a stick of incense and a candle, and say a prayer for him, and afterwards she felt not only more at ease with her work, but guided by his invisible hand. All the while, she never forgot the words that he had addressed to her not long before he died and, as she gathered the books that he had written and put them together away from the others, she promised herself that, when there was time, she would begin reading them. She was already tempted to do so. But she knew that if she started on that route, she would be spending years in that room without ever finishing her task.

Apart from the books, there were the paintings and the photographs that she would carefully pack into labelled boxes, with the intention of restoring them onto the walls once the refurbishment was finished. The record collection was the easiest to sort out. It was almost all jazz dating back to the early sixties. But there was one that she came across that stood out from the others, called 'The 5000 Spirits or The Layers of the Onion', by a group she had never heard of called The Incredible String Band. The colourful cover was faded and on the back of it was written, with a marker pen: To my best friend. Your brother. Mac. 1967. She made a mental note to ask her grandmother if Khun Chai had told her anything about the record and about this friend. She was so curious about this record that seemed totally out of place beside the Duke Ellington and the Miles Davis collection, that she put it on the old gramophone player one evening while she worked. As she listened, her head swaying gently, she imagined Khun Chai, as a young man in 1967, singing along to the oddly appealing music and the strange words of the songs.

One afternoon, in the bottom drawer of his desk she came across a dark brown leather folder. In it was a wad of A 4 sized paper. Thirty of the top sheets had been written on. The spidery scrawl became more illegible with each page. On the first one she read:

'How do I write about the love between two old people from totally different backgrounds? How would it end?'